MW00614623

THE BLACK SEA

A Joe Johnson Thriller, Book 6

ANDREW TURPIN

The Write Direction Publishing

First published in the U.K. in 2020 by The Write Direction Publishing, St. Albans, U.K.

Copyright © 2020 Andrew Turpin
All rights reserved.
Print edition — The Black Sea
ISBN: 978-1-78875-014-1

Andrew Turpin has asserted his right under the Copyright, Designs and Patents Act 1988 to be identified as the author of this work.

This is a work of fiction. Names, characters, businesses, places, events and incidents are either the products of the author's imagination or are used in a fictitious manner. Any resemblance to actual persons, living or dead, or actual events is purely coincidental.

<<<<>>>>

 Created with Vellum

WELCOME TO THE JOE JOHNSON SERIES!

Thank you for purchasing **The Black Sea** — I hope you enjoy it!

This is the sixth in the series of thrillers I am writing that feature Joe Johnson, a US-based independent war crimes investigator. He previously worked for the CIA and for the Office of Special Investigations — a section of the Department of Justice responsible for tracking down Nazi war criminals hiding in the States.

The other books in the series about his various war crimes investigations are all for sale on Amazon. So far, in order, the books are:

Prequel: *The Afghan*
1. *The Last Nazi*
2. *The Old Bridge*
3. *Bandit Country*
4. *Stalin's Final Sting*
5. *The Nazi's Son*
6. *The Black Sea*

I also have a second series, featuring former MI6 operative **Jayne Robinson** (who also appears in the Johnson books). This series so far comprises:

1. *The Kremlin's Vote*
2. *The Dark Shah*
3. *The Confessor*
4. *The Queen's Pawn*

If you enjoy this book, I would like to keep in touch. This is not always easy, as I usually only publish a couple of books a year and there are many authors and books out there. So the best way is for you to be on my Readers Group email list. I can then send you updates on the next book, plus occasional special offers.

If you would like to join my Readers Group and receive the email updates, I will send you, **FREE** of charge, the ebook version of another Joe Johnson thriller, ***The Afghan***, which is a prequel to the series and normally sells at $2.99/£2.99 (paperback $11.99/£9.99).

The Afghan is set in 1988 when Johnson was still a CIA officer. Most of the action takes place in Afghanistan and Washington, DC.

To sign up for the Readers Group and get your free copy of ***The Afghan***, go to the following web page:

https://bookhip.com/RJGFPAW

If you only like paperbacks, you can still just sign up for the email list at the above link to get news of my books and forthcoming new releases. A paperback version of ***The Afghan*** and all my books is for sale at my website, where you will find large discounts on bundles of my books. I can currently ship to the US and UK:

https://www.andrewturpin.com/shop/

Or if you live outside the US and UK you can buy them at Amazon.

Andrew Turpin, St. Albans, UK.

DEDICATION

This book is dedicated to my mother, Jean Turpin, a former nurse and midwife, who at the age of 90 was battling bravely with an aggressive form of cancer as this book was being written and edited. She still read every word of the draft version.

This book is also for all those doctors, nurses, and other healthcare professionals around the world who were working around the clock and risking their own lives to help those suffering from the disease that unexpectedly impacted us all so greatly during the run-up to publication in 2020.

"Death has become something different now. It's not something to be afraid of anymore. We're just serving out our days now. And after we die maybe we'll be with her once again."

A statement from two parents who lost their only child when Malaysia Airlines Flight MH17 was shot down over Ukraine in July 2014.

PROLOGUE

Tuesday, July 15, 2014
Chervonyi Zhovten village, Eastern Ukraine

The expanse of golden wheat, swaying gently in the breeze like waves heading for shore, stretched as far as the line of trees on the distant horizon. A handful of blue cornflowers and red poppies poked their heads above the blanket of yellow.

Overhead was an azure sky, a typical feature of Eastern Ukraine over the previous couple of weeks.

In the neighboring field, three rusty red combine harvesters were at work, operating in formation and throwing up clouds of dust as they chewed a swathe through the ripe heads of grain.

The temperature had risen to more than twenty-eight Celsius under a glaring sun, and Colonel Georgi Tkachev—he still liked to use his old rank—was feeling the heat.

Flies buzzed around his head, and sweat was dripping from his short, receding blond hair down onto his metal-framed sunglasses. The heavily built former intelligence officer swatted the insects away with a sharp flick of his left hand. He leaned against the door of his GAZ Tigr 4x4 armored vehicle and drew deeply from one of his favorite Ziganov black cigarettes.

In a corner of the wheat field, next to the dirt track where Tkachev's 4x4 was parked, were three vehicles that appeared at first glance to be olive-green battle tanks. They stood in a line, side by side, facing north toward the small city of Snizhne, a few kilometers away.

But these were no battle tanks. Their heavy-duty caterpillar tracks and solid steel bodies appeared similar to their battlefield brethren, but the array of technology mounted on the tops of the three vehicles told a different story.

Mounted on the one nearest to Tkachev was a green-painted rectangular board almost as wide as the vehicle and several meters long. It was supported by a hydraulic system that held it upright at an angle of about thirty degrees, pointing north. This was a target-acquisition radar with a range of more than eighty kilometers that could detect an aircraft flying as low as ninety meters.

The second vehicle had a chunky silver metal telescopic aerial that had been extended twenty meters high. This was a command post that contained an array of technology, including data display and control systems and computers. It was responsible for electronically directing the missile launchers to hit their chosen targets and to distinguish friendly aircraft from their enemies. It could also communicate via radio and satellite links with other distant command posts and with military headquarters.

The vehicle farthest away from Tkachev, the launcher, was the most fearsome of the lot. It had a swivel hydraulic unit on the roof onto which were mounted four identical slim green missiles, each five-and-a-half meters long with a pointed white tip and X-shaped fins at the rear.

The hydraulic system had been raised so that the four 9M38M1 missiles pointed north, in the same direction as the radar unit, which Tkachev knew was continuously scanning the skies ahead for potential targets.

The missile launcher, known as a Buk-M1 and code-named Grizzly by NATO countries, belonged to Russia's 53rd Anti-Aircraft Missile Brigade and was normally based at Kursk, about 550 kilometers farther north. A few other armored vehicles from the brigade stood amid a clump of nearby trees in an attempt to hide them from prying satellites and aircraft.

Tkachev's radio crackled with two loud squelch breaks. He raised it and listened.

"Target located," a disemboweled voice said in Russian through a flurry of static. It was the unit commander, who was ensconced in the command post vehicle in front of a circular orange radar screen at the center of a bank of controls. "Lock on."

Just half an hour earlier, Tkachev had had an animated conversation with the unit commander, who was less than happy with being told that his small unit would need to withdraw over the border into Russia as soon as the operation was completed. The commander couldn't see the reasoning, given his high hit rate over the past three weeks. What Tkachev didn't tell him was that his unit was going to be temporarily replaced with another one that was much more covert in nature and had objectives that he couldn't possibly reveal.

Tkachev could see a short, thin white vapor trail advancing across the skies to the north. He picked up a pair of binoculars and focused on it. There, in miniature but visible against the blue background, was the pale gray outline of the aircraft that was creating the trail.

He knew what was coming. He had seen it many times

now, particularly in the preceding weeks across various parts of Eastern Ukraine, which was held by pro-Russian rebels intent on destabilizing and defeating the Ukrainian military forces pitted against them. The Ukrainians were being taught a lesson, and so were the damned Americans who were helping them out behind the scenes.

Tkachev, like a few of his former colleagues in the highly secretive Spetsnaz subunit 29155 of Russia's GRU foreign military intelligence organization, had become a freelancer in order to provide the deniable and highly covert services required by the Kremlin. In Ukraine, he had recently been providing strategic guidance to the rebels and also directing the Russian units supporting them, including the Buk-M1 crew.

"Lock-on confirmed," crackled the level tones of the unit commander over the radio. "Destroy target."

"Destroy target. Roger," responded the officer in charge of the launcher vehicle.

Tkachev took an involuntary step backward and placed a hand above his sunglasses, giving his eyes some additional shielding.

A second later there was a roar, and an enormous burst of orange-and-yellow flame erupted outward from the base of the launcher, causing a mushroom of gray dust and dirt to explode from the ground behind it. Simultaneously, one of the giant missiles soared skyward at almost a thousand meters per second—three times the speed of sound—trailing fire and white smoke behind it.

Tkachev raised his binoculars again and watched transfixed as the 9M38M1 screamed toward its target, a Ukrainian Air Force Antonov An-26 military transport plane, which he estimated was flying at about twenty thousand feet.

The white vapor trail generated by the missile converged

relentlessly with the An-26 until, seconds later, there was a distant explosion, and an orange fireball appeared.

Tkachev caught a glimpse of large chunks of smoking debris plunging earthward. He lowered his binoculars as his radio crackled again.

"Target destroyed."

PART ONE

CHAPTER ONE

Tuesday, July 15, 2014
Portland, Maine

A CNN news bulletin was blaring from the television in the corner of Joe Johnson's kitchen. Two steaming cups of coffee stood on the countertop, and three empty suitcases were lying next to the door that led into the hallway.

Johnson had just retrieved the suitcases from a storage locker in his garage. By the following evening, they needed to be packed and ready to go. One belonged to him, the others to his teenage children, Carrie and Peter.

For the first time in nine years, he was preparing for a family summer vacation that involved more than just himself and the two kids and took them somewhere other than the Maine coastline. This time, not only were they going to Malaysia, but also two others were joining them.

One of them was his sister, Amy, who, ever since the death of his wife, Kathy, from cancer in 2005, had looked after the children whenever he happened to be away working.

This trip to Malaysia would represent a thank-you to her in many ways.

The other person was Jayne Robinson, whose role in Johnson's life had changed in recent months. Until April that year, he and Jayne had been freelance work colleagues on a number of war crime investigations, starting with the pursuit of an aging and notorious Second World War Nazi commander. But a few shared life-threatening situations during those investigations had drawn them closer together. And to Johnson's slight surprise, they found themselves rekindling the brief love affair they had had in Islamabad in 1988, when Jayne was working for the British Secret Intelligence Service, also known as MI6, and Johnson for the CIA.

Johnson poured some milk into the coffee mugs and pushed one of them across the counter to Jayne, who was looking tired. She had been up late the previous evening reading a guidebook about the Malaysian portion of Borneo, where they were heading for a couple of weeks to see orangutans in the jungle and spend some time on the beach.

From Borneo, the group planned to return via France, where they were going to spend two more weeks with one of Amy's friends, Natalia, who was renting a six-bedroom villa near Cannes for most of July and August.

Amy's husband, Don Wilde, had volunteered to stay home to look after the Johnson family's dog, Cocoa, a six-year-old chocolate Labrador.

Everything was set. Now they just needed to pack and get through the tortuous journey. The plan was to fly to Kuala Lumpur via New York's JFK airport and Amsterdam, then take a local connecting flight to Kota Kinabalu International Airport, in the Malaysian-controlled Sabah region of Borneo.

"I need this break," Johnson said. "I can't remember the last time I took so long off work. Probably when I was a kid selling ice creams between backpacking trips."

Jayne raised an eyebrow. "You really sold enough ice creams to pay for backpacking trips?"

"Yes. Thousands of them. I was immensely gifted." He threw her a sideways glance.

Jayne laughed out loud. "And modest. Enjoy this break, Joe."

The sound of footsteps clattering down the stairs echoed through the hallway and a few seconds later Carrie came in, her long dark hair trailing behind her. "Where's my suitcase?" she asked. "I want to start packing."

Johnson pointed. "You nearly fell over it."

"How hot will it be in Borneo? I'm trying to decide what to take."

"About eighty-five degrees," Jayne said. "Maybe ninety. T-shirts, swim gear, shorts, and sandals. Maybe one pair of jeans and a sweater. That's all you need."

Carrie gave Jayne the thumbs-up and exited as quickly as she had entered, picking up a suitcase on her way out.

Since Jayne had come to his home, a two-story Cape Cod-style property on Parsons Road, just off Back Cove, Johnson had admired the way she had fitted in so well with his seventeen-year-old daughter, despite not having children of her own. It had been harder to bond with his son, Peter, but she had managed to achieve that partly by driving him unasked to and from his school basketball games. As a Brit, she knew little about basketball, but she had learned quickly and often traded comments about the up-and-down performance of the Maine Red Claws, the local team that played in the National Basketball Association's minor league.

Johnson sipped his coffee. In some ways, it had come as a surprise to him when they had restarted their affair. Of course, he'd still felt attracted to her, just as he had two-and-a-half decades earlier. But he hadn't seriously thought she felt the same, despite the occasional flirtation after they began working together again in 2011. She enjoyed her city life in London, while Johnson had no regrets about moving to Portland from Washington, DC, where he had held a busy job as a senior investigative historian—effectively a Nazi hunter—with the Office of Special Investigations.

Would she stay with him in Maine long-term? Johnson didn't know, and didn't like to quiz her too much this early in their rekindled relationship. She was a very independent person, he knew that. But he hoped she would stay. She had settled in well, and one of her old friends from the UK, who had married the Maine secretary of state, was living nearby, which helped.

He stared at the TV. The news anchor finished reading an item about Hamas rejecting proposals for a cease-fire with Israel, then glanced down at his monitor.

"News is just coming in from Ukraine of a military transport aircraft that was shot down not far from the border with Russia," the anchor said. As he spoke, a ticker flashed across the bottom of the screen carrying the same news.

"It is being reported that the aircraft was a Ukrainian military transport and was destroyed by a missile believed to have been fired from within Ukrainian territory," the anchor continued. "A source within the Ukrainian government has blamed Russia for the attack, which is the latest in a series of rocket attacks on aircraft in the area. The government source said that the Igla surface-to-air missiles used by pro-Russian rebel forces in Eastern Ukraine were capable of reaching a height of only 11,000 feet, whereas the aircraft shot down today was at more than 21,000 feet. The source is accusing Russian forces of bringing a far more powerful missile launcher into Ukraine specifically to carry out the attack."

"Bloody hell," Jayne said. "That's another one shot down."

"Yes, there have been several in the past few weeks."

Right on cue, the anchor began to reel off a tally of the

various Ukrainian Air Force aircraft shot down during the previous two months, since the beginning of fighting in the Donbass region of Eastern Ukraine. There were ten of them. All of the casualties were aircraft targeted by pro-Russian anti-government separatist forces.

"We will update you on this story as more information becomes available," the anchor concluded.

"Vic will be tearing his hair out," Johnson said.

His old friend Vic Walter, a CIA veteran, had been appointed the previous year as director of the Agency's National Clandestine Service, generally known as the Directorate of Operations, and as deputy director of the entire organization.

Johnson and Vic had worked together for the CIA in Pakistan and Islamabad in the late 1980s. Although Johnson had left the Agency in September 1988 while Vic had stayed on and worked his way up the ladder, the pair had remained close friends.

In recent years, Vic had quietly drawn on Johnson's investigative expertise on a freelance basis on a number of occasions, for which Johnson usually enlisted the assistance of Jayne, who had left MI6 in 2012 to also go freelance. Most recently, the pair had unmasked the perpetrators of a terrorist bomb attack on the La Belle nightclub in Berlin in 1986, in which Vic's brother had been so badly injured that he had committed suicide several years later.

Johnson knew that Vic had recently been on a top secret visit to the Ukrainian capital, Kiev, along with the US secretary of state, Paul Farrar, and Vic's boss, the director of the Central Intelligence Agency, Arthur Veltman. The visit was to discuss cooperation with Ukraine in its ongoing conflict with the separatist rebels.

Based on his discussions with Vic, Johnson knew that any assistance would be of the "nonlethal" variety, including intelligence gathering. It might include technology that could stop Russian missiles, radar-jamming equipment, and devices to stop Russian interference with Ukrainian military communications, as well as items such as vehicles, night-vision goggles, and flak jackets.

Johnson took out his phone and logged on to the secure link he and Vic always used when they wanted to message, email, or call each other. They had each other's public and private keys so they could encrypt and read each other's messages. He began to tap away.

Vic, I assume you're under the gun given Ukraine. Just heard another Antonov was shot down today. Hope the Kiev visit went to plan. Keep going buddy. We're all heading to Malaysia/France on long vacation tomorrow. Will be in touch on return.

A few minutes later his phone pinged as a reply came back.

All going to shit here. DCI and Sec of State worried but sticking to previous plans re Kiev. Talks went well. More detail when we next meet. Enjoy vacation—wish I was going. Speak soon.

Johnson glanced back up at Jayne and read aloud Vic's reply.

"Sounds like he's on a high-wire act over at Langley," he added.

Jayne nodded, then furrowed her brow and ran a hand through her short, dark hair. She looked distracted.

"What's up?" Johnson asked.

"I was just thinking. Our connecting flight from Amsterdam to Kuala Lumpur, that's Malaysia Airlines, right?"

"Yes."

"What route do they take out of Amsterdam? What's the flight path?"

Johnson shrugged. "No idea. Presumably the shortest route. Over Eastern Europe, Russia, India. That way, I would guess."

"Over Ukraine?" Jayne raised an eyebrow.

Johnson shrugged again. He could see what she was thinking, and she was probably right. The route would logically go that way unless the airline decided on a major diversion.

He put his hand on Jayne's shoulder. "Don't worry. We're on a civilian airline, and we'll be at thirty thousand feet. There's no way the airline would take a route if they think there's any risk whatsoever."

CHAPTER TWO

Thursday, July 17, 2014
Azov Sea Port, Russia

There was a slight crunch as the driver of the white Volvo truck engaged first gear. Yuri Severinov, sitting a few meters away in the front passenger seat of his Mercedes 4x4, looked up at the noise and watched.

The truck driver and his colleague in the passenger seat both appeared to be humorless men with short-cropped military-style hair, wearing unmarked green battle fatigues.

The powerful Volvo was pulling a long, red lowboy semitrailer on which sat a tanklike armored vehicle, about nine meters long, painted khaki green and covered with black-and-green camouflage netting.

The truck began to move along the dockside, past a row of four gantry cranes and a stack of shipping containers, and down a track that led alongside a line of dark gray grain elevators that towered above the port like soldiers guarding a fortress. Shadows were being thrown across the dockyard by the morning sun, now starting to rise in the sky.

Severinov nodded to his driver, who immediately slid the Mercedes into gear and followed the lowboy as it moved along the rough concrete surface of the dock. It hadn't rained for a few weeks, and the semi's twelve wheels threw up clouds of dust on either side as it gathered speed.

Severinov eyed the cargo on the back of the lowboy. It was no simple armored vehicle. Rather, it was a Buk-M1 ground-to-air missile launcher, capable of bringing down very large aircraft flying at almost any altitude. The Buk had just been unloaded from a freight ship owned by Severinov, a billionaire oil and gas oligarch, who had brought the vessel from his Krasnodar oil refinery on Russia's Black Sea coast.

Two weeks earlier, Severinov had only a vague knowledge of the capabilities of a Buk-M1. But since he had received the secure phone call he had received from the Kremlin office of the president's special adviser, Igor Ivanov, his focus had been on little else.

Normally, Severinov's contact point at the Kremlin was Prime Minister Dmitry Medvedev's assistant, Mikhail Sobchak. But the call from the increasingly powerful Ivanov was something new and concentrated his mind. Ivanov was a former GRU officer who had a reputation for ruthlessness that was well founded. Once deputy prime minister, he was now an adviser in charge of special operations on behalf of the president and his small group of senior executives. Severinov knew from his contacts that Ivanov had been behind the organization of black operations and active measures to stir up hostility against the Kiev government in the Crimea and in Eastern Ukraine. He wasn't known as the Black Bishop for nothing among the cadre around the Kremlin powerbase.

When the call came, Severinov had been busy overseeing

a major maintenance turnaround, or temporary stoppage, at his Krasnodar oil refinery, near to Tuapse on Russia's Black Sea coast. The refinery, owned and operated by his oil company, Besoi Energy, manufactured gasoline and diesel fuels for distribution across southern Russia. But every three or four years, it had to stop production for a few weeks for essential maintenance. It was a logistical nightmare and involved flying in specialist maintenance engineering teams from overseas as well as Russia to help carry out the work.

Alongside his fleet of oil tankers, Severinov also owned a few other boats, including two yachts used for vacations and a small cargo vessel, the *Yalta*, which he sometimes moored at a jetty at the oil terminal adjacent to his refinery. He used the *Yalta* to bring in a variety of refinery equipment, materials and vehicles as required, mostly from the Russian port of Rostov-on-Don, more than three hundred kilometers north.

Ivanov knew of the existence of the *Yalta*—the Kremlin knew everything. His instructions, passed on from the prime minister and the Russian president, had been precise and extremely confidential.

Under cover of darkness, the Volvo truck and its highly sensitive cargo had arrived at the Krasnodar terminal two days earlier from somewhere farther down the Black Sea coast. The demeanor of the two men in unmarked military dress who were in charge of it had told Severinov not to bother asking any questions about their mission.

His task was to load the Buk onto the *Yalta* and to add extra camouflage netting to protect it from the prying eyes of Western spy satellites and aircraft. Then he was required to transport it across the Black Sea, through the Kerch Strait at the eastern end of the Crimean Peninsula, and up through the Sea of Azov—the saucepan-shaped sea directly north of the Black Sea, on the eastern side of the Crimea. The Buk was eventually offloaded at an anonymous industrial dockside at

Azov Sea Port, a few kilometers down the Don River from Rostov-on-Don.

The Kremlin also specified that Severinov carry out the task personally, not delegate it to one of his men, as he normally would do. It had left Severinov feeling somewhat demeaned, to say the least, but he had little choice in the matter.

The conversation with Ivanov had been civil, but the urbane Kremlin fixer left Severinov in no doubt: declining the job was not an option. Severinov's account with President Putin and Prime Minister Medvedev, once full of riches, had been heavily in the red for the previous couple of years after a number of blunders that had angered his paymasters.

Most recently, he had again, to his shock, come off worse in an encounter with American war crimes investigator Joe Johnson, who had, embarrassingly, exposed his part in the bombing of a Berlin discotheque in the 1980s, when he was working for the KGB. Johnson had also outwitted him in escaping from St. Petersburg over the border into Finland. This had followed previous embarrassments at Johnson's hands in Afghanistan, all of which reflected badly on the Motherland. As a result, the Russian president had given him a year to eliminate Johnson permanently. Already, three months of that deadline period had passed, and Severinov knew he could not upset the president any further.

Severinov and Putin had once both worked as equals for the KGB in Afghanistan during the 1980s but had then left the intelligence agency and gone their separate ways. Putin became a spearhead of the political elite who took charge as Boris Yeltsin's grasp on power weakened, while Severinov turned to business and enriched himself, thanks mainly to patronage from the president and his *siloviki*.

The president had expected a payback, of course, in the shape of utter loyalty and unerring completion of certain tasks when required. And that was where Severinov, initially successful, had fallen short more recently.

Severinov initially assumed that the Buk would be used somehow to assist the pro-Russian rebels who were running amok in Eastern Ukraine. He knew that several Ukrainian Air Force planes had already been shot down in the region, one as recently as two days ago. That was a good thing in his opinion. He felt that the destruction of the Soviet Union in the years after 1990 had diminished the Motherland on the international stage. There was no doubt too that in many of the peripheral former Soviet states there was a good deal of pro-Russian sentiment. Those rebels should be supported.

Of course, Russia couldn't be seen to be actively assisting the rebels, but the damned Americans were poking their noses in by assisting the Ukrainian government, so he failed to see why Moscow shouldn't do likewise.

However, despite his patriotic feelings, there was a moment when Severinov felt slightly uneasy as Ivanov explained, in confidence, exactly what the Buk would be used for. The revelation came with the usual implicit threat: if he disclosed the information to anyone, he would join the other *patzani*, or inmates, in one of the bloodied basement cellars of Butyrka, one of central Moscow's largest and most notorious prisons.

After he had learned their intention, it was obvious why they wanted him to transport the missile launcher on his somewhat battered freighter rather than use one of their sleek Russian navy vessels. They were clearly intent on a completely deniable operation.

The Kremlin knew well that the West tracked every Russian navy vessel like a hawk and almost certainly was doing likewise with the Buk units operated by the Russian military in areas adjacent to the Ukrainian border.

However, intelligence told them it was unlikely that the

same degree of intense surveillance applied to merchant vessels such as Severinov's freighter.

Severinov's task didn't end in the town of Azov. Ivanov had ordered him to accompany the Volvo from Azov Sea Port to an unofficial border crossing into Ukraine 220 kilometers north, very near to the Seversky Donets River and the border village of Severny.

The border crossing and the territory beyond were controlled by pro-Russian separatist forces and were therefore far safer than the checkpoints farther south that were closer but were controlled by the Ukrainian government forces.

At the Donetsk crossing point, he was to meet a former colonel of the GRU's Spetsnaz special forces, Georgi Tkachev, at a hut near to some houses down a country lane on the Russian side of the border.

Severinov had worked briefly with Tkachev on a handful of previous operations. In the past, the GRU had assigned Tkachev to a special subunit hidden away within military unit 29155, which in turn was part of the 161st Special Purpose Brigade.

But Tkachev was now an independent contractor deployed on covert operations by different factions within the government, mainly the Kremlin, though private sector employers also used his services.

At Donetsk, Tkachev would take charge of the Volvo and the Buk, escort it across the border into Ukraine, and return it the following day to the meeting point. From there, Severinov would be responsible for escorting it back safely on the *Yalta* to Tuapse.

Despite the Kremlin demand for confidentiality, there was one person with whom Severinov had discussed the mission: his old friend Leonid Pugachov, a colonel in the FSB with whom he had studied at university and joined the KGB

in 1980. Unlike Severinov, Pugachov had remained in the
intelligence service after the breakup of the Soviet Union,
switching from the foreign service to the domestic FSB. He
often gave Severinov informal assistance with operations in
return for very generous deposits into his bank account—
even at his level, FSB employees were not well paid.

In this case, the reason Severinov had mentioned the Buk
to Pugachov was because he didn't want any interference
from some overzealous FSB or police officer while transporting the launcher through Russian territory. He knew he
could rely on his old colleague, whose reach spread to most
corners of the FSB's empire, to prevent any inadvertent
holdups.

Now Severinov, wearing a long-sleeved black cotton shirt,
folded his arms as his driver followed the Volvo along the
bumpy track out of the shipping terminal and onto the
highway to Azov. They needed to take a route past Rostov,
then up the A-280 north through the mining city of
Novoshakhtinsk, parallel to the Ukrainian border.

On the sidewalk near the port entrance, a group of pupils
and a couple of teachers emerging from a school gate near the
port entrance stared at the oddly shaped cargo as it passed.

Severinov thought that his men had done as good a job as
they could in disguising the Buk—a necessary precaution.
From a distance, and to an untrained eye, the camouflage
netting made it look more like a regular army vehicle than
one of the most lethal portable ground-to-air missile systems
on the planet.

CHAPTER THREE

Thursday, July 17, 2014
  Chervonyi Zhovten village, Eastern Ukraine

The location was the same, but the scene was quite different from two days earlier. Georgi Tkachev climbed out of his Tigr and stood on the soil in the corner of the field. As far as he could see, there were short wheat stalks, as the combine harvesters had now cut down the crop for that year. Dust and chaff hung heavy in the still summer air.

To his right, where on his previous visit there had been three Buk units in a line, there was now just one: the launcher that he had escorted from the other side of the Russian border. All the men in the backup vehicles in the trees had gone: Tkachev didn't want them around for this particular mission, code-named Operation Black Sea.

He and his boss, Igor Ivanov, had agreed that the fewer witnesses for Operation Black Sea, the better.

Tkachev had assumed escort duties of the Buk launcher from a man he knew from a few past operations. Yuri

Severinov was one of those oligarchs of whom nobody took much notice of but whose face occasionally appeared in the business media. Tkachev knew his type: former KGB men who had acquired their wealth through their often long-standing political and intelligence service connections. In turn, those connections sometimes required the services of people like him. Indeed, one of his close former Spetsnaz colleagues, Vasily Balagula, had died working for Severinov earlier that year on an operation in Germany. Tkachev decided not to raise that subject with Severinov, however.

Tkachev had been slightly surprised to find someone of Severinov's stature delivering the Buk in person. Presumably he was under instructions from on high—most likely the same people to whom Tkachev reported. But why he was carrying out that role was something Tkachev didn't ask. Time was of the essence.

The launcher, now shorn of its camouflage netting, had been removed from the Volvo's lowboy semitrailer, which was now hidden among the nearby trees. It stood in the field next to the dirt track, more than half a kilometer from the narrow country road that ran north to Snizhne, a line of trees and bushes protecting it from the stares of passing drivers.

Tkachev, who was wearing a lightweight radio headset and microphone, walked over and glanced up at the top of the Buk, which was about three-and-a-half meters high. The four missiles pointed north and were raised at forty-five degrees, their white tips glinting in the sunlight. Then he levered himself up onto a foothold at the front of the vehicle and clambered into the cramped cabin.

The two men in unmarked fatigues who had come in the Volvo had introduced themselves as Dmitry and Andreas. They were now in the cabin, checking the control panel. The panel, made from gray metal, had two display screens and a series of yellow buttons and controls, including a red joystick.

The cabin was equipped with a radar system, but compared to the one in a Buk command-post vehicle, it was relatively basic. There was no ability to scan 360 degrees but rather just a more restricted frontal view. Similarly, there was no ability to distinguish between friendly aircraft, enemies, and civilian planes. Still, that was not important today.

The essential information that Tkachev required would be fed to him by another command-post vehicle stationed inside Russian territory. That vehicle not only had its own full radar system but also had access to Russian air traffic control systems. There would be no mistake made when it came to determining the target.

"Are you all ready?" Tkachev asked. He fingered a five-centimeter scar that ran from the left corner of his mouth up into his cheek, the souvenir of a knife fight many years earlier in Afghanistan.

Dmitry looked up and nodded. "Yes, we are prepared."

"Good. I will watch from outside and communicate from there." He tapped his headset.

Tkachev climbed out of the Buk, and Dmitry closed the armored trapdoor behind him. That would remain firmly shut during the firing process—essential given the large volume of heat, smoke, and dust generated.

Tkachev rolled the sleeves of his khaki camouflage shirt up to the elbow. On his left bicep was a circular blue-and-yellow insignia, showing a black bat flying above a globe symbol. It was the badge of the Spetsnaz of the GRU. Like his title of colonel, the badge was something he had clung on to unnecessarily, but it was to him a reminder of his life's journey, even his identity, and a source of immense pride.

Tkachev walked back to his 4x4 and glanced at his watch. There were still several minutes to go, he estimated. He pressed a button on his headset and began to speak in Russian.

"SNOWCAT, this is FIREFLY. Repeat, SNOWCAT this is FIREFLY. Do you read?"

"Affirmative, FIREFLY," came the response. "We have target on radar. Estimated arrival time six minutes. Airspeed 490 knots. There is only one birdie in the sky in that slot. Prepare yourselves."

"Roger. Six minutes. Will confirm."

Tkachev did a quick calculation. That was a speed of almost one thousand kilometers per hour. The plane was nearing their position fast. He swiftly switched circuits on his headset and rapped out instructions to Dmitry and Andreas.

"Check radar. Only one bird approaching. It should appear on screen inside the next two or three minutes. That is your target. Confirm."

"Roger, confirmed. Will update on sighting."

Tkachev felt his adrenaline surge. This was the key moment. He had to trust the two men inside the Buk launcher to carry out their job properly, but they appeared extremely professional, as he had expected.

He focused on his watch and waited, a pair of binoculars in his right hand. Almost precisely two minutes later came another squelch break. It was Dmitry.

"Bird on screen. I repeat, bird on screen."

"Good," Tkachev said. "That is your target. Go ahead."

"Okay. Locking on," Dmitry said.

Tkachev raised his binoculars to his eyes and scanned the sky. Eventually he located the plane, clearly outlined against the blue sky, a thin vapor trail streaming behind it. It was a large twin-engine Boeing 777 jet airliner, as expected, probably traveling at an altitude of about 33,000 feet. There was a pause of about eight seconds. Then Dmitry spoke again.

"Locked on."

"Good," Tkachev said, keeping his eyes glued to his binoculars. A thought flashed across his mind of the three hundred or so passengers and crew he assumed were on board: men, women, children, and babies. But then he forced himself to block it out and concentrate on the outcome he was aiming for.

"Proceed," came Dmitry's flat tones. It was as if he were requesting a sandwich in a down-market Moscow deli.

Away to Tkachev's right came the familiar roar and the enormous cloud of flame, smoke, dust, and debris as the 9M38M1 missile took off. Guided by its own internal radar system located in its nose cone, it streaked toward the Malaysia Airlines jet high in the sky above them and still in the early stages of its journey from Amsterdam to Kuala Lumpur.

Behind the rapidly ascending missile was a trail of white exhaust gases that hung almost motionless in the still air.

Through Tkachev's binoculars, everything was crystal clear. As expected, the missile didn't actually strike the airliner—that rarely happened, although if it had done, an impact fuse would have activated the seventy-kilogram 9N314 fragmentation warhead that was built into the midsection of the missile.

Instead, as Tkachev guessed would be the case, the missile's other fuse—a proximity fuse—kicked into life as its radar system detected that its target was very close. Tkachev saw the orange flash as the warhead detonated.

That explosion caused two layers of preformed fragments —bowtie-shaped and square pieces of steel—that were built in around the warhead to be propelled outward at massively high speeds. They formed a barrage of several thousand pieces of metal that slammed into the cockpit area of the nearby aircraft.

The devastating impact blew Malaysia Airlines Flight 17 apart.

Dmitry's voice came in Tkachev's earpiece. "Target destroyed successfully."

"I saw it. Now let's get the hell back into Russia."

He took his phone from his pocket and keyed in a secure message to Ivanov.

CHAPTER FOUR

Thursday, July 17, 2014
  Schiphol Airport, Amsterdam

Johnson knew something was wrong even before they had
landed in Amsterdam. The captain of their KLM flight from
JFK announced only that onward passengers to Kuala
Lumpur needed to check with their airline, as there were
ongoing issues with connecting flights. When he asked a
flight attendant for further details, she avoided eye contact
and told him to ask when on the ground.

As they made their way off the aircraft, it became obvious
that the issues were more serious than the usual causes of
flight delays.

Large numbers of armed police and other security guards
in berets and pale blue shirts were swarming the terminal, all
of them grim-faced. Groups of obviously distraught passengers were gathered together, some of them weeping openly.

It took Johnson only a few moments to find out from a

member of the airport's support staff what had happened. Malaysian Airlines Flight 17 to Kuala Lumpur—the same route his family and Jayne were due to fly later that evening— had crashed somewhere in Ukraine, the woman said. It was believed to have been shot down by terrorists, although no more was known at this stage. Because of the uncertainty, airport police had called in reinforcements.

"We do not yet know whether Malaysian Airlines will fly that route again tonight so I can't advise about your connecting flight," she said. "You need to collect your luggage, and we will keep you updated. I am very sorry, but I do not know more right now."

Johnson's first instinctive reaction was one of relief: it was not their flight that had been hit. Peter and Carrie, all of them, were safe. He immediately castigated himself for that selfish thought as he watched the people weeping around him.

His second reflexive thought—one that sent a slight shiver through him—was about the Russians. *Surely they weren't targeting my flight and made a mistake?* After all, he had a very long history with them, dating back to the Afghanistan war of the '80s. But he shook his head and dismissed the idea. They definitely weren't that incompetent.

Carrie, who was standing next to Johnson as the woman gave him the details, instantly burst into tears, and Peter looked as though he might do likewise. Amy gave a short shriek and stood open-mouthed while Jayne immediately took out her phone, checking for more information online.

"It's the bloody Russians," Jayne said. "Has to be. Why the hell are passenger jets flying over Ukraine with all that shit going on? I mentioned it yesterday, after we heard about that Antonov being shot down, remember?"

Johnson put an arm around each of his kids. "Let's wait

before jumping to conclusions," he said. "But I suspect you're right."

Jayne peered at her phone. "There's media coverage everywhere," she said. "They're reporting there are no survivors. Three hundred on the flight, according to this report. All dead."

Carrie grabbed her father's arm firmly, tears still trickling down her face. "I'm not going on that plane tonight," she said. "I'm not going to Borneo. Definitely not."

"Me neither," Peter said. "I want to go back home."

Johnson could see his children were not thinking logically in their panic and thought momentarily about trying to reassure them, but then he realized that was going to be a fruitless exercise. He ran a hand through the half circle of short-cropped hair around the side of his balding head, trying to think of what to do next.

"We don't want to just abandon our vacation after all that planning," Amy said. "Isn't there another route or another airline we could take to get there?"

But even before she had finished speaking, Carrie was shaking her head firmly. "No," she said. "I'm not getting on another plane. Not if they are being shot down."

Johnson put his hands up. "Listen, let's take our time deciding what to do. We'll get our bags. Then let's have a coffee and discuss it."

Forty minutes later they had collected their suitcases and made their way to the departures hall, which had been partially cordoned off with red-and-white police tape. Already, bunches of flowers had begun to pile up next to the Malaysia Airlines check-in desks, which were closed. A man was wandering around shouting something about his brother being on the crashed flight and where the hell were airline staff. At one of the closed check-in desks a teenage girl sat on a trolley, head in hands, weeping.

Amy trailed behind the rest of them, talking on her cell phone. Johnson turned to her just as she finished her call and put her phone back in her pocket.

"I just spoke to Natalia," Amy said. "Listen. She's heard the news about the crash. She said if we want to, we can go straight to Cannes and spend our whole holiday there instead of going to Borneo. There's plenty of space at the villa. We can either fly to Nice and hire a car, or we can get there by train. We don't need to fly if we don't want to."

Before Johnson could open his mouth, his children made the decision for him.

"Yes," said Carrie. "Can we do that? We'll go by train. I'm definitely not going to Borneo. You can go by yourself if you want, Dad, but I'm not getting on that plane, even if you give me a million dollars. No way."

Peter was nodding in agreement as she spoke, and Jayne threw Johnson a quick glance that said he wasn't going to win this debate.

She was correct. There seemed little alternative, although the idea of spending three and a half weeks with one of Amy's friends wasn't filling him with enthusiasm. "Okay," he said, reluctantly. "Cannes it is."

Johnson's phone pinged as a secure text message arrived. He glanced at the screen, tapped in his key and read it. It was from Vic and was extremely brief.

It's the Russians again. Stay safe en route to Borneo buddy.

Johnson didn't reply.

* * *

Thursday, July 17, 2014
Washington, DC

. . .

Some distance south of the Tomb of the Unknown Soldier, a white-haired lady hunched her back and, with a slight shuffle, walked along the broad pathway toward a solitary bench at the top of a slope. She took a seat on the right side of the bench and glanced down at the array of white gravestones that were spread out in neat lines on the grass beneath her vantage point.

This corner of section 35 of Arlington National Cemetery, only a couple of miles southwest of the White House and a short hop over the Potomac River into Virginia, was a good meeting place, in Anastasia Shevchenko's experience. She had used it a number of times when working at the *rezidentura* in Washington a few years earlier, and it was distant enough from the political buzz of Capitol Hill for the contact she was due to meet now to feel secure.

Shevchenko cast an expert eye around the cemetery. There had been no sign of trailing coverage as she had made her way on an extended surveillance detection route around downtown Washington and over the Arlington Memorial Bridge. She was confident she was black—she had seen nothing untoward.

In her right ear was a small earpiece through which she could hear her team of four covert SVR countersurveillance officers from the *rezidentura* who were placed at various points around the cemetery. None of them had given her an abort signal.

In theory, there was no reason for her not to be black, given she had entered the US only a few weeks earlier under a completely different identity. But the countersurveillance people were always cautious; they had aborted a couple of recent meetings, including one at this same location five days earlier on suspicion that the FBI were tailing them. There was no hard evidence of that, but the feds were professionals, and it was better to be safe than sorry.

Since her arrival in DC on July 2, she had spent most of her time at a rented apartment on Fifteenth Street NW, a block away from Lafayette Square. During the past few days she had been waiting for the confirmatory call that had finally come that morning.

A half hour or so later, the contents of the call were all over the television and radio news. A Boeing airliner carrying nearly three hundred people had been shot down over Ukraine. All passengers and crew were dead.

Shevchenko hunched her back again. She was normally anything but round shouldered. In fact, her slim, wiry physique was well toned for her age.

She took a phone from her pocket and made a pretend call, engaging some imaginary friend in an animated conversation that required her to pivot on her bench and scan the area behind as well as in front of her. Still there was no sign of any observers, no shadows behind trees or men loitering and smoking cigarettes. No women with prams or unusual-looking dog walkers.

Shevchenko replaced the phone in her pocket, next to a Czech passport identifying her as Tatiana Niklas, a fifty-eight-year-old teacher from Prague. The only accurate element of the passport was her age, which was spot on, but the rest of it was the identity of a woman who had died twenty years earlier.

Her black shoulder-length hair normally had only a few flecks of gray in the mix. But that would have been lost on any onlooker now. She had colored her hair a pale gray, almost white, adding at least fifteen years to her apparent age. Makeup had also lightened her dark complexion. She was fluent in Czech, having spent three years in Prague during the 1980s, and was confident she could cruise through any interview required at US immigration. After all, "Tatiana" was one of her longest-standing and solid legends, or false identities—she knew her background as well as that of a twin sister, and she often used the identity when recruiting agents for security purposes.

There had been no questions upon her arrival at Houston's George Bush Intercontinental Airport, which was a less obtrusive entry point than Washington's Dulles International or New York's JFK. She had been waved straight through. From there she made her way directly to Washington.

Major General Shevchenko was a key figure in Russia's foreign intelligence service, the SVR, so the steps she had taken to alter her appearance had been necessary. Just three months earlier, she had been ejected from the United Kingdom and bundled on a flight back to Moscow after being caught handling a mole she had cultivated in London. The mole, none other than the CIA's London station chief Bernice Franklin, had been uncovered following an investigation by one of the CIA's freelancers, Joe Johnson.

The failure in London had not gone down well with Shevchenko's direct boss, the counterintelligence deputy director Yevgeny Kutsik, while the overall director in charge of the SVR at Yasenevo, Maksim Kruglov, maintained a noncommittal silence. She guessed her ambitions to one day accede to Kruglov's throne had taken a severe knock.

But she accepted her fate and therefore laid low for a few weeks in Moscow.

Other intelligence agencies, sensing a moment of personal vulnerability, were quick to pick up on what had happened. During those weeks, she had a couple of extremely discreet approaches: a potentially lucrative one to spy for the Mossad and another from the German intelligence agency, the BND. In her disgruntled state, she had been slightly tempted by the former but had declined after two days of contemplation.

Then this opportunity to resurface in the US capital had come up, and all that had been forgotten.

Kutsik's attitude toward her when briefing her on the operation seemed clear: she was still well regarded, but likely in the last-chance saloon. He deliberately let slip that she had been chosen ahead of others who badly wanted the gig, such as Pavel Vasilenko, deputy chief of the American department, who had already done a lengthy stint in the Washington *rezidentura* a few years earlier. The SVR wasn't a "one strike and you're out" organization, but two strikes was a different story. She knew she couldn't afford another blunder; otherwise the wild dogs like Vasilenko who were snapping at her heels would have her on the floor.

Kruglov, who on the face of it had always supported her, had seemed much more conciliatory when she met him and even wished her good luck in Washington. But nevertheless, she was very aware that you were only as good as your last operation in this environment.

To her left, in her peripheral vision, Shevchenko caught a movement. There he was, her contact, whom she had cultivated during her previous stint in the US capital, when he had been significantly farther down the career ladder than he was now.

The man, now code-named TITANIUM, had visited Moscow a few weeks ago on a business trip for an international conference, and she had taken the opportunity to renew contact with him.

A key factor in her successful recruitment had been the scarcely disguised threat of blackmail. Again, based on observation and intuition, she had found out a long time ago whom TITANIUM was sleeping with, other than his wife. The surveillance team at the embassy had ascertained recently that he was still carrying on with that mistress.

In the process, the team had also somehow discovered

that he was on a long course of antidepressants and had been quietly and confidentially seeing a psychiatrist as well as his regular doctor. Another factor lay in the occasional unguarded hints that his political views were not always in alignment with his role.

In short, he was a powerful man in a vulnerable position, and in that vulnerability, Shevchenko saw an opportunity that she had taken. TITANIUM had been angry at the trap he had fallen into—she had made it clear he had no choice but to cooperate unless he wanted his personal business to get into the media. But at the same time he seemed to like the dollars that were now flowing into his numbered Swiss bank account and complied with her demands.

Shevchenko remained seated, her arms folded, as TITANIUM slid onto the bench next to her.

"Here we are again," he said.

Shevchenko returned her gaze to the middle distance in the direction from which TITANIUM had come. "Indeed we are," she said. "Are you certain you are clean?"

There was no obvious sign of anyone in the vicinity. The cemetery was quiet.

"I am certain as I can be."

"Good."

She knew that TITANIUM had a good reason to visit this section of the cemetery and indeed came here fairly frequently, which was why she had chosen it. It was unlikely that the FBI, knowing his habits, would follow him here. After all, his father, a Second World War air force bomber pilot, had been buried two years earlier little more than a hundred meters from where they were sitting. If only he knew what his son was doing.

TITANIUM cleared his throat a little. "I see your operation went according to plan. Devastating."

"It wasn't my operation. But yes. It was."

"The speculation has already begun, which is good. I have plenty of ammunition that you and your contacts can use to fuel that in the next few days."

"Give me the highlights," Shevchenko murmured, touching his forearm briefly and unnecessarily. "And keep your voice low." He was speaking a little too clearly for her liking.

"Right. There is only one real highlight, from which all the others can follow."

"And that is?"

TITANIUM leaned forward, resting his elbows on his knees and cupping his chin in his hands. He glanced sideways at the Russian. "Did you know that our secretary of state and the CIA director held a meeting with the Ukrainian president four weeks ago in Kiev? A long meeting with a lot of follow-up actions, promised by our president, which the secretary of state communicated."

Shevchenko had some difficulty in stopping herself from jerking upright in surprise. "*What?*"

"Yes. You heard correctly."

If true, this was a meeting that had gone so far under the radar as to be almost invisible. There had been no inkling at Moscow Center, the SVR headquarters, of such an event, although intelligence relating to some kind of military assistance had been picked up.

"What actions? Are you talking about intelligence or weaponry? Or both?"

She turned her head toward TITANIUM, who nodded once.

"Both."

"What type of weaponry?"

"Javelin anti-tank missiles. Firefinder missile detection radar. Humvee armored vehicles. Night-vision goggles. Flak jackets. You name it. Lots of stuff."

Shevchenko nodded thoughtfully and let her left knee stray sideways until it touched his, where she left it for a few seconds. "Ground-to-air missiles? Patriots or Stingers maybe?" The US defense manufacturer Raytheon was known to have sold its Patriot weapons system to a number of countries, including Poland.

"Not quite yet. Possibly Patriots to come. But don't let that stop you."

Shevchenko gave a quiet laugh. "No, it won't stop us. Thank you."

There was a pause as Shevchenko digested the implications of what she had just been told. This opened the door to significant opportunities and endless speculation that the White House, Pentagon, and State Department would struggle to deny convincingly.

"Do you have any documentary proof of the meeting? Memos, diary entries, follow-up emails?"

"I was anticipating that." TITANIUM reached into his pocket and removed a small flash drive. "There. Photos of memos and emails on that. But only for use if absolutely necessary. I would rather you didn't use them for obvious reasons—my security. I don't think it is necessary. This is all about the smoke, not the fire, in my view."

Shevchenko took the flash drive and pocketed it. "I agree. The smoke is the key thing. But this proof of the fire behind it will be useful internally at Moscow Center for my and your credibility, even if we don't use it externally."

"Anything else?" TITANIUM asked.

"Not for now. Let's meet again in a few days. Site GREEN?" That was at a golf course near to TITANIUM's home.

"Yes, site GREEN."

"I am going to work out some other potential locations. We also need to set up a better channel of communication.

Face-to-face meetings like this are high risk for both of us. I will give some thought to that and come up with a plan. It will involve using a covcom device, probably a phone app of some kind."

"Yes, covcom would be better. I agree."

"We need a place where we could come fairly close together to operate it, but without actually meeting. I know your schedule is hectic, but is there anything in your weekly routine that involves a regular stop outside the office, like a restaurant or bar?"

"You might find this amusing, but for years, I have fairly often stopped on my way home for a hot chocolate at a small café, a favorite place of mine. Maybe once every two weeks. It gives me half an hour of normality in my crazy working life, and I've stuck to it as I've risen up the ladder."

Shevchenko considered the idea. "That might be a possibility. I would need to structure it carefully to ensure security. We can discuss it further at our next meeting. Usual communication channels until then." The pair of them kept in touch using seemingly innocent text messages on burner phones that were changed regularly.

She scrutinized TITANIUM. "Are you okay? Not finding all this too stressful?"

TITANIUM gave a slight sigh. "I'm okay. Sort of. I don't find it easy, but it's fine."

He stood and nodded at Shevchenko, then turned and walked away in the direction he had come from. She pulled a pack of cigarettes from her pocket and lit one. She made a mental note to get some high-definition satellite photos from Yasenevo of the alternative meeting sites she had in mind, other than this one and the golf course.

"*Bozhe,*" she murmured as she crossed her right leg over her left, a prearranged signal that conveyed a *disperse* message to her lead countersurveillance officer from the *rezidentura* team.

God. *This little cookie is up to his neck in this*, she thought as she watched him disappear. *It's a spider's web.*

CHAPTER FIVE

Friday, July 18, 2014
  Cannes

The view from Natalia's holiday villa overlooking the Bay of Cannes to the right and Cap d'Antibes to the left was stunning under the morning sunshine. But Johnson was too distracted to truly appreciate the clear skies and blue seas of the Mediterranean stretching out in front of him.

To his relief, he had eventually persuaded his children to fly from Amsterdam to Nice, a two-hour journey, rather than take the ten-hour train trip they had initially favored. They had managed to get tickets on a flight that had arrived at half past eleven the previous evening and had then rented a car to drive to Natalia's villa, forty minutes away.

But during the evening, and then again this morning, both Johnson and Jayne had noticed a growing wave of social media coverage and speculation about the Malaysia Airlines crash. Although both of them only occasionally posted on Twitter or Facebook, they did follow the accounts of key news outlets, politicians, and intelligence analysts and kept a close eye on what was trending.

They sat on the patio of Natalia's villa, a few yards from a very tempting swimming pool, and flicked through the posts on their phones. The children were still asleep upstairs in guest bedrooms, while Amy and Natalia were chatting in the kitchen.

"There's thousands of tweets being pumped out," Jayne said.

Johnson nodded. "Facebook too. All kinds of dodgy theories."

In contrast to Johnson's, Jayne's, and Vic's instinctive reactions that the Russians were likely behind the crash, most of the social media posts were heaping blame on Ukraine's government, on the basis that the crash had happened on its territory. The Ukrainian military was accused of using either a fighter jet or a surface-to-air missile to shoot down the plane, either deliberately or in error.

But the more recent posts also were mentioning the possibility of a CIA plot to bring down the plane to discredit Russia and to try to generate further international sanctions against Putin's regime.

Johnson frowned as he scrolled down the tweets and cross-checked them against the hashtags that linked them together.

#KievDownedTheBoeing
#Kiev'sProvocation
#KievTellTheTruth

Those particular hashtags were so popular that two of them were listed among the top trending ones across the whole of the Twitter site. The posts linked to them all told the same story.

As Johnson read the posts, Amy emerged through a French door onto the patio, accompanied by Natalia, a slim, elegant woman. This morning Natalia's hair was tied up, and she wore a white cotton dress.

"We were wondering if you would like to take a stroll down to the beach," Natalia said. "There's a lovely little café I would like to show you. They do great coffee."

Johnson glanced up at Jayne, who imperceptibly shook her head, then back at Natalia. "That sounds good," he said. "But we're a little busy. The airliner crash last night has set the hares running."

"You're on vacation," Amy said. "We had a tough day yesterday. Don't you want to relax?"

Johnson paused. Relaxing with a coffee was exactly what he would like to do, perhaps followed by a leisurely lunch accompanied by a decent bottle or two of Chablis or Bordeaux. And then a siesta upstairs with Jayne.

But the aftermath of the Ukraine crash was pulling him in like some kind of centrifugal force.

"Not right now," Jayne said. "Perhaps we could go later?"

Natalia and Amy exchanged glances. "Fine," Amy said. "We'll go ourselves, then."

After the two women disappeared, Johnson jabbed his finger at his phone screen. "This is a troll campaign. No way this isn't coordinated."

The thousands of tweets had been pumped out from a whole variety of usernames, but most of them had similar hallmarks apart from the hashtags, particularly a slightly odd use of English in many instances.

Johnson began to check through news websites, many of whose stories quoted the tweets he had just been reading. But then he spotted a couple of stories on defense industry sites labeled as exclusive, with an additional tag of "Breaking News." Johnson knew of both sites and indeed occasionally read their news coverage: one of them was based in Prague, the other in Paris.

The first story to catch his eye was headlined "CIA Plot to Bring Down Plane," and the second, "Deadly CIA Plot To Shoot Down Plane 'Revealed'."

The stories mentioned a recent secret meeting in Kiev between the Ukrainian president Petro Poroshenko and US Secretary of State, Paul Farrar, together with the director of the CIA, Arthur Veltman, and the US national security advisor, Francis Wade. According to the reports, the meeting had been held at the request of US president Stephen Ferguson, a man often criticized for apparent weakness in the face of Russian aggression.

At the meeting, according to the reports, it was agreed that the United States would supply Ukraine with an array of weapons. The more detailed of the reports specifically listed Patriot ground-to-air missiles and possibly handheld Stinger anti-aircraft missiles, Javelin anti-tank missiles, as well as Firefinder missile detection radar and Humvee armored vehicles. Also in the package were night-vision goggles and flak jackets. The first delivery of weapons had already been deployed, the report said.

The articles gave no specific attribution to the information they were reporting, saying only that the details had come from high-level sources.

Johnson sat up in his chair. "My God. Look at this," he said, holding his phone so Jayne could read the story. "Patriots? No way. That can't be right."

There was little doubt that the Ukrainians would like the Patriot, one of the world's most advanced surface-to-air missile systems, built by US defense giant Raytheon. Not least, they needed an answer to the threat from the Russians, who were thought to be moving their Iskander short-range ballistic missile system into the Crimean Peninsula. The Iskander was capable of carrying a variety of warheads— including nuclear—and formed yet another serious threat to

Ukraine. But from his conversations with Vic, Johnson knew that Ukraine wasn't being granted its wish, at least not yet.

"Did Farrar actually go to Kiev for a meeting?" Jayne asked.

"Yes. Between you and me, Vic mentioned it, in strict confidence. But he says we aren't supplying Patriots to Ukraine, just lower-level support. And I know Raytheon has sold Patriots overseas, but definitely not to Ukraine."

Jayne raised an eyebrow. "So, is it bullshit? Or is it no smoke without fire? That's the problem with this stuff—nobody knows the truth."

Johnson inclined his head in tacit agreement. He clicked back to his Twitter account. Already the news stories were being quoted and referenced in a number of tweets, with a new hashtag attached to them: #MH17CIAplot. That wasn't trending yet, but Johnson guessed that before long, it would be.

A few other tweets from international news organizations were quoting senior politicians in the Netherlands, France, and Germany who were condemning the United States for its actions in providing the weapons systems to Ukraine. No doubt those comments would fuel further news coverage as the day went on.

A short quote from the front-runner for the Republican nomination in the 2016 presidential election, Maryland Governor Nicholas McAllister, also featured in two news stories. "My thoughts are with the victims of this terrible tragedy. It seems as though President Ferguson needs to apologize and explain what looks like another foreign policy disaster from the White House. I will be seeking a full investigation."

A US Defense Department spokesman and another from the White House were quoted denying that any surface-to-air missiles had been supplied to Ukraine. However, they had refused to comment on whether the reports of secret talks in Kiev were accurate.

"Langley is going to go ballistic over this," Johnson said. "And so is the White House."

"They need to make the denial stronger. It looks weak," Jayne said.

"That's the problem. They're denying the surface-to-air missiles aspect, but it's true that some weapons have gone to Kiev, so it's probably going to be difficult to believe them. The Agency has its fingers deep in a lot of pies, and people know that."

* * *

Friday, July 18, 2014
    Washington, DC

There had been no time for a proper internal inquest at Langley into how details of the Kiev talks with President Poroshenko had leaked; the call from the White House had come too quickly for that.

Vic Walter pulled himself upright in the black leather swivel chair, checked his watch, and glanced at his boss. Arthur Veltman's lips were pressed tight, and his arms were folded on the mahogany conference table at which they were both seated. As usual, he appeared anything but relaxed.

On the walls of the main conference room of the White House Situation Room, several video screens were silently showing live twenty-four-hour news channels with ticker-tape transcripts.

All the channels were carrying footage of the crashed Malaysia Airlines jet in Ukraine: there were videos and images of the crash site, across which pieces of still-smoldering plane wreckage were scattered. There were interviews with families of dead passengers and videos of bewildered-looking local people in the vicinity of the tragedy. Defense industry experts, relatives of the dead, and an assortment of talking-head politicians were either questioning whether the blame for the aircraft's demise should be placed on missiles supplied by the United States or openly criticizing the US.

Leading the charge was Nicholas McAllister, the front-runner for the Republican nomination in the next presidential election.

McAllister, the governor of Maryland, had been critical of President Ferguson on a number of other issues as his popularity gained momentum. There was a fifteen-second clip of him speaking during a press conference in Annapolis, in which he was asked for his view on the Ukraine crash.

"This out-of-control president has clearly demonstrated he has no proper grasp on critical foreign policy issues that are strategic to the United States," McAllister intoned, crouching closer to the bank of broadcast microphones in front of him and running a hand over his neatly coiffured gray hair. "He has a scattergun approach, throwing weapons and missiles at any regime that he thinks is aligned with his own interests. If it is shown that the Malaysian jet was shot down using arms supplied by his administration, his policy will have backfired in a massively spectacular way."

McAllister, accompanied by his platinum-blonde twin sister, Martina, a Republican state senator in Maryland, continued, "We all know that Ferguson is unfit for office. I have great sympathy for the innocent victims of his incompetence."

Martina, whom Vic viewed as a shameless attention seeker, led the applause after he finished speaking. Almost all of the reports showed the senator subsequently holding her own separate press conference at which she went a step further than her brother by demanding that Ferguson should face an impeachment inquiry over the part his policies and decisions had played in the shooting down of the airliner.

Vic glanced at Veltman and shook his head. This was not looking good for the White House.

President Ferguson's personal aide, Charles Deacon, an academic-looking man with neatly parted hair, black glasses, and a hook nose, walked in and greeted Veltman. He took a seat in a row of chairs placed against the wall while waiting for his boss, and began reading a file he was carrying.

"Come on," Veltman muttered, more to himself than to Vic. "Let's get this over with."

The two CIA men were unable to fiddle with their phones, their default way of dispersing nervous energy, because the security team had, as usual, locked their devices in a lead-lined cabinet in the Situation Room's reception area.

Veltman always reminded Vic of the builder who had constructed his house. His face was on the pudgy side, and he gave the impression of being slightly rough around the edges. But behind that demeanor and barrel chest was a razor-sharp intellect, which Veltman tried to convey by wearing a pair of donnish wire-framed glasses.

After the call had come two hours earlier, the two men had rushed the seven miles from the CIA headquarters building at Langley to the White House. But the president was already more than twenty minutes late for the briefing, and the wait was doing nothing for Vic's already anxious frame of mind.

Several months earlier, there would have been zero chance of Vic being included in such a meeting. But following his promotion to head of the Directorate of Operations at the end of the previous year, Veltman had asked him on a couple of occasions to join him for briefings with the president.

The destruction of the Malaysia Airlines jet had sent the

White House into the kind of adrenaline-fueled frenzy that Vic had previously only witnessed with mild interest from a safe distance. Now, though, he was in the thick of it.

As if to add gasoline to an already highly flammable situation, a few online media stories had just that morning revealed the highly secret talks that the secretary of state had held with Ukraine President Poroshenko, including their discussions about potential supplies of weapon systems. Since then, most social media channels had been jammed with tweets and posts speculating on this twist.

It was the kind of situation that Vic dreaded. He could almost predict the tone of the meeting that was about to take place.

Sure enough, about ten seconds later came the sound of Ferguson's voice preceding him through the open door of the main conference room.

The White House's Situation "Room" was something of a misnomer, as it actually consisted of a sprawling suite of rooms deep in the basement of the West Wing, of which the conference room was just one. Designed as a place for the president to receive classified information, monitor domestic and international crises, and conduct confidential video discussions with other world leaders, it comprised multiple conference rooms and smaller meeting rooms. Banks of communications equipment and screens were permanently manned by watch officers.

The president strode in, his national security advisor, Francis Wade, and Paul Farrar following in his slipstream. Behind them was another man Vic recognized, Brad Turner, who was chairman of the House Intelligence Committee, the main committee in the House of Representatives responsible for overseeing the US intelligence community.

Ferguson raised a hand in greeting to Veltman and nodded at Vic. He moved swiftly to his usual chair at the head of the table, the presidential seal mounted on the wall behind him, and sat.

Farrar, one of the president's right-hand men and also one of his close friends since their school days, sat to Ferguson's right, his normally pink, animated face looking gray and downcast. The darker-complexioned, more youthful-looking Wade sat to the president's left along with Turner, a fat man who smelled of cigarette smoke. Deacon moved from his perch against the wall and took a seat at the far end of the table.

The Situation Room was Wade's empire, given his security advisor's role, and he ran it like a fiefdom from his office in the northwest corner of the West Wing's first floor.

"This is a shitstorm," Ferguson said, without preamble. "Terrible enough that an airliner has been shot down—and by the way, I'm certain it's the Russians, not the Ukrainians, who did it. But then on top of that, how is it we had no warning that the Kiev meeting was about to leak?" He folded his arms and eyeballed Veltman.

"It's appalling, sir, and I'm also certain it was the Russians, probably using Buks," Veltman said. "You pose a good question about the meeting. We all believed it was watertight."

"Indeed we did," Wade said, his dark eyes flicking between the president and Veltman. "Given we held it in a private unmarked jet at Kiev airport with only two other attendees on the Ukraine side, I don't see how this could have happened."

"Clearly it wasn't watertight," Ferguson said, with a sideways glance at Veltman. "Now the only thing that looks watertight is the impression everyone now has that we directly supplied missiles to Ukraine that were responsible for shooting down a Boeing full of civilians. Have you seen the shit that idiot McAllister and his vile sister are spreading around?"

"Yes, we've seen it," Veltman said.

Ferguson pressed his palms together. "This shit that we provided the weapons and ammunition for one of the worst war crimes in modern history—I'm not standing for it. And I'm not standing for being set up as the fall guy for this either."

The president's voice was rising, and the veins on either side of his forehead were standing out like pieces of red cord. Vic could feel his stomach tightening in knots. He could clearly imagine how his boss was feeling right now.

"I would like to see some stronger denials out there," Veltman said. "Can that be done?"

"Karen's already doing that as strongly as possible, in categorical terms," Ferguson said, referring to his press secretary, Karen Packman. "And she's fudging the issue of the secret talks. But we can't outright deny the talks. And if you add in the willingness of people to believe anything on social media about the US supplying weapons to any aligned country that needs them, we're not going to cut much ice."

The president turned to Farrar. "Don't you agree, Paul?"

Farrar, a thickset muscular, man with wiry white hair, nodded. Normally energetic, he appeared unusually exhausted today. "I wouldn't be surprised if the Ukraine government is going soft on denying it because they would quite like to leave Russia with the impression that they actually do have Patriots," he said.

There was silence for a few seconds. Vic figured that Farrar was spot-on with his assessment.

Veltman leaned forward. "With your permission, sir, I would like to begin an extremely thorough investigation into who leaked details of those discussions."

"Well, I'm assuming the leak isn't coming from our end," the president said, his voice rising in tone again. "It's got to be coming from Kiev."

"You're probably correct, although we should keep an open mind."

The president tapped his fingers on the table. "Yes, go ahead with your inquiry. Leave no stone unturned. Get someone into Ukraine and do it. But I don't want the inquiry itself to become yet another story. I want it to be very low key, done out of sight, right under the radar. What I would like is for us to continue strongly denying the supply of missiles to Ukraine and to continue not commenting on the discussions with Poroshenko."

"Fine, we'll find a way to do that," Veltman said.

"I'd like to know exactly what Russia did," Ferguson said. "How are your sources in Moscow now? You lost a few good agents there last year, if I remember correctly, and more recently. Have you found replacements? Last time we had the conversation, you were working on some high-level SVR and FSB recruitments."

The president hadn't forgotten, then, but he wasn't likely to. Three highly placed Western moles within the SVR—two of them handled by the CIA, one by MI6—had vanished off the radar last year, presumed dead. All thanks to information provided to Moscow by the CIA's former London station chief, Franklin.

But in May, after the capture of Franklin, three more CIA assets in Russia had disappeared, while another working in the SVR's *rezidentura* in Buenos Aires had also been suddenly recalled to Moscow and was never heard from again. It was unclear whether Franklin was to blame for these latter four losses. Vic and Veltman thought not, but they had no evidence to back up their hunch, nor any other suspects to target.

Overall, their loss had left a major hole in the CIA's attempts to counter SVR activity and had caused a panic at

Langley. Everyone was paranoid about it, and many operations had been put on hold, presumed to have been blown.

"At the highest levels, the search for new assets is still ongoing, sir," Veltman said carefully. "Moscow station has to be extremely cautious, though, as you can imagine—FSB countersurveillance is red-hot right now. They know we're on the lookout. It's a slow burner."

The pressure was rising to land a major fish in Moscow—a high-level spy at head of directorate level in the SVR or FSB, or even deputy head—who could supply the Agency with valuable inside information.

Moscow station had been working hard on a number of individuals to replace those lost, but so far nothing had materialized. At lower levels, there had been slightly more progress. The pool of potential recruits was larger, salaries were lower, and temptation was greater. Of course, the quality of information received was correspondingly reduced.

"Keep the pressure up," Ferguson said, planting his elbows on the mirrorlike table surface. "But wherever you get the information, I want to know exactly who brought that airliner down and how and what missiles were used. I need to be able to deny that the CIA is carrying it out, at least until we have the proof we need. Do I make myself understood?"

There was another pause. "Yes, sir," Veltman said. "I get it."

The president nodded. "We need a one hundred percent guarantee that we get to the bottom of this, and quickly. If the Russians or the Ukrainians carry out some so-called investigation, it will be bullshit. Nobody will believe it."

"An air industry inquiry would be believed," Veltman said.

"Yes, an official inquiry will probably come from the Dutch Safety Board given that the flight originated there," Ferguson said. "But that will take months, years even. I need answers much faster—like yesterday. But I also need to be able to look the Russian and Ukrainian presidents in the eye, and anyone else, for that matter, and say we, that is, the CIA, are not carrying out our own private investigation on their soil."

"Yes, I get that," Veltman said. He had a slightly quizzical expression.

Vic was getting the feeling that the president was holding something back.

Veltman also appeared to be thinking the same thing. A second later he vocalized it. "I apologize for persisting, sir, but is there something we should know? Is there a specific reason you want it done so quickly and in this way?"

The president rocked back in his chair. "Yes, there is. Nobody knows this—yet—but it's because Paul's wife, Eileen, and their two kids were on that plane."

He looked at Farrar, who had turned a shade grayer and was staring down at the table.

"Eileen was godmother to my eldest, a friend to my wife. My family's like that with them." He held up his crossed forefinger and middle finger to illustrate how intertwined they were. "We need to find out who was responsible."

CHAPTER SIX

Friday, July 18, 2014
Langley, Virginia

When Vic and Veltman arrived at the suite of offices that occupy the seventh floor of the old CIA headquarters building at Langley, they found that Veltman's executive assistant, Kate, was just placing two cups of latte on his desk. She had fetched them from the Starbucks on the CIA campus—known to many of the employees there as the Stealthy Starbucks.

"I thought you might need those," Kate said as the two men walked in after returning from the White House. She brushed back her long blond hair as she headed for the door. "It sounded like a firestorm down there. Poor Paul."

"Thanks for the coffee," said Veltman, who had given her a brief flavor of the conversation from the car. She knew Farrar from his periodic visits to the seventh floor. "Yes, poor Paul. Firestorm sums it up. Ferguson was fuming. Hardly surprising."

Since his promotion to director of operations, Vic had been ensconced in an office next door to Veltman, complete with a connecting door. His room had a series of red and green digital clocks that told him the time of day in five key time zones, a series of monitor screens, and a row of windows that looked out over the sprawling Langley campus with its thousands of parking spaces and the heavily wooded Virginia countryside beyond.

The long, low-profile CIA headquarters building he was located in dated back to the early 1960s—and looked it too, although once inside it was a different story. It overlooked the newer campus buildings nearby, opened in 1991.

Vic had mixed feelings about his new role. On the one hand, he felt intense pride that he had climbed to such heights at the Agency, where he had spent his entire career. On the other hand, the new role was highly political and often felt like a high-wire act, with any number of people constantly conspiring to topple him off.

Now he sensed another challenge coming up. There was no way that Veltman was going to take responsibility for delivering the president's instructions.

"Very hard on Paul," Veltman said as he removed the plastic lid from the take-out coffee cup. There was no name written on the side, unlike every other Starbucks in the world. The baristas had been ordered not to ask for their customers' names.

"Yes," Vic said, sipping his latte. As usual, he sat in a black leather chair on the other side of Veltman's desk. He put his coffee down on the wooden surface. "What would be the odds of his wife and kids being on that plane? I thought when he came into the conference room he looked like a train wreck. Now we know why. Very tough."

Veltman nodded. "I'm not a great fan of his, but I do feel

so sorry for him." He strode to the window, placed one hand on the windowsill, and looked out.

"We've now got the mother of all jobs on our hands. We'll need to get someone into Russia and Ukraine, on the ground, to cut through the shitty lies that Moscow is already putting out."

He turned and leaned against the sill, nursing his coffee in his right hand.

"Agreed," Vic said. "It's no use trying to do it from here. And in the absence of a mole in Moscow, which is something we badly need right now . . ." He let his voice trail off.

"So who can we send?"

"There's no shortage of good people in Eastern Europe we could draw on. I could name a few in the Helsinki, Athens, and Istanbul stations."

Veltman took a long sip of latte and wiped his mouth with the back of his hand to remove the froth. "Remember what Ferguson said. No fingerprints. He wants deniability. I just can't see how that's going to work if we use bodies out of our Helsinki or Istanbul stations. Moscow Center would be all over them."

Moscow Center was the headquarters of Russia's foreign intelligence service, the SVR, at Yasenevo, south of Moscow. The SVR was created in 1991 when its predecessor organization, the KGB, was divided into two as the Soviet Union broke up. The other arm, Russia's internal intelligence service, the FSB, was based at the Lubyanka building in Moscow.

"It won't be easy to make it work," Vic said. "Although I do have one idea that—"

"Well, we're going to have to find a way to make it work," Veltman interrupted. "And I would like to task you with the little job of managing this particular operation." He gave a half grin, walked back to his desk, and sat down in his burgundy leather swivel chair opposite Vic. "It needs to be designed and executed to perfection. I wouldn't trust anyone else with it."

Vic had anticipated his boss's request. Being a long-term confidante of Veltman was something of a double-edged sword. His boss had unexpectedly given him the role of acting NCS director the previous September, despite the claims of other associate deputy directors who were more senior. He had then confirmed him permanently in the post in December. But with promotion came expectations, and Veltman was a demanding taskmaster.

"I was about to say that there is one angle we could take, and I have a person in mind," Vic said. He had been furiously trying to think of possible approaches.

"What?"

"We're talking about a major war crime here, with three hundred massacred. That's probably going to mean the case going to the International Criminal Court, if we can find the perpetrators."

Vic's view was that the ICC, based in The Hague and responsible for prosecuting international war crimes, including genocide, would have to get involved at some stage.

"Possibly. It's very early days to be talking about that. Ukraine would have to cooperate with the ICC and hand over jurisdiction to them."

"There's no question they'll do that. We know it's most likely the Russians who did it—so the Ukrainians will cooperate in trying to nail them. The way it would work is that a prosecutor from the ICC and his or her assistants would then carry out a preliminary investigation in Ukraine that could lead to a criminal prosecution."

"How does that help us?"

Vic leaned forward and opened his mouth to speak, but

Veltman got in first. "Don't tell me. We insert one of our guys into the ICC team on the ground."

Vic smiled. "You read my mind." It was literally what he had been about to say. This was why he got on so well with Veltman. The pair of them seemed to know each other's unspoken thoughts.

"It would be the perfect solution," Vic said. "The ICC will take forever to do their work. They are tortoises personified. Our guy would of course remain semidetached from the team, if not fully detached, and carry out his own much faster set of inquiries to meet the demands of our friend at 1600 Pennsylvania Avenue."

Veltman stood again and strode back to his window. He stood looking out in silence.

"I'm due to fly to London tomorrow to sort out the mess at the station there, then go on to Paris," Vic said. "Instead, I could go to The Hague first and visit the chief prosecutor, Fernando Morales—I got to know him quite well a couple of years ago."

Veltman turned, animated now, his right hand on his hip, his left running through the neatly groomed remains of his graying hair. "Good idea, yes. So what about the person for the job? There's that guy you used earlier this year to bring down our London station chief. The war crimes investigator. The same guy who nailed Watto."

This time Vic struggled to suppress a grin. "Joe Johnson, you mean." He had had conversations with Veltman about Johnson, although the two had never met or even spoken.

"Yes, Johnson. It was neat revenge, I thought, given Watto fired him from here in the '80s. Why are you smirking?"

"It's because you took the words out of my mouth—again. I was about to mention Johnson."

It was Vic who had brought in Johnson for the operation

earlier that year that started as a planned debriefing of an SVR defector heading to the West and ended by trapping Bernice Franklin. Veltman had been massively grateful for the work done, despite the embarrassment caused.

Franklin hadn't been the only recent senior casualty, though. Indeed, Vic's promotion had come about after his predecessor, Terry Jenner, had been forced to resign the previous year. That was also due to a successful investigation by Johnson and Vic into one of Jenner's right-hand men, Robert Watson.

Watson, now languishing in a federal prison, had spent years as chief of the Directorate of Operations' Near East Division, with a focus on projects such as the Pakistan drone program. But he was also a crook who had made millions on the side from illegal arms deals. His arrest in a Brooklyn subway station had been poetic justice for Johnson, whom Watson fired from the CIA in 1988 in Islamabad, where Johnson and Vic had first worked together.

"Johnson could do the job, couldn't he?" Veltman asked. "He sounds damned good. Isn't he a Russian speaker? I'll leave it up to you, Vic, but if he's good, and he's not Agency staff, it could resolve the issue of deniability."

Vic nodded. "He is damned good. He'd probably be occupying the office next door instead of me if he were still working for the Agency. And yes, he's fluent in Russian and knows the country. He has also done quite a lot of work for the ICC before, so to put him in that kind of role would not be a credibility stretch and would be a good cover story. Morales knows him." He paused. "I only have one doubt about him."

"What's that?"

"He can be a loose cannon at times. You never quite know what route he's going to take to get to the destination, if you know what I mean. This is going to be an intensely political, high-profile case. We can't afford to put a foot wrong."

"Well, I hope you're not getting your excuses in early. If you decide to go with him, you'd better make sure he doesn't put a foot wrong. Now if you'll excuse me, I have a meeting in three minutes. I'll let our White House friends know what we're thinking of doing before they call me."

Vic nodded and rose. "I'll let you get ready. I'll contact the NSA and get them to track where this stream of social media bullshit is coming from. There might be a common thread or a common author behind it all."

"Good," Veltman said.

Vic picked up his half-empty coffee cup and headed for the door. Halfway there he paused and turned back to Veltman. "I think Joe might be out of the country on vacation—he and his family were headed for the Borneo jungle to go see orangutans or something. It won't be easy to persuade him to do this."

"Screw the orangutans. You'll have to get him back out of the jungle, then. If he plays hard to get, let me know and I'll twist his arm."

Vic grimaced. "Sure. I'll give him a call first thing tomorrow and see what I can do."

CHAPTER SEVEN

Friday, July 18, 2014
    Cannes

Johnson pulled his cap farther down over his eyes and adjusted his sunglasses as he focused on the figure in the distance zooming past a moored yacht on a dangerously powerful-looking Jet Ski.

Peter, who had recently turned sixteen, had been out there on the millpond-flat Mediterranean for twenty minutes now and hadn't hit anything or anyone yet, so Johnson felt justified in relaxing at last.

He wiggled his toes in the sand and sighed. His book, Terry Hayes's *I Am Pilgrim*, lay open upside down on his chest. It felt good to be able to lie there and think of absolutely nothing, although he could feel his bare legs below his swimming trunks beginning to burn in the sunshine. The beach was relatively quiet; there were plenty of French families, but it seemed as though most of the Brits and Germans hadn't arrived for their vacations yet.

To Johnson's right, Carrie was lying flat on her back, her eyes closed and her Bluetooth earphones inserted, listening to some music while trying to get her tan underway. To his left were two chaise lounges, both of them empty because Jayne and Amy had gone for a walk along the seafront to check out the Old Port, with its marina full of luxury yachts. Natalia had decided not to visit the beach and had remained at the villa.

It was two o'clock, and the temperature was in the high eighties. Not quite hot enough to be uncomfortable, but bordering on it.

After the turmoil and stress of Amsterdam, Johnson was actually quite pleased the Borneo trip was off. While it would have been interesting, it would not have been relaxing. Now he could focus on enjoying his break and getting some quality time with Jayne and his kids. It was badly needed after a hectic first half of the year.

Cannes was something of a walk down memory lane too. Johnson had taken a long vacation along this section of the Côte d'Azur with his German girlfriend Clara while he was living in Berlin studying for his PhD in the early 1980s. He remembered the winding narrow streets behind the Old Port with their jigsaw puzzle of crammed restaurants and bars, with some nostalgia.

In his pocket, Johnson felt his phone vibrating. It wasn't a message; it was a call. He ignored it until it stopped. Then came another vibration as a voice mail arrived.

A minute later, the phone began vibrating again. This time, Johnson fished it out of his pocket.

"Shit," he muttered as he glanced at the screen. It was Vic, calling on the secure connection the pair of them always used. He waited for a few seconds, then jabbed at the red button to decline the call and shoved the phone back in his pocket.

Vic knew he was on vacation, so it had to have been something urgent. It would have to wait until after dinner, when it would still be afternoon in Washington. He would return the call then.

Two minutes later, the phone began vibrating again. This time Johnson keyed in his code number to accept the encrypted call, then answered it.

"Vic, I'm chilling out, trying to get a suntan," Johnson said without bothering to greet his old friend.

There was a pause, during which Johnson heard what sounded like a public-address announcement in the background.

"I'm at the airport—sorry about the noise. I thought you were in the jungle, photographing orangutans," Vic said.

Johnson didn't directly contradict him. There was likely only one reason why Vic was calling, and whereas Borneo was far enough away from Langley to be out of reach, Cannes possibly wasn't.

"There's beaches in Borneo. Where are you going? And why are you calling?" Johnson asked.

"The Hague. Then Paris and London. Listen, I just wanted a quick word about something that—"

"No, Vic," Johnson interrupted. Whenever Vic wanted a "quick word," it was normally to request a major favor. "The answer is no. You're going to ask me to do a job. I've just started a three-week vacation with my kids. So no."

He heard Vic cough, followed by another pause. The public-address announcement, which Johnson could now hear was a flight boarding call, was continuing.

"Actually, Joe, it's about that Malaysian plane being shot down, which I'm sure you can't have failed to notice, seeing as you've just flown to Malaysia."

"What about it?"

"I was having a chat about it with Arthur Veltman last

night. We're in something of a bind, a really major tight spot, and I need to discuss it with you. The thing is—"

Johnson sat up. He could feel his irritation mounting and consciously tried to keep his voice level. "Vic. You're not listening. My son's out on the water on a Jet Ski, having a great time. My daughter's enjoying her sunbathing, as am I. We're going to chill out. I might go swim a bit later. Then enjoy a beer. We're going somewhere nice for dinner tonight. So no. Flat no."

To his right, Johnson saw that Carrie had turned toward him and was staring, listening to his side of the conversation. She slowly shook her head.

"Okay, okay. I understand. Enjoy your break." There was a note of resignation in Vic's voice.

"Thanks."

"There's just one other thing. It's not just me and Arthur. There's a couple of other people who would like you to help them out."

"Who?"

"The president—Ferguson, I mean. And his secretary of state, Paul Farrar. If you just give me a minute, I—"

Johnson snorted. "Yeah, right. Nice try. Bye, Vic. Have a good flight."

He pressed the red button and ended the call.

As he did so, to his left he caught a glimpse of two women heading in his direction. Both were tall and lithe, unlike some on the beach, and were wearing crop tops and shorts, as if they were in their twenties. Jayne and Amy were very different in some ways—Jayne a Cambridge University international politics graduate turned spy, Amy an accountant who had studied at Philadelphia University. But when it came to fashion, they were out of a similar mold.

"Who was on the phone?" Jayne said as she sat on the

edge of the nearest chaise lounge to him. "You're looking annoyed."

"I am. It was Vic."

Carrie called out from her chaise lounge. "He was trying to get dad to do some work, as usual."

Jayne stared at Johnson. "He wasn't asking you to work, surely?"

Johnson nodded. "He was about to. I cut him off. He was starting to tell me some story about the president and Farrar needing my help. I was . . . abrupt with him."

"Good," Amy said. "You've done enough for him recently. He should know better than to call you on vacation."

"Yes, well, he *is* an old buddy, and he's doing a damned tough job."

Jayne reached over and put a hand on the nape of Johnson's neck. "Turn your phone off, put it in your pocket, and relax." She stroked a thumb slowly up and down.

He grinned at her touch and the instruction, delivered in that whisky-low voice that had always turned him on.

Then he did as instructed and sank back onto the chaise lounge. It was one of the ubiquitous lounges with a white plastic frame and a blue mesh covering seen on beaches all over the Mediterranean. Thousands of them dotted the long, narrow strip of sand that ran parallel with Boulevard du Midi Louise Moreau, the road that ran toward the Old Port.

He looked up to see Peter farther along the beach, returning his Jet Ski to the two bikini-clad girls who were manning the rental point. His son was clearly enjoying some banter with the pair of them; he still wore a wide smile when he arrived back at the family's beach encampment a few minutes later.

"Anyone like an ice cream?" Peter asked. The adrenaline rush from the Jet Ski ride and the chat with the girls had clearly put him in an upbeat mood. He caught his sister's eye.

"Come on, Carrie, we'll do the collecting if dad does the paying." He held out his hand.

Johnson gave a mock sigh and fished out a twenty euro note from his wallet. His son, nearing six feet now, bowed in humorous acknowledgment, and the two of them wandered off along the beach in search of a kiosk. They were growing up fast, both heading toward the end of their time at high school.

How much longer will they want to come on family vacations? Johnson wondered.

Thankfully, so far neither had given any hint that they wanted to stop, unlike some other kids their age he knew.

A couple of hours later, after a long swim in the sea and a doze in the sun, they began to pack up to return to Natalia's villa. Jayne was smiling as she tapped away on her phone, presumably sending a joking, light message to someone, when she suddenly stopped and held out the screen toward Johnson, who was brushing sand from his feet.

"Take a look at that," she said. Her smile had disappeared, and her voice had dropped a note or two.

Johnson peered at the screen. It was showing a news alert from Reuters.

"US Secretary of State's Wife and Children Killed in Ukraine Jet Crash," read the ticker-tape headline.

Johnson felt his stomach flip over. "Shit," he said.

He took the phone and tapped on the alert, and the full story loaded up.

WASHINGTON, DC (Reuters) — The wife and two children of the US Secretary of State Paul Farrar, were among the 298 killed when a Malaysia Airlines jet was shot down in Ukraine on Thursday, it emerged today.
US President Stephen Ferguson announced the news at a

White House press conference, at which he expressed his deepest condolences to his colleague.

Ferguson said Farrar was distraught at the loss of his wife, Eileen, 49, and his son, Eric, 19, and daughter, Naomi, 16. The trio had been en route to Kuala Lumpur to meet with Mrs. Farrar's sister.

The secretary of state was trying to continue working given the international diplomatic crisis that has erupted over the destruction of the Boeing 777, the president added.

Ferguson categorically denied mounting speculation that the missile used to shoot down the plane was a Patriot supplied to the Ukraine military by the United States. It is not yet clear who fired the missile or where it was launched from.

Some defense analysts believe the Russian military or pro-Russian separatist forces in Ukraine are responsible.

However, so far no evidence of this has been provided, and the Russian president Vladimir Putin has strongly denied the allegation.

"My God," Johnson said. He stared at the screen in silence for a couple of seconds, then handed the phone back to Jayne.

CHAPTER EIGHT

Saturday, July 19, 2014
Cannes

By half past two in the morning, Johnson had had enough. He had spent three hours wrestling with his conscience, and he finally realized he was losing the bout. He rarely seemed to come out on top in such duels, which always took place in the early hours of the morning and always left him feeling as though he had been hit by a truck the next day.

He turned over and over in an attempt to find slumber but found himself disturbed incessantly by the thought of the family of a man he knew of but didn't actually know, being wiped out in a plane disaster that Johnson and his family could easily have been involved in themselves.

It could have been us, but for the grace of God.

Next to him in bed, Jayne lay on her back, her face tilted toward him, her mouth slightly open, breathing lightly as she slept. He liked looking at her sleeping after they made love, which that night had been special as usual. She always seemed so peaceful, although Johnson had no doubts she had been just as troubled as he had been by recent events.

He found himself wishing he could doze off like her. She wasn't the one who had taken the call from Langley, though, and she wasn't the one who had angrily dismissed an old buddy who, it was now clear, was in need of some help.

Johnson picked up his phone from the bedside table, then slipped out from beneath the light summer duvet that covered the king-size bed on the second floor of the villa. He made his way onto the landing, where a night-light gave off a faint glow. He could hear the faint sound of steady rhythmic breathing—not quite a snore but bordering on it—coming from the bedroom opposite, where Amy was sleeping in the room next to Natalia's. Ever since childhood, his beloved sister, who was two years younger than him, had always insisted on keeping her door ajar at night and a landing light on. She blamed the habit on their father for telling the pair of them too many scary ghost stories when they were kids.

The two children were on the floor above, and Johnson knew for certain neither of them would have any difficulty sleeping. They had no worries other than when their next iPhone upgrade was coming or whether the gallery of photographs on their Instagram account made them appear cool enough when compared to their school friends.

Oh, to be young.

Johnson flicked on the flashlight on his phone and padded as quietly as he could down the polished wooden staircase and into the living room. There he turned on a small table lamp and poured himself a large scotch.

A half moon, bright as a searchlight in the clear skies above Cannes, was glinting in through the french windows that led out onto the patio next to the swimming pool. Johnson sat in a wicker chair next to the window and watched it for a while. He often found that contemplating the enormity of the solar system enabled him to see the bigger picture of the life he was enmeshed in on earth.

He had no idea what Vic actually wanted from him. But he could take a guess. He had already been involved in one fairly desperate venture into Russia that year, one that had brought him closer to losing his life than he would have ever admitted to his two children and Amy. At the age of fifty-five, he wasn't keen on getting involved in another.

Too old for that game.

But he knew instinctively, with a certainty borne of years of experience, that to resolve the problem the US was facing would require feet on the ground inside Russia and the pro-Russian area of Ukraine and the kind of intelligence gathering that just wasn't possible by using cameras on a satellite, remote tapping cell phones, using unmanned drones, and monitoring of emails.

Johnson took a large sip of his scotch and felt the stinging warmth spread down his throat. A minute or two later, the familiar slight feeling of light-headedness took him over.

He sometimes wished, in this kind of moment, that he could call his mother and get her view. Helena Johnson, originally from a Polish Jewish family, had spent two years of hell in the Gross-Rosen concentration camp during World War II before being liberated by the advancing Red Army in April 1945. She moved to the United States two years later and only finally passed away in 2001, nine years after Johnson's father, Bernard. Helena was always a source of inspiration and commonsense to her children, always seeking justice and truth in every situation.

Vic, you son of a bitch.

He had been so looking forward to this trip and quality time with his kids and Jayne. He knew that calling or messaging Vic would spell an end to it. Maybe his friend would give him an out. Maybe it wouldn't lead to another big commitment. Johnson tipped his head back and stared through the window at the moon, with the bright pinheads of the Aries constellation visible above it.

The tug-of-war going on inside him—between the voice of self-preservation and the responsibilities of a single parent on the one hand and the need to deliver justice and defend his country on the other hand—almost seemed physical.

This could and likely would be dangerous.

Damn you, Vic.

How many times had his friend done this kind of thing?

What to do?

Johnson already knew what he was going to do, though. It would be the same choice his mother would likely have advised.

He took out his phone and began to tap out a message.

* * *

Saturday, July 19, 2014
Moscow

The Black Bishop was having a good day, Igor Ivanov mused. He clutched his briefcase and waited outside the twin sets of dark wooden doors that led into the inner sanctum of the Kremlin—the office of his boss, the Russian president Vladimir Putin.

The Black Bishop tag was one that amused and pleased him. Dreamed up by some long-forgotten Kremlin political opponent as an intended insult, it had instead been counter-productive. It had left him with an aura of Machiavellian supremacy that gave pause to those who contemplated trying to backstab him. Nobody did. Not anymore.

The nickname also summed up quite neatly what his key

role at the Kremlin entailed: deploying the dark arts of manipulation, ruthlessness, and disinformation to further the interests of not just his master but also the Rodina, the Motherland.

Only three months earlier, Ivanov had been summoned to Putin's office to be told that he was to assume responsibility for some of the exceptionally heavy workload being shouldered by the prime minister. This would include the direction of the effort to maximize disruption against the Kiev government in the eastern part of Ukraine and also of plans to massively step up the operation to influence, destabilize, and infiltrate the United States. The use of media and social media disinformation was a key tool in that task.

There was no formal job description, as such—simply an understanding. And part of that understanding was that he could draw on the resources of the country's intelligence services, the SVR and FSB, as well as special forces, when required. The closest to a check and balance to this power base was that the president's approval was required for most significant operations. But it had been forthcoming without exception thus far.

Rather than being daunted by such a task, Ivanov reveled in it. He was energized to a degree that he could not recall previously, not even when servicing either of the two mistresses that he maintained in Moscow.

He and the president had agreed that, rather than take on some high-sounding, grandiose title, Ivanov would simply assume the tag of senior adviser. Putin's view was that it was low-key, attracting less attention and thus arousing less suspicion both at home and overseas. At least, that was the theory.

The arrangement and new responsibilities had not gone down well with everyone in the sprawling Russian intelligence community, particularly the prickly SVR director in charge at

Yasenevo, Maksim Kruglov, and his counterintelligence deputy director, Yevgeny Kutsik. But they had little choice, and Ivanov knew that Putin had a fairly critical view of Kruglov anyway, so if he needed to pull rank, it wouldn't be a problem.

The heavy doors swung open, and one of the president's aides held them as Ivanov walked across the parquet floor and the ornate Bokhara carpet to the chess-style table that jutted out at the front of his boss's main desk.

The president was wearing a thin smile that was almost as well pressed as his white shirt. That was a good sign, as was the fact that he was holding out his hand, which Ivanov shook firmly.

"Well done, Igor. Operation Black Sea went very well, I see. It was well executed."

"Thank you, Mr. President. It did go well."

"Take a seat. You can update me on wider developments too." Putin indicated to the beige leather chair at the left side of the chess table and sat himself down on the right.

Ivanov did as instructed and sat, placing his briefcase on the floor as he did so. He then laid his hands, palms down, on the edge of the table as he began to speak. "Sir, my only concern is that, as you probably have seen, the downed jet was carrying the family of the United States' secretary of state."

The president pressed his lips together. "Unfortunate for him. A coincidence. In other circumstances I might be tempted to say it's a pity he wasn't with them, but you're right to be concerned. There is likely to be retaliation, if they get a chance."

"Indeed."

"We will cross that bridge when we get to it. There is nothing we can do. I hope it doesn't disrupt our plans."

Ivanov nodded.

"I have seen the initial wave of Twitter posts," the president went on. "I assume all is going to plan on that front?"

"Yes. Completely to plan. Our friend Shevchenko had a good initial meeting with TITANIUM. The Twitter operation fully exploited the information we obtained."

"Who is handling the Twitter posts?" Putin asked.

"An old acquaintance of yours, Konstantin Gudovich." Ivanov was aware that Putin knew Gudovich, who had previously been a senior SVR communications chief and had often worked at the Kremlin.

"He's good. What's the next step?"

Ivanov explained that Shevchenko, code-named KARAKURT, was establishing a mechanism with TITANIUM to ensure timely and full supply of relevant material, including military and political intelligence. In turn, such information would be passed without delay to the Kremlin and, as appropriate, would be weaponized for use by the new troll factory that Ivanov had established in Rostov-on-Don, operating inside an innocuous-sounding company called the Web Marketing Group and employing a growing number of social media agents.

"Good," Putin said. "The US presidential election is less than two and a half years away, and I'm not having Democrats winning the White House—they are our biggest threat. Within twelve months, I want to have built our position of influence so that we are able to *vaporize* their chances." Putin steadily raised his hand into the air, as if to symbolize smoke rising.

"The recruitment of TITANIUM is very good for us," the president went on. "We must not waste it. I want us to be relentlessly negative toward all potential Democratic candidates. Understood?"

Ivanov nodded. "Fully understood."

"I want to undermine America's credibility internationally

and at home. The Ferguson administration must be discredited to the degree that voters swing completely the opposite way. At the same time, we build influence and we compromise the Republicans now through our active measures. We must ingratiate ourselves now; then we can capitalize on that and cash in and control them once they are in office."

Ivanov again nodded in agreement but did not speak.

Putin relaxed back into his chair. "Did the element of Operation Black Sea involving Yuri Severinov go to plan?"

"Yes, he delivered according to instructions."

"I am pleased to hear it."

"He gives us useful and deniable options, especially in the Black Sea region given his refinery operation and shipping fleet," Ivanov said.

"Yes. Continue to use him as you see appropriate. If he objects, tell him those are my personal instructions."

Ivanov reached into his briefcase and removed a slim maroon file, which he tossed onto the table. "I was reading Severinov's file earlier. There is a note that you instructed him three months ago to deal with the American investigator Johnson, who caused us such problems and embarrassment earlier this year and in Afghanistan last year."

He wanted to check that Putin remained of the mind to persist with his previous instructions.

Putin frowned. "Yes. The international media coverage of the Berlin incident was appalling." He leaned forward again and fixed Ivanov with his ice-blue eyes. "I am pleased you raised that. You can tell Severinov I want to know if he has made progress regarding Johnson. He is a thorn in the flesh. Tell Severinov I have not forgotten."

"Noted, sir. I will discuss it with him."

"Have you found a replacement for Vasily?"

Among the many problems that Johnson had caused was the death in Leipzig, Germany, of one of the Kremlin's most useful freelance covert wet-work specialists, Vasily Balagula, who had been under contract with Severinov at the time.

"I have someone in mind who I think will do a very good job. One of Vasily's old Spetsnaz team and the man who was deployed in Ukraine to handle Operation Black Sea: Georgi Tkachev."

"Yes, of course I know of Tkachev. He is outstanding. He has done some excellent work for this office. Good, I agree that you should use him." Putin paused. "There is one final thing."

"Sir?"

"It's about Operation Pandora. Have you made any progress with that strategy paper?"

"I have made a start, but it will take some time to complete, sir."

Putin frowned. "I want it as soon as possible. That is all. You can go."

The president stood and walked back to his desk.

CHAPTER NINE

Monday, July 21, 2014
　　Athens

Even at nine in the morning, the blinding light of Athens was harsher than Johnson remembered from his previous visit fifteen years earlier. Or maybe it was that his eyes were older and less able to adapt than they used to be. Either way, he found himself squinting as he emerged from the CIA car at the United States embassy on Vasilisis Sophias Avenue.

After his secure message to Vic in the small hours of Saturday morning to say he would consider doing whatever was required to help, things had moved far more quickly than he had expected, much to the distress of his children.

Vic had flown from Paris to Nice on Saturday morning and by one thirty that day was deep in a conversation with Johnson over lunch on the terrace of the InterContinental Carlton hotel in Cannes.

The discussion went almost exactly as Johnson had

privately predicted while sipping his scotch in the small hours of the morning in Cannes. Vic didn't mince his words.

"I need you to go back to Russia," he had said between mouthfuls of flamed *entrecôte de boeuf*. "The president is expecting us to deliver, and you're the best man I can think of outside the Agency to do this job. We don't have anyone reliable inside Russian intelligence right now, as you're well aware, although God knows it's not for lack of trying. So, we're going to have to do this from outside. The remuneration will be presidential too, I can assure you."

Johnson questioned whether the downing of the Malaysia Airlines jet was more a terrorist action than a war crime and therefore not within his usual remit. But Vic had brushed the argument aside.

"If this isn't a war crime, what the hell is it?" Vic asked. "Three hundred dead in a conflict between the government of Ukraine and pro-Russian separatists? I've just come from The Hague, and Fernando Morales has a similar view to mine. If he's keen to pursue this, who are we to argue? He intends to send a small investigative team to Ukraine and southern Russia immediately. If you are willing to do this job, you will be attached to that team, at least as far as the Russians are concerned. If challenged, that is your cover story. In practice, you're on your own. You probably won't even see the ICC people."

Johnson knew Morales, the ICC's chief prosecutor, reasonably well. It was a fair point that Vic had made: if Morales was taking the view that the disaster was worthy of ICC scrutiny at such an early stage, it would be difficult to persuade Vic otherwise.

So it proved. After another half hour of discussion, Johnson decided in principle that he would take on the job. The task of persuading the rest of his family and Jayne that this was a good idea was a different matter. Vic checked himself into the InterContinental and let Johnson do what was necessary.

He had little difficulty with Jayne, whom he approached first. As was always the case, she grasped the bigger picture immediately.

Jayne suggested that she should come to Athens with Johnson and Vic and help to run the operation. It made sense, and it was rare that Johnson and Jayne did not work in tandem on such investigations. The extent of her involvement in the medium term would depend on what emerged from Johnson's foray into Russia, of course, but planning for such involvement wasn't a stretch.

Jayne made Johnson promise that he would utilize the micro tracking devices that both of them used to keep tabs on each other's movements while on operations. The tiny trackers, installed in a heel of their shoes, had proved invaluable more than once and allowed their movements to be followed on a secure smartphone maps app.

Johnson agreed to Jayne accompanying him to Athens once Amy had indicated she was happy to remain in Cannes and take care of Carrie and Peter, alongside Natalia. Johnson was unable, for obvious security reasons, to explain to his sister exactly what the operation was about, but clearly indicated its importance.

Unsurprisingly, the two children proved a greater challenge. Over dinner on Saturday evening, there were vocal objections from Carrie and Peter, partly caused because Johnson, once again, was unable to explain exactly what his task would be, where he was going, or why. He found himself creating a supposedly hypothetical case of a man—he had Paul Farrar in mind—who had lost his family in a plane bombing and needed help to find the perpetrators. That was as far as he was prepared to go in terms of detailing his mission.

How would that person feel, and wouldn't he need all the help he could get to bring the criminals to justice? Johnson asked.

Eventually, he talked them round, as he usually did when it came down to an argument over securing justice and the vital part he could play in it. He didn't like to just dictate what he was going to do, rather feeling that it was important they all discuss it together. Johnson took considerable pride in the values he had instilled in his children and their ability to prioritize their options in life accordingly.

At lunchtime on Sunday, Johnson, Jayne, and Vic had taken an Aegean Airlines flight to the Greek capital.

The Athens station, located on the top floor of the enormous square US embassy building, was one of the largest CIA operations in Europe, partly because it had a massive telecommunications complex that acted as a regional hub for the Agency. It transmitted the top-secret messages that flowed daily from Langley to CIA stations beyond Greece, and vice-versa. The Athens station also acted as a logistical support base for smaller CIA stations in the Middle East. The heavily fortified embassy sat behind a high metal fence with an array of surveillance cameras and several guards.

Vic had decided to travel to Athens for two key reasons. First, the CIA's chief of station in Moscow, Ed Grewall, known to everyone inside the Agency as Sunny, was passing through, and the chance to discuss the Ukraine situation with him was too good to pass up.

Second, a friend of Vic's, Valentin Marchenko, an assistant director of the Foreign Intelligence Service of Ukraine, the SZR, was in the city for briefings with the Agency's Athens chief of station. It made sense for him to also meet with Vic, Johnson, Jayne, and Sunny.

Vic assured Johnson that both Marchenko and Sunny would be invaluable allies for any operation that involved an incursion into Russian territory. Marchenko in particular would also pick up intelligence on the activities of pro-Russian forces in Eastern Ukraine.

After checking in at the station, Vic, Jayne, and Johnson spent half an hour with Sunny, a genial, thoughtful man of half-Indian descent with a neatly trimmed beard. He agreed with the general strategy to pursue a below-the-radar deniable visit into southern Russia and advised in broad terms on the approach. He then disappeared with Vic to a separate secure room for a further half hour of private discussions—no doubt for him to update Vic on how recruitment of high-level agents in Moscow was progressing, Johnson assumed.

Once Vic, Johnson, and Jayne had finished with Sunny, they headed out in an old Fiat on a one-hour surveillance detection route through central Athens to ensure they were black prior to their meeting with Marchenko.

The SDR was necessarily lengthy because of the high risk of Russian surveillance. From its *rezidentura* at the modernistic Russian embassy in Nikiforou Litra, two miles north of the US embassy, the SVR maintained a robust presence in Athens. Putin saw Greece as a prime target, given that its relations with the European Union were worsening.

"The Greeks and the SVR keep all of us Americans under surveillance," Vic said. "No trust. I don't want to risk a hotel or bar for this conversation."

Once they were certain they were clear, they drove to the meeting place that Vic had arranged: the parking lot on top of the pointed nine-hundred-foot limestone peak of Mount Lycabettus that dominated the neighborhood of the same name.

Marchenko, who looked like a taxi driver with a pack of Marlboro Reds and a ballpoint pen in his shirt breast pocket, led them on foot along a dusty footpath close to a modern yellow-and-red steel amphitheater at the top of the hill. Eventually they came to a long rustic bench, tucked between faded pine trees, that looked east across Athens. The flat-roofed US embassy building was clearly visible below them, less than a mile away.

Johnson and Marchenko remained standing while the others sat on the bench. As Vic and Johnson began to explain the objectives of the operation, Marchenko lit one of his Marlboros, blowing smoke into the tree above his head. He confirmed that the Ukrainians would be more than happy to give whatever assistance was required in what was essentially an anti-Russian mission.

"We're not interested in the crash site," Johnson said. "That will be swarming with military, police, government officials, and so on. It's not even necessarily the missile launch site we need to see. It's more about how the missile got to the launch site, who took it there, and who fired it."

"First, I want to say we are not planning a holiday here," Marchenko said, as he lit his second Marlboro. "This is a war zone. You have separatist militias in Eastern Ukraine, you have Russian military giving them support, and you have Ukraine military fighting them. It will be dangerous." He glanced first at Vic, then at Johnson.

"Second, a Buk missile launcher is a big unit," Marchenko continued, tugging impatiently at his pointed graying goatee. "It is difficult to hide completely while transporting it, especially on the ground. We have a geo-location team already working hard on this. They are analyzing social media outputs from people in that area. People often post pictures of unusual things they see, whether it is vehicles or anything else. It's open-source information, available to anyone. I expect results soon."

"Excellent. Thank you," Vic said.

Jayne glanced behind her to ensure they remained unobserved. "We will also need access to whatever recordings your surveillance teams have picked up of radio, cell phones, and other traffic involving Russian military and intelligence operatives in that area," she said.

Marchenko's black eyes flicked between the other three. "We are completely on top of all that, as you would expect. The Russians consistently underestimate us, and they are careless in their talk."

"We will also need one or two armed close-protection officers for Joe," Vic said.

The sides of Marchenko's mouth creased slightly outward for the first time, the closest Johnson had seen him come to a smile. "I will enjoy that. I'm good at close protection, when needed."

"You will come with me?" Johnson asked, raising his eyebrows. He had been expecting that Marchenko would delegate the task to one of his more junior operatives, and had been considering whether he should take Jayne along, given that she was fluent in Russian in addition to other languages.

"Yes, just us two for this operation—we will travel faster that way. I also have a good contact in Rostov-on-Don, a guy named Stepan, one of ours. He will also be able to assist us. I know that territory very well, and it is not just about close protection. You need someone who has military and intelligence service expertise. Especially if we need to protect you from *moskali* scum in Russian territory—in the danger zone."

Johnson knew that *moskali*, the literal translation of which was Muscovites, was the standard Ukrainian derogatory term for Russians.

Vic folded his arms. "I think that sounds like a good plan. I will be briefing my director, and if this goes well, I will ensure you are given the appropriate credit. Jayne and I can remain at Athens station and run the show from there." He looked at Jayne. "Is that okay with you?"

Jayne nodded in agreement. "Yes, that makes sense."

"How do we get into the danger zone, as you put it?" Johnson asked. "And when will we go?"

"We will fly from here into Rostov under cover, with false passports," Marchenko said. "You will also need identification from the ICC. Can you get that?"

Johnson nodded. He had been to Rostov a couple of times before, and it made sense that Marchenko wanted to take that route. "I already have ICC identification from my previous work with them, but it's in my real name. They will courier new papers to me tomorrow."

"And I have agreed with the ICC prosecutor that he will give Joe a separate letter of support," Vic said. "The document is also coming tomorrow."

"Good," said Marchenko.

The Ukrainian was a few inches shorter than Johnson at about five feet nine, and looking down on him, Johnson could see droplets of sweat gathering on his balding head. The temperature was warming up as the sun climbed higher.

"I am thinking we will leave here on Wednesday, in two days, to give us time to prepare," Marchenko continued. "From Rostov we will go by car, which my network there will provide. It is not far to the Ukraine border from there, and the area where the Boeing came down is close by. I believe that is where the missile launcher would have come across the border from Russia. They would have taken the shortest route."

Johnson privately sighed to himself. The territory Marchenko was talking about was right at the center of the fighting that had been going on between the pro-Russian separatist forces and Ukraine army units.

What am I getting into?

"Can we get weapons?" Johnson asked after a few moments of silence.

"We will get them in Rostov, with the car," Marchenko said. "I just want to be clear—this operation will not be without risk."

He's not joking.

Johnson glanced at Vic, the trace of a wry grin on his face, then back at Marchenko. "I suppose you're going to say we have no option?"

Marchenko nodded, his goatee bobbing up and down. "You are correct. If you want to find out the truth, you have no option."

CHAPTER TEN

Tuesday, July 22, 2014
Washington, DC

TITANIUM placed his cup of coffee next to the open laptop on his kitchen countertop and scrolled down the intelligence report that had landed in his secure in-box at some uncivilized hour while he was still asleep. It was the President's Daily Brief, the top-secret document that was produced by the Director of National Intelligence's office and went directly to the president and a small number of other high-level officials.

President Ferguson had recently ended the traditional practice of receiving his daily brief in a black leather folder with the presidential seal at the top in gold. Instead, the brief arrived in digital format for him to read on his tablet or laptop. The digital format made it easier to distribute the report, and as a result, a few more people in the higher echelons of government now received copies. That suited TITA-

NIUM, as it had made it more difficult to trace him as a mole.

TITANIUM was looking to see if there was anything on a specific subject. Eventually, he spotted an item with the tagline he was seeking near the bottom of the dense document, written in small font.

He picked up his bowl of breakfast muesli and began to eat as he read the paragraph.

MALAYSIA AIRLINES CRASH UPDATE — CIA has arranged to receive output from an urgent independent undercover investigation due to start tomorrow (July 23) into the Flight 17 disaster. Objective of investigation, part of an International Criminal Court initial inquiry, is to determine precisely where and in whose territory the missile was launched from and who authorized and fired it. The investigation also aims to determine the source of information contained in social media posts regarding the meeting between the SoS, the NSA, and the Ukraine president (see appendix B below for summary of posts' content). Updates to follow.

During his time in the US Army, TITANIUM's colleagues always used to say he had balls of steel. It was true, back then, up to a point: he had been courageous, and that was why he had been able to reach the heights he had achieved in his career. Now, despite the image he projected publicly, he knew that it was no longer the case. In fact, a shiver ran through him as he read the report.

It didn't require an expert in US intelligence and political matters to read between the lines of the phrasing. *Part of an ICC inquiry?* Extremely unlikely. This was going to be a classic CIA deniable operation.

As he expected, the Agency was going to try to hunt down

whoever leaked the secretary of state's talks with Poroshenko. It seemed certain the starting point for that inquiry had to be in Kiev, which was always as watertight as a sieve.

And who was going to conduct the investigation? TITANIUM would make it his business to find out. It should be easy enough, given the contacts he had carefully cultivated over the years at various levels within the White House and CIA, although he would need to be extremely careful in his approach. The risk of discovery was increasingly markedly.

He flicked down to appendix B, but the Twitter and Facebook posts quoted were the same as those he had seen previously. Nothing new there.

TITANIUM logged out of his US government email account and turned off his official laptop computer. The next step would be to pass on the information he had seen to Tatiana, whom he had decided was something of a smiling viper. She was sharp as the razor wielded by the Turkish barber he occasionally visited in DC.

TITANIUM would transfer the bare bones of this new information using an old-fashioned text message on his burner phone once he was well away from any government building and certain that he was not under surveillance from the FBI's counterintelligence bloodhounds. Then he could pass more details to Tatiana at their meeting scheduled for Saturday.

TITANIUM put his laptop into his briefcase and finished his muesli. It was his usual breakfast, always consumed at home at about six o'clock before he left for his habitual twelve- or fourteen-hour day in the office. Sometimes, if there was an evening function to attend, it could stretch to sixteen or more hours.

The long days were one of the factors that had triggered his depression. However, he had to admit, the loss of his father a couple of years earlier, issues with his children, the problems within his marriage, and the guilt over his affair that had been compounded by Tatiana's blackmail were also major and cumulative factors.

Now he had the guilt of betraying his country to add to all that. The money that Moscow paid him formed a sizable recompense, of course, and would add up to a very large financial bonus once he retired. But he nonetheless found it difficult.

The truth was, he felt he had done well to continue doing his job to a high level under the circumstances.

With some of the more complex, lengthier material he had handed over to his Russian handler, it had been necessary to take photographs of the documents on his laptop screen. For that purpose, he used the camera on a smartphone after having removed the SIM card and disabled the Wi-Fi connection, and he also removed the battery, apart from when he needed to use it.

But a photograph wasn't required in this case; given the document's brevity, a simple summary would suffice. He knew that the information would be of considerable interest in Moscow.

Any investigation into the destruction of the Boeing would be something the Kremlin would want to stop dead in its tracks, especially if it took place covertly on Russian soil. For Moscow, it would be critical that the truth remain permanently concealed.

So whatever the Russians chose to do to stop an investigation from succeeding, he would do his best to help facilitate, working quietly behind the scenes. Putin and his cronies might be a bunch of crooks, he reflected, but they always paid very well for the information he provided.

CHAPTER ELEVEN

Tuesday, July 22, 2014
Washington, DC

"*Dermo*," Anastasia Shevchenko swore as she read the text message. She could feel the hairs rising on the nape of her neck.

Then she reread the message, first checking the time it had arrived. Quarter to seven that morning, and it was now half past eleven. For security reasons, she only turned on the burner phone when she wanted to check for messages or send one herself. The last thing she wanted was for it to be tracked.

> *Objective of investigation, part of an International Criminal Court initial inquiry, is to determine precisely where and in whose territory the missile was launched from and who authorized and fired it.*

Below the excerpt TITANIUM had sent her from the President's Daily Brief was another line.

Have discovered from my source at Langley that the investigation is being handled by an independent, Joe Johnson. Worked for the CIA many years ago. A war crimes investigator. Will provide more information when we meet. This is no doubt a deniable CIA operation.

Shevchenko put the phone down and leaned back in her chair, thinking furiously.

Surely Johnson wasn't *really* working on this investigation that TITANIUM was flagging, was he? It briefly crossed her mind that TITANIUM might know her real identity and therefore her past history with Johnson.

But no, that was highly unlikely.

In fact, it took very little thought to realize that it made sense that Johnson was working the investigation. The downing of the Boeing in Ukraine was undoubtedly a major war crime, and it made logical sense for the CIA to want to investigate it, but at arm's length, so it could be denied if required. The speculation on social media that a Patriot missile took down the plane made the undercover route the sensible one to adopt. The lower the profile, the better. She would have done exactly the same herself.

Joe Johnson was an independent war crimes investigator, and—she had to admit—a damned good one too, as she had found out to her cost in London earlier that year.

She walked to the window of her seventh-floor apartment in the historic Woodward Building, a refurbished Beaux-Arts Revival apartment building dating back to the early twentieth century. She had rented it using her Tatiana Niklas cover.

From the window, she could see southward down Fifteenth Street NW to the towering obelisk of the Wash-

ington Monument that honored the United States' first president, less than a mile away. The White House itself was a
block away, and to her amusement, the FBI's headquarters,
the J. Edgar Hoover Building, was just a fifteen-minute walk.
If only they knew.

Johnson might be damned good, but she was damned
good too. And it seemed he had been assigned to an operation that would surely, inevitably, take him into Russia.

Perhaps, then, this investigation could be more of an
opportunity than a threat—and not just for her but for her
old colleague and longtime lover, Yuri Severinov.

If she was going to be honest, she had become slightly
weary of Severinov, who in the past had been damaged by
Johnson even more than she had been. But she felt sorry for
him, not least because he was under very heavy pressure from
Putin to dispose of Johnson following the embarrassing reve-
lations that the American had unearthed in Afghanistan and
Berlin.

Without question, she would now have to report the
Johnson development to Yasenevo, as she couldn't run the
risk of them finding out via another channel. That meant the
Kremlin would be informed in short order too and was
certain to put even more pressure on Severinov.

She therefore decided to inform Severinov first, thus
giving him a little thinking time to put plans in place before
the heavy hand of Putin descended upon him once again.

To help keep their communications secure, she and
Severinov had recently set up an anonymous email account,
also under the Tatiana Niklas name, to which they both had
access.

Inside the account, they had created a draft email that
they used almost like a chat room. Both of them wrote new
text inside the email—their messages and replies. But the
email remained in the draft box and was never sent to

anyone, thus drastically reducing the likelihood that it might be discovered.

Shevchenko opened her laptop and logged on to the email account.

Then she clicked on the draft email, which was headed FC Dynamo Moscow Fixture List. The visible part of the email consisted, indeed, of the scheduled games for the forthcoming soccer season involving Dynamo Moscow that she had copied and pasted in. Moscow had five major soccer teams in Moscow, but Dynamo was the team she and Severinov had often watched during the Soviet era and had continued to support ever since.

Dynamo Moscow was affiliated with the Ministry of Internal Affairs, the police, and the KGB during that period, and the Dynamo sports club, of which it was a part, was a natural home for KGB officers for both social and work reasons.

The actual messages between Severinov and her were far down the email, below the fixture list. They included a large number of exchanges, including recent ones in which she had been complaining about her boss and another in which she had been flirting a little with Severinov, who had written a couple of fairly crude messages indicating he wanted to get laid.

There she wrote a new message.

You will not believe this: Have learned from my new friend here that CIA is to carry out deniable investigation into the Malaysian jet crash. Guess who they have hired? Joe Johnson! Little more known at this stage, but will find out more. Johnson is certain to make an undercover visit to crash/launch site and in my view also certain to get into Russia. This must be an opportunity for you to terminate? CIA also investigating social media blitz blaming Americans

and Patriot missile. Unclear if Johnson will handle that
aspect. Am informing Yasenevo—have no choice about that.
But perhaps you can put plans in place quickly?

Underneath, Shevchenko added another line containing her new burner phone number.

That's in case you need me urgently, she wrote.

Then she saved the draft email with its new paragraph and closed the application. It was certain that Severinov would find the message soon, as they had each committed to check it at least twice a day.

Her next task was to dispatch a similar but official message to her direct boss at Moscow Center, the counterintelligence chief and SVR deputy director Yevgeny Kutsik, and to the overall SVR director, Maksim Kruglov. She shouldn't really pull rank by sending it to Kruglov but couldn't resist, largely because it irritated Kutsik, whom she disliked.

Shevchenko preferred old-fashioned methods of communication with Moscow Center. Ideally, she liked to use dead-drop sites where handwritten coded messages or flash micro memory cards containing encrypted files could be left for collection and onward transport by anonymous couriers traveling on scheduled flights. Those were the most secure methods, in her experience.

However, because of the speed with which her move to Washington had been arranged, those essential building blocks of an intelligence officer's life had not yet been put in place.

Her fallback method was another slightly old-fashioned technology, steganography, which enabled her to conceal a digital message inside a standard electronic JPEG photographic file or an MP3 music file. Anyone viewing or listening to the file would not be aware of the message contained within the lines of code written into it. Her usual method of transmission was to upload the files to a password-protected account within a photograph-sharing site. From there, a technician at Moscow Center could download and decode it.

An app on her laptop provided all that she needed, complete with a range of large, high-definition photographs of tourist scenes in and around the US capital, each about eight MB in size and therefore providing plenty of data within which to hide her message.

Although steganography wasn't Shevchenko's preferred communication tool, its advantage was that it was so far out of fashion that the counterintelligence people at the FBI and CIA were not so closely focused on it as they might have been. So the chances of escaping detection were high.

She started up her steganography app and typed in a short one-paragraph message containing the relevant details about Joe Johnson and the Malaysian jet inquiry. Then she encrypted the message and selected a photograph of a tourist riverboat on the Potomac River.

With two clicks of her mouse, the message was embedded into the JPEG file. Next, she logged on to her photograph-sharing site, also under the Tatiana Niklas name, and selected a folder marked "DC Vacation," into which she uploaded the newly doctored image.

Shevchenko knew that within a few minutes, the file would be downloaded at Yasenevo, the message would be extracted and decrypted, and it would be available on Kutsik's laptop for secure reading.

CHAPTER TWELVE

Wednesday, July 23, 2014
  Rostov-on-Don Airport

The smell of hot tarmac greeted Johnson and Marchenko as they walked out of the Aeroflot Boeing 737 and onto the steps down to the apron at Rostov-on-Don airport. The temperature was warmer than Johnson had been expecting but not dissimilar to that inside the plane, which seemed to have a faulty air-conditioning system. The journey from Athens had been a long one, requiring a two-hour layover and change of planes in Moscow, as there were no direct flights.

But thankfully, Johnson's long-standing cover identity, the nonexistent Philip Wilkinson, had stood up to scrutiny at passport control in Moscow.

The CIA's Athens forgery department, located in the basement of the embassy, had done a good job in producing a high-quality six-month Russian business visa that gave Johnson an unlimited number of entries and exits. For good measure, they had also inserted a visa into his second false passport, in the name of Don Thiele, which he was carrying to use only in emergencies.

He had acquired the Wilkinson and Thiele identities after leaving the Office of Special Investigations in 2006. They both included a US passport, credit cards, a bank card, a driver's license, and a birth certificate—all of them acquired through a contact who was a former police officer. The address linked to the documents was an abandoned house in rural New Hampshire.

The photograph in the Wilkinson passport showed Johnson with a shaven head, so before leaving Athens he had taken a razor to his remaining hair. He was also wearing a pair of black-rimmed glasses with plain glass and a dark-blue unbranded baseball cap. They were subtle changes, but hopefully they would be enough.

Johnson was also carrying his new International Criminal Court identification and letter of support, but the border control officer in Moscow asked only if his stay was for business or leisure. There were no questions about the specifics of his trip, so Johnson did not require the additional documents.

Marchenko was also traveling under a false identity, that of Lithuanian business executive Henrikas Venclova.

"Russian immigration and passport control is a joke," Marchenko said as they walked through the airport building. "They have a real problem with illegal immigrants. For 250 euros, any guy in the street can buy a Lithuanian passport with a Russian visa that will get you in. Pah."

Johnson had to privately concur with him.

Compared with Moscow, the airport in Rostov was looking a little neglected, explained by the fact that it was only three years away from being replaced by a larger international airport, scheduled to be built eighteen miles to the northeast.

As they exited the airport, Johnson saw that the arrangements Marchenko had made with his SZR contact in Rostov, Stepan, had worked. The vehicle he had promised, a rugged navy-blue Lada 4x4, was waiting outside the low-slung white terminal building. A nervous-looking girl in her twenties handed him the keys and a small black backpack.

"There are two phones in the bag. Stepan says to give him a call if you need anything else," she said, then disappeared toward the bus station.

Once they were sitting in the Lada, Marchenko unzipped the backpack and took out the cell phones.

"Russian phone," Marchenko said, handing one to Johnson. "A burner."

Johnson took it and switched off his main phone.

"Are the guns in the bag too?" Johnson asked.

"Two Makarovs, with six spare magazines. Do you want to check them?"

Johnson took the two compact pistols, both semiautomatics, removed the eight-round magazines, and pulled back the slides, ensuring the chambers were empty. Then he replaced the magazines, which were loaded with 9mm rounds, as were the spare magazines. The pistols looked well maintained. Hopefully they wouldn't be needed, he thought, but it was reassuring to have them. He handed them back to Marchenko, who put them in the bag and zipped it shut.

Marchenko's main phone beeped and he checked the screen, then tapped on it and scrolled down what was clearly a document of some interest, his brow furrowed in concentration.

"Our geo-location team has come up with a result to get us started," Marchenko said. "There were a string of posts on social media in the few hours prior to the Malaysian jet being shot down, especially on Twitter and Facebook. They show a white Volvo truck cab pulling a lowboy semitrailer with a military armored vehicle covered with camouflage netting through towns and villages on both sides of the border. However, my team identified the cargo not as an armored vehicle but as a Buk missile launcher."

"Can they send us the posts, and do they have locations for where the photographs were taken?" Johnson asked. "They can probably get street addresses through users' account IDs and IP addresses."

"Yes, they are emailing them," Marchenko said. "They are also sending several locations that the semitrailer appears to have passed through, including the crossing point into Ukraine near a village called Severny, next to the Seversky Donets River. They have also identified where the missile seems to have been fired from."

He looked up and grinned at Johnson. "Good start, eh?"

It was a decent start, Johnson thought. It would be even better if Vic's contacts in the NSA could pinpoint the source of the posts on Twitter and other social media platforms that were blaming the United States, the CIA, and Ukraine for shooting down the jet. Determining who was behind this blame campaign, and where they were located was crucial if they were to clear the US of fault. Before he left Athens, Vic had assured him they were working on it, but so far no results had been forthcoming.

"Yes, it would seem promising," Johnson said. "However, I want to talk to actual witnesses. Where are these locations?"

"There are a few on the A-280 north of Rostov on the route to the border crossing they used at Severny. That is about 220 kilometers from here. Then there are more sightings on the Ukraine side too."

Johnson fingered the old bullet wound at the top of his right ear. "So the Severny border crossing is in the hands of the pro-Russian rebels?"

"Yes. It is right now."

"We'll need to be damned careful, then. They seem a trigger-happy bunch."

Marchenko hesitated. "Yes, they are. We could get to the likely missile launch site by crossing the border farther south, where Ukraine has control, perhaps at Marinovka. The missile launch site is now back under Ukrainian control too."

"But then we won't find any witnesses who saw the missile launcher cross the border from Russia. That's the proof my president will need if he is going to accuse the Russians of providing the missiles—rather than the CIA," Johnson said.

Marchenko flipped the car keys in the air and caught them. "True. That's what we'll have to do, then. We'll head for the Severny checkpoint first thing tomorrow."

Johnson sat still for a few seconds, watching as Marchenko fastened his seat belt.

Then Marchenko inserted the keys and pulled away from the curb.

* * *

Wednesday, July 23, 2014
Moscow

The email account that Severinov shared with Shevchenko as a means of communication seemed like an old-school way of keeping in touch, but when combined with a secure virtual private network, it worked well—particularly when either of them was in sensitive, highly monitored locations, such as Washington, DC.

Upon reading the message that his long-time lover had left, Severinov walked to the window of his office on the ground floor of his residence in Moscow's Gorki-8 district and gazed down at the garden. The Moscow River curled its way past the end of it, and he never tired of the view.

This looked like an unexpected opportunity to kill two birds with one stone. Any investigation into the machinations behind the shooting down of the Malaysian airliner would be negative for Russia and for the president, he knew. So proactively trying to stop it dead in its tracks would earn him much-needed bonus points at the Kremlin.

It was also an opportunity for personal revenge on Johnson, who had humiliated both Severinov and his FSB friend Leonid Pugachov only a few months earlier in St. Petersburg.

He returned to his desk and called Pugachov, who was always full of practical common sense on any matter related to security and could be trusted completely to keep any information Severinov gave him confidential.

There were a few seconds of silence at the other end of the secure phone line as Pugachov, who was in his office at the Lubyanka in Moscow, digested what Severinov had told him.

"Is Johnson really going to come back into Russia so soon after the last narrow escape?" Pugachov asked. There was a distinct note of incredulity in his voice.

"Anastasia is rarely wrong," Severinov said. "The question is more about exactly when and where he returns, and under what identity."

"Let's think this through," Pugachov said. "They are far from stupid. They will know where the Boeing was shot down, and it is likely they have worked out roughly where the missile came from. Therefore, they will want to visit the launch site to try and gather evidence and will probably want to try and find witnesses. My guess is that they will also want to know how and where the missile got into Ukrainian territory."

Severinov agreed. "Yes, but how do they get there? That is

the key for us now, to head them off. I think Rostov is the most likely. They wouldn't fly into Donetsk or Luhansk—they are controlled by the rebels; it would be too risky. They won't come from Kiev—that is eight hundred kilometers. And they can't come up through the Crimea from Sevastopol because of the fighting."

"Volgograd?" Pugachov suggested.

"A possibility, but unnecessarily far. Rostov is the nearest major entry point to the crash site and the launch site."

Pugachov cleared his throat. "It's the most likely, yes. And if so, probably via Moscow. Did Anastasia say when this inquiry is likely to start?"

"No information on that. But I would expect they will come very soon, before the evidence is destroyed by the GRU. We need to stop them."

"We? Why do you need to get involved?" Pugachov said. "Your part in this exercise was not a large one. You were the delivery mechanism."

"You are forgetting two things, my friend. First, I am under orders from the president to dispose of Johnson. This may be my best chance, possibly my only chance, to do that while he is on Russian soil. Second, if this investigation succeeds, and if it exposes me as playing any part in the jet disaster, it will be the gulag for me. It would be all over the international media. I have unfortunately embarrassed the president enough in the past couple of years. I sense his patience is running rapidly dry."

Severinov could hear his own tone of voice. Flat, factual, and probably depressed. That was how he felt. Shevchenko's news from Washington concerned him. He knew the feeling: it was the fear of failure, because this was an opportunity he could not mess up.

Pugachov remained silent for several seconds. "You may be right," he said eventually.

"I am right. I cannot afford to screw this up, Leonid."

"So, in the absence of Vasily, who do we bring in to carry out the wet work, assuming that is needed?" Pugachov asked.

"There is one man who is in favor at the Kremlin. Someone who would be a more than adequate replacement for Vasily. That is Georgi Tkachev."

"I know of Georgi. Former GRU Spetsnaz, like Vasily."

"He worked with Vasily on a number of operations—Afghanistan, Georgia, Chechnya—and has been in the Crimea. He is out of the same mold. A very tough operator—I would not like to be on the wrong side of him." Severinov didn't mention Operation Black Sea and the Malaysian Boeing, as he doubted Pugachov knew about Tkachev's role in that.

Pugachov gave a slight chuckle. "I have seen reports about him. Good with guns and knives. Knows how to use missiles."

"That is why the president's office likes him. And, like me, he gives them deniability. And given that it was Johnson who put a bullet into Vasily, he might be quite motivated."

After another ten minutes of discussion, Severinov felt they had drawn up a workable strategy. Pugachov was going to utilize his contacts in the FSB's Border Service division to check through international passengers arriving at Russia's airports, particularly Rostov, Moscow, and St. Petersburg. There would be a focus on all male passengers aged forty-five to sixty-five and especially those whose tickets were booked after the Malaysian jet crash.

Officers on passport control duty at the airports and at Russia's land borders with Ukraine were to be given Johnson's details and photograph. The FSB teams posted at those locations were to be instructed to detain Johnson if sighted. Pugachov was also going to alert his military contacts who were responsible for providing support to the pro-Russian rebel forces in Eastern Ukraine. If any of them came across

Johnson, they would hold him until Severinov, Pugachov, or an FSB support unit could remove him.

Meanwhile, Severinov was going to call Georgi Tkachev and arrange a flight for him from Moscow to Rostov. Pugachov and Severinov were also to travel together to Rostov, where Pugachov would arrange a meeting with the regional police chief to request support as required.

"Thank you, Leonid," Severinov said as they finished the call. "Let's hope we get the bastard this time."

CHAPTER THIRTEEN

Thursday, July 24, 2014
Severny, Russia-Ukraine border

The potholed lane wound its way westward past a few roughly constructed houses made from cinder blocks, wooden planks, and corrugated iron roofs. Some of the homes looked better kept, but generally speaking they reminded Johnson of some of the wood-framed shantytown homes he had once seen a decade earlier at Umoja Village in Liberty City, a neighborhood of the greater Miami area.

He glanced up and down the street. Despite their appearance, some of the homes had TV satellite dishes and relatively new cars parked outside.

After a while, the road surface, made from crushed stone, came to an end. From that point onward, the street was a completely unsealed mess of dust and gravel. Marchenko pulled onto the side of the road and killed the engine. A row of ducks emerged from a bush and waddled across the street ahead of them. The grass on the side of the road grew long and straggly, and weeds were sprouting from the cracked cement base of a bus stop.

"The border post is about a kilometer farther on," Marchenko said. He took his phone from the holder on the dashboard where it was secured and tapped at the screen.

"This is the location where a couple of the Twitter posts originated, according to my team," Marchenko said. "There's no actual house numbers, though."

He turned the phone and showed Johnson one of the images that his team at the SZR had sent him. It was a screenshot of a Twitter post that showed a photograph of a white Volvo truck cab pulling a long lowboy, which was carrying a large military armored vehicle. The truck was shown outside a long single-story white-painted hut with a green corrugated iron roof.

The caption accompanying the photograph was in Russian and read, "Military machinery on the move this morning. It looks deadly." It was dated July 17, a few hours before the Boeing was shot down.

Johnson glanced up. The same green-roofed hut, looking even more rustic in real life than in the photograph, stood twenty yards from where they were now parked. Next to it, a telegraph pole was lurching at an angle, seemingly in danger of collapse at any point.

"Very good work," Johnson said. The SZR team had moved quickly to trace the photographs online, certainly more quickly than Vic's team at Langley had done. Both the SZR and Marchenko had gone up in Johnson's estimation.

"You can see it is not a normal armored car from the shape beneath the camouflage netting and the tarp," Marchenko said, pointing to the photo. "It's too bulky on top, for a start. That's where the missiles are placed. It's a Buk missile launcher, for sure. You wouldn't pick it up from satellite photos taken from above because of the camouflage—

which I am sure was the intention. But at street level, it's quite obvious if you know what you're looking for. See, here's another photo."

Marchenko flicked his screen and showed it to Johnson. This image showed the lowboy slightly farther down the street. In the foreground was a Mercedes 4x4, following the Volvo, with the passenger-side window wound down. A man wearing a long-sleeved black shirt was leaning out of the window, apparently gesticulating at whoever had taken the photograph. Perhaps it had been an instruction to stop taking pictures.

Johnson took the phone from Marchenko and studied the screen, then pinched it between his thumb and index finger to enlarge the photograph of the man in the Mercedes. He leaned forward in his seat and again enlarged it.

However, the photograph was slightly blurred, as if the person who had taken it had moved the phone or camera slightly as the shot was being taken. Now, even when fully enlarged, the man's face in the 4x4 remained unclear.

Johnson explained the problem to Marchenko as he scanned through the other screenshots of the lowboy taken at different locations during its journey. There were four more of them altogether, and in two others the Mercedes was visible, although the passenger window was up and the occupant not visible behind the darkened glass.

All the photos had come from a Twitter account, but the handle was a meaningless combination of letters and numbers, with no indication of the owner's actual name.

"We need to find the person who took this photo," Johnson said, returning to the original image he had seen. "Perhaps whoever it is has other, clearer photographs we could see."

"Why?" Marchenko asked.

"I would like to know who that is in the Merc." He jabbed

with his finger at the phone screen and handed the device back. "It's the only picture we have of an actual person. Can you send the pictures to me?"

Marchenko looked at him. "Sure." He tapped on the screen and forwarded the secure email he had received to Johnson.

Johnson opened the car door. "I think we should knock on a few doors and find our photographer. Do you want to do the talking?"

"Of course."

Marchenko locked the car and joined Johnson as he made his way through the gate of the nearest property, up the path, and to a rickety front door with peeling green paint. Johnson knocked and a young woman in a gray T-shirt holding a toddler's hand opened the door and eyed the two men.

"Hello, I am hoping you can help me," Marchenko said in Russian.

The woman shrugged. "What do you want?"

Marchenko showed her the image that had been forwarded to him. "I am trying to find the person who owns the Twitter account that posted these photos."

"Are you police?" The woman looked suspiciously at Marchenko. "You don't sound like it."

"No. Definitely not police. I'm just interested."

She glanced at Johnson. "And you don't look like you are from around here."

"We are working together," Johnson said, trying to keep his part of the conversation as brief as possible.

The woman looked at the photo again, just as her toddler began to cry and cling on to her leg.

"There is only one person I know here who uses Twitter," she said. "It is Mikhail at number 42." She pointed down the street in the direction Johnson and Marchenko had come from.

Marchenko thanked her. Johnson could hear the toddler wailing as they walked along the street.

Number 42 did have a satellite dish attached to the roof, which Johnson took as a promising sign. It clearly belonged to someone who was media savvy. The owner, a man in his forties, answered the door quite readily.

"Are you Mikhail?" Marchenko asked.

The man nodded, and Marchenko went through his explanation, showing him the screenshot of the Twitter post.

"No, it is not my photograph," Mikhail said, shaking his head firmly.

Johnson eyed him keenly. He looked away.

"All right," Johnson said. "Do you know who might have posted it?"

Again the man shook his head.

As they walked back along the street, Johnson turned to see the man leaning against his doorframe watching them, his arms folded and legs crossed.

"Shall we try more houses?" Marchenko asked.

"Yes, it must be someone around here. Let's not give up."

They knocked at three more doors, all of which drew blanks, and were about to walk through the gate of yet another property when Mikhail from number 42 appeared from behind a red corrugated-steel bus stop on the other side of the street.

Johnson turned as he approached.

"I think I may be able to help you," Mikhail said. "It was my post. I wasn't sure if you were police or FSB to begin with. The man in the Mercedes shouted at me when I took pictures, so I was a little worried. But now I can see you are not Russian officials. I hate them. All of them."

"You are correct. We are not FSB and certainly not Russian either," Marchenko said. "We're actually private investigators, and we're trying to trace someone connected to the military equipment you photographed." He explained the issue with the blurred photo and asked Mikhail if he had any others that showed the Mercedes more clearly.

Mikhail removed his phone from his pocket and began to scroll through some images. Eventually he held up the phone for Marchenko and Johnson to see; it showed another picture of the 4x4, this time in somewhat better focus.

"There, try that one. I think it is the Russian army scum taking weapons into Ukraine to kill more of those poor people. They are *filth*. Complete *shits*."

Mikhail kicked the ground in disgust and scrolled to another photo. "There, look at that. The truck carrying the armored vehicle stopped just down the lane, and the man in the Mercedes also stopped and got out and spoke with another military-looking man who was waiting for him. Definitely a Russian."

Johnson took the phone and again enlarged the images. One showed the man leaning out of the 4x4's window. It still wasn't pin-sharp, but it was possible to clearly make out his features.

"My God," Johnson said softly.

It was Yuri Severinov.

"You know that man?" Marchenko asked.

"I certainly do," Johnson said. "It's someone with whom I have had problems with before. He's an ex-KGB man, now involved in oil and gas. But what the hell was he doing here with the Buk?"

Johnson flicked to the next photo, of Severinov standing next to the Mercedes deep in conversation with the military-looking man that Mikhail had mentioned. The man, with short, receding blond hair, was wearing battle fatigues with the sleeves rolled up. He had a noticeable scar on his left cheek that ran down to his mouth.

Then Johnson noticed a badge on the man's left sleeve,

over his bicep. It was a circular blue-and-yellow logo with a black bat flying above a globe symbol.

He pointed at the badge. "See that?" he asked Marchenko.

He knew what that meant: the man was from the Spetsnaz of the GRU.

"Special operations, this one," Marchenko said.

"Could your people find out who that is?" Johnson asked.

"I will ask them to run the photo through their database. There's a good chance they can get an ID if he's GRU Spetsnaz."

Johnson was about to ask Mikhail to send him copies of the photographs when he heard a distant squeal of brakes.

He glanced up to see two white Russian police cars, with blue stripes along the side and lights on the roof, pull to a halt about 150 yards away on a bend farther up the lane.

* * *

Thursday, July 24, 2014
    Rostov Oblast

The needle on the speedometer rose to 154 kilometers per hour as Pugachov pushed down hard on the accelerator of the gray BMW X5 that he had borrowed from the FSB's Rostov-based car fleet. The rear end of the unmarked 4x4, an aging but powerful model, quivered a little as he moved into the overtaking lane of the M4 divided highway heading north and steered past a Porsche.

In the passenger seat, Severinov was focused on his laptop screen, which showed a series of photographs captured from airport security video footage at Moscow's Sheremetyevo International Airport and at Rostov-on-Don Airport.

The images were of two men. The first was tall wore

black-rimmed glasses and a dark-blue baseball cap; he had a visible slight nick at the top of his right ear. The second was shorter and balding, with a gray pointed goatee beard.

"The tall one is definitely the *ublyudok*, the American bastard," Severinov said. "The second, I have no idea."

"My men also have no idea about the second one, so far," Pugachov said, hunched forward as he concentrated on the highway. The traffic was heavy. "But they are working on it."

Since the phone call had come in from Pugachov's office at the Lubyanka, they had already covered more than 150 kilometers, most of it at a dangerously fast pace. According to the satnav perched on the dashboard, they still had another 23 kilometers to go to Severny, on the Ukraine border.

A police station near the Ukraine border had taken a call from a young woman who reported two suspicious men, one of them who looked foreign, knocking on doors near to Severny and asking odd questions about photographs posted on Twitter of a Russian armored vehicle. The police had passed on the details to the provincial FSB office in Rostov, which in turn had reported the details to the Lubyanka. The report had come just after Pugachov had alerted the FSB in Moscow and Rostov to look out for anyone matching Johnson's description.

The woman had given a description of the two men that seemed to match the photographs from Sheremetyevo and had also given details of the vehicle they were traveling in, a blue Lada 4x4, including the license plate.

Upon hearing the details, Severinov's antennae for trouble had immediately begun to flash bright red. He knew that he and Pugachov had to move quickly, so they set off without Georgi Tkachev, who had agreed to help but was still in Moscow, awaiting a flight to Rostov.

The radio on the BMW's dashboard squawked, and Pugachov pushed a button.

"Pugachov."

"Sir, we have trawled through our airline passenger database here and have more details of Johnson's route to Rostov."

"Go ahead."

"He flew from Athens on the Aeroflot service to Moscow, then connected to Rostov."

"Athens?" Pugachov said. "Under what name?"

"We've been through the passenger manifestos. Only one possibility. Philip Wilkinson. A US passport holder. The only American on the flight."

"Any details of the other man?"

The radio crackled explosively, so Pugachov repeated his question.

"A man named Henrikas Venclova. Lithuanian passport. But likely to be a false ID."

"Of course. Anything else?"

"Yes. Police are searching for the Lada near Severny. And also, we have found a record of a Joseph Johnson traveling to Athens from Nice airport on Sunday on a scheduled Aegean Airlines flight. Before that, Johnson flew the previous Wednesday, just over a week ago, from Amsterdam to Nice, having transferred from a flight originating in New York."

Severinov glanced at Pugachov. "Four days in Nice. Interesting. Ask if they can find out what he was doing there, who he was meeting. And did he travel alone on those other flights?"

Pugachov repeated the question to the FSB caller.

"Yes, sir, I have got that. We will make some checks. I will liaise with the SVR on this one. Over."

Pugachov flicked a switch on the radio and ended the call, then turned his attention back to the highway, accelerating once more as the BMW entered a long, straight section.

Some time later, the radio squawked into life again. It was Pugachov's FSB colleague again.

"We have had contact from police in Severny," the officer said. "Johnson and the other man have been spotted in the village."

"Have they stopped them?" Pugachov snapped.

"No. They drove off with a local man down a lane. The police are trying to track them. A woman pointed them in the right direction, but they have not yet found them."

Pugachov slammed the palm of his hand on the top of the steering wheel, causing the BMW to swerve slightly.

Severinov glanced at the car clock, then at the satnav, which was telling him that at the current rate of progress, they would arrive in Severny in six minutes.

* * *

Thursday, July 24, 2014
Rostov Oblast

Instinctively, both Johnson and Marchenko edged into the shadows thrown by a small cluster of trees that stood between them and the two police cars.

The passenger doors of both vehicles opened almost simultaneously, and two officers in pale blue shirts got out and looked around them. Then they walked up the path of the house next to their parking place. The two drivers also got out and stood next to their cars.

"Shit," Marchenko said. "We need to move."

"Yes, but how?" Johnson asked. "They are blocking our way out. We can't just try and drive past them. My gut feeling is that—"

"They are looking for us," Marchenko interrupted.

Johnson nodded. "That's my guess."

"You are in trouble?" Mikhail asked.

"Not in trouble. But we want to avoid police," Johnson said.

"I can help you. Where is your car?"

Johnson glanced at Marchenko, who gave a slight nod and pointed down the lane toward the green-roofed hut.

"Down there," Marchenko said.

"Is the car good off-road?"

"Yes. It's a Lada 4x4," Johnson said.

"Come quickly, then. There is another route out of here down a dirt track," Mikhail said. "I will show you." He crossed the lane so that the bend in the lane and the line of trees alongside it took him out of sight of the two police cars, then strode rapidly toward the Lada, Johnson and Marchenko following behind.

They jumped into the Lada, with Marchenko behind the wheel, Johnson in the passenger seat, and Mikhail in the rear.

Marchenko pulled away, following Mikhail's instructions to head left in a southward direction down the gravel lane. As they did so, to their right, Johnson caught a glimpse of the first woman they had met running from her house down the path toward her gate, waving and shouting in the direction of the policemen.

CHAPTER FOURTEEN

Thursday, July 24, 2014
Rostov Oblast

"Move," Johnson said, turning around and looking through the rear window. "That damn woman we first spoke to was alerting the police. Doesn't look good."

A cloud of dust flew up behind the Lada as Marchenko accelerated hard down the gravel track, heading south away from Severny village. After about a hundred yards, the gravel turned to dirt, which created even more dust.

The Lada bounced up and down on the rough surface. It was dry now but had been badly rutted by heavy vehicles during previous wet spells.

To their right was a row of trees and empty grasslands beyond.

"Their patrol cars will struggle on this surface," Marchenko said.

"Let's hope so, because we're leaving a huge dust trail," Johnson said. He thought about removing the two Makarov pistols from the black backpack that lay at his feet but, given that Mikhail was in the car, decided against it. He could access them quickly enough if things got desperate.

The land they were traveling through was uncultivated wasteland, with just a few random trees and bushes, long grasses, a couple of rusty abandoned tractors, and mounds of earth, as if some kind of excavation work had begun but then had been abandoned.

After about half a mile, there was a rusted steel sign with faded white lettering on a pale green background that in both Russian and English read Customs Control Zone. Below that, on another sign, was some more wording in Russian, but the sign was so rusted that Johnson could not make out what it said.

There was no sign of a customs point or border line or fence of any kind, so the sign seemed somewhat incongruous. Next to the sign, a narrow track that was overgrown with weeds led off the main track in a westerly direction.

"That is into Ukraine, down there. It's the border," Mikhail said, pointing down the track.

"Shall I go that way?" Marchenko asked.

"No. It's dangerous. You can get shot at. There has been a lot of fighting between the Ukraine army and the rebels. The Russian army has been helping the separatists. They come in black or green unmarked uniforms, usually at night."

Johnson realized he needed to get the photograph of Severinov in the Mercedes from Mikhail and asked him to send it via text message.

"What's your number?" Mikhail asked.

Johnson read out the number of the Russian burner phone. Mikhail keyed it into his own phone and sent the picture.

"Thanks. Got it. Where does this lane go?" Johnson asked as they continued down the dirt road. The Lada bounced into a particularly large pothole, causing his head to bump into one of the roof struts.

"Three kilometers of dirt road, then back to the highway," Mikhail said. "Then you can escape."

The police, in a normal sedan, would indeed have difficulty catching them on this bumpy surface, Johnson thought. He jumped as his phone rang. It was Vic, calling at the most inconvenient time, as usual. But given their arrangement to keep communications to a minimum, Johnson assumed it had to be urgent.

He tapped in his key to access the encrypted call.

"Vic, this is a very bad time," Johnson began. "We're running from a local police patrol. Can I call you back?"

"No. Listen," Vic said. "Turns out the NSA has been working with an anti-Putin hacker in Moscow. They've got a series of IP addresses and from that a physical address for the posts about the jet crash."

"Where?"

"Rostov-on-Don. They're all coming from there. All off the same proxy server. It's got to be Russian shit—must be coming from the Kremlin."

"We've just come from Rostov, dammit."

"I know, but you need to get back there. I'm going to text you the street address. I need you to check it out. It's critical. We need to prove it's the Russians. Okay?"

Johnson battled to avoid rolling his eyes. This was crazy.

"I'm not going back to Rostov. We were just there, and if the cops have been alerted to look for us, the highway back is going to be swarming with them."

There was a pause. "Joe, you're going to have to give it a try. This is critical."

Johnson sank into his seat. Maybe if they could ensure the police patrol didn't tail them, they might have a chance, as it seemed very unlikely they had gotten close enough to see the license plate. He groaned.

"All right, Vic," Johnson said in a resigned tone. "We'll give it a try. If you don't hear from us again, you'll know what's happened. Don't say I didn't warn you."

"Thanks. Inform me of your movements when you can."

"Sure, Vic. Just one bit of news. Seems like our old friend Severinov played a part in transporting the Buk missile launcher into Ukraine. He was in a 4x4 escorting the semi-trailer it was on. I've got photos—I'll forward them to you. Will tell you more when I know more."

"*Severinov?* Do you know what—"

"Vic, I can't talk. Speak later." Johnson ended the call.

He quickly summarized Vic's call to Marchenko, who shrugged but said nothing.

The more Johnson thought about it, the more he realized that if the National Security Agency had found something significant, then it was indeed important to follow up. Based at Fort Meade, Maryland, the NSA's role was concentrated on obtaining so-called signals intelligence, especially by tapping into and monitoring phone, email, and internet traffic. In turn, this information was used to inform and assist other US intelligence agencies, including the CIA and FBI.

A few seconds later, Johnson's phone beeped as a secure message arrived from Vic. It contained a street address and a postal code in Rostov as well as a short note adding that the office operated under the name Web Marketing Group and was thought to be on the second floor.

The dirt track continued through heavier scrub and bushes and eventually emerged back onto the paved highway near a gas station.

"Let me out here," Mikhail said. "I can't come any farther with you. You are on your own. I'm pleased to help—I hate what's going on in Ukraine—but I'll be in big trouble if the police or the FSB find me with you."

Marchenko braked to a sharp halt. "There you go, my friend. And thank you. You have saved us from a police cell. Good luck."

Mikhail nodded and got out. "Good luck to you too," he said. He shut the door and started running toward some nearby houses.

Marchenko had his foot back on the accelerator as soon as Mikhail had gone. Johnson forwarded the photographs of Severinov, the missile carrier, and the unknown GRU Spetsnaz officer to Vic and Jayne and, as an afterthought, to Marchenko.

* * *

Thursday, July 24, 2014
Rostov Oblast

Severinov held on to the edge of his car seat as the BMW screeched to a halt next to a gas station just as a white police car emerged from a dirt track right next to it.

"That must be our police crew," he said.

But Severinov knew immediately from the police vehicle's speed, which was no more than a crawl, that it had lost its target. He wound down the passenger window to hear the sound of metal dragging on the ground below the police car's chassis; the vehicle had clearly suffered some damage.

"So Johnson is nowhere to be seen," Severinov said, slumping back in his car seat and throwing up his hands.

"The idiots have lost him," Pugachov said.

The police car stopped. Both Severinov and Pugachov

undid their seat belts, climbed out, and walked over to the driver, who wound down his window.

Pugachov showed the driver his FSB identification card. "Pugachov, FSB. You are the crew detailed to track the American, Johnson?"

The driver studied the card and, upon seeing Pugachov's rank, snapped upright in his seat, his brow furrowed. "Yes, sir, we are."

"So what happened? Where the hell is he?"

"He was going too fast over the dirt road," the police driver said. "They have a 4x4. We couldn't keep up. We wrecked our exhaust when we hit a pothole. I am sorry, sir."

Severinov folded his arms. "Did he actually come this way? Could he have gone west into Ukraine down one of those tracks?"

The policeman looked away. "We were not close enough to see, but the dust being thrown up by his car led this way, not toward the border. He must have come in this direction."

Severinov swore under his breath. "So what next, then?"

"We have the license plate. Reported by a woman in the village. An alert has already gone out to all cars," the police driver said. "If that Lada is spotted, it will be pulled over. I can assure you of that."

"Do you know what the American was doing here? What he wanted? Who he was with?" Pugachov asked.

"According to the woman who spoke to us, he was with another man, shorter, with a goatee. But when he left, she said one of her neighbors also went with him, a man named Mikhail Turgenev."

"*What?*" Severinov said.

"Yes, this Turgenev lives nearby; he was with them. All three left in the Lada. The woman saw them—she was the one who alerted us in the first place, who called the police. Then she also saw them drive off in the Lada. According to her, Johnson's companion was asking questions about who in the lane had taken photographs of an armored car and an escort vehicle that had appeared on Twitter. The woman told him to try Turgenev's house as he was the only person she knew who had a Twitter account. The next thing she knows, Turgenev is leaving with them in the Lada, just as we arrived. Unfortunately, we didn't know exactly where Johnson was— we stopped too far up the lane and had just started knocking on doors when we heard her shouting at us to come quickly."

Severinov narrowed his eyes. Now alarm bells were ringing at full decibels in his mind. If Johnson had seen a photograph of the Buk missile launcher passing through the village en route to Ukraine, that was bad news. Had he also seen pictures of him, Severinov, and of Georgi Tkachev, accompanying the launcher?

Bljad. Sonofabitch.

Visions of a flood of international media coverage implicating him in the destruction of the Malaysian jet and the deaths of three hundred people filled his mind, followed by a sinking feeling in the pit of his stomach at the renewed wrath such a development would incur from the Russian president.

Tkachev, whose flight from Moscow had now arrived in Rostov, would also be furious.

"Find this Mikhail Turgenev then too," Severinov said. His voice suddenly sounded hoarse and cracked a little. "If he posted such pictures on Twitter, he is a fool. Go back to his house, see if you can get his cell phone number, and put a trace on his phone. If he's with Johnson, you will then find him too."

"Yes, good idea, sir," the policeman said. "We will do that."

Pugachov leaned down and put his face to the car window. "You need to make sure you get all your resources thrown at this. I can speak to your commanding officer if necessary."

"There is no need. I can do that. There is only one problem."

"What?" Pugachov snapped.

"Sir, we have an issue with the number of patrols out there—there are not many."

"Why?"

"It is always like this, not just today. It is continuous. We are flat-out, mainly dealing with the criminals who have come to the region from Ukraine. We have also lost some officers who have gone over to fight for the separatist rebels. It is difficult. I am not making excuses. I am just informing you of the situation across the Rostov Oblast."

Severinov felt his anger rising. He bent down beside Pugachov to look the police officer in the eye. "You can tell the remaining patrols to get their priorities straight—and *I* am the priority now. Forget the criminals from Ukraine. I want that car found. This criminal we are seeking is the most urgent case on your list."

He walked back to the BMW, his fist clenched in his pocket, and sat in the passenger seat. A few seconds later, Pugachov joined him.

"So where do you think the American has gone?" Severinov asked, glancing at his old colleague. It felt like a guessing game.

"I don't know. If he's investigating the Malaysian crash, then he might head over the border to the crash site."

Severinov gazed through the windshield into the distance. "It's possible, but I'm not sure about that. Would he risk going into a war zone?"

"Probably not," Pugachov said.

"And the crash site is going to be very busy with officials, police, military, you name it. He won't find out anything new there."

"What about the missile launch site?"

"That is more likely, yes, but again, what will he find? It is going to be deserted apart from maybe some faded vehicle tracks in the dirt."

Pugachov nodded, conceding the point.

Severinov remained silent for several seconds, visualizing southwestern Russia in his mind. "If he came into Russia via Rostov, maybe he is going to leave the same way? I can't see too many other options."

Pugachov placed both hands behind his head. "I agree. Let's head back to Rostov. I'm going to call my office there, and we'll get the airport, airlines, and port on full alert first, in case he tries to get out that way."

"Yes. And we can get Tkachev to help us out when he arrives. He will have his own special solution for Johnson."

PART TWO

CHAPTER FIFTEEN

Thursday, July 24, 2014
Rostov-on-Don

To Johnson's relief, they made the journey back to Rostov-on-Don without any signs of surveillance or interception by police. He made continuous checks for trailing coverage, but so far they seemed to have gotten away with it, thanks to Mikhail.

Using the coordinates provided by the NSA, Johnson guided Marchenko to a street in central Rostov, Bol'shaya Sadovaya Ulitsa, three blocks north of the River Don. He pulled the Lada into a parking space at the side of the street behind a five-story office building constructed in an ornate style that contrasted with some of the grimmer Soviet-era buildings around it.

"Is that it?" Marchenko asked.

"It would seem so," Johnson said. "But before we do anything else, let's dump this car somewhere safe. That woman in Severny might have given police the plate number."

To Johnson, this all felt a little like going into the lion's den.

"You're right," Marchenko said as he lit up another of his Marlboros. "In this country, you still never know who is an informer and who isn't. Times have changed, my friend, but habits haven't."

"Can your people get us a different car?" Johnson asked. "I don't want to take any risks."

Marchenko drove to a quiet residential street six blocks away, where they removed their things, including the back-pack containing the two Makarovs, from the Lada and locked it.

Marchenko then called Stepan, his SZR contact who had supplied the Lada and, after a short negotiation, arranged for it to be swapped for another vehicle. He also sent the photo-graph of the Spetsnaz GRU officer who had been with Severinov to SZR headquarters in Kiev, asking for an identi-fication.

Johnson ditched the blue baseball cap he had been wearing and exchanged it for a black one with the yellow-and-blue badge of the FC Rostov soccer team he had bought from a supermarket near to where they had parked. He also removed the battery and SIM card from the Russian burner phone, as he assumed all communications would be moni-tored and therefore didn't want to run the risk of them trian-gulating his location from connections his phone made to nearby masts.

Then they walked by a circuitous route back to the office building identified by Vic, which was next to a small plaza in which stood a bronze statue of one of Russia's heroes of the 1812 Patriotic War, a general of the cavalry, Matvei Platov, together with his horse. Johnson couldn't help but reflect that Platov would struggle to recognize the type of vicious civil war now being fought not far away across the Ukraine border.

Their first job was to carry out a reconnaissance of the office building, which had a sign at the front door that read Platov Business Center. It was an old-fashioned brick structure, with several exits and floor-to-ceiling sash windows, as well as balconies on most floors. It housed several companies, and a brass nameplate on the wall near the entrance showed that the Web Marketing Group was indeed located on the second floor as Vic had indicated.

Platov Business Center had a twenty-four-hour concierge desk inside the front reception area, at which sat two men. Perhaps for that reason, there were no obvious burglar alarms or intruder detection devices, at least as far as Johnson and Marchenko could see.

Johnson also identified a set of parking bays among some trees behind the office building where they could park a getaway vehicle when the time came. It was secluded yet offered quick access to the main traffic arteries that ran through central Rostov and the highways out of the city.

Stepan, a greasy-haired man in his forties, turned up with a colleague about twenty minutes later in a dark-gray Škoda Yeti at a prearranged point nearby. The colleague headed off on foot with a set of fake license plates for the Lada, which he was intending to drive away and store in a lock-up garage.

"Get in," Stepan said, indicating toward the Yeti. "I'll take you to our safe house for now. You can use this car later when you need it. Just be careful, though. FSB surveillance here is patchy but can be persistent. They are difficult to counter on their home territory."

Stepan, it emerged, was officially a cultural attaché at the Ukraine consulate, but that was just a cover for his espionage role as an SZR officer, which had kept him exceptionally busy since the start of the conflict in Ukraine earlier that year.

The safe house was only a couple of kilometers from the office building they were targeting, but before heading there,

Stepan drove on a ten-kilometer surveillance detection route through the suburbs of Rostov.

When he was satisfied there was no tail, he finally approached the safe house, one of several three-story town houses on a narrow street conveniently located just two blocks away from the consulate in Pereulok Khalturinskiy. He explained that the SZR used the safe house for covert meetings with agents and as a base for operations across the Rostov Oblast. Johnson took some comfort from the fact that he was clearly good at his job.

The safe house had an integrated drive-in garage with a shutter-style door made of black metal that Stepan opened with an infrared clicker when they drew near.

"So, what are you two guys going to do about this office building?" Stepan asked once they were safely upstairs in a high-ceilinged reception room. "Are you going in there tonight?"

Johnson shrugged as he sank into an armchair. He felt conflicted between the need to do the White House's bidding on one hand and protecting himself on the other.

"Our NSA believe that the disinformation about the Malaysian jet is coming from there," Johnson said. "My boss is desperate to get to the bottom of it; so is our president. I am guessing that Poroshenko is probably also keen to know the truth. But . . ." He let his voice trail away.

"But what?" Stepan asked, looking alternately at Johnson and Marchenko. "You mean you're worried about being on the FSB and police radars?"

"That's the issue," Johnson said. "But I'm struggling to think of another way to get the proof."

"Aren't you going to regret it if you leave without trying?" Marchenko said. "It'll be difficult to come back. And the FSB don't know exactly where we are."

Johnson nodded but didn't reply. Marchenko was correct —it would be extremely tough to leave then try to return at a later date.

"Security doesn't appear to be as tight as I expected," Marchenko said.

"No, not at first glance, anyway. I've seen much more difficult challenges," Johnson said.

"You're right. Tonight it is, then."

Johnson shrugged. He could feel himself bowing to the inevitable. "I guess so. Then we head straight to the airport and out of here. Job done."

He turned to Stepan. "So, how do we get in, then? Do you have any suggestions, or should we go for the break-and-enter option?"

"I have an idea," Stepan said. "Listen to this and tell me what you think." He began to detail his plan.

* * *

Thursday, July 24, 2014
Rostov-on-Don

Severinov and Pugachov were two-thirds of the way back to Rostov when the call came in on Pugachov's radio from the FSB office. The police officers they had met near the border had found Mikhail Turgenev and had taken him to the nearest station for questioning.

From what Severinov knew of police procedures, the questioning process in the cells was unlikely to be a happy or painless one for Turgenev.

Shortly afterward, there was another call, this time from Georgi Tkachev, who had arrived in Rostov and was heading to the FSB's offices. They agreed to meet there as soon as Pugachov and Severinov could make it.

An hour later, they were sitting around a plain wooden table in a meeting room on the first floor of the monolithic four-story building, which stretched along almost an entire 170-meter block in central Rostov, north of the River Don.

In the center of the table was a conference call phone from which was emanating the tinny voice of the policeman that Severinov and Pugachov had met near Severny.

"There are two key points," the officer said. "First, we immediately confiscated Turgenev's phone and found five relevant photographs on it, all of which show a long semi-trailer with an armored vehicle on it. I can see exactly what the vehicle is, and I am sure you know it too. I don't need to spell it out. Also, some of the photographs are of a Mercedes 4x4. In a few, Mr. Severinov can be seen leaning out of the window. Two of the images show the vehicles stopped at the side of the lane, and Mr. Severinov is standing next to another man in fatigues, wearing a GRU Spetsnaz badge."

"*Da, da*. He is one of ours. Continue," Pugachov said, glancing across the table at Tkachev.

"Turgenev subsequently used the phone to send the photographs by text message to another phone, I believe belonging to Johnson, the American. I have that phone number for you."

"Give it to me now," Pugachov snapped, reaching for a pad of paper and a pen. "Go ahead."

He wrote down the number that the policeman gave him.

"Thank you, good job," Pugachov said. "Anything else?"

"We have persuaded Turgenev to squeal a little more. He thinks that Johnson and the other man are going to Rostov. There was a phone call during the short time he was in their car, and he said Rostov was mentioned. That is all he knows."

There was a pause, and then the policeman added,

"Believe me, we have taken all steps to ensure he has told us everything that he does know."

Severinov pressed his lips together. He had a good idea what the policeman meant by "all steps."

"Is that it?" Pugachov asked.

"Yes, that is all the information I have. I have extracted copies of the photographs from the phone, and I will email them to you. I have deleted the originals, and we will put traces on the phone as soon as we can. I am going to find some charge to press against this man, Mr. Turgenev. He's in the cells."

"What charge?"

"I don't know yet. But it will be serious enough to put the bastard behind bars."

"That is your business, officer," Pugachov said. "I will be in touch if I need anything else." He ended the conference call.

Severinov immediately stood up. "Can your telecoms people trace that number?"

"Yes," Pugachov said. "I've got the team leader waiting outside." He nodded toward a man who was waiting in the corridor on the other side of the glass door that separated them.

He beckoned the man in, introduced him to Severinov as the leader of the FSB's telecommunications team, and explained that they needed him to urgently prioritize tracking the cell phone number being used by Johnson.

"We will get onto this immediately. As long as the phone is active, there is a good chance we will have him," the telecommunications officer said. He nodded and left.

Shortly afterward came a call on Pugachov's cell phone from Rostov police headquarters to inform him that there was still no sign of the Lada. Pugachov instructed the police to call in reinforcements and to step up a street-by-street search of the area for both the vehicle and the two men.

"Good, Leonid. I'm certain Johnson is in this city," Severinov said. "I think he's got what he wanted, those photographs, and he will be trying to fly out as soon as he can. We will get him when he breaks cover."

CHAPTER SIXTEEN

Thursday, July 24, 2014
Rostov-on-Don

It was just after ten thirty in the evening when Stepan parked the blue-and-white Gazprom gas network maintenance van in the bay behind Platov Business Center that Johnson had earmarked earlier in the day.

The fake van, which the SZR kept in their lockup garage, was normally used for surveillance operations in and around the city, and Stepan had no hesitation in making it available to Johnson and Marchenko.

"There are thousands of these vans," Stepan said. "People don't blink when they see them. It's the perfect cover for us. And their customer service people are so lazy, they don't answer the phone when people call, so even if anyone wanted to check if it was a genuine Gazprom van or not, they wouldn't be able to."

Johnson had operated from many similar surveillance vans

during his long career; he had to concur with Stepan that it was indeed a perfect cover.

This particular model of van, an adapted Volkswagen Transporter four-wheel-drive automatic, had a potent twin-turbocharged 196 horsepower diesel engine instead of the usual 89 horsepower unit. It had been equipped with three one-way windows at the rear and both sides that were coated to appear like a shaped steel panel from outside but offered visibility from inside. Peepholes were built into the side and rear panels.

The bar across the roof with orange-and-white flashing hazard lights also had hidden cameras and microphones installed, offering both video and audio feeds to the monitors inside the van.

A rack inside that contained several genuine items of gas industry equipment, including a few handheld gas-monitoring devices the size of large old-fashioned cell phones in rugged rubber protective cases. There was also a selection of protective white hard hats, all carrying the Gazprom logo.

Stepan gave Johnson his cell phone number in case of emergencies. He had also provided Johnson and Marchenko with Gazprom jackets, complete with company logos, flashlights, and fake identity badges. Their plan was to set up an operation to find and deal with a nonexistent gas leak at Platov Business Center. That would give them a perfect excuse to enter the building.

A few lights were still showing on the second floor; obviously employees of the Web Marketing Group were driven hard. However, by ten minutes to eleven, they had gone out and the floor was in darkness.

At just after eleven, Johnson watched as Marchenko, wearing one of the hard hats, strode around to the front of the building and disappeared into the reception area. His job was to hoodwink the concierge and get them in through the front door.

Within five minutes, Marchenko reappeared, a faint grin on his face. "We are okay to go in. I've explained that we are both gas engineers and need to check all appliances in the kitchens on each floor as well as the gas meters in each office, as there is a risk they may be leaking. The concierge wants us to include the reception area in our test because he is quite concerned about the possibility of breathing in methane."

A few minutes later, Marchenko and Johnson, also wearing a hard hat, walked into the front lobby, both brandishing gas detectors. Marchenko, worried about Johnson's American accent giving him away, didn't bother introducing him, and Johnson just gave a very curt nod of acknowledgment.

Marchenko then made a show of carrying out a gas test near the front desk, which he pronounced negative.

"*Da*," grunted Johnson in response as he pretended to tap a note into his phone.

"We will need to go to the upper floors next," Marchenko told the duty concierge, a dapper man in his sixties who wore a waistcoat and a black tie. "You don't need to accompany us. If there is gas, it will not be safe. Can we access the various offices?"

The man looked doubtful. "I can't let you go in those offices unaccompanied. I will have to come."

"What about if a visitor comes in down here?" Marchenko asked.

The concierge indicated toward a buzzer on his desk. "That will sound an alert on my pager if I am not in the lobby," he said.

He seemed determined, so Johnson was thankful when Marchenko didn't argue. Better to go along with it and think of a solution later.

"Don't turn any lights on or off," Marchenko said,

waving the flashlight he had taken from his jacket pocket. "It might trigger a spark. Dangerous if there is gas in the air."

The concierge picked up his own flashlight from the desk. He ignored the elevators and led the way up the staircase behind his desk and through some swinging doors into a landing area. There was another set of double doors opposite with a small plate on the wall that read Web Marketing Group. The concierge removed an electronic pass card from his pocket, pressed it against a sensor next to the door, and pushed it open. He turned on his flashlight.

Johnson and Marchenko also turned on their flashlights and followed him through. They found themselves in a cavernous open-plan office that stretched the full width of the rear of the building, full of identical bench-style desks with PCs and monitors. There had to have been at least a couple of hundred workstations, Johnson calculated. If they were all churning out false tweets and other social media content, this was an industrial-scale operation.

At the far rear of the room were five individual offices with glass panels and doors that separated them from the open-plan area. They had to be for management, Johnson assumed, and they had to be his starting point.

But how to get rid of the concierge? The old guy was heading toward a kitchen in the far-left corner of the office area, with Marchenko in tow, and it seemed highly unlikely he was going to leave them unattended.

Johnson pondered for a couple of minutes, but he could think of only one way to do this. He took his Russian burner phone from his pocket, surreptitiously reinserted the battery and SIM card, and dispatched a text message to Stepan, who was still outside in the Gazprom van.

In office. Need to distract concierge for as long as possible. Go to reception desk now and press buzzer until he comes. Keep him talking.

Johnson looked carefully at the PCs as he walked down a central aisle between the rows of desks, swinging his flashlight from one side to the other as he went. All of them were turned off.

He continued into the kitchen, where the concierge was showing Marchenko the gas oven and boiler and a meter in a cupboard attached to the wall. Marchenko told him to stand well back while he did a pretend check using his handheld gas detector, which he again pronounced negative; then he began an examination of the meter.

Johnson's phone vibrated as Stepan replied. *Ok.* He then slipped the battery and SIM card out of the phone again.

A few minutes later, the concierge reached into his pocket and removed a small black pager, which he examined then replaced in his pocket.

Shit. He's ignoring it.

"Are you finding anything?" the concierge asked Marchenko.

"We need to do a lot more checks. It may take some time," Marchenko replied.

The concierge again reached into his pocket and scrutinized the screen of his pager. "I am sorry, it appears that I have a visitor downstairs at the reception desk. He keeps buzzing me." He furrowed his brow and looked first at Marchenko then at Johnson. "Can I leave you alone for a few moments while I go and check who it is? Will you stay here?"

"That's no problem," Marchenko said. "You go and deal with your visitor. We will be some time doing checks in this area. We won't move. Take as long as you need."

The concierge nodded, made his way back to the office entrance, and disappeared through the doors.

"I'll tackle the management offices first," Johnson said as soon as the concierge was out of sight. The beam of his flashlight picked out the largest office, farthest away from the kitchen. He walked over to it and went in.

There was a desktop computer that Johnson could see from the winking LEDs had been helpfully left in sleep mode. He placed his flashlight on the desk and reactivated the computer by moving the mouse. The screen lit up. This was a good sign—perhaps management were less careful about computer security than their employees, for whom leaving a PC switched on was probably a firing offense. That was often the case, in his experience.

However, although the screen activated, it went straight to a log-in page, requiring a name and password.

Johnson looked around. On the desk was a pile of letters addressed to a Konstantin Gudovich, managing director, Web Marketing Group. It was good to know he had the boss's office, and that gave him a name to try, but the password was another problem. He checked a corkboard that hung on the wall, full of various yellow sticky notes and other bits of paper held by thumbtacks. But there was nothing that indicated a password.

He pulled open the three drawers beneath the desk one by one, but again, there was nothing helpful. A dark-green metal filing cabinet stood against the wall, and Johnson pulled open the top drawer. Only a couple of computer equipment boxes were inside, one for a Bluetooth mouse and another for an external USB hard drive.

He tried the other two drawers, but they contained only pens, paperclips, a stapler, and other stationery supplies.

Johnson stood, picked up the flashlight, and swung it around the office for several seconds. Then he returned to the first drawer and picked up the hard drive box; it was too much to hope that there might be a disk inside containing a backup of the computer's hard drive, but perhaps it was worth checking. Sure enough, it was empty.

Then he tried the mouse box. Inside was a thin instruction leaflet, on the cover of which was a word thinly scribbled in pencil: Sadovaya. That was the name of the street outside.

Johnson put the leaflet back into the box and placed it back in the drawer, which he closed.

He stood thinking for a few moments. *Sadovaya*. It could be meaningless, but on the other hand, if the owner had set up the computer and the Bluetooth mouse together, maybe he had scribbled the password down somewhere convenient. You never knew.

Johnson went back to the PC keyboard and in the name box typed in *konstantingudovich* and in the password box, *sadovaya*. An error message popped up. Incorrect log-in or password.

He tried again, this time using *konstantin.gudovich*. The error box reappeared, and alongside it was another message warning that the account would be frozen after five incorrect attempts to log in.

For his third try, Johnson typed in *Sadovaya* using a capitalized S.

The computer screen went momentarily blue, then the familiar sight of a Microsoft Outlook email in-box appeared in front of him.

Despite the tension, Johnson couldn't resist grinning to himself. Sometimes it paid not to dismiss the obvious. However, time was now running short. Johnson guessed that Stepan downstairs would not be able to keep the concierge occupied for too long; the man had been quite visibly concerned about leaving him and Marchenko alone.

He removed a small 500GB hard drive and USB cable from his pocket and plugged it into the PC tower, clicked onto the disk management app, then proceeded to copy the documents and email folders onto the drive, praying as he did so that Stepan was going to be up to the task demanded of him.

There was 134GB of data to copy. A blue bar appeared on-screen, indicating progress with the task. It began to inch slowly from left to right.

While he was waiting, Johnson clicked over to the documents folder and checked its contents.

There were a number of subfolders, all of which were labeled with what appeared to be hashtag names. Most consisted of people's names and were meaningless to Johnson, although he thought a couple were Russian politicians.

However, Johnson almost jumped in his seat as one near the bottom of the list caught his eye; it had the hashtag *#MH17*.

He felt a jet of adrenaline shoot through him.

Johnson clicked on the folder, which had about a dozen Word documents inside it, all labeled with other hashtags. The first was named *#MH17CIAplot*. The next three had the tags *#KievDownedTheBoeing, #Kiev'sProvocation,* and *#Kiev-TellTheTruth.* The rest were in a similar vein.

Johnson opened the first one with the *#MH17CIAplot* tag. It appeared to consist of an email that had been copied and pasted into the document and included what were quite obviously three draft tweets written in English. They all had different wording, but each had the same central message and a set of hashtags suggesting the CIA was responsible for downing the Malaysian Boeing by supplying Patriot missiles to Ukraine in a plot cooked up by US Secretary of State Paul Farrar, and the Ukraine President Petro Poroshenko.

The address at the top of the pasted email had been deleted, and there was no signature at the bottom, but there was a brief note above the email.

Issue these as soon as possible, as discussed.

In the absence of any identification in the pasted email, Johnson clicked on the Word document's properties tab. All the fields were empty, apart from the author's name in the Summary tab. It read IGOR IVANOV.

"Sonofabitch," Johnson muttered. He knew exactly who that was.

Johnson checked the other Word documents. The next four were similar to the first, all authored by Ivanov. The sixth, however, was not a copy of an email but contained what seemed to be text typed directly into the document. A different author's name was written in capitals in the properties box: KARAKURT/DC.

Johnson stared at it for a moment, then checked the remaining documents. They too had the same author: KARAKURT/DC.

He felt himself tense up. This looked like some sort of code name. "*DC?* My God," he said out loud involuntarily.

Right then, a flashlight beam appeared on the office wall, and Marchenko put his head around the door. "Any progress?"

"Yes, I think so. Maybe huge progress. Let me finish. I'll tell you in a minute. Go back to the kitchen and keep a lookout."

Marchenko did as requested.

Johnson took out the phone, reinserted the battery and SIM card, took a photograph of the documents on-screen, and texted them to both Vic and Jayne. Then he did likewise with the properties tabs, showing the names IGOR IVANOV and KARAKURT/DC. Better to be safe and send the data while he had the chance, just in case problems arose further down the line. That was the first lesson he had learned upon joining the CIA many years ago, in 1984. Intelligence was worthless unless it was in safe hands.

He toggled back to the disk management app. The copying process was nearing completion, but he guessed it still had a minute or two to run.

Now they just needed to get out of there as quickly as possible. There was still no sign of the concierge returning.

Johnson removed the battery and SIM from the phone.

CHAPTER SEVENTEEN

Thursday, July 24, 2014
Athens

Jayne stood at one end of the long rectangular reflecting pool that ran parallel to the southwestern facade of the US embassy's chancery building and watched the water spouting from the simple piped fountain halfway along it. The building's modern architecture, with its white marble external columns that were clearly intended to echo those of the nearby somewhat more archaic Parthenon, was more inspiring than some embassies she had seen over the years.

The American flag fluttered from a tall pole to her left, behind a statue of George C. Marshall, the US secretary of state whose aid program helped bring prosperity to Greece after World War II.

"I feel like a swim in that," Jayne said to Vic, nodding toward the pool.

Vic stood smoking a cigarette. It was the first time she

had seen him smoke, although she knew from Johnson that he occasionally did so when he felt stressed.

The barrage of social media posts about the Malaysian jet destruction had continued since the disaster, albeit at a slightly reduced rate. The venom contained in them, however, was not diminished.

Just that morning, a raft of new tweets had appeared, still under the same hashtags, though the most often used was *#MH17CIAplot*. They were all relentlessly placing the blame for the 298 deaths at the door of the White House and President Ferguson.

Many relatives of the deceased passengers had been reposting the messages, piling pressure on their own governments, particularly those in Australia and the Netherlands, where most of the passengers were from. In turn, questions were being asked via diplomatic channels, causing further embarrassment for the president.

Newspapers and other US media that were supportive of his Republican rivals who were jockeying for position ahead of the next presidential election in 2016 were picking up on the social media coverage and becoming increasingly critical. Many pointed the finger of blame at the president for interference in the Ukraine-Russia conflict, arguing that it was yet another case of the CIA trying to pick winners.

Consequently, the White House was calling on Veltman at Langley to deliver a result. Vic had described the conference call that he had joined that morning, involving Veltman and Paul Farrar, as the most intense so far.

There had been some progress. Vic and Jayne had earlier that day received the photographs from Johnson that showed the Buk missile launcher, Severinov, and the unknown GRU officer. It enabled Vic to claim some progress on the conference call, but it was obvious that he needed more.

"Anything from the NRO yet?" Jayne asked. The National

Reconnaissance Office was the United States's spy satellite intelligence agency, based at Chantilly, Virginia, half an hour's drive southwest of Langley. It worked closely with the CIA.

Upon receiving the images from Johnson, Vic had immediately sent them to the NRO with a request to match them with photographs of the same spot taken at the same time from the array of surveillance satellites in orbit above Ukraine and Russia at that time.

His hope was that by capturing images of the missile launcher lowboy from above, the NRO would then be able to accurately track its previous and future movements across Russia and Ukraine.

Vic shook his head. "They're quick, but they'll need a bit longer than that."

Jayne scrutinized Vic's face, which looked a little drawn.

"Are you okay, Vic?" she asked.

He shrugged and stubbed out his cigarette in the soil beneath a potted shrub, then looked around like a guilty schoolboy to ensure nobody was watching. "I'm okay. Been better. It's too hot out here. Let's go back indoors."

They were halfway up the steps that led from the neatly manicured pool area when their phones beeped almost simultaneously.

Jayne, who had her phone in her hand, got to the message first.

"It's Joe," she said. "Photos of documents."

"Must be important if he's taking a risk like that, sending them by text," Vic said.

Jayne didn't reply, but she knew he was right. Why did he have to underline the risk bit, though? Since she and Johnson had become a couple again earlier that year, her view of his reward-to-risk balance on such operations had changed a little.

"Let's read them in the office," she said.

They took the elevator to the CIA station on the top floor and headed straight to a secure meeting room where they could talk in private.

They both scanned through the documents on their phones, enlarging them when needed.

Jayne leaned forward in her chair. "Where has he got this stuff from? Look at this metadata box—it says DC. Is that where these draft tweets are originating? And who or what is KARAKURT?"

Vic didn't speak for a couple of seconds, then pursed his lips. "KARAKURT isn't a surname. It has to be a code name. It's the Russian equivalent of the black widow spider."

Jayne, who was fluent in Russian, had a sudden memory of a nature documentary she had watched long ago. Vic was correct.

"This is a joke," she said.

"I wish it was a joke. But to me it looks as though—"

Jayne interrupted. "It looks as though whoever leaked the Kiev talks isn't in Kiev. They're in bloody DC."

* * *

Thursday, July 24, 2014
  Rostov-on-Don

Severinov was slumped in a chair in the FSB's first-floor meeting room, staring at the peeling paint on the walls and the cracked plaster in the ornate rose that surrounded the garish lighting fixture in the center of the ceiling. The FSB had a fearsome reputation in every city across the country, but there was little money in the building maintenance budget, and it certainly showed.

Tkachev sat opposite him chatting to a former GRU colleague whom he had brought in, Anatoly Nikolsky.

Severinov checked his watch. Maybe he should tell Pugachov, who was in the neighboring room making a phone call, that it was time to go home and get some rest.

But he didn't get the chance. The telecommunications team leader burst through the glass door and into the room without knocking.

"We've got a trace on the Johnson phone number," he said, struggling to get his words out. "Nothing all evening—he was off-line. Then we picked up seven text messages sent, three of them short, four with bigger chunks of data. Probably photographs. There was one short message received. We just managed to get a fix on the number. A few seconds later it went straight off network again."

Severinov jumped out of his chair. "Where?" he demanded.

"Not far. A couple of kilometers farther along Bol'shaya Sadovaya Ulitsa, out here." He pointed toward the street outside the office building.

"*What?* You mean he's just down the street?" Severinov said, his hands on his hips.

"It looks that way, yes."

"*Mudak.*" Shithead.

Severinov strode to the door, yanked it open, and hollered down the corridor. "Leonid, get here now. We've got Johnson."

After a few seconds, Pugachov's head appeared around the door of the office next door. Severinov didn't give him time to speak.

"It's Johnson. Let's go. Get some men and a car. We've probably got minutes at most."

Pugachov dashed into the meeting room and grabbed his

jacket and the Makarov semiautomatic that was lying next to it on the table.

He turned to the telecoms team leader. "What's the street address?"

The man gave him the details and added that the building was called Platov Business Center.

"I know it," Pugachov said. "There's several businesses in there. Which one?"

"Don't know."

Pugachov picked up the phone and dialed a number.

"We need three cars and six men, armed, at the rear door, within two minutes. It's urgent," he snapped. "Make one of the cars my BMW. We'll need pursuit drivers for all three. I've got the target address. Platov Business Center."

Pugachov looked at Tkachev and Nikolsky. "I need you both too."

Tkachev nodded. "Of course. We've got a Mercedes out there."

Pugachov slammed the phone back onto its cradle and strode toward the door. "Right, let's go."

* * *

Thursday, July 24, 2014
Rostov-on-Don

It was twenty minutes before midnight when the files finished copying onto Johnson's portable hard drive. He pulled the cable from the USB socket, pocketed the drive, put the computer back into sleep mode, and ran out the door to the kitchen, where Marchenko was keeping an eye on the double swinging doors at the far end of the room.

"Let's go. Quick. I've got the lot," Johnson said. "This stuff is unbelievable. I'll tell you in the van."

They both strode toward the exit, their flashlight beams lighting their path, just as the concierge came back in. He stood still, looking surprised, as the two men approached him.

"You have finished already?" the concierge asked.

"Yes, all done," Marchenko said. "Our colleague outside has found the leak—it's at the rear of the building, not internal. So you're all clear. We're going to go and help him. Thanks for your assistance."

"What about the other offices?" the concierge asked.

"No need," Marchenko said. "It's all okay. We're leaving now."

The concierge moved to one side as the two men walked past him, then he followed them across the landing and down the stairs. He stood watching as Johnson and Marchenko left through the front entrance.

As soon as they were out of sight, they both broke into a run, heading across the small plaza, which was dimly lit by orange streetlights and the glow from a brighter spotlight that was trained on the statue of Matvei Platov and his horse. Beyond the statue, the white Gazprom van remained parked at the rear of the building.

They were past the statue and within twenty yards of the van when from the main street behind them there came the whine of powerful car engines being thrashed at high revs, followed by a screech of brakes. Johnson glanced over his shoulder to see two gray sedans and two black ones scream to a halt outside the front of the building.

A stream of men, most of them wearing black clothing and carrying guns, jumped out of the cars and ran into Platov Business Center. Behind them, striding at a slightly more sedate pace, were four other men—one of whom, Johnson was certain, was Yuri Severinov. He would have recognized the gait anywhere.

Marchenko also turned and saw them. "Bastards. That's got to be the FSB," he said. "That asshole concierge must have tipped them off. But how?"

They both sprinted the remaining distance to the van, yanked open the sliding rear door on the passenger side, and climbed in. Before the door was shut, Stepan had the engine running.

"Go," Marchenko yelled. "There's FSB at the front of the building."

"Not just FSB," Johnson said. "Severinov was there too."

Stepan pushed his foot down hard on the gas.

As the van began to move, two men dressed in black appeared around the side of the building, from the direction of the front door, and began to run toward them, sprinting hard.

But they must have realized they were too late. The van was rolling away when Johnson saw the men stop, turn, and sprint back toward the line of cars. Then he lost sight of them.

Stepan reached the end of the street, only fifty yards away, and turned right to head back to the safe house.

By the time he had made the turn, they heard the sound of sirens in the distance.

Johnson and Marchenko, who were both on a long bench seat, hung on to the driver's and front passenger's seats in front of them as Stepan accelerated hard along a long, straight street with two lanes in each direction. He went through a red traffic light and across a junction, narrowly missing two cars crossing in the other direction, and gunned the van up the next junction, where he took a sharp right, now heading toward the river.

Johnson could see that the next junction would take them

straight over Bol'shaya Sadovaya Ulitsa, the busy main street on which Platov Business Center was located. His guess was that if they could make it over undetected and into the streets nearer to the river and the safe house, they might have a chance.

The light turned green just at the right time as Stepan approached, and he accelerated again. Johnson glanced at the speedometer, which was showing eighty kilometers per hour, well above the limit of forty.

As they crossed the junction, forcing a couple of youngsters on the pedestrian crossing to break into a run to get out of the way, Johnson glanced right to see a gray BMW and a black car, the latter with blue lights flashing, heading toward them about 150 yards away.

After another few seconds, Stepan swore loudly. "They are behind us. Hold on."

He swung right at the next junction, now on a street with elegant low-level stone buildings, and again floored the gas pedal. The powerful 196 horsepower engine responded instantly.

Johnson could see through the rear one-way window that the leading gray BMW was turning the corner but was held up for several seconds by a taxi that had stopped to let people out. With a long continuous blast of its horn, it eventually swerved around the taxi after the traffic cleared and resumed the chase.

The delay had bought the van a couple of hundred yards, but the BMW was closing in on them.

"We are struggling," Stepan said, unnecessarily.

There was silence for a second. He was right. Despite the firepower beneath the VW van's hood, it wasn't going to hold off an FSB car for long.

"We will have to carry out a maneuver," Stepan added.

"What maneuver?" asked Johnson.

Stepan hunched over the wheel, trying to concentrate on driving and talking at the same time. "I am going to do a left soon, then a quick right-left-right onto narrow streets. We should be out of sight for a few seconds. When I shout, you must open the sliding door as I make the final turn, when I am moving slowly, and jump out. It is important you slide the door shut as you go. Roll as you land so you don't get hurt. There is an alley right there with a recess a couple of meters along it. You need to get into the recess, fast as possible, and go flat against the wall. If you are quick enough, they won't see you as they pass. Understood?"

"Yes."

"Good. Then when the cars have gone, you run forty meters to the end of the alley. You will see the safe house across the street. Knock three times on the door. The safe house duty manager, Valeriya, will let you in. Then you must take the Škoda from the garage and drive to the Ukraine border at Marinovka. That checkpoint is under Ukraine army control—not the Russian rebels."

"That makes sense," Marchenko said. "Good plan." His voice sounded cracked and reedy.

Stepan turned his head and glanced at Marchenko. "Valentin, you can negotiate with the army to either escort you from Marinovka to Kiev or give you a safe route. Understand?"

"Yes. How will you escape, then?"

"There is a narrow street where I can crash the van into some railings. That will block the street; then I can run off through a park and past some buildings where it is difficult for them to follow. I think I can lose them and get back to the safe house. I should be back there within five minutes. If I'm there before you leave, I will come with you to Kiev. If not, just go. Don't wait for me."

Stepan wrenched the steering wheel left and the van's

tires squealed as it lurched onto a side street. Johnson feared for a moment that the van would topple over. Forty yards farther on, Stepan did the same on a right-hand turn, just as the gray car appeared in sight through the rear one-way window. A few seconds later, he took a left, then accelerated hard, the boom of the van's exhaust echoing against the walls of the buildings that lined the narrow street.

"Get ready," shouted Stepan.

Marchenko grasped the handle of the van's sliding door, poised to exit, with Johnson right behind him, holding the edge of the seat to get enough leverage to launch himself out.

The van's tires squealed again as Stepan turned right.

"Go!" Stepan shouted as he braked, slowing the van momentarily.

Marchenko pulled the handle and slid the door back in one motion, then from a crouching position rolled out onto the sidewalk. Johnson copied his movements, getting as low as he could but simultaneously putting his right hand around the outside of the sliding door and grabbing the handle so he could slide it shut as he left the van.

Johnson managed to pull the door across as he left the van —but not quite hard enough. It clanged and almost shut but then sprang open again as the van accelerated away. Johnson swore as he hit the pavement, banging his elbow and shoulder sharply in the process and causing a wave of pain to shoot up his arm.

He focused on getting back to his feet and following Marchenko, who was already moving smartly into the alley entrance, which was directly next to their landing point just as Stepan had described.

But already he could hear the sound of the pursuing car's engine whining as it approached.

CHAPTER EIGHTEEN

Thursday, July 24, 2014
  Rostov-on-Don

"*Bljad*," Severinov swore as the FSB driver who was piloting Pugachov's BMW took the corner. The white van with the Gazprom branding ahead of them was moving far more quickly, and accelerating much faster out of the corners, than he expected a commercial van to do. Clearly whoever was driving was an expert and definitely not a gas company employee.

The red taillights of the van vanished around a left-hand corner ahead of them, and Severinov, sitting in the rear seat behind the driver, leaned forward and craned his neck to get a better view.

There was no doubt: Johnson and another man, presumably the supposed Lithuanian Venclova, were in the van. The concierge in the Platov building had taken one look at the photograph of Johnson that Severinov had shown him and confirmed it was him. The concierge said that he and another man had both claimed to be Gazprom engineers and had just left, heading toward the rear of the building where they had a company van.

They had immediately set off in pursuit of the pair.

"Move," Severinov muttered. The FSB driver slammed on his brakes and turned the wheel sharply as they came into another right-hand bend, causing the car's tires to shriek loudly. He heard the van doing likewise ahead of them.

"We are getting closer," Pugachov said from the passenger seat. He had surrendered the driver's seat to the FSB man, who he said was a better pursuit driver, but Severinov was not so sure, based on what he was witnessing.

They were indeed drawing nearer, but not close enough. And then there was the issue of what to do if they did catch up. There was little chance of the BMW physically shunting the sturdy two-and-a-half tonne van off the street.

Severinov grasped the sides of the driver's seat in front of him as they rounded the corner. The van was visible almost fifty meters ahead.

He caught a glimpse in his peripheral vision of a sharp movement in an alleyway to his right as they rounded the corner but ignored it, focusing instead on the van ahead. The getaway van shot straight over the next junction without stopping, narrowly missing two cars and triggering a barrage of horns.

The BMW followed, negotiating the junction with only a little more care, and then as they rounded another right-hand corner, Severinov was astonished to see the Gazprom van skewed at a forty-five degree angle across the street in front of them, its nose buried in a metal fence next to a gate that led into a park. The driver's door was hanging open, as was the sliding rear door on the passenger side.

"Over there," Severinov said as he caught a glimpse of a

figure disappearing through the gate, which was illuminated by a streetlight.

The driver braked hard to a halt next to the van, which was blocking the street, and Severinov, Pugachov, and the driver climbed out just as the other two black FSB cars and Tkachev's Mercedes arrived behind them.

Neither the van driver, nor Johnson, nor Venclova were anywhere in sight. Presumably they had all run off into the park.

Severinov sprinted toward the park entrance, pulling his Makarov from his waistband and flicking off the safety.

There, in the dim glow from a couple of lights on the right edge of the park, he saw someone running hard next to some bushes in the direction of a group of buildings. As he ran, he appeared to throw something into the bushes.

Was that Johnson? Severinov couldn't tell in the gloom. It didn't matter. He dropped to one knee, took aim, and began firing. After a couple of shots, the man's legs collapsed from under him, his arms flew out sideways, and he crashed head-first onto the gravel path, where he lay still in the shadows.

Got the bastard.

Severinov, followed by Pugachov and a couple of the FSB men, ran into the park and up to the man lying facedown on the path. He flicked on the flashlight on his phone and saw that blood was pouring from a bullet wound at the back of his neck. Severinov turned him over and did a slight double take.

The bullet exit wound in the front of the man's neck was far larger than the entry hole. The round had blown out his entire Adam's apple area and destroyed his lower jawbone. Death must have been almost instantaneous.

But the dead man definitely wasn't Johnson, and Severinov didn't recognize the face.

So, where the hell was Johnson?

Severinov quickly calculated distance and times and

doubted that Johnson could have escaped the park quickly enough to avoid being seen. He must have gotten out of the van earlier somehow.

He ordered two of the FSB men to run to the other visible exits and check if they could see him. Meanwhile, Severinov retraced his steps a short distance and, using his phone flashlight, began searching in the bushes for whatever the man had thrown.

After a few minutes, he found a phone beneath a holly bush. The screen was badly cracked but was still live and displaying several recently dialed numbers.

Using his own phone, Severinov took a photograph of the numbers on display and turned to Pugachov.

"Leonid, can we get these numbers checked by your telecoms team?"

Pugachov nodded and also took a photograph of the numbers, which he immediately sent to FSB headquarters.

Severinov went through the man's pockets, but there was nothing that identified him. He had half expected that. He also flicked through the apps on the phone, but again there was nothing that would help. The email app had not been activated. It appeared to be a burner phone.

The two FSB men returned, saying there was no sign of Johnson.

"*Pizdets*," Severinov said. Dammit. This felt like something of a dead end for now, just when it was clear they could not afford it.

He grimaced, closing his eyes in frustration, but then in the same instant recalled something.

He turned to Pugachov. "Leonid, I think Johnson might have jumped out of the van before the crash. I saw movement down an alley just after we turned a corner. The van's sliding door was open too."

Pugachov put his hands on his hips. "You may be right.

Let's go back there and look around. Maybe someone saw something."

"Either way, he's still going to be in this area. We need to seal off all routes out of the city center area and alert all local police patrols."

"I'll get that done now."

Pugachov removed his phone from his pocket and tapped on a number.

* * *

Friday, July 25, 2014
Rostov-on-Don

The metal shutter of the garage door clattered and rattled as it rose. Johnson winced at the noise. It was far from ideal to be making such a racket at well past midnight given they were trying to make a rapid, unobtrusive exit from Rostov.

Marchenko, next to him in the driver's seat of the Škoda Yeti, turned on the headlights and let out the clutch as soon as he had enough headroom to exit the garage. He moved out sharply into the street, right in front of a man in dark clothing on the sidewalk just a few yards away.

In the dim light thrown off by the streetlights, and because he was on the side of the car farthest away, Johnson didn't realize immediately who the person was, but Marchenko did.

"That's a damned policeman," he muttered. "Now of all times." He swore under his breath and accelerated down the street.

Johnson looked in the Škoda's passenger-side mirror as the car sped off. The policeman did not appear particularly animated; it looked as if he was probably on a routine night patrol. He certainly wasn't reaching for his radio or notebook. But he was standing, hands on hips, watching them.

It was understandable that Marchenko didn't want to stop and run the risk of the policeman pulling them over for driving across the sidewalk without checking for pedestrians. But on the other hand, to speed away like that might be inviting trouble.

It was too late to worry now, though.

Their priority was to cover the route to Marinovka as swiftly as possible and get out of Russia. The dashboard satnav showed it was 140 kilometers away. Beyond that, it was another 840 kilometers to Kiev. Altogether, they were looking at more than fourteen hours of driving—more if there were difficulties through the rebel-held areas.

Johnson and Marchenko had wasted no time upon arriving back in the safe house. Within ten minutes, they were ready to go and in the Škoda. They had managed to grab water, two flasks of hot black coffee, and snacks provided by Valeriya, a young woman who was the safe house night manager. Marchenko had thrown a few pieces of emergency equipment into the trunk, including several lengths of rope, two sleeping bags, and raincoats, in case they were needed.

As Stepan had instructed, they didn't wait for him. Johnson just hoped he had managed to escape as intended, although he had a feeling that something had gone wrong, given he hadn't made it back to the safe house within the five minutes he had indicated.

Soon, Marchenko had the Škoda heading west along Ulitsa Tekucheva, the long, straight divided highway that led out of the city.

The car headlights picked out the white-and-black concrete posts bordering the road, and on both sides, lights from high-rise apartment buildings glowed in the darkness.

Johnson cursed to himself.

What am I doing?

For the second time in a few months, he was on a hell-for-leather escape bid out of Russia, with his life potentially at stake, having gotten most of the information he wanted but with Severinov still at large. He felt a momentary stab of frustration that he still hadn't nailed the Russian.

Johnson didn't know for sure how Severinov and the FSB had found out they were at the Platov building, but he didn't want to risk reinserting the battery and SIM card into his burner phone, just in case the brief messages he had sent to Vic—vital as it had been to send them—had been the cause. He also didn't want to risk using either his main phone or Marchenko's.

That meant he could not let Vic and Jayne know of his next planned move, although the tracker in the heel of his shoe meant they should probably be able to work it out before too long.

Johnson turned to Marchenko. "Have you driven this route to Kiev before?" he asked.

"Yes, a couple of times."

"When was the last time?"

"That's a good question. A few years ago. Before the fighting started."

Johnson paused for a few seconds, wondering whether to vocalize what was running through his mind. The broad grass strip that divided the two segments of the highway, with its floodlit burger billboards mounted on posts and neon signs promoting electrical goods, reminded him of the interstate that wound its way through Portland. That seemed a long way away now.

Eventually, he spoke. "What are our chances?"

Marchenko shrugged but didn't reply.

* * *

Friday, July 25, 2014
  Rostov-on-Don

The alley, needless to say, was empty. "This is where I saw movement," Severinov said. "If they did jump out here, then they probably ran off down there and out the other end."

He and Pugachov walked along the dark alley, no more than a couple of meters wide and about forty meters long, until they emerged at the other end on another street, which was also deserted. Opposite them were several three-story town houses, mostly with integrated garages.

"I think they've got to be hiding somewhere around here," Pugachov said. "But where? We can't get police to search every property, and not in the middle of the night."

Pugachov's phone rang. He glanced at the screen, answered the call, then listened carefully. In the silence, Severinov picked up enough of the conversation to know that the caller was from FSB headquarters and that there had been a development.

"We're in that area," Pugachov said to the caller. "Can you get me the address? And get it cross-checked with the police." He nodded at Severinov, animated now, and ended the call.

"They've checked the phone numbers called by that dead guy's phone. One of them was for the cell phone for Johnson that we had, another was for the Ukraine consulate, and the final was for somebody else's cell phone, which they and police are now trying to triangulate."

The two men walked back down the alley to the BMW that Pugachov had parked in the street nearby. One of the other FSB cars remained parked next to it.

As they were about to get into the car, Pugachov's phone rang again. Again, there was an animated conversation.

After it had finished, Pugachov gave a small fist pump. "The other number was for someone who is currently at a house on the street we've just been near, at the other end of the alley. Johnson's phone is still switched off, but he could still be at that house."

He walked to the FSB vehicle in front of his and instructed the driver to follow him.

Two minutes later, they were parked in the street a short distance away from the town houses they had seen just earlier.

"It's number twenty-two, the one with the black garage door," Pugachov said, pointing. "Police are coming."

A few minutes later, two unmarked police cars pulled up behind Pugachov's BMW. A uniformed officer got out and walked to Pugachov's car window, which Pugachov wound down.

"Mr. Pugachov?"

"Yes."

"Sir," the officer said, "before we take any action here, you need to know something. This is the same address from where we had a report from one of our beat officers a short time ago. He was on a routine foot patrol and noted a vehicle leaving the garage at number twenty-two at high speed. It came out over the sidewalk without looking and nearly knocked him over, he said. He was annoyed and thought it unusual, wondering why the rush at midnight. He wasn't able to speak to the driver because they took off too fast—no way were they going to stop. So he messaged in a short report with the license plate. It was a gray Škoda Yeti. Two men in the vehicle, sir."

"The bastard's gone," said Pugachov. "But good work, officer. Get in the house and check it now anyway. Get an alert out to traffic police to stop that Škoda if they spot it too."

"Yes, sir."

"And can we check the cameras on routes out of Rostov? Especially those heading toward the airport, toward Ukraine, and toward the port."

"There are license plate recognition cameras on most of the main routes. Don't worry, sir, we'll track him. Let me get this house raid moving." The officer removed his radio from his belt and pushed a couple of buttons. There was a squelch break, and he began to bark out a series of instructions.

Severinov felt his blood pressure rising, his disappointment turning rapidly to anger. "*Dermo*," he said, his voice tense. He turned to Pugachov. "As soon as we get a trace on that Škoda, I want Tkachev and his colleague after Johnson. They won't make a mistake. I want you to give them a shoot-on-sight order. I've had enough of this shit."

Outside, the police officer beckoned to his colleagues in the car behind theirs. Three of them got out and went to number twenty-two. Severinov watched as they knocked on the door. Nobody answered, and after they had tried a couple more times, one of the officers used a large sledgehammer to smash in the door. The officers disappeared inside.

While the officers were searching the property, Pugachov made another call, this time to Tkachev, who had returned with Nikolsky in the Mercedes to the FSB offices on Bol'shaya Sadovaya Ulitsa. He gave Tkachev the Škoda's details and asked him to be ready to leave immediately, as soon as a sighting came through.

Pugachov finished the call, and both he and Severinov climbed out of the BMW and stood on the sidewalk, waiting for the police to finish searching the house.

A message came in on Pugachov's phone, and he stood reading it for a few moments. "Hmm, new information has just come in," he said.

"What?" Severinov asked.

"Remember my guys found out yesterday that Johnson had come from Nice to Athens to Rostov?"

"Yes, of course." Severinov said, a little impatiently.

"The reason he was in Nice was because he was on vacation in Cannes with his family—his two teenagers and his sister. And that British bitch, the MI6 agent, Robinson. You know, the one who also caused us problems a few months back. Seems she and Johnson are an item. The sister and the kids are still there, sunbathing on the beach, but not Robinson, it seems. I'll find out where she went."

Severinov turned and stared at Pugachov. "You know all that?"

"Yes. Have to give the SVR the credit, though. Their boys dug it all up."

"Interesting," Severinov said. "Yes, find her. Could be useful to know. And as for Johnson, the stupid bastard will be wishing he'd stayed in Cannes by the end of tonight."

Pugachov chuckled.

A couple of minutes later, the three policemen emerged from number twenty-two, frog-marching a young woman and a man who had handcuffs fastening their wrists behind their backs. The woman was limping heavily and struggling to walk. As they passed Severinov, he could see blood was coursing down her face from a large cut above her right eye, and her left eye looked to be swollen, purple, and closing up fast. The officers bundled both of them into one of the patrol cars.

The officer who had originally spoken to Pugachov hurried back toward them, talking on his radio. When he had finished the conversation, he came up to Pugachov and Severinov.

"The woman was the person the dead guy in the park had called," the officer said with a thin smile. "Her phone was in the house. I got her to talk, after a little persuasion. She said

Johnson was here, along with another man, traveling under the name of Henrikas Venclova, a Lithuanian, but he is actually Valentin Marchenko, an assistant director of the SZR. They are both in the Škoda—I have just heard the car is heading west out of town. Our control center logged it on our camera network."

"West? Toward Ukraine?" Severinov said. He jerked upright in his seat.

"I don't know, but Ukraine is probably the best guess, yes," the officer said.

Severinov turned to Pugachov, his hand unconsciously moving to rest on the Makarov in his waistband. "Ukraine makes sense, especially if he's SZR. Right. Get Tkachev after them. We'll follow."

Pugachov grabbed his phone from his pocket.

CHAPTER NINETEEN

Friday, July 25, 2014
Rostov-on-Don

The Russian Armed Forces had many Spetsnaz, or special forces, brigades that were controlled by the GRU, the country's foreign military intelligence agency.

But few had quite as notorious a reputation as the highly secretive subunit hidden away within military unit 29155, which in turn was part of the 161st Special Purpose Brigade, headquartered behind tall concrete walls in eastern Moscow.

Although now a freelancer, Georgi Tkachev was proud to have been a member of that subunit. It was a clandestine bunch of about only twenty operatives with a variety of unique skills acquired during long experience of hands-on combat. The unit had, for many years, been tasked with delivering results in situations where normal military tactics were either inappropriate or would too obviously leave the Kremlin's fingerprint.

There were few more dedicated teams of assassins

anywhere in the world, especially those who specialized in both semimilitary operations, such as the covert destabilization of Crimea and Moldova, and the surgical killings of individual traitors who had betrayed Russia's secrets to foreign governments.

Among his contemporaries in 29155, Tkachev stood out as exceptional. It was for that reason that he had been noticed by the rising Kremlin star, the president's special adviser Igor Ivanov, and had become first choice in recent months for a series of special operations closely watched by the president and his close-knit team.

Tkachev, who at forty-one was as fit as most of his colleagues a decade junior, had earned his reputation in some of Russia's bloodiest conflicts, including Afghanistan, Chechnya, and only in recent months, Crimea. For this latter campaign, he had been privately told he would receive a Hero of Russia medal, the country's highest honor, from President Putin at the next scheduled ceremony.

He saw himself as significantly superior to his international rivals, in particular the arrogant American idiots at the US Army's Delta Force, or the US Navy SEALs.

Tkachev's skill lay in four key areas: guns, as he had been top of his Spetsnaz training year group in both rifle and pistol shooting; in close combat, in which he had proved himself deadly with knives; explosives; and, finally, anti-aircraft missile systems.

But Tkachev was no prima donna. Quite the opposite. He couldn't afford to be. The truth was that despite his operational successes, he remained a lowly paid soldier and lived in a two-bedroom apartment in southern Moscow with his wife and two teenage sons.

His hope was that by following Ivanov's suggestion and leaving the GRU to go freelance, he would exponentially increase his earnings, given that he would be paid directly by his masters at the Kremlin and would not be stuck on a Russian army pay scale.

Ivanov's argument was that if Tkachev operated as a freelancer, the Kremlin would have a looser hand to deploy him as it saw fit. The operation to shoot down the Malaysian jet had been the most recent of those deniable jobs.

Tkachev sipped from a bottle of Coke. He and Nikolsky were sitting outside the FSB's offices in their unmarked gray three-liter, twin-turbocharged, Mercedes C-Class, awaiting further instructions from either Severinov or Pugachov following the failed pursuit of the Gazprom van.

The two men had worked side by side on any number of jobs on behalf of subunit 29155 and had gone freelance at about the same time. They trusted each other like brothers.

Nikolsky glanced sideways at him. "Do you make love to that?" he asked, nodding at the 9mm pistol that lay on Tkachev's lap.

"Lighter touch than most women," Tkachev grinned, wiping a hand across his face. He hadn't shaved since starting the Malaysian jet operation and now had significant stubble. "Lower maintenance too. Definitely lower than my wife."

Nikolsky laughed. "And mine," he said.

The pistol, a Gryazev-Shipunov GSh-18, was Tkachev's favored option when it came to handguns, partly because its magazines carried eighteen rounds. He had never had problems running out of ammunition the whole time he had used the weapon.

Behind his seat, lying on the floor of the Mercedes, was his VSS Vintorez silenced 9x39mm sniper rifle, his weapon of choice in most situations because it was so quiet. It fired its rounds at subsonic speed, thus avoiding the loud snap heard with many alternatives. Next to it was a long black canvas bag that held three rocket-propelled grenades and a one-meter tubular steel RPG-7 launcher tube.

Tkachev's phone rang. He glanced at the screen. "I think we could be on the move," he said, stabbing at the green button with his index finger. It was Pugachov.

"Hello, Leonid," he said, flicking on the speakerphone so Nikolsky could hear.

Pugachov spoke quickly and succinctly, as usual, and the task sounded straightforward. Head west out of the city on the A-280. Liaise closely with Pugachov and Severinov, who would be following as quickly as possible. Overtake the Škoda before it reached its likely objective: the Ukraine border. Kill both occupants.

That would be a neat revenge for the life of Vasily Balagula, someone for whom Tkachev had had the greatest of respect.

Nikolsky had slipped the car into gear even before Pugachov had finished speaking.

Yes, Johnson would meet his Maker at some point soon. It was just a question of when.

* * *

Friday, July 25, 2014
    Rostov Oblast

The text message beeped loudly on Marchenko's phone after they had been driving west out of Rostov for about forty minutes.

"Read that for me," Marchenko said, pointing to the phone, which rested in a cradle on the dashboard. "I need to concentrate on the highway."

Johnson grabbed the phone and tapped on the alert showing on the front screen, which was glowing brightly in the darkness. The message was from the safe house manager,

Valeriya.

FSB or police smashing down door. Many men. Don't reply.

Johnson swore, then read out the message.

"Shit, she won't last long. You know what they're like," Marchenko said.

"Just hope she can hold out a little while—twenty minutes, half an hour would be huge for us," Johnson said.

"Doubt she'll go longer than five minutes. Slim whisper of a girl. They'll break her in half if she doesn't talk." Marchenko gripped the steering wheel and accelerated again, taking the Škoda's speed up to above 150 kilometers per hour. "Take the battery and SIM out of that phone. They'll have hers by now, with that number on it."

Johnson complied with the request.

The divided highway here was straight and fast, with two lanes in each direction, and the blacktop surface was smooth. There was little traffic. Johnson checked the satnav and did a quick calculation. In about fifteen, maybe even ten minutes, they should be at a junction of the A-280 where they needed to turn sharply right and head north.

From there, it would be another seventy-five kilometers to the border. Maybe forty-five minutes, perhaps quicker, depending on progress and driving conditions.

He leaned back in his seat, thinking.

"Assuming she talks, then—"

"She will talk," Marchenko said firmly.

"Okay, when she talks, within the next ten minutes, police and Severinov and the FSB will know what direction we have come and what car we're driving. We have had a head start of forty minutes. They will struggle to catch up."

"Yes, but they could alert local police out here, or border

patrols. Although to be honest, they are very short of men, and there's even fewer at this time of the night."

"That's the problem, I agree. So what do we do? I think we need a change of vehicle," Johnson said.

"How?"

A Shell gas station appeared ahead of them, its forecourt bathed in light, and a couple of cars and lorries stationary next to the pumps.

"We could hijack a car at a gas station," Johnson said, patting the Makarov in his waistband.

"Risky. A gas station would have cameras. Many car owners carry guns too. Don't want a gunfight."

Johnson shrugged. He gazed out the windshield into the blackness. The headlights picked out the occasional clump of trees as they flashed past, but otherwise there was nothing.

The Škoda made faster progress than Johnson had been expecting, and after another ten minutes of driving, a large signpost appeared ahead of them, indicating that the A-280 continued southwest to the Ukraine border at Maksimov. However, they needed to turn right toward Kuybyshevo and the Marinovka border checkpoint.

Marchenko slowed sharply as they approached the turn. On their right, Johnson saw a picnic area and a large gravel car pull-off, dimly lit by a couple of streetlights. A man had parked his car next to one of the picnic tables and was busy urinating into a bush. The parking lot was otherwise deserted.

"Stop," Johnson said sharply. "Turn in there."

Marchenko braked harder and turned into the car park.

"Pull up behind that car," Johnson instructed, pointing toward the vehicle, a silver Audi sedan. "We're going to swap cars with that guy. Turn the engine off and bring the key. It will buy us some time—maybe just enough."

Marchenko did as he was told, and Johnson, acting now

almost on instinct, got out, pulled the Makarov from his belt, flipped off the safety, and approached the man, who was concentrating on peeing into the bush.

"Hey, friend," Johnson said loudly. "I need to swap cars with you. Give me your keys."

Startled, the man jumped and turned, spraying urine in Johnson's direction in the process.

"What the hell?" he said, scrambling to close his fly. "Who are you? What are you talking about?"

"Give me your car key," Johnson repeated. "We are swapping vehicles. If you are lucky, you might get your car back sometime. But not tonight. Throw the key on the ground near my feet, then go around to the back of the Škoda and sit on the ground."

He raised the Makarov and pointed it straight at the man, making it clear he was serious.

The man finished zipping up his pants. "*Svoloch.*" You bastard.

Marchenko came up behind Johnson. "If I were you, I would cut out the swearing and do what you are told."

The man, outgunned and outnumbered, appeared to realize he had no choice. He slowly reached into his trouser pocket, took out his key, and tossed it toward Johnson, who reached down and picked it up. The man slouched his way to the rear of the Škoda and sat on the ground. Johnson followed him, the gun trained on him the whole time.

"Good man," Johnson said. He turned to Marchenko. "Get our things from the Škoda, and check that there is plenty of fuel in the Audi. Then get this guy tied up. We can't risk him alerting someone. There's rope in the trunk. I'll cover him."

Marchenko did as Johnson asked. "Tank is almost full," he called from the driver's seat of the Audi.

"Good. Now tie him up. Somebody will come along and

find him by morning. I don't want anyone contacting police until then."

Again, Marchenko did as Johnson asked, tying the man's arms behind his back and his ankles together. They stuffed a piece of rag in his mouth and used another piece of rope to secure it in place. Then they lifted the man into the rear seat of the Škoda and shut the door.

"We should put the car a little farther forward, behind those trees, so it can't be seen from the highway," Marchenko said.

"Good idea."

Marchenko moved the Škoda, leaving the keys in the ignition, then returned to the Audi.

"Let's get the hell out of here," Johnson said.

* * *

Friday, July 25, 2014
  Rostov Oblast

Despite their FSB pursuit driver flooring the gas pedal remorselessly, Severinov and Pugachov found themselves at least ten minutes behind Tkachev as they continued along the A-280.

They drove largely in silence, which gave Severinov too much time to ruminate yet again on the lost opportunities he'd had in the past to rid himself of the eternal thorn in his flesh that Johnson had become.

In Afghanistan, the previous year, he had had a chance, but the American had slipped through his net, triggering a torrent of criticism from the Kremlin.

To Severinov's even greater despair, Johnson's investigations into war crimes he had committed during the 1980s in

Afghanistan against the mujahideen had also made public his ancestry. Both his father, Sergo, and his half brother were the bastard sons of former Russian leader Josef Stalin by different women: Severinov's grandmother and mother, respectively.

Both women had been seduced by Stalin, who knew but didn't care about the fact that Severinov's mother was married to Stalin's own son. It was a tangled history of incestuous family relationships that Severinov tried, often in vain, to bury at the back of his mind. He just didn't want to think about it, but at the most inopportune moments, it popped up in his mind like some kind of dark ogre.

Eventually, Tkachev called Severinov when he reached the junction where the highway ran north of the A-280 toward Kuybyshevo and the Ukraine border checkpoint at Marinovka.

After a brief discussion, they agreed that the road north to Kuybyshevo had to be the route Johnson would take. Heading farther southwest made no logical sense, given that the border there was controlled by Russian rebels and would put Johnson into potentially deeper trouble. They agreed that Marinovka, which was controlled by Ukrainian forces, was almost certainly the objective.

Severinov confirmed that they too would follow the Kuybyshevo road and try to catch up as best they could.

As Pugachov's BMW drew near to the same junction, about twelve minutes later, the car radio crackled into life and the police control desk from Rostov came on the line.

The duty sergeant explained briefly that a motorist had stopped to drink a coffee at a picnic pull-off at that same junction. He had heard banging from a Škoda parked near some trees and, on investigating, had found a man tied up in the rear seat. He had freed the man and had called police.

The police switchboard had asked to speak to the victim, who quickly informed the duty officer that his car, a silver

Audi A4, had been stolen by two men. One of them, definitely a foreigner, was armed with a pistol.

The switchboard officer, fully up to speed with the chase taking place along the A-280, had put two and two together and immediately called the operational team.

"Send an officer to the car park," Pugachov said. "We are nearby but will not have time to stop. Make sure he takes a statement from the victim and that the Škoda is secured. We can deal with it later."

"Will do, sir."

"And can you alert and redirect any other patrols onto the route heading toward Marinovka? It's vital we stop the Audi before it reaches the border."

The duty sergeant hesitated before replying. "Sir, I have already issued that instruction. However, we do have a problem in that region. It is remote, and it is the middle of the night, and we just do not have any patrol vehicles nearer to the border than yourselves. You are closer than any others."

"You have got to be joking, man," Pugachov exploded.

"Sir, I am very sorry. We have significant issues with manpower, and it is the middle of the night, sir."

Pugachov didn't bother replying. He immediately ended the conversation, called Tkachev, and explained what had happened.

"Georgi, at all costs, do not let Johnson cross that border," Pugachov said. "Do whatever it takes."

"Understood," Tkachev replied. "We're doing 165 kilometers an hour—going like a greyhound on heat. We'll catch him."

CHAPTER TWENTY

Friday, July 25, 2014
  Marinovka, Russia-Ukraine border checkpoint

The long line of red taillights of cars waiting to get over the border was visible as soon as Marchenko reached the brow of the hill. There, on the plain ahead of them at the end of a ribbon of blacktop, was the checkpoint. Its collection of flat-roofed prefabricated buildings and the corrugated steel canopy that formed a high arch over the highway were all highlighted in the darkness by a mish-mash of headlights, streetlights, and floodlights.

Two tall girder-style telecom pylons towered above the checkpoint like sentries on duty, both illuminated faintly by the glow from below.

"Shit," Johnson said. "We can't get into that line; we'll be like sitting ducks if the FSB catch up with us."

"I know. No chance," Marchenko said. "Hold on."

He accelerated as they came down the slope toward the checkpoint. As he neared the back of the line, he steered into the oncoming traffic lane and gunned the Audi, swerving around a motorbike chugging up the slope toward him.

The sudden acceleration forced Johnson back into his seat, a wave of adrenaline shooting through him as Marchenko drove past perhaps forty vehicles on the wrong side of the road. Some of the waiting drivers began honking their horns. Hardly surprising, Johnson thought, given that they had probably been there for half an hour or more.

"I'm going to talk my way through it," Marchenko said, hunched forward over the steering wheel.

He braked to a halt about ten meters from a row of waist-high concrete barriers that stretched across the road, with two narrow gaps between them to allow traffic to move in either direction. Three Ukrainian soldiers, all brandishing rifles in a firing position, began advancing toward the Audi from behind the barriers, yelling at them to raise their hands.

Behind the soldiers, the blue-and-yellow horizontal-striped flag of Ukraine—the colors representing the sky and the wheat fields—hung from a flagpole and waved in the night breeze, illuminated by a spot lamp.

To their left, the burned-out shells of two military trucks lay in the long grass near to a large sign that in Russian read "Bon Voyage." Johnson assumed the destroyed trucks were the legacy of fighting at the checkpoint between the pro-Russian rebels and Ukrainian forces.

Marchenko jumped out, raised his hands above his head, walked boldly toward the soldiers, and began speaking in his native Ukrainian, most of which Johnson struggled to understand. The soldiers lowered their guns after Marchenko showed an identification card, which Johnson presumed was his SZR credentials.

Seeing that the atmosphere was easing, Johnson got out of the passenger door and began to reach for the passport in his pocket, in case the soldiers demanded to see it.

Suddenly, from behind him came more honking of horns. Johnson turned and in the distance saw another car speeding down the hill toward them, also on the wrong side of the road, its headlights on full beam, its engine whining.

There was a shriek of rubber squealing on tarmac as the car braked to a halt around forty meters away. Johnson could now see it was a Mercedes sedan. As it stopped, the rear driver's side door flipped open, and in one movement, a man rolled out and into a dip at the side of the road that was covered by long grass.

In the same instant, the front door opened and the driver also rolled out, clutching something close to him.

Johnson felt a rush of adrenaline inside him. He spun round and shouted at Marchenko. "It's FSB! Run."

The two men sprinted for the concrete barriers. To his right, he could see the three soldiers also running in the same direction.

The first gunshots came just before he reached the left-hand gap between the barriers, the multiple *thwack* of a semiautomatic rifle firing echoing in his ears. Johnson dived to the ground just before he reached the barriers, just as a bullet smashed into the top of the cement structure a couple of feet away, sending slivers of concrete splattering into his face.

He rolled sideways behind the barrier, finally reaching the cover he was seeking, as another round hummed past him and clanged into the corrugated steel structure of the check-point building. More shots were smacking into the concrete barrier away to his right, but Johnson also saw muzzle flashes from the rifles being fired by two of the Ukrainian soldiers, who were now fighting back.

From the line of cars waiting to cross the border there came screams and shouts from onlookers and the high-pitched wailing of a child.

Johnson remained flat on the blacktop behind one of the three-foot-high concrete barriers that ran across the highway.

He looked up. Marchenko had managed to scramble behind the far end of the same concrete barrier but was lying with his back to it, clutching his shoulder and moaning.

The two Ukrainians were continuing to fire, aiming their rifles through narrow slits between the concrete blocks, blazing rounds in the direction of the Mercedes and the Russian gunmen.

In between shooting, one of the soldiers was signaling to his colleagues behind him, calling for reinforcements.

However, the third Ukrainian soldier was lying beyond Marchenko in the vehicle gap, flat on the ground, legs and arms sprawled out at a weird angle, with blood pouring from a large wound at the back of his head. The dead man had dropped his rifle, which was close to the edge of the concrete barrier, only a yard or two from Marchenko's grasp.

"Grab that rifle," Johnson shouted. "Throw it over here." He could see Marchenko was possibly too badly wounded to use it himself, and the Makarov in Johnson's belt was useless in this situation.

Marchenko reached over, grabbed the rifle butt, and pulled it toward him, visibly wincing. Johnson crawled over and took the weapon. Now he could see blood coming from a wound at the top of Marchenko's left shoulder, where it appeared that a round had hit him.

But there was no time to play nurse. Johnson knew they had to get through the border post and onto Ukrainian soil, still twenty yards behind them. He tried to calculate the angle of fire coming from the Russian side and the protection given by the concrete blocks. The Russians had an advantage because their position was elevated compared to the checkpoint.

"We'll have to crawl, roll, whatever," Johnson shouted.

He squinted through an inch-wide gap between two of the concrete blocks. It didn't allow him to see much. No wonder the Ukrainians were struggling to contain the Russian marksmen.

Behind him, from the Ukraine side of the checkpoint, came the sudden roar of a large diesel engine. Johnson turned to see a large dark-green eight-wheeled armored personnel carrier heading toward them from the Ukrainian side of the covered canopy over the checkpoint.

The APC, which Johnson recognized from its boat-shaped body as an amphibious BTR-4 model painted with camouflage markings, reached the center of the checkpoint. As it did so, there came the unmistakable hiss and whoosh of a rocket-propelled grenade. Johnson instinctively covered his ears and flattened himself to the ground. A fraction of a second later, the checkpoint office behind him disintegrated in a flash of orange, the blast sending debris flying in all directions. Johnson could see little through the smoke that now covered the area.

But the APC kept coming. Then, as it drew level with the concrete barriers, the machine gun mounted on top of it erupted in a continuous rat-tat-tat of bullets.

There came another whoosh, and an RPG cannoned into the front of the APC with another deafening explosion. The heavily armored vehicle looked undamaged, but it slowed and stopped, and its machine gun stopped firing. Johnson was unable to see if the gunner was injured.

He could see that now was his chance. He doubted that the Russians would remain in position with the APC now in the fray. The cover provided by the Ukrainian vehicle was their best chance of getting over the borderline.

He leaned over, pointed in the direction of the checkpoint, and shouted in Marchenko's ear. "We go now!"

But Marchenko shook his head firmly. "Not safe. Wait."

* * *

Friday, July 25, 2014
   Marinovka, Russia-Ukraine border checkpoint

For a moment, when the RPG flew into the border checkpoint, making a huge orange explosion, the scattering of debris, and creating a cloud of black smoke that rose upward, Tkachev thought he had killed Johnson.

But then the smoke began to clear, and he could see that rather than landing his RPG just behind the concrete barrier, where he was certain the American was still hiding, he had overshot and hit the office behind it instead.

Tkachev cursed and was about to reload his RPG-7 launcher when he saw an armored personnel carrier emerging from beneath the canopy over the road. A few seconds later, the mechanical clattering of machine gun fire began, and rounds started whistling over his head.

"*Dermo*," he hissed. If they were bringing in the heavy artillery, this might be game over. Although in the darkness, they clearly didn't know precisely where he was. The firing seemed quite random.

But Tkachev wasn't giving up yet. Neither he nor Nikolsky had seen Johnson and the Ukrainian, Marchenko, retreat to the checkpoint from where they had originally seen them take cover, behind the concrete barriers. So they assumed they were both still there, although it was difficult to be certain given the poor light.

Tkachev had an ideal position to assess his target. He was positioned higher than the checkpoint yet had a concealed position in a dip in the ground, behind some tall grass. The angle allowed him to look down on the checkpoint. Tkachev shoved the next rocket into the launcher. Perhaps if he could land a direct hit on the APC, he might disable the machine gun, and the resultant confusion could give him a few moments to have one final try at Johnson. He could use the third grenade to flush Johnson out and then take him out with the sniper rifle, which lay on the ground next to him.

Tkachev thought through his options. Whether the RPG failed or succeeded, he would need to escape afterward. There was no chance of retrieving the Mercedes now—it was too out in the open on the highway, and they would be mown down by the APC's machine gun.

The things in his favor were that the Ukrainians wouldn't dare to stray more than a very short distance into Russian territory, and also Severinov and Pugachov were not far away now and could pick them up.

Tkachev knew this area well, having only a couple of months earlier quietly helped to arm one of the Donetsk People's Republic separatist battalions that was based just over the border. So if, under cover of darkness, he and Nikolsky could escape on foot across the countryside on the Russian side of the checkpoint, they should be easily able to make contact with and meet up with Severinov and Pugachov.

Tkachev put his head slightly above the ridge that was giving him cover. Yes, he had a clear line of sight to get a hit on the APC, which was clearly visible in the light from the checkpoint. He took aim, then carefully pulled the trigger. His grenade scored a direct hit on the front of the vehicle, which stopped moving a second or two later.

Nikolsky looked across at him from his position a few meters away and gave a thumbs up.

Tkachev pointed behind him. "I will fire one more grenade to try and flush out Johnson, then hit him with the Vintorez. Then we leave on foot."

Nikolsky again gave the thumbs up.

Tkachev pushed the third and final grenade into the launcher and again raised his head slightly above the ridge.

Slowly, he took aim, concentrating on getting his elevation just right—slightly above the line of the concrete barriers, but in front of the now smoking ruin of the checkpoint office. If he could land it in the right place, his expectation was that the blast would either finish off Johnson or force him to break cover and run for safety.

He pulled the trigger and watched as the grenade flew into the checkpoint. This time his aim was better, but the missile still exploded farther away than he had intended.

Tkachev swore and grabbed his rifle, placed it in position on the soil ridge in front of him and, using the telescopic sight mounted on the top, carefully took aim.

Just as he applied his eye to the sight, he caught a glimpse of two shadowy figures rising from behind the concrete barriers and running away from him toward the canopy and the checkpoint.

Tkachev was certain they must be Johnson and Marchenko and desperately tried to steady his rifle and the sight so he could get an accurate shot off. After what seemed like an eternity but was actually no more than a second or two, he stilled the gun sufficiently. The crosshairs were firmly pinned on the back of the taller of the two figures running on the right, whom he was certain was Johnson.

Tkachev squeezed the trigger.

CHAPTER TWENTY-ONE

Friday, July 25, 2014
  Marinovka, Russia-Ukraine border checkpoint

It was only after Johnson had yelled a stream of obscenities at Marchenko that he agreed to move.

Marchenko's face was distorted with the pain he was obviously feeling from his wounded shoulder, but he eventually nodded. "Okay then, we go."

Johnson was about to glance over the top of the concrete barrier, just to double-check that they weren't about to commit suicide by standing up, when there came yet another whine and whoosh of an incoming RPG.

Both men hit the ground behind the barrier, covering their ears and turning their faces toward the concrete shield, away from the checkpoint buildings. Johnson curled himself into a ball and hoped for the best.

This time the grenade struck the ground between them and the now wrecked checkpoint building, which was still smoking from the previous blast. Johnson felt the searing heat from the resultant explosion and half expected that he would be frazzled or blown into the next life.

But when the bits of concrete and tarmac thrown up by the explosion had fallen back to earth, to his surprise he quickly discovered he could move and wasn't injured. The RPG had landed too far away, nearer to the building than to him, and three large steel drums that were standing on the concrete had also helped to shelter them.

By this stage Johnson's body was awash with a cocktail of fear and adrenaline. The only thing that mattered now was getting to the safety of Ukrainian soil.

He rose to his feet, grabbed Marchenko by the collar, and dragged him upward. "Move now. Come on, run," he shouted.

The two of them ran side by side, around the steel drums, toward the checkpoint and the canopy. Although it was only twenty yards or so, it felt much farther. Behind him, Johnson could hear the chatter of the armored personnel carrier's machine gun restarting.

As he ran, it immediately struck Johnson that sprinting side by side like that, they were easy targets for the Russians behind them, who had rifles. When they reached within five yards of the checkpoint barrier, Johnson shoved Marchenko in the back, powering him to the ground, and yelled to him.

"Get down, crawl!"

Marchenko uttered a guttural sound of pain as he hit the pavement, and Johnson simultaneously dived to the ground himself, taking most of the remaining skin off his knees in the process.

As he landed, a couple of yards to Johnson's right, a pane in the main checkpoint window exploded into fragments as a large-caliber round hammered into the office, punching a large hole in a wall opposite, followed by another round that shattered the door next to the smashed window.

To both right and left, Ukrainian soldiers were diving for cover, cursing and shouting as they did so.

Johnson got his head down and tried to ignore the chaos, crawling as fast as he could beneath the red-and-white hydraulic checkpoint barriers, Marchenko somehow doing likewise.

When he reached the far side of the canopy, Johnson glanced over his shoulder. Although the checkpoint was burning and smoking, and the Ukrainian soldiers were shouting at each other, the shooting had suddenly stopped, and he could see he was now well out of the line of sight of the Russians. That gave him enough confidence to finally get to his feet.

A Ukrainian soldier cautiously approached them, a rifle at the ready, and pointed to Marchenko's injured shoulder, which was bleeding heavily, and his chin, which he had also scraped. His goatee beard was smeared red, and blood was dripping from it. The soldier spoke a few words that Johnson didn't properly understand, but it was clear he was asking if Marchenko needed treatment.

On the far side of the checkpoint, the gunfire had finally stopped.

Marchenko nodded and took his SZR identity card and passport from his pocket and showed them to the soldier. When he realized Johnson didn't speak Ukrainian, the soldier switched to Russian and guided them toward a small prefabricated hut that formed the medical room.

A nurse in the medical room stemmed the bleeding from Marchenko's shoulder and patched it up with heavy bandages. He had been lucky the round missed the bone. She also stuck a large gauze bandage on his chin and disinfected Johnson's scraped knees.

When she had finished, Johnson approached the soldier, who was waiting for them.

"Can we get our vehicle through the checkpoint if it's not been shot up?" Johnson asked the soldier. He hoped the man would not ask about the car's ownership or request to see registration documents. It wasn't possible to see the vehicle from where they were standing, but given the gun battle, Johnson gave the car only a fifty-fifty chance of being intact.

The soldier went to check the Audi. He returned after a few minutes to say the car had taken rounds through the rear window and trunk lid and was a mess, but it otherwise appeared drivable. Another soldier would bring the car through the wrecked checkpoint for them. Thankfully, there were no questions about ownership documents. Johnson figured the soldiers did not want to get involved in SZR business.

Johnson sat on a chair in the medical room waiting for the nurse to finish with Marchenko. A clock on the wall read half past two. He suddenly felt exhausted, both physically and from the mental stress.

Yes, there had been significant progress in his investigation. He had unearthed the missile launcher that had destroyed the Malaysian airliner and more importantly had identified Severinov as one of the key people who had delivered it. Hopefully the SZR or Langley would be able to obtain an identity for the other man.

Just as critically, he had uncovered what appeared to be a coordinated leak from Washington of information that was allowing the Russians to put together a highly effective social media disinformation campaign.

But Johnson realized he couldn't relax: even from here, they still had another 850 kilometers to go to the Ukraine capital. And that was assuming they could safely get through territory where forces fighting for the pro-Russian separatists were active.

Johnson groaned as it dawned on him that he would have

to drive the full distance—there was no way Marchenko was going to be able to do it in his current condition.

And he didn't know how far Severinov's or the FSB's tentacles stretched into Ukraine.

They weren't out of this mess yet.

* * *

Friday, July 25, 2014
Rostov Oblast

"I need to apologize for screwing up this operation," Tkachev said. "We were too late getting to the checkpoint. Any earlier and we would have caught the bastard."

Severinov, who was sitting next to Tkachev and Nikolsky in the rear of the gray BMW, was surprised at the apology. He had been expecting Tkachev, who had previously struck him as somewhat arrogant, to blame anyone but himself for the failure. He remained silent for a couple of seconds.

He and Pugachov, who was in the front passenger seat, had picked up Tkachev and Nikolsky at the side of the highway about two kilometers back from the checkpoint, on the Russian side of the border, over the brow of a hill, out of sight of the Ukrainians.

The two former Spetsnaz operatives, clearly highly embarrassed, had phoned to report the mission failure as soon as they had retreated away from the checkpoint to safety. Johnson and his SZR friend appeared to have escaped over the border into Ukraine.

There was no way the pursuit could continue given the strong Ukrainian army presence at this particular border crossing. Severinov had to concede that Johnson and Marchenko had chosen their escape route wisely.

Now all four of them were en route back to Rostov through the darkness. The headlights picked out the strip of blacktop ahead as the FSB pursuit driver piloted them toward the A-280 junction.

The driver had turned on the radio news a few minutes earlier. The station, based in Rostov, was already reporting a rocket attack and shooting at the border checkpoint, without giving any further details. Drivers waiting to cross the border had phoned in to report the incident.

"I could just say it's unfortunate, one of those things, bad luck, or something," Severinov said. "But Johnson must have had a delay while changing cars, so you should have been able to gain ground on him. And I'm also surprised given your background that you failed at the checkpoint with the RPGs and sniper rifle."

He glanced at Tkachev. But the Spetsnaz GRU man said nothing.

"I've been pursuing Johnson for some time," Severinov said. "And the whole episode has been highly damaging to me and my business. There are plenty of people in the Kremlin, from the president downward, who are getting very irritated by the fact that we haven't got rid of him. I'm not going to let this go. I'm assuming you don't want to let this rest either—it's not going to look good on your record."

"You know our motto in the GRU," Tkachev said. "Greatness of Motherland in your glorious deeds. With the emphasis on deeds. We never rest."

Severinov did know the GRU's motto. He had it inscribed on a plaque in his house because he found it inspiring, even though he had served in the KGB. "Right. The Motherland is one thing. Success would also earn you a huge amount of credit inside the president's office," Severinov said. "So what do we do?"

"There are a couple of rebel leaders operating inside Ukraine whom I could call on to help me."

"No. We won't need rebel leaders for what I have in mind. We are not going to widen this operation. I want you to take direct responsibility for it—that way it is more secure. And here is what I would like you to do. I have recently acquired some intelligence that could help us."

Severinov began to run through what he had in mind.

After listening for about twenty seconds, Tkachev turned his head toward him. "Are you serious?"

"Yes, I'm deadly serious."

CHAPTER TWENTY-TWO

Saturday, July 26, 2014
Washington, DC

TITANIUM's house, on a tree-lined street in Chevy Chase, one of Washington, DC's suburbs favored by the wealthy elite, was undoubtedly less lavish than some of those owned by his contemporaries who worked on Capitol Hill. But he had lived there for fifteen years, and although his wife occasionally looked for alternatives in places like McLean and Great Falls, they had always decided to stay put. They liked the neighborhood, which was only seven miles north of downtown, just over the border into Maryland.

Now he found his house had another advantage: it backed onto the rolling fairways and greens of the golf course at Chevy Chase Club. For private members only, the club was where TITANIUM occasionally socialized and, even more rarely, took out his clubs for a round. His job was so busy and he had so little free time that playing regular golf was not an option.

But TITANIUM needed simply to hop over a fence at the bottom of his garden, and he could stroll along the edges of the fourteenth and tenth fairways toward the clubhouse. Wrapped around the building was an extensive parking lot that was accessed from Connecticut Avenue.

It was there that he had arranged to make his next transfer of documents to Tatiana, who had code-named the meeting location site GREEN.

The timing worked well, as he often took a stroll around the course first thing on a Saturday morning to try and clear his head following the invariably crazy schedule of the work week. Any onlooker who took the slightest interest in his schedule would not have noticed anything out of the ordinary.

TITANIUM found himself having to ignore the underlying resentment he felt every time he met his Russian handler. Although they had met a few years earlier, when she was working in Washington, she had recruited him relatively recently while he was on a trip to Moscow. And she had done so in the most Machiavellian way, which had left him feeling extremely pissed but unable to do much about it.

Initially, he had thought her approach had been on spur-of-the-moment but now he knew it was no such thing. She was clearly a strategist, not simply an opportunist.

For her age, which he guessed was a couple of years older than him, Tatiana was very lithe and fit. She was still surprisingly attractive too, despite having dyed her hair white to make herself look older.

The one thing that had made TITANIUM feel better about the whole thing was that the political objectives the Russians seemed to have in the US were fairly well aligned with his own views, which had changed in recent years. Not that he would ever admit that to his employer, of course. In fact he scarcely discussed it with anyone.

So although he had been coerced, he tried to rationalize it by telling himself it didn't matter because the information he was handing over was being used to good effect and was putting the president and his party under increasing pressure.

From now on, his objective was a drip-drip of material so that by the time of the presidential election in late 2016, the political damage would hopefully have been done—and at the same time, his bank account in Zürich would be massively fatter than it was now.

The intention, though, was to not do too much too soon. There was a long way to go.

TITANIUM kept an eye on the parking lot as he walked up the gravel path that led from the tenth tee. The nondescript white Toyota Camry stood in a bay on the southern side of the clubhouse, not far from the top of the path. Sure enough, at the wheel, appearing to adjust her makeup in the mirror, was a woman with shoulder-length pale gray hair.

TITANIUM saw her straightaway and sat on a bench about twenty feet away, where he took his phone from his pocket and began to tap on the screen. He was accessing a function, buried inside a common social media app, that allowed him to securely send a document wirelessly to another nearby phone with the same function.

As soon as he saw the connection with Tatiana's phone, TITANIUM tapped on the send button, and the transfer was done.

The document, in PDF format on US Department of Defense–headed paper, concerned secret flights to Kiev that had taken place over the previous two days. They involved two United States C-130J Hercules military transport aircraft and two similar aircraft operated by the Royal Air Force, of the United Kingdom.

The document detailed the cargoes carried by the aircraft, which consisted of an array of military equipment, including the items he had listed for Tatiana at their previous meeting. They included Humvee armored vehicles, Javelin anti-tank missiles, night-vision goggles, Firefinder missile detection radar, and flak jackets. There was also body armor, helmets, other military vehicles, thermal vision devices, heavy engineering equipment, advanced radios, patrol boats, rations, tents, counter-mortar radars, uniforms, first aid equipment and supplies, and other related gear.

When the document had been transferred, TITANIUM sent a short accompanying message.

> *Feel free to speculate that the C-130Js were also carrying Patriots and other missiles. DOD AND WH will deny it but will struggle to convince anyone. Proof the flights took place is clear, per air traffic control records.*

A few seconds later a message came back from Tatiana.

> *Thank you and understood. I am planning different meeting site next time. List to follow immediately. Will inform you of choice prior to meeting.*

Today he and Tatiana had agreed not to come in closer proximity than required to transfer the document and not to actually speak. There was no need.

A few seconds later another message arrived containing a list of three different meeting places in the northeast area of Washington, all of them with a color code: site YELLOW, site RED, site BLUE.

MEMORIZE AND DELETE, it said at the bottom.

TITANIUM did as instructed, memorizing the locations and color codes, and then deleted the message.

Once the message exchange had been completed, TITANIUM rose from his bench and walked back the same way he had come, along the side of the fairway, back over his fence, and into his garden.

Yet again, it felt a little like pulling out the pin from a grenade and throwing it into his own camp.

* * *

Saturday, July 26, 2014
    Athens

"So who the hell is KARAKURT?" Johnson asked as he slumped back onto his pillow in Jayne's hotel room. Making love to her again had eased some of the tension he had been feeling since escaping into Ukraine in the early hours of the previous day.

Jayne brushed back her dark hair from her face and propped herself up on an elbow. He liked the fact that she was completely unselfconscious about her body with him.

"Good question," she said, reaching out and gingerly placing a hand on his left knee, which had a square bandage covering a deep scrape from where he had dived to the ground at the Marinovka checkpoint. "You're looking a little battered."

"I'm feeling battered."

"Although it didn't seem to impair your efforts just now." A faint smile crossed her face, and she flicked her tongue across her lips.

Johnson laughed. "You obviously pressed the right button."

"But to your point, I have no answer. KARAKURT? I don't know. My guess is that's got to be the handler, not the agent. The material is coming from someone at a high level in DC. Whoever it is wouldn't be dealing directly with Igor

Ivanov, and definitely not with a troll factory in Rostov, that's for sure."

Johnson nodded, trying to think. After very little sleep in the previous forty-eight hours, it was a battle.

From Marinovka, he had driven the Audi hard to Kiev, stopping only for coffee and bathroom breaks and a two-hour sleep at a gas station once they had gotten out of pro-Russian territory and into safer areas. After they had reached Kiev, he had taken Marchenko to a hospital to be properly treated.

It was only then that he headed for Kiev's Boryspil International Airport, from where he had thankfully managed to get a seat on a budget airline flight to Athens that departed late on Friday night. The severely battered Audi had been left in the long-term parking lot at the airport. Johnson just hoped its owner had a decent insurance policy.

Johnson moved closer to Jayne, who had been staying at the hotel Airotel Stratos Vassilikos since his departure to Rostov. "If Ivanov is running this operation, rather than Yasenevo," he said, "then it's coming from Putin's office. Ivanov is the new tsar in that department—he's got Putin's ear, I gather. So it's likely the SVR have someone highly capable in DC as the handler. It's not going to be some junior at the *rezidentura*. Vic needs to get his and the FBI's counter-intelligence people moving on this."

Jayne ran her fingers along Johnson's forearm. "My worry is that this isn't just about a few damaging tweets. If there's a Russian agent in the Defense Department or the White House, then what other material are they passing over? The Twitter stuff is likely just the tip of the iceberg."

Johnson's phone rang. He leaned over and picked it up from the bedside table. It was Vic.

"No chance of a break," Johnson said, holding back a sigh and jabbing at the green button to answer the call.

"Are you still with Jayne?" Vic asked, without attempting

to make pleasantries. "I don't want to know what you two are up to, but you both need to get in here—I'm at the station. We've got to make a plan, and then I need to talk to Veltman so he can brief the president. The bastards are chewing at my heels. So come on. Then we'll need to get on a plane back to DC."

"Okay, okay," Johnson said. He rolled his eyes at Jayne, then hauled himself out of bed and planted his feet on the carpet. "We're on our way."

By the time they had gotten ready and walked the five hundred yards to the embassy, another hour had passed. Vic was visibly anxious, and Johnson soon found out why.

"Take a look at that," Vic said, thrusting his phone at Johnson. "While you two have been working out, these have come through."

Johnson deliberately avoided catching Jayne's eye and instead focused on the screen. It was showing a series of tweets from someone with an anonymous-looking username, all of which carried the hashtags *#MH17CIAplot* and *#Kiev-DownedTheBoeing*.

He read the first one, which showed a photograph of a US C-130J Hercules transport plane and a caption above it.

US President Ferguson sends secret military flights to Kiev with more Patriot missiles and launchers and other weapons for Ukraine forces—ten days after Malaysian Boeing is shot down. More carnage looms. #ButcherFerguson #Killer-Ferguson.

The second showed a photograph of wreckage of the Malaysian jet and another caption.

Dishonest killer President Ferguson intent on triggering war between Russia and Ukraine as America fuels arms race by sending in lethal cocktail of weapons to Kiev. #Warmonger-Ferguson.

There were a few more tweets in a similar vein, mostly repeating the themes in the first two.

"They're not stopping, despite your visit to the troll factory," Vic said. He flicked his phone screen to a news web page and showed it to Johnson. It was open at a story headlined "US Caught Sending Illegal Anti-Aircraft Missiles to Kiev." The text below outlined in some detail the contents of four C-130J aircraft that had been dispatched from the United States and the United Kingdom to Ukraine, containing a huge array of weaponry. The US cabinet member responsible for coordinating the delivery of armaments was named as Paul Farrar, secretary of state.

"A lot of mainstream media are quoting these tweets, and because they're not getting a categorical denial from Washington saying that the flights never took place, they're running with it," Vic said. "Even if journalists don't believe it, they're not certain. No smoke without fire and so on."

"How much of it is true?" Jayne asked.

Vic grimaced. "Actually, the White House won't admit this publicly, but the list of weapons and equipment is spot on, apart from one item."

"The Patriots," Johnson said.

"Correct. That is utter bullshit. But the rest was so accurate it could only have come from a highly placed source."

Johnson stared out the top-floor window of the CIA station toward Mount Lycabettus.

"Does Ed Grewall have anyone in Moscow we could tap for the identity of this KARAKURT?" Johnson asked. "Or for the actual agent?"

He turned back to Vic. There was no doubt about it: the most likely way of catching whoever was responsible for the leak was for an SVR officer who had been recruited by the CIA in Moscow to somehow find out and supply the name or code name they needed.

"Now you're on the same track as me," Vic said. "Solely between us, there is one person who Sunny's team has very recently recruited inside Yasenevo. A person disaffected with the Putin regime after a stint in DC. The team has planted the seed with this agent about getting KARAKURT's identity. Now we have to wait and see if it germinates."

"What department is he or she in?"

"It's a he. American desk, Directorate PR. The deputy chief."

"Might be promising."

"I hope so," Vic said, checking his watch. "But it's early days. In the meantime, Veltman wants us on a conference call in ten minutes for an update."

The call didn't start for another half hour because Veltman was waylaid by an urgent phone call from Farrar. When it did, Vic and Johnson quickly briefed the director on the events in Rostov and at the border. Then they discussed the latest batch of tweets that had surfaced that morning.

"Given it is now clear the leak is coming from the US and not Kiev, unfortunately, we're going to have to get the feebs involved," Veltman said. "Although you can guarantee they will screw it up."

Like many at Langley, Vic's boss wore his antagonism toward the FBI like a badge of honor. It was more of an ingrained cultural attitude at the Agency than anything justi-fied by facts. However, the two organizations had to work closely together; unlike the FBI, the CIA did not technically have the authority to carry out criminal investigations inside the United States or carry out law enforcement functions. If Langley wanted any investigation of that kind, they had to involve the FBI, although in practice, the Agency sometimes pushed the boundaries.

"There is one feeb I'd like to involve," Vic said. "Simon Dover."

Dover was the FBI's executive assistant director and headed up the bureau's Criminal, Cyber, Response, and Services Branch. Vic had known him since Dover was a supervisor in the FBI's counterintelligence division, running an assortment of espionage investigations on which Vic had also worked. It was Dover who had helped Johnson and Vic to trap Robert Watson, Johnson's old CIA boss and nemesis.

"Yes, Dover's a good operator. Call him in," Veltman said.

"Good. I'll brief him when we're done here," Vic said.

"Listen," Veltman said. "I would like all three of you, including Jayne, to come back to DC tonight and help with this. I think your work there has been done."

Veltman's tone of voice brooked no argument.

"Tonight?" Vic asked. He glanced at Johnson and then Jayne, checking their responses.

Johnson threw up his hands and shrugged. That would put a decisive end to his remaining hopes of a vacation with his children, then. Jayne inclined her head in agreement.

"Yes. Tonight," Veltman repeated.

Vic nodded. "Fine. We'll get packed."

"Good."

Vic leaned back in his chair and stared at the video screen. "Before we finish, can you just level with me, Arthur," he said. "How many people knew about that Ukraine meeting between Farrar, Poroshenko, and yourself?"

Veltman looked at the floor. "I don't know. Probably a dozen at Langley."

"No, I mean outside Langley," Vic said.

Now Veltman was looking outright embarrassed. "Look, there's the White House team, and, I discovered last night that Brad Turner had informed the House Intelligence Committee."

Vic pressed his lips together. "The intelligence committee? Are you joking? There's twenty-two people on that."

"No. Sadly I'm not," Veltman said. "Turner came clean after we pushed him hard. The committee members were only given the basics, but they had enough. He said it was all in confidence and that he had no choice if the CIA's budget proposals for next year were to get through because most of his colleagues just did not grasp the scale of the challenge facing the Agency from the Ukraine situation. Sounds as though some of them have been objecting hard to the increases we want given the resources we're throwing at it. He made them all sign special nondisclosure agreements, but—"

"They're not worth the paper they're written on," Vic said.

"Precisely."

Johnson shook his head. "This is going to be a hunt for a needle in a haystack," he muttered.

* * *

Saturday, July 26, 2014
  Athens

"You are joking, Joe, aren't you?" Amy said.

Johnson put a finger in his left ear and tried to hear what his sister was saying against the torrent of noise near the check-in desks at Athens International Airport.

"I'm really sorry, Amy," he said. "There's a major crisis going on, right up to White House level, and they need me."

He had just explained, as briefly and clearly as he could,

the outline of why he and Jayne were now heading to Washington, DC. Behind him, a long line of passengers was waiting at the British Airways desk for the same flight, via London's Heathrow Airport.

"Give me a call when it's quieter," Amy said. "I can take care of the kids, no problem. Me and Natalia can keep them entertained—there's no shortage of things to do here. They'll just be disappointed, that's all. They wanted a vacation with their dad."

"I'm hoping I can get back for part of the vacation," Johnson said. "I'm hoping it won't take too long."

Hoping, hoping, hoping, he thought as he ended the call. *Some hope.*

Jayne and Vic were standing near the entrance to airport security, waiting for him, as he put his phone back into his pocket and hurried to join them.

Vic was reading a message on his phone, frowning as he did so.

"Bad news?" Johnson asked as he caught up with them.

Vic looked up. "Not really, just more delays. The NRO's saying it will take them longer than they thought to get the satellite results back on the images of the Buk launcher. Something to do with the timing of the photographs and weather conditions—cloud cover, that kind of thing. They need to carry out enhancement work. And nothing back on identifying the GRU guy yet either. But the good news is Dover is getting things moving on our mole in DC."

The departures board behind Vic refreshed, and a gate number appeared for the first leg of their British Airways flight.

Johnson pointed it out, and the three of them walked through the barriers into the security check area.

It seemed to Johnson that there was a long way still to go in this investigation. Without doubt, a Russian penetration agent, seemingly with links to Severinov, was operating inside the US political and security system who had already landed several heavyweight punches on the Ferguson administration.

Obviously, if they didn't get to the bottom of it soon, there was a severe danger of a knockout looming.

CHAPTER TWENTY-THREE

Saturday, July 26, 2014
Cannes

It was going on ten thirty when Amy finally attracted the eye
of the waiter who had been serving them and called for the
check. The pizza restaurant was something of a tourist trap
and would not have been her first choice, but both Carrie and
Peter had voted for it, and they needed cheering up, so she
and Natalia had agreed. In any case, the view from their
table, depicting the brightly lit marina with its array of
superyachts, was a fascinating one.

Some of Europe's most well-heeled tycoons and their
families were sitting around tables on the upper decks of
their boats, drinking, laughing, and eating until late into the
evening.

Before coming to the restaurant, the four of them had sat
on the beach near the Radisson Blu hotel, drank a Coke each,
and watched the sun go down along with a crowd of others
who were catching the last few rays of the day.

The sidewalk that ran past the restaurant carried a continuous stream of tourists. Amy guessed that many of them would be heading toward the hillside bars and restaurants of Le Suquet, one of Cannes's oldest and most seductive neighborhoods, dating back to Roman times.

From beneath their maroon canopy, the four of them had a ringside view of the action. The temperature was still more than eighty degrees, even this late into the evening, and on another night she could have sat there for much longer and worked her way through another bottle or two of the Château de Saint-Martin rosé that they had enjoyed with dinner. But Natalia couldn't drink any more because she had to drive home.

"Dad would have enjoyed that wine," Carrie said. "He likes a glass or two."

Amy straightened her low-back red T-shirt and smiled. "He does. I am sure he would rather have stayed here and helped us drink it."

"That job of his is extremely annoying sometimes," Carrie said. "It seems to get in the way at the worst possible times."

Peter nodded. "Like now."

Amy exchanged glances with Natalia, who raised her eyebrows a fraction. She wasn't smiling and clearly agreed with the sentiments the Johnson children were expressing.

"Your dad's job isn't just a job," Amy said. "With him, it's more of a mission sometimes. It's something he feels deeply about, achieving justice if people have done something seriously wrong that has affected a large number of people. I think he feels obliged to try and help if there is a situation where he is called upon. He has a very special set of investigative skills. Not many people could do what he does."

Carrie shrugged and said nothing. Amy had heard similar sentiments from her before, but that had always been when they were at home and when Joe was away working overseas somewhere. He hadn't been called away during a vacation before, and Amy had to sympathize with his daughter.

Five minutes later they were in Natalia's car, a Renault station wagon, heading home eastward along Cannes's iconic Boulevard de la Croisette, lined with palm and pine trees, which followed the line of the beach in the direction of Antibes.

Natalia turned left just before the yacht club and began the windy climb up the hill toward the rented house on Avenue du Mont Rouge.

In this area of Cannes, the houses grew grander the higher one rose, many of them hidden behind stone walls covered in ivy and creepers and with driveways that curved away beyond electronically controlled entrance gates. The plots were large and the property price tags astronomical.

Natalia braked to a halt at a junction and then turned left.

Avenue de Mont Rouge was the next on the right, about a hundred meters up ahead. Natalia turned off, but when she rounded the first bend in the street, she found the way blocked off by a red-and-white roadwork barrier. A large blue Électricité de France van with red and white stripes along the side was parked facing back down the hill, illuminated by the orange glow from an overhead streetlamp. Four workmen in dark coveralls were standing next to the barrier, talking.

"Dammit," Natalia said. "What's happening here? There's no other way up to the house." She braked to a halt behind the van and wound the window down as one of the workmen looked up and saw her. He walked slowly over to the Renault, scratching his head.

"Do you live up there, madam?" the workman asked, pointing up the hill.

"Yes, halfway up," Natalia said. She spoke fluent French, something that Amy, whose language skills were more limited, found deeply admirable.

"I am sorry, madam, but we are having to do a repair here, which means no cars will be able to drive up there for the next two or three hours. Are you able to leave the car here and pick it up later, or in the morning?"

Natalia gave a grunt of annoyance in response. "I guess so, if we have to. Shall we park here?"

"Yes, that's fine. I do apologize."

Natalia turned to Amy, then glanced at Carrie and Peter in the rear of the car. "Did you understand that? We need to leave the car here. They're doing repairs."

"Annoying," Carrie said. "Why do they do that at nighttime?"

"Good question," Amy said. "Anyway, there's no choice. Out you get."

They all climbed out of the Renault and began to walk together past the van. The man who had approached initially stepped out in front of Natalia.

"Could I just check your names, and which property you are from?"

They all paused while Natalia gave him the four names and the house number.

Just as Natalia finished speaking, Amy became aware that the other workmen were approaching them from behind. She half turned and saw the man nearest to her, who had a large scar on his left cheek, holding something in his right hand that in the light of the streetlamp looked like a gun.

To her left, she thought she heard Natalia, or it might have been Carrie, gasp loudly.

Then she felt something touch her lightly at the top of her back, where her bare skin was exposed above her T-shirt.

The next thing she knew she had dropped to the ground on her back, as if someone had sharply pulled a rug from under her. All of her muscles were spasming hard, an intense pain was shooting through them in waves, and her brain felt as if it was being shaken hard inside her skull. She wanted to shout and get up, but she couldn't move or speak, and she had a vague awareness that to her left, Natalia, Carrie, and Peter had also fallen. Inside her there was a deep instinct to do something to help them, but that was impossible.

After a short time, the spasms and shaking stopped, and a hand pushed something into the side of Amy's neck. She wanted to reach up and stop them, but she was unable to. Almost immediately, she felt herself sinking down and down.

Then everything went black.

PART THREE

CHAPTER TWENTY-FOUR

Sunday, July 27, 2014
  Dulles International Airport, Washington, DC

As soon as the British Airways Boeing touched down at Dulles, Johnson's phone beeped with a few text messages and also two missed call alerts from Natalia.

He glanced at the texts, one of which was a secure message from Marchenko.

I am recovering faster than expected. All ok. My team have ID of GRU officer. Name is Georgi Tkachev. Was in a special unit of Spetsnaz unit 29155. They are killers. He is now an independent operator. We believe he has been ringleader of pro-Russian violence in Crimea and Eastern Ukraine in recent months. We guess working directly for Kremlin.

It was unsurprising that Severinov had such an individual now working for him. Tkachev was obviously Balagula's replacement. Johnson wondered whether Tkachev had been behind the attack he had just narrowly escaped from at the Marinovka border checkpoint.

The other text messages were from a couple of Johnson's friends in Portland, and he ignored the two missed calls. They could wait until they were through the airport and he could call Natalia back in a more relaxed situation.

Meanwhile, Vic also had calls to deal with. He walked through the airport ten yards behind Johnson and Jayne with his phone glued to his ear, catching up on a series of voice messages.

Vic's CIA driver was waiting for them at the arrivals pickup level outside the terminal in a black BMW. Vic climbed into the front passenger seat, while Johnson and Jayne rode in the back.

Johnson showed the others the message from Marchenko about Tkachev, and Vic immediately forwarded the detail to his team, asking them to try and dig up what other information they could.

When they were a couple of miles along the eastbound Dulles Toll Road, Johnson's phone rang. He removed it from his pocket and glanced at the screen. It was a Russian number, beginning with +7.

Johnson sat upright and stared at the screen. What was this? He debated momentarily whether to let it go to voice mail but then changed his mind and hit the green button.

"Hello?"

There was a short silence at the other end of the line. Then came a heavily accented voice, speaking in a slow rhythm.

"I've got Amy."

Johnson found himself momentarily unable to speak. His heart felt as though it had been clamped tight in a vise. Then he managed to gather himself. "Who the hell is this?"

He glanced up to find Vic had turned his head, listening. Jayne was doing likewise.

"You know who I am, Joe. We've had a few encounters. Don't you recognize the voice?" There was a mocking lightness in the caller's tone now.

A shock wave went through Johnson, and his entire body tensed. It was Yuri Severinov.

"What do you mean, you've got Amy?" Johnson uttered in a low tone.

Vic's entire body swiveled around at lightning speed as he registered what had been said.

Johnson silently mouthed one word to him—"Severinov."

Vic immediately went into operational mode and made a circling sign with his left hand, which Johnson took to mean to keep the Russian talking. He knew exactly why.

"I mean what I say," Severinov said. "I've got her."

"You—"

"Listen. This is going to be very brief. If you want your sister back, I want your investigation called off. I want a public statement from the White House and the CIA admitting that they have been conspiring with the Ukraine government to supply a large variety of weapons, including ground-to-air anti-aircraft missiles. I also want them to confirm that any future planned shipments of weapons will be cancelled—there will be no more military equipment for Ukraine from the United States."

"I can pass the message on," Johnson said.

The initial wave of panic had passed, and Johnson was starting to recover his thought processes. He glanced at Vic, who was now tapping furiously on his phone keypad, presumably sending a message to Langley.

"But you know very well that a statement like that has nothing to do with me," Johnson continued. "It won't be my decision. I have no influence over what the White House, the president, or the CIA do or say about anything."

"Yes, yes. I thought you might say that. But you, my friend, are going to have to find a way to persuade them. You are well placed with the CIA, thanks to your newly promoted friend, Mr. Walter, is that not correct? He is the one who is a highflier at Langley, and you appear to be his number one choice for this type of investigation. So get him to listen and get the people above him to listen—otherwise your sister will die."

Severinov paused and then added, "And she will not be the only one."

A fresh spike of adrenaline rushed through Johnson. "What do you mean?"

"I mean what I say. Because I do not just have your sister. I have your children too."

Johnson struggled to process what he was hearing. He could feel drops of sweat beginning to roll off his forehead, and his chest tightened.

He had to be lying.

"I don't believe you."

He feared for a second that he was going to pass out and forced himself to concentrate.

"I don't really care whether you believe me or not. I have the three of them: Amy, Carrie, and Peter. If there is no White House and CIA statement within the next seven days, they will all die. If we do see a statement, they might live long enough for you to come and get them."

"Just tell me where you are now," Johnson said, his voice rising sharply. "I'll come right now. Where the hell are you?"

"Goodbye, Joe. Nice to speak to you. I will be in touch. You've got seven days."

The call ended.

Vic muttered something inaudible from the front seat,

then slapped his hand on his thigh. "I don't think that was long enough."

"Bastard!" Johnson spat the word out. "I'll kill him. How the hell . . . he's got both my kids. And my sister."

He sank into his seat. "I don't believe this. And he's threatening to kill them. I have to call Natalia now."

Even as he spoke, it briefly crossed Johnson's mind that this could all be a bluff, a ploy to extract a rapid concession from the government. Maybe Severinov didn't really have his kids.

Jayne voiced the same thought almost simultaneously. "Is he for real? Or this just bullshit?"

Johnson tipped his head back and stared at the roof of the car. He wished it was just bullshit, but all his instincts told him this was no ploy. Severinov was no fool. He was a long-term survivor in the shark pool of Russian politics, business, and intelligence agencies. They didn't bother with idle threats.

"No, it's not bullshit," Johnson said. "But he must know Washington doesn't bow to this kind of threat from kidnappers or terrorists or whoever. It's bound to be a no."

"You're right," Vic said. "It'll be a waste of time even mentioning it to the White House. They'll just say they can't because if they give in to one threat, there'll be a dozen more the following day from a whole list of other bloodsuckers."

"So what's he after, then?" Jayne asked.

Johnson paused as Severinov's words ran through his mind.

If we do see a statement, they might live long enough for you to come and get them.

"Me. That's what he's after," Johnson said as he searched for Natalia's number on his phone. "My kids and my sister are the bait, and I'm the fish. He's trying to reel me in."

* * *

Sunday, July 27, 2014
  Washington, DC

"It was the most agonizing thing I've ever experienced by a long shot. No joke, my whole body was rigid and out of control, and my legs went from under me. I was thrown on my ass and fried like a piece of meat. I honestly thought my brain was going to explode. I was shaking like I was in a tumble dryer." Natalia's voice, a little tinny as it came through the speakerphone, was trembling, and then Johnson heard her begin to cry.

"Sounds like you were Tasered," Jayne said. "I had it done to me once in a training exercise at MI6. That's what it's like."

"Yes, I think that's what happened," Natalia sobbed. "Then they jabbed me in the neck with something. I remember seeing Peter next to me on the ground, but nothing else. A few seconds later, I passed out."

Johnson tugged at the old bullet wound at the top of his right ear and stared out the window of the BMW as they turned northward onto the Beltway, the circular interstate that ran around the capital, in the direction of Langley. He found himself fighting back tears but somehow forced himself to stay focused.

Natalia next described how she had regained consciousness next to her car on Avenue de Mont Rouge, just a hundred yards away from the house in Cannes, to find herself alone. There was no sign of Amy or the children, and the Électricité de France van and men were gone. She had no idea how long she had been unconscious but suspected it must have been at least three-quarters of an hour, possibly longer.

She had great difficulty walking back to the house, but she reached it eventually and made an emergency call. Now the house was swarming with French police officers.

"I can't understand how or why it happened or how they could just vanish unseen," Natalia said. "Your children and your sister are gone, and I invited you all here. I'm so sorry, Joe—I feel like it's all my fault."

She burst into tears again.

"It's not your fault," Johnson said. "It's mine."

Why the hell didn't I see this coming, he thought. *Shit*.

It was a classic old KGB modus operandi. If you can't get the man, get his family.

"How is Don taking it?" Natalia asked.

Johnson had had a long and difficult phone conversation with Amy's husband earlier and explained what had happened.

"He was shocked and distraught, as you'd expect," Johnson said. "But I've told him it's being dealt with at the highest levels and he's accepted that and isn't going to say anything publicly—for the moment."

"What are the police saying?" Jayne asked. "They've had hours now. Have they found any signs of where they went to?"

"They know nothing," Natalia said. "They have no clue. No witnesses, no trail to follow, no sign of the van, no sign of anything. There's no CCTV up and down that street and none in the neighboring streets. It's a quiet street and it was late at night, and they must have had well over an hour to make their getaway."

"We need to think this through," Vic said. "It may not help if the police launch a massive publicity campaign. It could be counterproductive."

"The police chief here says they are not going to do that immediately."

"Good. Try and encourage them to keep it low profile for

the time being," Vic said. "Natalia, we'll make inquiries from
this end and call you back very soon. Hold tight, and keep
your phone with you."

They ended the call.

Vic shook his head. "I'm going to talk to my DGSE coun-
terpart and make sure they stop police from broadcasting this
everywhere unless we're sure it's going to help." The DGSE,
the Direction Générale de la Sécurité Extérieure, was
France's equivalent to the CIA.

"Vic, if it's going to bring my kids and sister back, they
can go as big with it as they want to." Johnson was now
fighting his instinct to shout and rage.

"If we need to launch an operation to get them back, we
want to keep it as under-the-radar as possible," Vic said.

"For God's sake, Vic. This is my family." Johnson paused.
"I'm getting on the next plane back to France." He banged his
hand on the car seat. "I'm going to damn well go and find
them myself."

"Whoa, wait, Joe," Vic said. "Stay calm. You're going to be
more useful here right now. This is going to be a chess game:
we need to outthink them, not run after them. We've no idea
where they are, so we need to find that out first."

Johnson clenched his fists tight but said nothing. He
knew Vic was right. There was probably little he could do
that the local French police weren't doing in terms of looking
for physical clues. But Severinov was too smart to have left a
trail.

"It might be time to see whether we can get Sunny to
provide anything of value from his Moscow recruits," Vic
said, tapping away on his phone screen. The phone beeped as
a message arrived, which Vic scrutinized.

"We can push hard at this end too—in DC," Jayne said. "If
there's someone leaking stuff to the SVR, then there will be a
handler, a link in the human chain, who may know what is

going on. We should get the FBI's counterintelligence boys onto it straight away."

Vic waved his phone at her. "Already done. I spoke to Dover from Athens to tell him what has happened regarding our mole and what we needed—he's just messaged me. We're not going to Langley anymore. We're going to the J. Edgar Hoover Building right now. Dover is there waiting for us."

CHAPTER TWENTY-FIVE

Sunday, July 27, 2014
Washington, DC

It had been several years since Johnson had last been inside the monolithic concrete J. Edgar Hoover FBI building at 935 Pennsylvania Avenue. This time, he was astonished at how the place had deteriorated.

First, the CIA driver had to take a detour through the underground parking lot to get to their designated space because the ceiling of one of the parking ramps was disintegrating and had apparently dropped chunks of cement on cars passing beneath. Then there were cracked ceilings in the corridor leading to the fourth-floor rooms in the counterintelligence division where they were meeting Dover. Paint was peeling from the walls of the meeting room, and the carpet was stained and threadbare.

Johnson noticed Vic glancing at the signs of neglect with disdain. It wasn't something he was used to on the seventh floor at Langley.

"Looks as ugly inside as it does outside," Johnson murmured. "And that's saying something."

Vic just nodded.

However, despite the working conditions and despite having to come into the office on a Sunday, Simon Dover looked to be in an upbeat mood when he arrived. He enthusiastically shook hands with Vic, Jayne, and Johnson.

A white-haired FBI veteran, he had gotten to know Vic in 2002 while working as a supervisor in CD, as the counterintelligence division was known internally. Promotion had taken him to a different though related role in CCRSB, but he was still an influential figure in counterintelligence, where his contacts were strong and there was a very significant crossover with his current role. So Vic still used him as a first port of call on many issues.

Dover had brought along his colleague Iain Shepard, a wiry man with a runner's physique who was the recently appointed executive assistant director in charge of CD.

"Apologies for being a little late," Dover said, rolling up the sleeves of his powder-blue shirt. "We've both just been briefing Bonfield about all this. He had questions." Robert Bonfield was the FBI director, in charge of the entire organization from his office on the seventh floor.

Dover looked directly at Johnson. "Vic's told me about your children and sister. We're all sorry to hear that. If there's anything we can do to help in tracking them down and bringing them back, rest assured we will."

"Thanks," Johnson said. "There may well be given the direct links between Severinov's demands, the leaks we've seen out of DC, and the president's policy here. I appreciate the offer."

He felt like telling Dover that his kids were *all* he cared about right then, but he held back.

"Take a seat, all of you," Shepard said. "That's if you can

find one that meets the description. Federal funds don't reach this far into the building." He pointed toward several unpadded chairs grouped around a chipped wooden table.

When they were seated, Shepard waved a hand at Dover. "In terms of tracking down our mole and whoever's doing the handling, Simon told me what you need. As it happens, we've recently upscaled our surveillance operation on the Russian diplomats in the embassy who we believe are SVR. It's been round the clock for the past two months. Good timing for you. There are currently 116 Russian diplomats in DC. We've been watching a dozen in particular. Of those, we think a couple are the hotshot handlers—we're all over them and making life generally difficult for them to do anything without us knowing about it. If they buy a tube of toothpaste, we know the brand."

"What about others?" Vic asked. "Illegals, or those who might have come in under false IDs?"

"They're difficult to monitor. Sometimes impossible. So we've got a parallel strategy to deal with that possibility, although we're applying it to their known handlers as well."

"What is it?"

"Focusing on their countersurveillance guys. We think four, although maybe six, of the supposed diplomats are actually countersurveillance experts, so we have to be damn careful. They rarely make mistakes."

He gave them a quick briefing on the Russian countersurveillance teams—the eyes and ears for the handlers, the SVR officers who actually held the covert meetings with agents. It was their job to position themselves at strategic locations around a meet site and call an abort if they saw anything untoward.

"Have you seen anything yet?" Jayne asked.

"Not specifically," Shepard said. "But we've been looking for patterns."

"What sort of patterns?" Jayne asked.

"The Russians are quite aggressive in their CS. They will use a team and try and lure our surveillance guys into traps so they can be spotted—narrow streets with no cover, open areas. So what we've been looking for is several of their CS guys heading to the same area of DC at roughly the same time in preparation for a job. They won't all converge at once; that's too obvious. But there have been recent signs they are working on something. We think there was an abort in Arlington Cemetery and another in Prospect Hill Cemetery and possibly one in Chevy Chase, near a golf club. All appeared to be called off. The CS team converged, then disappeared again, with no sign of an actual meeting. Unless we were too late in getting there, of course, which is a possibility. It's dangerous to get too close."

"Is it possible these CS forays are decoys?" Dover asked, glancing at the others with laser-blue eyes. He sat up straight in his chair. "Meanwhile, the real meets could be elsewhere. Or are they just practice runs?"

Shepard shrugged. "It's possible they are decoys, yes. But we think we're achieving good coverage of their team, at least those operating out of the embassy. And if they're practice runs, then we just need to persist until we get the real thing. We'll be out again first thing in the morning. I was planning to join the team in the control van. It will be well back from the action, out of sight. I like to do that sometimes. You can join me if you want to, although it'll be a little cramped."

Shepard looked around the room, looking for assent. Vic and Jayne nodded, then finally Johnson did too, although he by now felt he was operating on autopilot. He was struggling to keep his focus on the meeting. All he could see in his mind's eye was a picture of his two children and his sister, tied up, arms lashed behind their backs, gagged, in the back of some van or truck, being taken to a secret hideaway in France or Italy or somewhere.

Or is it worse than that?

It was the not knowing that hurt the most.

In Johnson's vision, Severinov and a row of his Russian friends were there, grinning at the kids, goading them, tormenting them.

Johnson fought to stop the red mist from rising inside his head.

Bastard. If he could have reached out and killed Severinov right then, he would have.

CHAPTER TWENTY-SIX

Monday, July 28, 2014
  Mediterranean Sea

Roughly 4,500 miles to the east of the US capital, a boat bounced a little as it struck a wave. Amy, Carrie, and Peter rose and fell with it, the rope that bound their hands tight behind their backs chafing their skin as it tugged at them.

Carrie, who was sitting between her brother and her aunt on the bench that ran along one side of the cabin, felt her stomach heave once again. She retched hard. But by now, there was little left to vomit up.

Trails of dried puke ran down the front of her blue T-shirt, and a pool of it lay on the cabin floor in front of her, sloshing around with the motion of the boat.

Her head was spinning. She felt dizzy with confusion, exhaustion, and hunger, and the fear that had risen inside her when she had regained consciousness refused to go away.

This is a nightmare.

Only it wasn't.

Her only memory of those final moments near Natalia's house was of seeing Peter and Natalia crash to the ground next to her before she utterly lost control of her own limbs and fell flat on her back, writhing and spasming out of control, like a puppet on a string. One of the men dressed as an electricity worker pushed something into her neck. After that, nothing.

She had awoken in her current position, already tied up. The cabin was below deck level—she knew that because of the gloom and because there were steps going up at the far end of the room. There were no portholes to let in light. They had been released periodically in order to eat snacks and go to a tiny chemical toilet in a cubicle at the rear of the cabin.

The men had confiscated their phones. Carrie could see them on the floor in a corner of the cabin, their batteries and SIM cards removed and lying next to the handsets.

She had seen five men so far, all muscular military-looking guys dressed in black. All carried guns, and all had fairly similar short haircuts. They rarely spoke to their captives but did talk among themselves in a serious, businesslike manner.

The one she saw the most was the man with a large scar on his left cheek whom she recalled seeing behind her just before she lost consciousness. He had short blond hair, was starting to go bald, and smoked a lot.

The men had said nothing about where the boat was heading, nor how long the journey would take. Carrie assumed the boat must have left from the Cannes port while they were still unconscious, or maybe from another more secluded mooring nearby. They could be on any one of the thousands of yachts and boats in the area.

She knew they had been traveling the whole time because of the continuous motion of the boat, and she knew that it was now late in the day, because the shafts of light that spilled into the cabin when the men opened the door were becoming dimmer and softer. So they must have been on the move for nearly two days now, and they had to have been some considerable distance from Cannes. But she had no idea in which direction they were headed.

Carrie's best guess was that the men were Russian. Her dad sometimes spoke Russian words when he jokingly wanted to show off his language skills, and these men sounded similar, quite guttural. Also, she knew her dad had been to Russia earlier in the year, and he had left them in Cannes to go to Russia. She had heard him discussing it with Jayne.

But why the hell have they taken us?

This had to be something to do with her dad and his job —nothing else made sense. It wasn't a random kidnapping. But what was it, then?

She didn't dare talk or discuss the situation with her brother or aunt, because one of the men had told them in heavily accented English that they would immediately be gagged if they spoke. He waved a pistol in their faces in a threatening manner as he did so. Carrie had no doubt he would do what he said. A reel of duct tape and a few dirty rags lay on the bench opposite them. She imagined the rags would be stuffed in her mouth and the tape wound around her head, like she had seen in so many films.

And she knew for certain that if that happened, she would die, because she couldn't stop throwing up. She would choke on her own vomit.

Neither Amy, to her left, nor Peter, to her right, had said a word. But she could see from the expressions on their faces that they too were terrified and exhausted. Amy's face had gone gray, her hair was a mess, and she suddenly looked like a grandma, not an aunt.

Carrie's hunger was also growing, despite the vomiting. The men had given them dry cereal bars, bananas, and water, but nothing else. Carrie had vomited it all back up again, although the others had kept it down.

These men would surely not bother to give them food if they intended to kill them. That gave her some hope, but the things she had read about Russian gulags, prisons, torture, brutal killings, and mass graves filled her with dread. She had slept briefly in her seated position but mostly felt too stressed and uncomfortable to relax sufficiently to fall asleep.

Carrie glanced at Peter. His expression was one of pure dejection. She nudged him and tried to smile some sort of encouragement but just couldn't.

She turned to look at Amy but knew that her aunt wouldn't be able to get them out of this mess. Her only hope now was her dad.

* * *

Monday, July 28, 2014
Moscow

The American department, spread across much of the third floor of the SVR's Y-shaped headquarters building just south of the Moscow ring road, was probably the most influential and best resourced of all the directorates that made up Russia's foreign intelligence service.

Pavel Vasilenko stood outside his private office for a moment and surveyed the extensive floor space swallowed up by the department. Hundreds of worker bees busy compiling, analyzing, and probing for information on Russia's main enemy were spread out across the open-plan area and private offices in front of him.

He had held the deputy's role for the previous three years since returning from a stint in the *rezidentura* in Washington,

DC. He had enjoyed the posting up until the moment when his ten-year-old son, Timofey, who had been at home in St. Petersburg with his mother, had fallen severely ill. The illness had unfortunately coincided with an important but not critical SVR operation in the US capital, and the SVR's leadership had not permitted him to return home for another two weeks.

As a result, his son had died before he could make it back to see him. Vasilenko had carried his anger at the regime silently, unlike his wife, Katerina, who had been consumed by her bitterness and regularly vented to him in their private moments. He knew, from his casual conversations around the diplomatic circuit that the Americans, the Brits, or even the Israelis, were highly unlikely to have behaved in the same way toward their staff.

Maybe it was coincidence, or, far more likely, the result of those conversations, but one day he had been tapped on the shoulder while watching his ice hockey team, HC CSKA Moscow, play at the Ice Palace indoor arena.

The approach came from an American whom he recognized from the US embassy, a man named Ed Grewall who had since been promoted to chief of station. The conversation began with a request for a few pointers on the finer points of the sport. Before long, the topic of discussion had diverged into politics. Vasilenko had cut the encounter short for fear of being spotted, but they had agreed to meet again, in a more private location.

Long before that meeting took place, Vasilenko decided that if an offer was made, he would accept it. He would work quietly but determinedly against the Putin regime. The chain of events relating to his son were the major but by no means the only factor in his decision. He disliked the culture and environment that had evolved in Russia under the president and his predecessor, Boris Yeltsin, following the breakup of the Soviet Union. When Grewall approached him, there was finally a chance to do something about it.

Vasilenko had exceptional access to most communications and intelligence regarding the US and, just as importantly, to the sources of much of the material. It was his job to ensure that before it was packaged for dispatch to the Kremlin, it was sanitized and contextualized and sense-checked. Going the other way, he also kept a close watch on what information was sent from Yasenevo to operational SVR officers and illegals—agents operating undercover without an official diplomatic status at an embassy.

He returned to his office, a somewhat spartan, functional room around five meters square, and sat down at his computer. A series of PDF files of that day's outgoing traffic were open, and he began going through them.

They included a batch of material relating to the Ukraine crisis and the ongoing part the US played in stoking the fire there. Well, that was top priority, and all hands were on deck dealing with that. It was destined for the *rezident* at the Russian embassy in DC. He signed it off and moved onto the next.

This was interesting. A batch of high-definition satellite images of three locations in Washington, two of which were cemeteries. The photographs were so detailed that it was almost possible to read the carved inscriptions on the gravestones that were lying flat.

The complex label at the bottom of the images told him that they were to be sent to KARAKURT, who he assumed was an SVR agent in DC. Strict compartmentalization of information on a need-to-know basis within the SVR, even at Vasilenko's level, meant that he did not know KARAKURT's true identity.

However, a note at the bottom of the electronic file said that the agent was being run by Directorate KR, the external counterintelligence arm, with inputs from Directorate S, which ran illegal agents not officially registered as Russian embassy employees. That meant KARAKURT was almost certainly not on the embassy staff.

Vasilenko paused for a moment. The true name of KARAKURT would be a snippet that the CIA would love to get their hands on. Exactly how he could obtain that detail was currently eluding him, but 'he would put his mind to finding a way and pass it on.

Vasilenko made a mental note of the location names, all of which were fairly close to each other in the northeastern area of DC: Mount Olivet Cemetery, the US National Arboretum, and Glenwood Cemetery. He would pass them on as soon as he had an opportunity; they might be nothing, or they might be of some significance. Either way, they would get him off to a good start with his new unofficial paymasters.

There was nothing to indicate why KARAKURT wanted the photographs, but his best guess was that it was part of research for a new covert meeting place.

Cemeteries were, in his view, excellent meeting locations. He had used them himself because they were generally quiet and because visiting a relative's gravestone alone, perhaps to clean it or to lay flowers, was a perfect and natural excuse to engage in a conversation with someone nearby who was also ostensibly just a lone mourner.

Vasilenko did not know who KARAKURT's agent was—that information was also strictly restricted—but he assumed it was someone with significant stature inside the US government machine.

He signed off the documents and moved on to the next ones.

CHAPTER TWENTY-SEVEN

Monday, July 28, 2014
Washington, DC

The insistent knocking woke Johnson from a deep sleep that
had been a long time coming.

For hours, images raced continually across his mind of his
two children. He imagined them tied up, exhausted, and
terrified, with black-clad Russian special forces soldiers
pointing guns at them. That was the best-case scenario. The
worst was something that took him to a very dark place, a
vision that he had to force himself to parcel up in an imaginary box and throw away the key.

So it had been well past three o'clock in the morning by
the time he had surrendered to exhaustion and somehow
buried his continuing anxiety about his children sufficiently
to nod off.

Now he jerked awake and turned his head. Jayne, lying
next to him in the spare room of Vic's house in the Palisades
neighborhood, also flicked her eyes open.

Vic and his wife, Eleanor, a generous woman with long black hair, had invited them both to stay overnight at his place, and they had been mightily thankful for that.

"What?" called Johnson, his voice cracking and croaking. "You heard any news?"

The door opened silently, and Vic's face appeared around the side of it.

"Yes, you'd better come and look at something," Vic said. "Two overnight cables just came in."

Johnson swung his legs from beneath the quilt and grabbed the blue terry-cloth robe that Vic had lent him. He beckoned to Jayne, who also climbed out of bed and put on a robe.

"What have you got?" he said as they followed Vic out the door.

Johnson glanced at his watch as they walked. It was twenty past six.

"I'll show you." Vic led the way down the stairs to his home office at the rear of the house. Early morning sunlight was streaming in through the window that overlooked the garden, and the large monitor attached to Vic's laptop was glowing brightly.

"Have a look at that," Vic said, pointing.

Johnson peered at the screen, which was displaying a classified CIA cable, numbered 24X1B and marked Top Secret, Operational Immediate.

"It's from the NRO," Vic said. "They've traced the path of the Buk from the photos you got in Ukraine and matching satellite imagery."

The National Reconnaissance Office had worked quickly. Johnson read down the text.

Missile launcher, towed on semitrailer by white Volvo truck, was taken via highway from Russia/Ukraine border to Azov

Sea Port, then by ship, a freighter named the Yalta which is
registered to Besoi Energy, across Sea of Azov to the Kras-
nodar oil refinery, near Tuapse on Russia's Black Sea coast.
Oil refinery is also owned by Besoi Energy. Imagery after the
Yalta arrived at Krasnodar port is not optimal due to heavy
cloud cover, and we lost track of the Buk. There was no subse-
quent trace of the truck.

A satellite map, printed below the text, had a yellow line that traced the path of the missile launcher across land and sea.

"This is Severinov's refinery," Johnson said. He knew from his research that the Russian oligarch owned the Krasnodar fuel manufacturing plant.

Even as he spoke, another picture of his children and his sister flashed inside his head, this time of them chained inside a drafty industrial unit surrounded by oil pipes and valves and stopcocks. Again, he battled to hold down the surge of anger he could feel rising inside him; it felt like a volcano trying to erupt.

"Do you think the bastard could have taken my kids there?" He turned to look at Vic, who shrugged.

"It's a long way there from Cannes," Jayne said. "Must be fifteen hundred or maybe even a couple thousand miles. I don't know. Seems unlikely. Severinov must have several potential sites where he could keep them."

"But we can't rule out the refinery," Johnson said. "He's obviously got a shipping fleet—there's that freighter, the *Yalta,* and he must have oil tankers. You can guarantee he's got other ships or boats too. What about yachts or speedboats? He's an oligarch, so he's likely to have one. There were hundreds moored in Cannes."

"Possibly," Vic said. "I'll get our energy analysts to see if we can find out exactly what he has in his fleet."

Johnson nodded. "Anyway, this material from the NRO is more solid evidence of what Severinov's been doing. He's up to his eyeballs in the Malaysian jet crash."

Johnson paused and glanced at Vic. "You said two things. What's the other?"

Vic stepped over to the PC and toggled to another CIA cable.

This one, also marked Top Secret, was a very short missive from Ed Grewall in Moscow.

> *Information received from SOYUZ includes request for high-def satellite imagery received from SVR operative KARAKURT in DC. True ID not yet known. Pictures of 3 sites required: Glenwood Cemetery, National Arboretum, Mount Olivet Cemetery. Reason not known, but surmise potential covert rendezvous sites.*

"SOYUZ is Sunny's new America's desk asset at Yasenevo," Vic said. "He works the American desk."

Good cryptonym, Johnson thought. Soyuz was a Russian spacecraft, upgraded many times since its first launch in the 1960s and still operating.

"Can we get Dover and Shepard to put their surveillance guys on these three locations?" Johnson asked.

"Already done—I sent them both a message half an hour ago."

"Good. But we still don't know who the hell's KARAKURT," Johnson murmured as he stared at the screen. "Perhaps SOYUZ can search for that the next time he's in orbit around Moscow Center?" He didn't smile.

* * *

Monday, July 28, 2014

Yasenevo, Moscow

Vasilenko emerged from the corner office of his boss, the American department chief and SVR third deputy director, Fyodor Unkovsky. It was eight o'clock in the evening, and he had just been handed yet another assignment. It was now unlikely he would get home before midnight.

Unkovsky had ordered him to put in place a surveillance operation on the perceived Republican front-runner for the United States presidency, Nicholas McAllister, currently the governor of Maryland. According to Unkovsky, the instruction had come directly from the office of Vladimir Putin and was delivered via a phone call from the Black Bishop of the Kremlin, Igor Ivanov.

Somehow, Vasilenko doubted that Unkovsky's version of events was wholly accurate. Unkovsky was notorious for invoking the president's name, and more recently Ivanov's name, every time he wanted a job done quickly. It was a classic tactic, but Unkovsky had played that card far too often, particularly over the past two years since Putin officially acquired the power to make such direct requests of the SVR without first consulting the Federal Assembly. It was obvious he was fabricating the source of many of his requests. The problem was, nobody could tell which were genuinely from the Kremlin and which weren't.

But either way, it did make logical sense to know much more about McAllister well ahead of the election given that he might win the White House. If there was something that could be used to advantage, perhaps in a blackmail scenario— whether it be political, business, or sexual in nature—the Kremlin would not want to let the opportunity slip.

So Vasilenko could hardly argue. He now faced a difficult negotiation with the *rezident* in Washington, whose already overstretched team would have to cover the additional workload.

Vasilenko strode along the dimly lit corridor that led from his boss's private office, past a row of portraits hanging on the wall of the first three directors of the SVR since its formation in 1991: Yevgeny Primakov, who later became prime minister of Russia; Vyacheslav Trubnikov; and Sergei Lebedev, who got to know Putin when they both served in the KGB in East Germany in the 1980s.

They were the faces of experience, political skulduggery, survival, and patronage. Men who had survived dark nights of treachery by dint of sleight of hand, swiftness of thought and, on occasion, speed of trigger or glint of knife.

The faces in the portraits gazed across the corridor at another large photograph that hung on the opposite wall, this time an aerial shot of Washington, DC, with the White House visible in the top left of the image and Capitol Hill in the lower right. The picture had been there since well before Vasilenko had joined the American department. It was a constant reminder of the main enemy.

As he reached his own office, Vasilenko realized that sometimes fate worked in mysterious ways. Here, hidden behind his irritation at the late night that lay in front of him, was an opportunity.

It would make sense if this operator KARAKURT, whoever he or she was, doubled up on duties in DC and managed the surveillance work on McAllister alongside the existing operation to collect intelligence on the US relationship with Ukraine. If McAllister was indeed destined for the White House, then it would be logical to tie the two operations together.

That would also give Vasilenko the perfect excuse to determine the true identity of KARAKURT and to form a personal connection with him or her.

He didn't bother entering his office but continued to the stairwell, descended one flight and, working off a hunch, made his way along another long corridor to the far end of the building, where Directorate KR, foreign counterintelligence, was based and where one of his longer-standing contemporaries in the service, Deputy Director Yevgeny Kutsik, had his office.

As Vasilenko approached, he could see from the gleam of light emerging from beneath Kutsik's solid wooden office door that he had not gone home. That was typical; the man was well known for being an utter workaholic.

He knocked.

"Come in."

Vasilenko entered to see Kutsik sitting in an enormous black leather swivel chair behind an oak desk. There was no chair in front of it, the window blinds were pulled down as always, although the sun hadn't yet set, and the only light in the room came from a circular desk lamp to Kutsik's left. Kutsik was notorious for making his guests stand: a deliberate ploy to keep their visits as brief and uncomfortable as possible, and to underline his authority.

"Yes?" Kutsik glared at him from above a pair of rimless half-moon glasses. The desk lamp threw a dark shadow from his nose across the right side of his face.

There was a folder on Kutsik's desk. From his elevated angle, Vasilenko could just about read the upside-down title on the front, which was in a small font: Operation Pandora.

That's a new one. What is that about? It was forbidden at Yasenevo to have readable documents visible to those who did not have clearance to see them. As ever, the chiefs seemed to live by slightly different rules.

"I've just had one of those requests from Fyodor," Vasilenko said. He wanted to ask what Pandora was but knew better.

"What was the request?" Kutsik asked. As he spoke, Kutsik appeared to realize that the Pandora file on his desk was visible and smoothly nudged another folder with his elbow to cover it up.

"Something that came direct from the president or Ivanov," Vasilenko said. He went on to explain the nature and the urgency of the demand that had apparently come from the Kremlin.

"Fyodor mentioned that we already have an operation running in DC in relation to Ukraine, which I know you are overseeing," Vasilenko continued. "My thinking is that it would make sense to combine surveillance of McAllister with the work already underway. If McAllister wins, then it will be his policies on Ukraine that we will need to influence. We need to know what he is doing and thinking on that front."

Kutsik frowned. "I don't like combining operations. It's dangerous. It puts both operations at risk of compromise by contamination. If one gets blown, the other might too. Much better to compartmentalize them."

"I agree, normally. But in this case, I think it critical that we don't run any risk of letting something important slip through the net. The McAllister work would feed into yours on Ukraine and vice versa. What capacity does your operative have?"

Kutsik shrugged. "Not exactly overloaded. The operation's only been running for a month."

"My biggest concern is that the president's office gets the idea that we've missed something by not cooperating efficiently, that we've missed a trick. Then we both lose."

Kutsik rocked back in his chair and placed both hands behind his head, staring at the far wall. It was impossible to tell what the man was thinking. Vasilenko had known him for twenty-five years, and he remained just as inscrutable now as when he had first met him.

After at least a minute of silence, Kutsik leaned forward and folded his arms on the desk, eyeballing his visitor.

"*Da*. Yes. I agree. I will speak to KARAKURT and gauge her opinion."

A woman.

That narrowed the field very significantly. There were very few women in the SVR capable of operating successfully undercover in the West. Vasilenko knew better than to directly ask for her true identity. Besides, now that he knew the officer was female, he had another method of working that out. He only had a couple of people on his mental short list, one of whom was a clear favorite.

"Thank you," Vasilenko said. "Let us talk again when you have done that."

Kutsik nodded once and looked down at the paperwork on his desk. The meeting appeared to be over.

Vasilenko was about to open the door and leave when Kutsik spoke again.

"By the way, as of tomorrow I will no longer be in this office."

Vasilenko turned in surprise. "No longer here?"

"No. Kruglov just told me that he wants me to run Directorate PR, and to become his official number two. I thought you would want to know. There will be a formal announcement in the morning."

PR was political intelligence and was another key arm of the SVR. And if Kutsik was being promoted to Kruglov's official deputy, that was a major career milestone, making him a very clear favorite to succeed the director when the time came.

"Congratulations. Many congratulations," Vasilenko said. He walked back to Kutsik's desk and shook his hand.

"Thank you."

"Who will take over your role?" Vasilenko asked.

"That is not yet decided," Kutsik said, his face impassive. "I am playing a part in deciding my successor. We are discussing it."

There was no hint that he himself might be in the frame for the counterintelligence chief's job, but Vasilenko pondered it nonetheless. He would dearly like that position, which was highly sought after. But as was the case with so many things at Yasenevo, it was probably best not to ask.

"Good," Vasilenko said. "Thank you for letting me know in advance. I appreciate it. I will wish you good night."

Kutsik nodded and went back to his paperwork. Vasilenko made his way back to his office and logged back onto his laptop computer. Then he navigated to a secure web page on the SVR's intranet, to which he had been given temporary access by the security department two days earlier to help him resolve an internal disciplinary issue involving nonattendance at work by one of his senior staff. It was a searchable registry of those who had used their electronic identity tags to enter the Yasenevo parking lot. Virtually all employees traveled to work by car, as was evident from a quick glance at the sprawling hectares of tarmac lots around the Yasenevo buildings. So the database was effectively an attendance register.

He knew what name he needed to check and keyed it into the search box at the top of the page.

Within seconds, the data he needed was on the screen in front of him.

Yes, that made sense. She had begun using the parking lot on April 25, after her return from London. She had stopped using it on June 28. Vasilenko had seen her a few times in different parts of the building during that two-month period. Since then, she seemed to have vanished. Well, that also aligned with the month that Kutsik had mentioned in relation to how long his operation had been running.

A woman he disliked was handling one of the gemstones in the crown of Russia's informants inside the United States. It was an exceptionally high-profile role, and success would put KARAKURT back on course toward the director's office following her enormous screwup in London earlier in the year.

That was a role that Vasilenko wanted. Not for patriotic reasons, as had been the case earlier in his career, but more because it would put him in an even stronger position to secure intelligence of use to Grewall.

KARAKURT was Anastasia Shevchenko. It had to be her. But what the hell was Operation Pandora?

CHAPTER TWENTY-EIGHT

Monday, July 28, 2014
Washington, DC

TITANIUM left the secretary of defense's luxurious office complex, the blandly labeled Room 3E880, on the third floor of the concentric Pentagon building. He tucked his leather document case tightly under his left armpit and walked a few yards along the corridor in a westerly direction.

The office, located on the northeast corner of the outer E-ring of the building's massive five-ring structure, was where he usually met the defense secretary, Philip Monterey. The view eastward from Monterey's panoramic office window stretched over Columbia Island and the Potomac River toward the Washington Monument and the White House.

To the west was the green expanse of Arlington Cemetery, where his father's remains lay and from which direction a hijacked American Airlines Boeing 757 had come when al-Qaeda terrorists had flown it into the side of the Pentagon building on September 11, 2001, killing a total of 189 people.

Indeed, one of his best friends, who was a Pentagon employee at that time, had been heading north into Washington on Interstate 395 that morning. As he reached the top of a hill, he had a clear view of the Pentagon below him in front of the city, just as the Boeing appeared to his left, as low as it could be without touching the ground, and struck the huge building with such devastating results.

But now TITANIUM thrust all of those thoughts to the back of his mind. What he had just heard during his routine weekly briefing with Monterey was something he now had to pass through to the woman he knew as Tatiana Niklas as quickly as possible.

He knew that it would have a similar effect to throwing a large bucket of gasoline onto an already blazing bonfire—a bonfire that had been started by shooting down the Malaysia Airlines jet over Eastern Ukraine.

The details, which included a US military strategic and tactical plan for Ukraine and the full draft of a bill that was destined for Congress, would have to wait until they could meet face-to-face and he could hand over the material on a small flash drive.

He could send the main points in summary by text message from his burner phone. However, he definitely wasn't going to risk doing so from within this building, which was bristling with all manner of detection and monitoring devices.

He quickened his pace as he made his way past Room 3E944— where the deputy secretary of defense, Lynn Williamson, worked—and along a broad, brightly lit corridor lined with wooden panels and photographs of past US military heroes, generals, war planners, and political leaders.

Eventually he came to an elevator that took him down to the elite Mall Entrance to the building, outside which was the VIP parking lot where Monterey and his high-ranking military and civilian colleagues were delivered early each morning by their drivers.

TITANIUM's car, a black Mercedes S-Class, was waiting in the lot, its engine running. He climbed into the car, gave his driver a brief instruction, and fastened his seat belt.

He glanced at his watch. Yet again he was late taking his medication for his depression, so he grabbed a bottle of water from the holder in the door, removed a capsule from his pocket, and swallowed it with a swig of liquid.

It was only when the car had exited the complex onto South Washington Boulevard, heading toward the Arlington Memorial Bridge and the route to Capitol Hill, that TITA-NIUM took his burner phone from a pocket inside his brief-case. He inserted the battery and SIM card and began to tap out a short message.

By the time the car had crossed the river and was rolling along Constitution Avenue NW, the message had been dispatched, the phone had been turned off again, and the battery and SIM removed.

Now he had an hour and a half to spare before his next meeting on Capitol Hill, one that he knew would last until past eleven that evening. The truth was, it was the last thing he felt like doing. He therefore felt that he deserved the treat that was awaiting him at his next port of call—a long-standing friend-with-benefits whom he was due to meet at their usual spot, a rented condominium in a red brick apart-ment complex just south of Logan Circle.

He knew that the arrangement was driven by his poor relationship with his wife and his depression and was just as risky and likely counterproductive in a different way as the game he was playing with the manipulative Russian Tatiana.

Indeed, the two were in many ways tied together because Tatiana had effectively blackmailed him into his current situ-ation after she found out about the friends-with-benefits arrangement. In his present frame of mind, though, he didn't care; risk was something he thrived on, and he liked the adrenaline rush it brought. The rewards were just as nice too, albeit in a different kind of way.

* * *

Monday, July 28, 2014
    Washington, DC

Johnson was sitting in Vic's living room with Jayne, debating whether to give Natalia another call to check whether the French police had made any further progress, when his phone rang. It was Vic.

"Got any good news?" Johnson asked as his opening gambit. He turned his phone to loudspeaker mode so Jayne could hear.

"Funny you should ask that. Yes. I just got off the phone with Sunny. His new agent came up with the goods. I've got the likely identity of our friend KARAKURT."

Johnson sat bolt upright in his armchair. "Who is it?"

"Anastasia Shevchenko."

"*Shevchenko?* She's KARAKURT? Are you sure?" Johnson bit his bottom lip and glanced at Jayne, whose mouth had dropped open slightly.

He had been wondering at the back of his mind what had happened to Shevchenko since he and Jayne had managed to discover the identity of her agent Bernice Franklin in London a few months earlier.

"They seem certain, yes."

"Well, screw me. The obvious questions, then: Where is she? What name is she operating under?"

Where is she so I can bleed her dry and find out where the hell my family is.

Vic cleared his throat. "They don't know that. It's been difficult enough to get the identity. Sensitive. You know how it is."

Johnson stood and walked around Vic's living room, holding his phone in front of him. He recalled that Shevchenko had previously worked in the SVR's Washington *rezidentura*, so she knew the city. She could be anywhere.

"There is of course one person who will likely know where she is," Johnson said, the irony striking him.

"Who?"

"The same bastard who's got my kids and sister. Her lover."

Vic grunted. "Well, we'd better give him a call and ask him."

"Lowest form of wit, Vic."

"What?"

"Sarcasm."

As the two men lapsed into uncharacteristic silence, Jayne spoke.

"I just had a thought," she said. "Quantum."

"Quantum?" Johnson asked.

"Yes. Wasn't Quantum put into some refineries in the Middle East and other sensitive locations?"

Even as she spoke, a light bulb went off inside Johnson's head. The Quantum program, run by the NSA's Tailored Access Operations hacking division, involved extensive covert installations of malware—or special spy software—on target computer networks and routers and sometimes even hardware on PCs. Its controversial tools could tap into email programs and apps, copy documents and files, and change data if required. It enabled the TAO to monitor organizations and individuals seen as a potential threat to the United States.

To the best of Johnson's recollection, about one hundred thousand installations had been made covertly on computers across many countries. The technology was even capable of operating on computers not connected to the internet by utilizing micro radio transmitters installed on motherboards or in USB sockets.

"I think you're correct. Genius, Jayne," Johnson said. "Vic, did you hear that?"

There was a pause. Then Vic spoke. "Yes, I heard. How the hell did you know about that, Jayne? Never mind. Thing is, I have no idea whether that Krasnodar refinery was on the list or not."

"But some refineries were included," Jayne said. "I recall that from an MI6 briefing not long before I left. We cooperated with the NSA on that program, and GCHQ was heavily involved. There was a huge concern about an oil crisis in the Middle East and the impact it might have on the US and Europe's fuel security, which is why refineries were targeted. The aim was to try and get advance warning of anything that could signal a fuel crisis—big drops in Middle East gasoline production for example. But some Russian refineries were also a focus."

"I agree, it would be a surprise if a key Russian refinery was not included," Vic said. "But let me check with the NSA. I'll give Alex Goode a call."

Alex Goode was an old friend of Vic's and a senior officer at the National Security Agency's enormous headquarters building at Fort Meade, a forty-five-minute drive northeast of Washington. Vic and Johnson had deployed Goode and his team on a few previous investigations where there had been a need to intercept cell phone, email, or other online data or calls.

"If we can get into the refinery system, Severinov's laptop or PC might be accessible," Jayne said.

"In which case the TAO might be able to use Quantum to find out where my kids are too," Johnson said.

"Don't get your hopes up, Joe."

Johnson shrugged. At the top of his mind was the seven-day deadline that Severinov had imposed. What he needed was a foundation on which to build some sort of strategy to solve the problem. It was impossible not to mentally cling onto anything that might conceivably bring Carrie and Peter back.

"Got any other news?" Johnson asked.

"Yes. It's not good, though. Have you looked at your Twitter account recently?"

"Not for a couple of hours."

"I thought not. Can you check it out now?"

"What are we looking for?" Johnson asked.

"Search for the MH17 hashtags."

Jayne was tapping on her phone screen, and after a few seconds she thrust it at him.

"Take a look," Jayne said.

Johnson took the phone and read a series of tweets, all with a similar theme and with now familiar hashtags.

US to send another $1bn of Patriots to Ukraine.
First US shoots down a jet, now it gives $1bn more missiles
Warmonger Ferguson to send $1bn more Patriots to Ukraine.

And so it went on, all the tweets from anonymous-looking accounts with odd names and labeled with the *#MH17CI-Aplot* and *#KievDownedTheBoeing* hashtags.

A deep chill ran through Johnson. How would Severinov react to news of more missiles for Ukraine? He had demanded that the US should not send any more assistance or arms to the Kiev government, and he now had Amy and the kids.

"Shit," Johnson said. "Looks like more crap from the troll factory. Where the hell's all this billion-dollar stuff coming from?"

He handed the phone back to Jayne, who began tapping away on it.

"Good question," Vic said. "It unfortunately happens to be true—up to a point. I can tell you that there is a secret plan at the White House and the Pentagon to put together a further $1 billion military aid package for Ukraine, mainly loan guarantees but also more military equipment. It's early stages now, though a bill will go to Congress at some point fairly soon. But there are categorically no Patriots involved, I can tell you that. Where the hell this information came from is a mystery—it's top-secret stuff at this stage. Once again, it's been leaked, and the spin that's being put on it in the context of the Malaysian jet disaster is causing major problems. Search for tweets by Nicholas McAllister."

"I already have," Jayne said, her face serious. "McAllister and others in the Republican camp are all tweeting about this, criticizing the administration. His sister, the twin, she's in on it too. The news channels are picking it up too, and they're rehashing the Malaysian jet bombing."

"So it's everywhere?" Johnson said. He felt his stomach turn over.

Jayne reached over and squeezed his shoulder.

"Damaging stuff," Vic continued on the phone. "I've been speaking to the White House. They're telling me the president is going ballistic over this. They're going to put out a forceful denial immediately, saying the Patriot allegations are rubbish. And another thing—I've just had a message from Veltman. There's a meeting with the president that he and I have been called to tomorrow morning at the White House.

Veltman wants you to go along too, Joe. We need to hash out a plan for dealing with all this. Veltman wants the president to know we're on top of it."

Johnson paused and sat down in his armchair again. *Veltman wants, Veltman this, Veltman that.* Normally, the chance of meeting the president for the first time was something he would have grabbed with both hands. But right now, it was the last thing he wanted. His knees felt a little wobbly.

"Vic, the president may be going ballistic," Johnson said. "But that's nothing compared with how I'm feeling."

Johnson felt droplets of sweat begin to roll down his forehead. All he could think of were the words on the phone call he had received the previous day.

I want your investigation called off and a public statement from the White House and the CIA . . . any future planned shipments of weapons will be cancelled . . . I have the three of them. If there is no White House and CIA statement within the next seven days, they will all die.

"I'm sure you haven't forgotten, Vic, but if that military package for Ukraine goes through—whether there's Patriots or no Patriots involved—Severinov's going to kill my kids and sister."

CHAPTER TWENTY-NINE

Tuesday, July 29, 2014
Washington, DC

The call from Alex Goode came in on Vic's cell phone as they were in the car on the way to the White House.

Vic, having convinced Johnson to come along, had decided to drive himself rather than use a driver so they could talk more freely. Jayne had volunteered to remain at Vic's house and hold an update call with Natalia in Cannes.

Vic put the call on loudspeaker so that Johnson, in the back seat, and Arthur Veltman, in the front passenger seat, could hear. "The NSA has had that refinery on the monitoring list for some time," Goode said. "Our TAO team has compromised its router. We've had Quantum tools on it and on the PCs, packet sniffers operating and so on. We've been crawling all over the digital traffic both in and out."

"And? Is there anything?"

"No. We've been over the records overnight. Nothing out of the ordinary. Just the kind of routine material you'd expect from an oil refinery. Tons of emails about oil prices, gasoline prices, industry gossip, tanker bookings, equipment orders, and repairs. Workers doing a bit of gambling online and downloading the odd bit of pornography, but you expect that. Severinov has a work PC, which he uses fairly regularly, and we've hacked into that, but there's nothing that stands out. With a few exceptions, like him ordering crates of scotch or a new Mercedes, everything on his PC there is related to the refinery. However—"

"Are you sure?" Johnson interrupted. "There's nothing buried in private folders in his email or hidden on encrypted drives?"

"We are fairly certain there's not."

Johnson bowed his head momentarily. "Shit. But hang on a minute—if he's only got refinery files on that PC, he must have another private laptop for his personal email accounts and files, right? Otherwise, how is he communicating with Shevchenko? For God's sake, as far as we know they're sleeping in the same bed when they get the chance—he must have some means of keeping in touch when he wants to get laid, if nothing else."

Goode chuckled. "Yes, that was what I was about to say when you interrupted. That's the next job. We haven't got Quantum on his personal computer—yet. If he's connecting to the refinery routers with it, using their broadband, we could get our tools on it, I hope."

"How long could it take?" Johnson asked.

"Anything from hours to weeks."

"*Weeks?*"

"I'm just being honest, Joe. It's tricky sometimes."

There was a couple of seconds of silence.

"What's the likelihood that he or his IT security people spot it?" Johnson asked. His immediate concern was that if the Russian realized his laptop was being attacked, he might retaliate by hitting back at the nearest obvious target—Johnson's children.

"Our people are expert at covering their tracks," Goode said. "Don't worry."

Johnson stared up at the car roof for a few seconds and said nothing. *Don't worry.* What sort of goddamn stupid comment was that?

"Thanks, Alex," Vic said, breaking the silence. "Keep us posted if you get anything else of interest." He ended the call.

Immediately after the call with Goode had finished, Vic had another catch-up conversation with Simon Dover to update him on progress and to ensure his team was continuing to maintain subtle surveillance on the three sites identified by Ed Grewall's SVR mole at Yasenevo. They were, but there had been absolutely no sign of any covert activity or meetings taking place at any of them.

"Don't get too close," Vic warned. "We don't want to run the risk of them spotting surveillance and aborting for another site we know nothing about."

"Don't worry. We're managing it," Dover said as he signed off.

Johnson sank back into the black leather car seat. Too many people with no clue what this was like telling him not to worry. He rarely felt depressed, but he was feeling as though a slight fog was building up in his mind, and his usual reserves of adrenaline had dried up.

It seemed as though the lives of his kids and sister and the success of the operation now lay far too much in the hands of others for his liking.

Maybe it was time to change that.

* * *

Tuesday, July 29, 2014

Krasnodar oil refinery

The army of workers swarming over the forty-meter-high silver tubular-steel hydrocracking unit at the Krasnodar refinery reminded Severinov of worker ants struggling to build a nest. Their vans and trucks were parked untidily on the concrete road that ran through the middle of the extensive tangle of vessels, tubes, pipes, and valves that made up the site.

Workers were going up and down the steel ladders that ran up the sides of the hydrocracking unit and around the walkways that encircled it.

Severinov looked out of the floor-to-ceiling plate-glass window of the refinery's management office that sat in the center of the site and watched as a new length of piping was slowly hoisted into place by a giant crane that had been brought in by ship from Barcelona. Some of the teams working on the hydrocracker were from London, others from Milan and Aberdeen. They worked on a shift basis, two weeks on, two weeks off, with round-the-clock activity to ensure the project was completed as quickly as possible.

The refinery managing director had established the work program and ran it, but Severinov nevertheless liked to spend some time on-site during such crucial periods to keep an eye on progress.

Spread across a huge 730-hectare site, the refinery, dating back to 1935, was still going strong, although it had undergone a massive transformation over the years. It was now capable of producing 150,000 barrels per day of high-quality gasoline and diesel fuel.

The site included many buildings and units, some of which were not currently being used and others that had been turned into storage units.

One of the disused buildings, near the southern perimeter of the site and a safe distance away from any maintenance workers, was particularly securely locked—and with good reason. Only a very small number of people on the site knew what was concealed there.

Next to it was another similarly disused building, and that was where Severinov planned to keep Johnson's kids and sister when they arrived.

He glanced around the private office, which was deserted. He walked to the door and checked the adjoining open-plan space where his administration staff worked. They had gone home for the evening, leaving him alone. He took out his laptop, which he regarded as a much safer option than using the desktop PC, and started it up.

Severinov logged on to the virtual private network through which he accessed the email account that he shared with Shevchenko. He then opened up the usual draft email that they used for communications.

A new message from Shevchenko briefly informed him that she had received fresh information from her agent in Washington about a planned $1 billion aid program for Ukraine. Well, he knew about that already—he had seen the various tweets that had gone out earlier that day, presumably from the office in Rostov. There had been so many that he couldn't possibly have missed them.

Severinov typed out a quick reply, which he kept businesslike.

Saw tweets about $1 billion program. Good work. New information from this end. My men took Johnson's two children and sister from vacation property in Cannes + bringing them to Russia by yacht. I spoke to Johnson + demanded US abandon military aid to Ukraine in return for family's release. That will not happen of course. After a few days I

will give Johnson a false location for them inside Russia. 100
percent Johnson will try to rescue them + I will kill him. The
$1 billion aid will help me—I can argue US is increasing not
cutting Ukraine aid program + raise threat to kids. But it is
important you keep up pressure with new information. If
Johnson does not take the bait and attempt rescue I will kill
or maim one of the kids to start with and teach him the hard
way. Keep me updated.

He saved the message and logged out of the email
account.

CHAPTER THIRTY

Tuesday, July 29, 2014
Washington, DC

Johnson stared out the window as Vic steered the car off Seventeenth Street NW at the White House's southwest entrance, the usual route CIA staff used when they attended meetings in the Situation Room. Vic braked to a halt in front of a vehicle gate next to a pedestrian security kiosk and waited until a guard had checked all their passes and identification documents. He then waved them through to a small parking lot in front of the old executive office building adjacent to the West Wing.

There seemed to be zero progress on any front. As they walked in, Johnson was pleased he wasn't in Vic's or Veltman's shoes right now and carrying the weight of the CIA's responsibility on his back.

Normally, the prospect of meeting the president would have energized and excited Johnson, but right now, all he could think of was his children and sister.

Jayne had called as the car came within sight of the White House to say she had spoken to Natalia to get an update. French police did have a breakthrough of sorts: an eyewitness who said he had seen a van, which he thought might have been from Électricité de France, pulling up at the quayside in Cannes late on the night of the kidnapping. Two men carried large boxes from the van onto a yacht. The man had thought little of it and continued walking. Beyond that, there was no further information.

It was better than nothing, Johnson reflected as they walked up West Executive Avenue, the small street between the old executive office building and the West Wing, and turned right into the west basement entrance.

After going through the usual set of stringent security measures, they went downstairs to the basement. They placed their phones in the lead-lined security box and were shown into a small conference room within the Situation Room suite where the president's personal aide, Charles Deacon, was waiting for them. He shook hands with Veltman and Vic, whom he clearly already knew, and introduced himself to Johnson.

After twenty minutes, the unmistakable figure of President Ferguson appeared at the door, accompanied, as Vic had predicted, by three men in dark suits, all of whom Johnson recognized from photographs and TV coverage. There was National Security Advisor Francis Wade, Secretary of State Paul Farrar, and Brad Turner, chairman of the House Intelligence Committee.

All the men briefly shook hands. Ferguson gave Johnson an appraising look for a couple of seconds, appearing to size him up; perhaps that was his usual way with people he hadn't met before.

"We've only got ten minutes," the president began. "I need to get to the Treasury for a budget meeting. I'm very unhappy to see all the Russia-driven Twitter and media coverage about our Ukraine aid plans—it's giving Putin ammunition on a plate, not to mention McAllister. So, Arthur, what's the latest?" He turned to Veltman and folded his arms.

Veltman gave a quick update on initiatives to uncover the mole, summarizing the intelligence from Moscow about likely rendezvous sites, FBI actions to surveil them, and the identity of Shevchenko. He also outlined the evidence unearthed by Johnson about the Buk missile launcher.

"In summary, that's where we are at," Veltman said.

"But you're no nearer finding the traitor who's leaking all this?" Ferguson asked in a level tone.

"We believe we're making progress, sir," Veltman said.

Ferguson placed both palms flat on the gleaming wooden conference table. "Our entire Ukraine strategy is at stake here. I expect concrete results soon—I have invited President Poroshenko to join me in addressing a joint session of Congress to officially propose the $1 billion package of loan guarantees, plus another $291 million in other military equipment. But we can't do that while this chaos is going on." He tapped the table firmly with his fingers.

"With this speculation and criticism swirling, it will make it damn frigging hard to persuade Congress to support anything," Ferguson continued. "That is why I want to be able to announce at the joint session that we have caught the traitor responsible for all the groundless leaks, rumors, and damaging speculation. Understood?" He fixed his stare first at Veltman, then at Vic.

Then Ferguson leaned forward and turned his gaze on Johnson. "Mr. Johnson, we haven't met previously, but I know your record. I know from Arthur what your role is in this investigation, and I thank you for that. I value the deniability it gives me and the rest of our team. I also understand from

Francis that your family is currently in a potentially highly dangerous situation and that demands have been made for their release."

"Mr. Wade has informed you correctly, sir," Johnson said. "The biggest concern is we don't know where they are right now, and their lives are at risk."

Johnson paused for a moment. "Severinov has told me that in return for their release, he wants our investigation called off. He also wants some kind of public statement from the White House saying that we have been conspiring with the Ukraine government to supply weapons, including anti-aircraft missiles. That's effectively asking us to admit shooting down the Malaysian Boeing. He is also demanding any future shipments of weapons to Ukraine to be cancelled. It's obviously being driven by the Kremlin, sir."

"Yes, it is," Ferguson said, his eyes fixed on Johnson, his voice devoid of emotion. "And you, of course, will understand I unfortunately can't give in to those demands. Our suspicion is that Russia is planning an invasion of Ukraine soon, just as it has done in Crimea. Thanks to your efforts, we now have proof it shot down the Malaysian jet, killing three hundred people, including Paul's family." He nodded toward Farrar, who sat impassively, arms folded.

"We can't back down in the face of such aggression," Ferguson continued. "It would set a precedent that we would regret for evermore. I am sorry."

Johnson's scalp tightened sharply at Ferguson's words, and he felt momentarily dizzy. He knew that would be the president's standpoint, but he found it impossible not to react. He noticed the president scrutinizing him carefully.

"I understand, sir. I know you have no alternative."

"But Mr. Johnson, Joe, I can promise you this," the president continued. "Once Arthur and Vic's teams have located your kids and your sister, you will get maximum assistance and advice, and we will do whatever is needed to extract them."

Wade nodded. "We can allocate special forces, SEAL teams, who are already in the Mediterranean."

Johnson leaned back in his chair, imagining Carrie and Peter and Amy tied up somewhere horrific and a SEAL team fast-roping silently down in the darkness from a helicopter. Then gunfire, bullets flying, knives being drawn; the screaming, shouting, and silence. The SEALs were damned good; they had pulled off all manner of exfil operations against the odds. But who knew what might happen in any given scenario?

No. That wasn't the way he would do it. It seemed to carry too much risk to his family.

"Sir, thank you. Yes, I understand. I knew that's what you would say," Johnson said. "But my whole life I've been an independent, resourceful operator. I'm also something of a control freak—sometimes that's a weakness, sometimes it's a strength. I'll bear in mind what you're saying, but when we find out where my kids are, I may want to take part in the exfil myself, perhaps with a very small team, a couple of people. Any support that is available will be very helpful, however. Let's see when the time comes—if it comes."

He paused as the president, his eyebrows now slightly raised, continued to look at him.

"And if there is any blood on the floor, it will be Severinov's," Johnson added.

CHAPTER THIRTY-ONE

Wednesday, July 30, 2014
Fort Meade, Maryland

The brightly lit but windowless room stretched forty yards in front of Johnson, who stood at the bottom of a short flight of stairs that led down from the high-security entrance lobby. An array of open-plan desks ran down the right side of the room, most of them occupied by scruffy-looking men in T-shirts and jeans and slightly better dressed women, all glued to large computer screens.

At one desk, a group of six people were gathered around a man at one PC, all of them engaged in a heated debate that seemed to require a lot of pointing at the screen, swearing, and arm waving.

"They'll be hacking Beijing," Vic said from behind him.

"Don't joke about it," Goode said. "They probably are."

Once Goode had established it was feasible to get into the Krasnodar refinery's network, he had invited them to

Fort Meade to guide the team doing the hacking in order to ensure they got precisely the information they needed.

However, the process to get into this inner sanctum of the strictly segregated Tailored Access Operations wing of the NSA complex had been a tortuous one. Vic, as a fairly regular visitor, already had the required security clearances, and he had been previously scanned by the retinal recognition systems in place at the entrance.

But Jayne, even though she had been to Fort Mead previously while working at MI6, and Johnson had to undergo lengthy visitors' clearance procedures that took the best part of an hour. The door to the special TAO wing, known as the Remote Operations Center, was a fortress-style steel affair that required a special six-digit passcode and was protected by armed guards.

Goode explained that more than six hundred of the TAO's one thousand or so employees were based in the Remote Operations Center, which was tucked away inside the enormous Fort Meade complex.

"They're mostly young geeks," Goode said.

On the way in, Johnson could not fail to notice that not only was the campus heavily protected by barbed wire and attack dogs, but also the numerous security police were armed with weaponry that included grenade launchers and machine guns. Two armored personnel carriers were parked near the tallest of two black glass office buildings.

Goode pointed at a man and a woman who were approaching from the far side of the room. "These two have been running the fuel security program—the refinery and oil and gas production company specialists."

The man and woman, whom Goode identified only by first names, Seb and Anna, both appeared to be in their thirties, but were dressed like students, in hoodies and jeans.

They carried iPad-style tablet devices, didn't smile much, and both appeared tired.

Seb led the way to a separate room at the rear of the open-plan area that housed six computer terminals. Anna sat down at one of them, and Seb pulled up a chair next to her. The others remained standing behind Anna.

"I've been into the Krasnodar refinery's router already today," said Anna, fingering her blonde bob. "Your man Severinov is logged on to the network with a company PC and also with what appears to be a private laptop."

She adjusted her thick black glasses and pointed to a tree-like diagram on the screen. "This shows all the currently connected devices. And this one, a Windows laptop, is his machine." Her finger moved to a square near the bottom of the screen, marked SeverLENO8153.

"I noticed he was using a specific internet email provider," Anna said. "So the last time he logged on to it, I routed him to a bogus web page that looks and functions like the real thing, using diverts. But I used the page to pop a piece of software onto his laptop that enables me to control it remotely."

She turned and gave a faint smile. "People think we use spam emails, but that's old hat these days. It had a low success rate."

"Interesting," Jayne said. "When I came here a few years ago, this stuff was still under development."

"Yes," Anna said. "It's quite a refined tool these days. I can access his apps, but if he's doing something else on there, he won't know I'm doing it. It might slow his machine down fractionally, but he won't notice the difference. Now, what do you want?"

"Can we go through his emails first?" Johnson asked.

Anna nodded and toggled to Severinov's email in-box. They spent the next three-quarters of an hour trawling through the in-box, which contained thousands of emails, doing searches for a variety of keywords. However, none of them threw up anything linked to Shevchenko, Johnson's children, or the Malaysian airliner. There were plenty to and from friends and business acquaintances, many from his secretary with business-related issues and appointment queries, and a lot that were about his travel plans.

"Can we do similar searches through his files—his documents, spreadsheets, PowerPoint slides, photographs, and so on?" Johnson asked.

Anna obliged, but twenty minutes later, there was still no sign of anything that might be helpful.

"Hmm. Looks like he's being very careful," Seb said.

Jayne took a step forward. "Does he have other email baskets or folders? We didn't check those. His drafts basket, or junk? We had a few cases at MI6 where our targets were using draft emails as a kind of message board. Everyone in the gang had a password and could write messages in there. The emails were never sent."

"Hang on a moment," Anna said. She clicked on the email subfolders tab.

"There's a drafts folder. I'll try that."

She clicked on the folder. It contained four emails, three of which had labels in the subject line and one that didn't, which she clicked on first.

It was a copy of a newspaper report on an FC Dynamo Moscow game, which had clearly been copied and pasted into the email. Anna scrolled down to the end of it. "Not much use," she said.

The next email was headed "Assets List" and consisted of a long list of various businesses, oil production fields, power generation plants, the Krasnodar refinery, and many other properties and sites across several countries.

"Just in case he forgets what he owns," Johnson said. The others laughed.

"What else do we have here?" Anna said, scrolling down. "FC Dynamo Moscow Fixture List 2013-14. That won't be much use either."

"No, it won't. It must be his team," Johnson agreed. He folded his arms and glanced at Vic, who shrugged.

Anna turned around. "We're not having any luck here. Do you want me to see if I can check if he's had any other devices running on the refinery network? Cell phones or whatever?"

"Yes, let's not leave any stones unturned," Johnson said.

"Wait, before you do that," Jayne said. "Can you open up that fixture list email? I'm looking at the right-hand column. It says it was modified yesterday. But last season must have finished weeks ago, so I'm wondering why he's written something into the email."

"No problem," Anna said. She reached for her mouse and clicked on the email. Sure enough, the email contained a list of matches for the entire soccer season involving Dynamo Moscow.

"Scroll down, please" Jayne said. "Can we find what was modified yesterday?"

Anna did as asked. She got to the bottom of the fixture list and stopped. The final game listed was on May 15 against Spartak Moscow.

"Strange. Is there anything else on there?" Jayne asked. "Keep going down."

Anna did so. There was only white space. But then, just as Anna slowed her scrolling, a line of text came up at the bottom of the screen.

Saw tweets about $1 billion program. Good work.

Johnson put his hand on the back of Anna's chair and leaned over her shoulder. "Wait, what's that?"

Anna scrolled down farther, and more text became visible.

New information from this end. My men took Johnson's two children and sister from vacation property in Cannes + bringing them to Russia by yacht . . . "

The message continued for several sentences. The entire group clustered around Anna's computer said nothing for several seconds as they read it.

Jayne broke the silence. "Bloody hell."

"Fucking bastard," Johnson finally said. His voice was cracking and rose in volume. "I'll kill the son of a bitch."

"Can you screenshot those?" Jayne asked.

"No need. It's all being recorded," Seb said.

"Good. Scroll down further."

Anna continued to scroll down, and more messages came into view. They were obviously part of a conversation Severinov had been having.

Then one appeared with a reference in crude Russian slang indicating Severinov was desperate to get laid. *Are you ready for it, Ana?*

The reply read: *Ready anytime!*

"Ana?" Johnson spat the word out. "Anastasia, of course. It's that bitch Shevchenko."

"Keep going down," Jayne said, a note of impatience in her voice.

Another older message appeared.

You will not believe this: Have learned from my new friend here that CIA is to carry out deniable investigation into the Malaysian jet crash. Guess who they have hired? Joe Johnson! Little more known at this stage, but will find out more . . . "

Again the message went on for a few sentences. Below it was a US cell phone number with a short note.

That's in case you need me urgently.

Vic put his hands on his hips. "She's got some nerve. We'll need to inform Dover and Iain Shepard as soon as we're finished here. She's in DC—the feebs can shut her down."

Jayne pointed at the cell phone number. "We'll need to find her first. Can we get a trace on that number? That must be hers."

"Yes," said Seb. "We'll get onto that immediately." He tapped the number into his tablet.

Johnson turned to Vic. "He doesn't say where in Russia he's taking my kids or when. But if he's got them on a yacht, that fits with what French police picked up about the Électricité de France van and men carrying boxes onto a yacht. Can we trace yachts heading from Cannes to Russia these past few days? He might be taking them to his refinery. I need to get over there."

"Yes, we can check," Vic said. "There'll be thousands of yachts in the Med, but we can whittle them down. We'll get the NRO to do it. And there's no point in you going to the refinery or anywhere else until we know where the kids are. Keep calm, buddy. We're close."

"My team can help with the yacht," Goode said. "We can get satellite images and check recordings of coast guard shipping communications where the call timings match up with the position of the yachts we're targeting."

Behind Johnson, there was a loud cry of annoyance from Anna.

The entire screen had gone black.

"Shit," Anna said.

"What's happened there?" Johnson asked.

"Don't know," Anna said, her voice now downbeat. "His laptop's either been turned off or has been disconnected from the network."

"Does it mean he knows we've been in his laptop?" Johnson asked. He felt his chest tighten.

Anna hesitated. "I don't know."

CHAPTER THIRTY-TWO

Wednesday, July 30, 2014
Washington, DC

Shevchenko had always found that lowering her already husky voice by a note or two gave it a seductive quality that many men found irresistible. Although she didn't like ingratiating herself with her superiors, she had to admit it worked equally well when the objective was not seduction in the sexual sense but rather professional advancement.

Thus, when the call came to her secure phone from Igor Ivanov, the subtle change in inflection happened almost without her realizing she was doing it. It was built into her DNA by this stage, a part of her professional makeup.

"I have got something coming down the wire that should keep you amused, and the president too," Shevchenko said.

She was standing next to the floor-to-ceiling plate glass window in her apartment's living room, gazing out at the Washington Monument obelisk that pointed to the sky like some kind of a giant white marble missile.

"What might that be?" asked Ivanov. "Is it related to the aid for Ukraine?" The Kremlin ringmaster had sounded impatient when he first came on the line, but now the ice was thawing rapidly.

"Yes, exactly. It's the original source documents," Shevchenko said. "By tomorrow night I will have met TITANIUM, and I should have a copy of the Defense Department's strategy and tactical document for Ukraine, and also a copy of the draft Ukraine Support Act—that includes the $1 billion loan guarantees and other military support. He's nervous about handing them over, but he will do it. This should form the foundation for further active measures against the presidency and against the government generally."

"Nervous?"

"Yes. Understandably. But don't worry. It will be fine."

She tried to purr in the best way she knew how, although if she was deep-down honest, it particularly went against the grain to do so with men like Ivanov, whom she disliked. To her, he represented all that was worst about the Kremlin.

There was a grunt of approval at the other end of the secure line to Moscow. "The president will be happy to see that."

Shevchenko could almost hear the brain cogs whirring as Ivanov calculated exactly how to claim the credit with the president for her coup. It was the sound of self-aggrandizement and treachery.

"The sooner we get those documents, the better," Ivanov said. "You obviously have levers to pull with this asset, TITANIUM."

"You could say that. Blackmail, greed, hubris. Then there's his mistress, his bank account, and his career. I could go on."

"And you think TITANIUM will be our route to influence McAllister as the election draws near?"

"Of course," Shevchenko said. "We're currently serving up

ammunition on a plate for McAllister. All he has to do is keep firing it at the president. He's doing it rather well too. He already feels indebted to us because of our social media offensive, from what I can gather. We just need to take our opportunities to compromise him and his family when we can over the coming year or so. I will manipulate TITANIUM to make sure he generates those opportunities."

"I would like to see an occasional business visit to the McAllister team from one or two of our oligarchs, that kind of thing," Ivanov said.

"I agree. Business-related visits only," Shevchenko said. "Nothing official, nothing from our government, and definitely not the president. We need to be subtle."

There was a brief rasping sound at the other end of the line. Was that Ivanov chuckling?

"Classic *kompromat*," Ivanov said. "Slowly draw him in, make the relationship gradually more conspiratorial. Almost without him realizing."

Much as Shevchenko disliked Ivanov, his thinking was spot-on. "If they don't inform the FBI," she said, "that's a green light to continue and take the relationship deeper."

"And they obviously haven't so far."

"No, although we've given them little reason to so far, to be fair. That will change quite soon, I feel."

"Good," said Ivanov. "All you have to do now is slowly reel them all in. Just make sure you don't screw up."

Bozhe, he's so patronizing. "I will try not to, sir."

"There may be a benefit for you from this, and sooner than you think," Ivanov said.

Shevchenko furrowed her brow. "What do you mean?"

"Have you heard about the latest development at Yasenevo?" Ivanov asked.

Now she felt even more confused. What had occurred

that she had not been notified about? Was this idiot playing games with her? Knowledge was power.

"I have been a little out of touch here," she said. "I have been keeping communications with Yasenevo to a minimum."

"Of course. You couldn't be expected to know. Yevgeny Kutsik is changing roles. He is moving to run Directorate PR and to be Kruglov's official deputy. That, of course, leaves a vacancy at the head of counterintelligence, and Kruglov asked me if I had an opinion. I told him that I thought you would fit that role very well, and he agrees. I think you will be hearing more from him very soon about this. It depends, of course, on you not making any slipups there in Washington, given what happened in London."

Shevchenko found herself taken aback. She had not heard that Kutsik was moving roles. If true, however, heading counterintelligence would be her ideal next move at Yasenevo and would give her a big push toward her ultimate career objective: Kruglov's office. She had assumed the debacle in London had torpedoed that opportunity.

"Thank you, it is the first I have heard of all this. I would be honored to be offered that role. I think the relationship with TITANIUM is at such a stage that someone else could take it over if I needed to move on. I have done the groundwork."

"Yes, I am sure that someone from the embassy could run him, or even better, we can put an illegal in place. By the way, you are not hearing about the counterintelligence role from me. Wait until Kruglov tells you officially. Do not mention it to anyone. It is not confirmed. Understood?"

"I understand. Thank you."

"Oh, just one other thing. And believe me, I am trying to help you here, not interfere. I think you would be well advised to end your relationship, your affair, with Severinov. That is my advice."

The Black Bishop ended the call.

Shevchenko continued to gaze out the window for a few moments. She felt slightly stunned by what Ivanov had just told her, both about the counterintelligence role and about Severinov. She also felt deeply irritated by his patronizing tone.

The Directorate PR chief's job was presumably almost a done deal, otherwise he certainly would not have mentioned it in that manner, even with the added caveat about not making further mistakes.

She therefore needed to make doubly sure that everything went to plan here with TITANIUM.

And then there was the comment about Severinov. Her first reaction had been surprise that Ivanov knew they were a couple. But that was a stupid thought; he knew everything. True, Severinov certainly wasn't in favor at the Kremlin these days, but she hadn't known it to be quite so bad. Perhaps Ivanov was trying to give her a heads-up on which way the wind was blowing for Severinov.

The fact was that her feelings for him had never been that strong in the first place. It had been more to do with power and money than a full-on love affair. She didn't see him very often—a bit like her semidetached husband—and when they did meet, he was always too distracted by his business and the machinations of the Kremlin to be interested in her needs. Maybe Ivanov was trying to do her a favor.

Shevchenko put down her secure phone and removed her burner from her handbag. She inserted the battery and SIM card and quickly tapped out a message.

Site BLUE tomorrow 7.30pm.

She sent it to TITANIUM's number. That timing seemed about right to her. The meeting site she had decided upon closed at eight in the evening, when there would likely be wardens or security guards about to make sure that visitors left. But any earlier than seven and the volume of visitors would almost certainly be higher, even on a Thursday evening. The weather forecast was clear, so that was not an issue.

Shevchenko had already completed the preparations required, including acquiring a vehicle and purchasing a pair of long-handled bolt cutters from a hardware store.

She mulled over whether to bring in a countersurveillance team from the Russian embassy to provide cover for her meeting but decided against it—she would carry out this one solo. They were like bulls in a china shop anyway and more likely to give her away than protect her, with their accidental radio squelch breaks and grunts in the bushes. Definitely not the best team she had worked with.

A minute later she received a one-word reply from TITA-NIUM. *OK.*

That was it, then. TITANIUM was in up to his neck now. There was no escaping. She hoped that before too long, Nicholas McAllister would be similarly entrapped.

* * *

Wednesday, July 30, 2014
    Fort Meade, Maryland

The NSA moved quickly. Less than an hour after Seb had logged Shevchenko's cell phone number into their system, an aide came running into the operations conference room where Seb and Anna had taken Vic, Johnson, and Jayne for coffee.

The aide, a young man wearing a pair of tracksuit bottoms

and a New York City Marathon finisher's T-shirt, held up an iPad for Seb to see.

"We picked up this a few minutes ago from the number you gave us," he said. "The phone was online for a couple minutes, then went off again. It's a text message."

Johnson moved behind Seb so he could see the iPad.

The message read: *Site BLUE tomorrow 7.30pm.*

Below it was a short response. *OK.*

"We captured the corresponding cell number of the person who sent the reply," the aide said, pointing to a number at the bottom of the screen. "Like the first number, that also appears to be a prepaid SIM card. A burner. We can't find a registered user."

"Did you pin down a location?" Seb asked.

"They weren't online long enough."

Johnson glanced at Vic. "Site BLUE. What the hell. Where is that? Perhaps one of the three sites we got from Ed, but which? Or could it be somewhere else?"

Vic shrugged. "Good question. Last time I checked with Dover and Iain Shepard, they had the three under surveillance but had picked up nothing from any of them. Maybe it is somewhere else."

Johnson could feel his levels of stress rising. They simply could not afford to get this wrong. He still had no confirmation of exactly where his kids had been taken, and he needed to get Shevchenko in a situation where he could extract the information from her.

Once again, he had the feeling that things were running well out of control.

"We'd better get down to see Shepard and Dover," Johnson said. "We'll need a watertight plan to monitor all of those sites."

* * *

Wednesday, July 30, 2014
  Washington, DC

The array of large-scale maps and high-resolution satellite
photographs spread out across the chipped meeting room
table were in three groups, one for each of the sites
pinpointed by the intelligence received from Ed Grewall in
Moscow: Mount Olivet Cemetery, the National Arboretum,
and Glenwood Cemetery.

Johnson glanced around the room, the same somewhat
timeworn place within the FBI's J. Edgar Hoover Building
where they had met Dover and Shepard a few days earlier.

Apart from himself, Jayne, Vic, Shepard, and Dover, three
counterintelligence surveillance team leaders also sat around
the table.

All three locations had been put under surveillance two
days ago, following the information passed on by Grewall, but
nothing significant had been seen. In the absence of any positive indication of which was site BLUE, it was agreed that
the three locations would be monitored equally.

Shepard had called the meeting to devise a firm plan for
each of the three sites.

Two of them, the National Arboretum and Mount Olivet
Cemetery, were adjacent to each other, separated only by the
busy Bladensburg Road, a three-lane divided highway that ran
through northeast Washington. The other, Glenwood Cemetery, was a mile and a half away to the west, near the
McMillan Reservoir.

Shepard's plan was to have two surveillance trucks in
place, both disguised as construction workers' vehicles, one
covering Mount Olivet and the Arboretum, the other Glenwood. These would act as control units for the surveillance
officers being deployed and also for the four surveillance

drones equipped with cameras that he planned to use. Other FBI officers, including special agents with arrest authority, would be placed in nearby streets along with a few Metropolitan Police Department officers.

It was going to be a difficult operation, Johnson could see. Attempting to put in place a surveillance operation without it being obvious to anyone with Shevchenko's street skills and antennae for trouble was a serious challenge.

"If site BLUE is actually not any of these places, then we'll have to hope Shevchenko or our mole will switch on their phone so we can triangulate them," Shepard said.

Out of the corner of his eye, Johnson caught sight of both Dover and Vic simultaneously shaking their heads.

They were right to be concerned. The chances of getting a successful triangulation that was precise and quick enough to catch an intelligence officer of Shevchenko's expertise was exceedingly slim.

It was still not known what identity Shevchenko was using, other than it wasn't her true name. There was no record of her entering the United States. The Department of Homeland Security had now sent investigators scurrying to all corners of the organization in a desperate search for details of the fake passport she must be carrying, but so far to no avail.

"I'm guessing her appearance is completely different," Johnson said. "New name, new look. She's a mistress of her dark art, that's for sure—as we know well."

"At least when we do catch her she won't have diplomatic immunity this time, unlike in London," Jayne said.

While the others started finalizing details, Johnson took Vic to one side. "Are you going to be able to get me a weapon? I don't have one, but I have a gut feeling it may come in useful. Beretta ideally. Maybe for Jayne too. She likes the—"

"Walther PPS," Vic said, with a slight grin.

"Good memory."

"I should be able to get them," Vic said as they rejoined the group. "Leave it with me."

Johnson tugged at the old wound at the top of his right ear. The injury had occurred while saving Vic's life when the two of them were targeted by a KGB sniper while on a cross-border trip from Pakistan to Jalalabad in neighboring Afghanistan in 1988. He had pushed Vic into the safety of a doorway as the gunman opened fire, but a round had clipped the top of Johnson's right ear, leaving a small nick, a scar for life.

He scanned the room. There seemed to be a lot of people involved in the scheduled operation against Shevchenko, although they would be spread across multiple sites.

"I'm assuming all of the people on your list know what they're doing in this type of situation?" Johnson asked Shepard. "There's no doubt Shevchenko will immediately abort if there's even the slightest hint of anything unusual in the air, a vibe that she doesn't like. She's probably going to have a CS team there as well."

Given his kids' lives were on the line, Johnson was concerned that if Shevchenko had countersurveillance people in the vicinity, also looking out for coverage, the chances of them noticing the FBI team and calling off Shevchenko's meeting with the mole increased.

"They're all quality operators. The best," Shepard said. "Don't worry. They'll all be invisible until the rendezvous is underway. The last thing I want to do is cause her to abort. We'll get photos with the drones, then we go in. Too late for her to stop at that stage."

Behind him, Dover was nodding.

CHAPTER THIRTY-THREE

Thursday, July 31, 2014
   Tyance, Russia

Carrie thought that her heart was going to burst through her chest, it was pumping so hard and so loud. She turned over so her brother and aunt couldn't see her face and cried hard, silent tears for the third time that day. Surely this had to end. Where were these men taking them to?

After the second day on the boat, the Russians who were guarding them had brought thin rubber mats of the type that Carrie had used in the gym at school and laid them on the cabin floor. They had then allowed her, Peter, and Amy to lie down to sleep rather than force them to do so sitting on the hard bench.

But their hands and ankles had remained tied with plastic fasteners of the type her dad used to keep his electric cables together. They only cut the ties to allow them to eat or use the toilet, and then replaced them with new ones after they had finished. They still weren't allowed to talk to each other.

Most of the time, and always when their wrist or ankle ties were off, one of the men sat in the cabin with a gun in hand, reading a book or listening to music through earphones, and often smoking. Usually it was the man with the scar on his cheek and the receding blond hair.

The chances of escaping were zero. All they could do was survive, and Carrie tried to do that by thinking of nothing at all, by blanking her mind. It worked for a while, but before too long the fearful thoughts returned.

Both Amy and Peter looked awful. Their hair looked greasy and messy, their skin slightly gray, and their eyes unfocused and full of anxiety. Carrie knew that she must look equally haggard.

One thing Carrie was sure of was that they had gone a very long way. Her best guess was that they had been on the boat for four nights, although she felt so disoriented she couldn't be completely sure. Most of the time, the boat moved smoothly, but sometimes when she could hear the wind whistling outside, it bumped up and down and rolled as the sea became choppier. Occasionally she heard prolonged deep-throated honks from ships' horns in the distance.

At least after the second day she had managed to keep some food down as her body gradually got used to the movement of the boat.

She lay on her side for some time. After an hour or so, she got the sense that the boat had slowed, if not stopped. There was a slight bump as it hit something, followed by another. Then came the sound of shouting from somewhere outside.

The man with the scarred face, who was sitting with his gun, jumped up and disappeared up the stairs and out of the cabin.

Carrie sat up and looked at Peter and Amy, both of whom had also sat up on their floor mats. She still didn't dare speak, so instead she shrugged.

A few minutes later, the man with the gun reappeared, picked up a pair of scissors, and cut their ankle ties, though not the ones binding their wrists in front of them.

"Out, move," he said in heavily accented English. "Go up the steps." He stood pointing the gun at them and jerked his head in the direction of the exit, indicating to them to go.

After pausing for a second, Amy led the way, and Carrie and Peter followed behind her. Carrie struggled to walk in a straight line, her sense of balance disturbed.

The door emerged into a smart, modern cabin with a bar and fully equipped kitchen at one end and luxury padded sofa-style seats and a dining table with a champagne bucket on top at the other.

"Keep going. Out on the deck," the man with the gun behind them ordered.

They continued through the dining area and out through a wide door at the rear onto the open deck of the yacht. The glare of the sun hurt Carrie's eyes after so long in the gloomy cabin belowdecks. This was a large modern luxury boat, similar to those she had often seen in the marinas around Portland Harbor back home and more recently in Cannes. There was a hot tub at the rear and also an inflatable dinghy with an outboard motor.

But then she glanced up and saw the scene beyond.

This was no fancy marina. Rather, it looked as though the yacht had been tied to a jetty in a harbor on the edge of an industrial area. There were massive circular oil tanks of the type she had seen at the Turners Island oil terminal, off the Fore River in Portland.

A narrow river ran into the harbor, and crossing it was a rusty iron railway bridge and a road bridge. Warehouses with corrugated iron roofs stood on the jetty, and beyond were more jetties with large commercial ships moored next to them. Several large cranes were being used to load the ships.

A tangle of large gray pipelines ran along the jetty and up the left-hand side of the river toward more white circular oil tanks that were visible in the distance.

There was a large rusty sign on the side of one of the warehouses, written in a language that Carrie assumed was Russian. It was definitely written in the Cyrillic alphabet; she knew that much.

This must be Russia.

My God.

The man with the gun indicated to them to walk along a gangplank onto the jetty, where a black Mercedes 4x4 stood, its doors open.

Peter turned around to look at Carrie. The look in his eyes made her instantly burst into tears.

* * *

Thursday, July 31, 2014
    Washington, DC

At precisely twenty minutes past seven, Anastasia Shevchenko made her final check up and down Channing Street NE, ensuring that she was unobserved. Then she patted the SIG Sauer P365 9mm pistol in her pocket and climbed out of the maroon Toyota sedan she had recently bought for cash in the Congress Heights neighborhood.

She opened the rear door of the car, which she had parked beneath a tree, and removed a bunch of flowers. On the floor, beneath the seat, was the pair of bolt cutters that she had used late the previous evening when preparing for this meeting. Then she locked the vehicle with the remote fob.

From there, Shevchenko consciously hunched her back and walked for a few meters until she came to an alleyway no wider than a car, paved with red bricks. If anyone had happened to look at her, they would have seen a white-haired lady wearing a broad-brimmed straw hat and sunglasses, shuffling along.

She turned into the alleyway and followed it northward between two houses. There were garages behind the houses, and she also passed the slightly run-down backyards of more houses that faced the main street, North Capitol Street NE, that ran parallel to the alley on her left side.

On her right was a long brick wall topped with spiked metal railings. It was too high to climb over, but behind it was her destination: Glenwood Cemetery.

A woman on a bicycle rode along the alley toward her carrying groceries in a wicker basket on the handlebars. Shevchenko stiffened a little until the woman had passed. From one of the backyards came the sound of some kids playing. A dog barked loudly.

She straightened her sunglasses, then made her way toward an old wrought-iron double gate that stood in a gap in the wall. The gate was padlocked shut with a rusty metal chain and clearly had not been used for many years.

Shevchenko glanced in both directions along the alleyway. There was nobody in sight, no sign of trailing coverage.

She had visited the site the previous day, but there had been too many people around, although she was certain none of them had been surveillance. So, she had returned after midnight, when it had appeared clear, and made a few preparations to facilitate her plan. They included using her newly acquired bolt cutters to slice through the chain on the gate. She had then carefully put the chain back in position, ensuring that the link she had cut was not visible to passersby.

All she had to do now was move the chain and padlock, slip her hand through the iron bars, pull back a bolt, and slide the gate open so she could pass through. She closed it again behind her, replacing the padlock and chain.

Shevchenko could have used the main entrance to the cemetery on the far side of the site, about five hundred meters away on Lincoln Road NE. But after careful research, she had decided this was a far better option, in her view.

She knew that TITANIUM would come through the main entrance, and she had choreographed the meeting in her mind so that it would be a chance and very brief encounter. Both parties would converge from different directions at the place within the cemetery that she had specified.

Just ahead of her, behind some ivy-clad trees, was a gray tarmac road, no more than the width of a car, that curved around to the left. The road wound its way all over the site, allowing cemetery staff and mourners access to the graves. She made her way onto the road and, her senses now in overdrive, walked past a line of tombstones dotted among the trees. The only sounds came from the constant background hum of the busy traffic on North Capitol Street NE and some kids yelling at each other in the alleyway.

Shevchenko glanced at her watch and took the opportunity to simultaneously check around her, as if pausing for breath. It was twenty-eight minutes past seven. She continued walking but at a slightly slower pace. The timing had to be just right.

Fifty meters ahead of her up the hill on the left side of the road, beneath a cluster of trees, she could see the meeting place: a row of six ancient mausoleums. Four of them were built from red brick, two from stone, like miniature houses set into the grassy bank behind them, each with their own padlocked front door.

She continued toward them. And then she saw TITANIUM, ambling slowly in her direction down the hill, an upright figure in a brown wool ivy cap and sunglasses, wearing a blue shirt and jacket, his top button undone and, she was thankful to see, his tie removed. That would have been too much. He was alone; there was no sign of anyone else in the area.

Shevchenko continued at a similar pace and, as they converged, she saw him slip his hand into his jacket pocket and remove something that she knew would be a flash drive.

They drew level.

"Good to see you made it on time. All clear?" she asked.

"Yes, all clear. Here you go."

He passed her a tiny flat black drive that she assumed contained copies of the documents.

As she took it, Shevchenko became aware of a buzzing noise above her, quite distinct from the background traffic hum.

She looked up, and then she saw it.

A black drone was hovering above them, stationary between two trees and clearly visible against the clear sky behind it. It was perhaps twenty meters high, maybe more. She felt as though she had received an electric shock.

"*Dermo*. Shit," she muttered. "It's a drone. Go. Leave. Back the way you came. Now. I will be in touch."

TITANIUM followed her glance and did a slight double take. "Oh my God," he muttered. Without a further word, he turned on his heel and strode back the way he had come.

She looked up again, and the drone was still there. It was no child's toy—she knew a surveillance drone when she saw one. This was a large device with eight rotors and a camera slung beneath.

What the hell? This meeting was as secure and tight as she could have possibly made it. Someone, somewhere, had leaked it. It momentarily crossed her mind that TITANIUM had somehow betrayed her, but then she dismissed the thought. He couldn't have—it would be a suicidal move. He was in too deep.

Acting on instinct, she removed the SIG Sauer from her pocket, flicked off the safety, took aim, and fired two successive shots at the drone. The first missed, but the second smashed straight into the body of the device, scattering black fragments in the air. The machine twisted sideways, then fell like a wounded bird onto the grass between the trees.

For a second, Shevchenko considered going and grabbing it, but she abandoned that idea. Instead she turned and sprinted back the way she had come. When she reached the gate, she yanked it open and ran out into the street.

CHAPTER THIRTY-FOUR

Thursday, July 31, 2014
Washington, DC

The tall, erect figure ambling down the hill, wearing a brown wool cap and sunglasses, looked vaguely familiar to Johnson. He and Vic, together with two FBI counterintelligence officers, were poring over a monitor that showed a video feed coming from a drone hovering over Glenwood Cemetery.

But it was Vic who beat him to it. He jumped off his stool in the back of the FBI surveillance van and pointed at the monitor screen. "That's Wade! Can you see? It's goddamn Francis Wade."

"Can't be," Johnson said. He peered at the screen for a few seconds, watching the man walk toward a row of elegant old brick and stone-built mausoleums. The more he looked, the more the man in the wool cap and open-neck shirt did indeed look like the national security advisor.

"Do you really think—" Johnson began.

"He *is*."

Vic turned to the dark-suited FBI counterintelligence team leader who was in charge of the van. "Can you tell Shepard it's Wade?"

But the officer, one of the three who had been in the planning meeting at the J. Edgar Hoover Building the previous day, was already pushing the call button on his radio.

A second later, Johnson spotted the person he was now certain would also be in the cemetery: Anastasia Shevchenko. The feed from a camera transmitting from the drone showed a stooped woman in a straw hat walking with a slight limp and converging on Wade from the opposite direction. It wasn't possible to see her face because of the broad-brimmed hat, but Johnson knew it was her.

"And tell him that's Shevchenko," Johnson said. The officer nodded as he began feeding the news into the radio mouthpiece, followed by a stream of instructions to his colleagues.

Johnson, Vic, and Jayne had elected to join the FBI surveillance van team based outside Glenwood Cemetery, which Shepard and Dover thought would be the least likely of the three sites to be the rendezvous point for Shevchenko and her mole.

Shepard was in the other surveillance van, a mile and a half away near Mount Olivet Cemetery and the National Arboretum, while Dover was in a car on the other side of Glenwood so he could quickly move to any of the locations if required.

The two FBI chiefs had taken the view that Mount Olivet and the Arboretum were the likely options because road access was better and faster and there were more potential exit and escape routes. However, after studying the maps and satellite photographs, Johnson had not been convinced.

Now Johnson stayed glued to the monitor as the two figures on the cemetery path reached the mausoleums at the same time. He saw Wade, assuming it was him, pass something to her, which she took, and then almost in the same second she looked upward, straight at the camera.

"Shit, she's seen the drone," Johnson said. "Probably heard it."

Shevchenko appeared to say something to Wade, who immediately turned around and walked back up the hill, away from her. She glanced up at the drone again, then took something from her pocket.

"It's a bloody *gun*." Jayne's voice rose sharply as she spoke, standing next to Johnson in the van.

Shevchenko raised her arm, and a couple of seconds later, the screen went black.

"She's hit the goddamn drone," Johnson said, reflexively feeling his waistband for the Beretta that Vic had given him. "Now how do we track her?" The plan had been to use the drone for that purpose, if necessary.

"We'll have to get after her on foot," Jayne said. She turned to the FBI surveillance officer. "What routes are there out of the cemetery? Gates? Holes in the fence? Where would she go?"

"Only the main entrance, and we've got that closed down now," the officer said. "Other than that, over the iron railings. They run right round the site."

"Nothing else?" Johnson asked.

"Just a padlocked gate in the railings on this side of the site. It's only about a hundred yards from here, along the alley, at the end of Douglas Street. She won't get over that."

The van was parked in Evarts Street NE, on the opposite side of the cemetery to the main gate, near its northwest boundary. Next to the van there was an alley, which Johnson knew ran parallel to North Capitol Street on one side and the cemetery on the other.

"A gate?" Johnson queried. That had not been mentioned

in the planning meeting. "Who have you got on this side of the cemetery?"

"There's two men, one at either end of North Capitol. Out there." He waved his arm toward the street. "They'll close her off immediately if she comes this way, which I doubt. The railings and the gate are both too high."

Johnson tried to calculate their options. The team leader might be correct, and his men probably did have all exit routes closed off. And maybe the railings and gate were too high. But he was also certain that someone as professional as Shevchenko would have worked out escape options other than the main gate if the worst happened.

He looked at Vic. "Should I go out and see if I can spot her coming this way? I don't want her somehow splitting the two men you've got on North Capitol."

"Yes," Vic said. "Good idea. I'll wait here."

The team leader also nodded. "Fine. Go ahead."

"I'll come," Jayne said.

Johnson nodded. "Let's go. We'll aim for the gate first."

He opened the rear door of the van and jumped down onto the ground, followed by Jayne. They both ran down the alley, past a row of backyards, in the direction of the gate.

As they reached a bend in the alley, the cemetery came into view ahead of them, with its boundary wall and iron railings.

As Johnson rounded the bend, he caught a glimpse of someone emerging from the cemetery and running down Douglas Street NE, perhaps sixty or seventy yards away, toward North Capitol Street. All he could tell was that it was a woman with white hair.

"That's got to be her," Johnson muttered. He broke into a full sprint along the alley, losing sight of the woman who had run out of his line of view.

As Johnson ran, to his left, from the direction of the cemetery, he heard the distinct sound of a gunshot.

What was that? But there was no time to find out now.

By the time Johnson reached Douglas Street NE, Shevchenko was nowhere to be seen. To his left, a rusty wrought-iron gate into the cemetery hung open.

"There," Jayne said, pointing across the other side of North Capitol Street, a busy three-lane divided highway.

Johnson looked just in time to see the woman scrambling through what appeared to be a vertical slit in a chain-link fence. There was now no doubt: nobody but Shevchenko would have run in such desperate fashion. She must have taken her life in her hands dodging the heavy traffic to cross the street.

Where the hell were the two FBI agents?

Like a magician onstage, Shevchenko vanished from view into clumps of bushes and greenery.

Johnson didn't hesitate. He ran the short distance to the end of Douglas Street and looked for a gap in the traffic on North Capitol. He decided to take a risk and, with the nearest car approaching, ran out with his hand held up in a clear signal to stop. It worked. The car braked hard, as did another slightly farther back in the neighboring lane, and he and Jayne made it to the other side.

The black chain-link fence that bordered the sidewalk had been cut from the bottom up with a pair of bolt cutters or other similar tool, right behind a small tree so the damage was less visible to passersby. The cut, about four feet high, allowed the metal fence to be pushed back like a curtain so a person could get through.

Johnson, mindful that Shevchenko had a pistol, took the Beretta from his waist, flicked off the safety, and scrambled through the hole in the fence, Jayne right behind him.

Ahead of him, Johnson briefly heard the rustling and

crashing of Shevchenko pushing through the bushes, followed by the sound of running footsteps.

The Russian had obviously planned this escape route carefully.

Johnson held his Beretta ready as he fought his way through the bushes and emerged onto a long, narrow area paved with old broken concrete that stretched a couple of hundred yards to the other side of the otherwise grassy site. Sticking up at intervals from the paved section was a row of thirty-foot-high cylindrical gray concrete towers.

Johnson knew from his study of the satellite photographs and map that this was the disused McMillan Sand Filtration Site—a decommissioned water treatment plant dating back to the early 1900s and now awaiting redevelopment.

Where was Shevchenko? He heard her footsteps ahead, then caught a glimpse of her as she ran with surprising speed around the second of the towers before dodging behind the concrete structure, once again out of his line of vision.

"She's there," Johnson called to Jayne, who emerged from the bushes behind him. "You go to the left of the towers; I'll go down the right."

He took off past the first of what he could now see was a row of ten towers ahead of him. The concrete surface was rough and broken, with weeds protruding from wide cracks, and he had to be careful not to trip.

Come on, catch her.

Flashing images of his children crossed his mind as he ran.

As Johnson approached the second tower, he caught his toe on a protruding piece of pavement and only just managed to avoid tumbling headfirst. As he recovered his balance, there came the unmistakable crack of a gunshot ahead of him, followed immediately by another shot and the whine of a ricochet as a bullet glanced off the tower no more than a yard to his left, sending slivers of concrete flying into the air.

Johnson felt something hit him on the top of his head.

"Shit," he muttered as he threw himself to the ground. Looking up, he saw Shevchenko emerge from behind what looked like a derelict red brick control house and sprint around the fourth tower, fifty yards ahead. Johnson raised his gun in front of him and fired, but he had no time to steady himself and take proper aim. The shot went wide as Shevchenko disappeared from view again.

He hauled himself to his feet and put his hand to his head. It felt wet and, when he lowered his hand, it was smeared with blood.

But he ignored it and ran forward again.

To his left, he saw Jayne running parallel to him on the other side of the towers, holding her gun in front of her. In his peripheral vision, he saw her drop to one knee, raise her gun, and fire a couple of rounds in succession. She swore loudly, jumped up, and continued running again.

It was obvious that the best chance they had of hitting Shevchenko was as she broke cover to run around each of the towers. But it was easier said than done. The fifty-yard lead that the Russian had, coupled with the uneven surface, made it extremely hard to shoot accurately on the run. Johnson knew he could stop to fire, like Jayne had just tried to do, but that could cost him another fifteen yards each time he failed to hit his target.

Perhaps his best bet was to gamble on outrunning her before she exited the site on the other side. But God, she was in better shape than he would have given her credit for.

Johnson ran hard past the fourth tower, firing yet again on the run as he saw Shevchenko duck around the sixth. Again he missed and she disappeared from view.

Dammit.

To his left, Johnson heard Jayne loose a round, followed by a couple of curses. This was ridiculous.

He kept going, and again Shevchenko appeared on his side, still running hard as she rounded the next tower. Johnson again raised his Beretta and, finding himself on a piece of flatter ground, took better aim and fired three shots in rapid succession.

The first round missed badly, but his second and third whined into the area around Shevchenko's ankles or feet. The Russian stumbled, tripped, and fell headfirst, landing flat on her front.

Got the bitch.

"She's down," Johnson yelled, hoping Jayne would hear.

Johnson charged toward Shevchenko as she tried to haul herself upright.

As he drew nearer, Johnson could see that Shevchenko was no longer holding her gun. She got to her hands and knees, desperately scanning the ground among a clump of weeds to her right, trying to spot it.

Shevchenko launched herself sideways from her position on all fours toward what Johnson assumed was her pistol somewhere in the weeds.

"Hands up! Hold it!" Johnson screamed as he drew close. She was now a sitting duck, and if he wanted he could blow her away, but he instinctively held back from doing that.

"Don't move!" Johnson yelled, even louder. Now he was near enough for her to know her game was up. She slumped to the ground, giving up on her battle to get to the pistol, which Johnson could see was still a good ten feet away from her. It must have skittered across the concrete when she fell over.

Johnson came to a halt, his Beretta trained on Shevchenko, just as Jayne arrived, also with her pistol in firing position. He could feel blood trickling down his forehead and into his eyebrows.

"*Bljad,*" Shevchenko muttered.

"Lie down and turn over on your front," Johnson ordered. "Arms stretched out." He could see that her ankles and feet were uninjured; the rounds he had fired must have hit the ground near her, not her limbs.

"*Poshël ty*," she shouted.

Johnson took a step toward her.

"I said lie down on your front," he yelled, pointing the gun rock-steady straight at her. Now his adrenaline was flowing like a river.

The Russian just stared at him for several seconds, her eyes blazing with fury.

Johnson lost patience. Moving his aim slightly to Shevchenko's right, he pulled the trigger, and the round smashed into the rough concrete no more than a foot from her midriff, sending dust, cement fragments, and dirt splattering all over her and making a large hole in the ground.

She jumped like a rabbit; then, slowly, realizing her game was up, she turned over on her stomach and spread her arms out to either side in surrender.

"Do you want to search her?" Johnson asked Jayne. "She might have a backup gun."

Jayne sat astride Shevchenko's lower back so she couldn't move, and searched her thoroughly.

Eventually, she found a small zipped pocket that had been sewn into the waistband of Shevchenko's slacks and undid it.

"Here you go," Jayne said, turning toward Johnson.

She held up a small flash drive.

* * *

Thursday, July 31, 2014
Washington, DC

. . .

The walk back up the narrow cemetery road toward the main gate, in reality little more than four hundred yards, seemed more like four hundred miles to Francis Wade.

As soon as he had seen the surveillance drone and realized the Russian, Tatiana, was visibly spooked by its appearance, a dark cloud had descended over him as surely as if someone had flicked a switch in his brain. The adrenaline rush that had lifted his spirits as the time of the meeting approached vanished. This was bad news.

A black-and-white movie of possible consequences began to play out in his head as he walked. Discovery would mean everything unraveling like a ball of wool: his treachery at work, his betrayal of his country and his boss, his stupid long-time affair, and the disloyalty to his wife.

He saw the recriminations that would quickly come, the shame, the interrogation, the media coverage, and almost certainly the long prison sentence to follow.

It was too much.

As he continued along the curved road past the cemetery's red brick chapel in the center of a small traffic island, he stopped and looked carefully ahead of him. The late evening sunshine was casting long shadows from the tombstones across the freshly mown grass.

He could see nobody, so he continued toward the exit, now a couple of hundred yards away and partially concealed by a cluster of trees that grew on both sides of the road.

But then, as he emerged from the trees, his line of vision cleared. In the shadows near the main gate, behind a ring of white statues of angels that stood on a large traffic circle, he saw two black cars that hadn't been there when he had entered the site.

Next to one of the cars were two men in dark suits wearing sunglasses. One was speaking into a handset, and the other, standing alert with legs apart, had a gun in his hand.

Wade decided there and then what he would do.

He stepped off the road, walked calmly to the nearest tombstone—this one was fashioned from dark granite, with a rounded top—and sat down next to it.

What better place could there be?

Then he removed a small Heckler & Koch handgun from his pocket, clicked off the safety, put the barrel in his mouth, and pulled the trigger.

* * *

Thursday, July 31, 2014
Washington, DC

Shevchenko's jaw was aching and badly bruised from where she had banged it on the ground when she fell, and it felt as though she had also pulled a hamstring in the process. Certainly the back of her thigh was hurting.

Bozhe. God. *What a mess.*

The meeting with TITANIUM had only been intended to last a few seconds. How the hell had she gotten it so wrong? How had she screwed it up so spectacularly?

There had been absolutely no sign of surveillance on her way into the cemetery. Nothing, in fact, until that drone had appeared out of nowhere. How had they found her?

And how had this guy Johnson, who was no more than a private investigator yet was now pointing his damned pistol in her face, somehow gotten the better of her?

It defied all logic.

Who on earth had leaked it? The thought swirled around in her head as she lay chest down on the rough concrete ground. There was a traitor of massive and audacious proportions operating somewhere in the small circle of SVR people who were in the know about TITANIUM.

And she knew that a second failure of this magnitude inside a few months would wipe from the slate every trace of her previous long line of successful operations against Russia's main enemy. She was done for.

The gulags of the Stalinist era might have disappeared, but she knew she could face a spell in the modern equivalent —one of the horrific penal colonies like the institution in Karelia, in northwest Russia. She knew men who had emerged from there broken and beaten, with unspeakable stories of being tortured and raped to the sounds of Lyube and Putin's other favorite rock bands.

Or she might face the classic Russian solution—*vysshaya mera nakazaniya*, VMN, or the supreme degree of punishment. It meant the same in any language: a bullet in the back of the head, despite Russia's official bar on the death penalty.

Even if the worst didn't happen, it was certainly the end of the promotion that had been right in her grasp. She'd never take over Kutsik's role as deputy director in charge of counterintelligence at Yasenevo now. Her career was dead.

In this game, you were only as good as the last operation.

Dermo, dermo, dermo.

From her prone position, with Johnson's pistol pointing at her head, she had no choice but to accept it when his British sidekick, Robinson, sat on her back and searched her.

Inevitably, Robinson found the flash drive, which Shevchenko should have thrown away but, in the panic to escape the cemetery, hadn't done so. That was unprofessional.

After Robinson finished her search, Shevchenko turned her head and glanced up at Johnson, who picked her gun out of the weeds and then began a conversation on his phone.

Now it was Robinson's turn to point a gun at her head

while Johnson talked. He was probably calling the FBI, who would doubtless come running with their handcuffs ready.

Blood was dripping down the side of Johnson's face from what looked like a deep cut on his head. A pity the damage hadn't been greater.

Shevchenko knew she had no diplomatic immunity this time, unlike the episode in London. They could prosecute her, but she doubted they would. The far more likely outcome was that she would be kicked unceremoniously out of the United States, which would maximize the publicity and use her as an example of all that was bad about Russia. Putin would despise her for it.

There had to be a way out of this. There must be.

Think, come on, think.

She racked her brain, trying to come up with a solution. And then it struck her—it was the obvious way out. A way she had been slightly tempted to go down before.

But now, unlike then, there was no downside and no true alternative—not anymore.

CHAPTER THIRTY-FIVE

Thursday, July 31, 2014
  Washington, DC

With Shevchenko now safely on the ground and Jayne's gun pointed at her, Johnson walked over to where the Russian's pistol was lying in some weeds. He picked it up, flicked on the safety, and put it in his pocket.

Blood was running freely down the side of his head from the cut, which he assumed had been caused by a flying fragment of concrete from where Shevchenko's bullet had ricocheted off the side of the tower.

Johnson then walked several yards away, out of Shevchenko's earshot, and called Vic. Very quickly, he told him where they were and what had happened.

"I want to get the questioning underway quickly," Johnson said. "We need to find out if she knows where Severinov has got my kids. That's top priority."

"Yes, I agree, Joe." Vic, who was still in the FBI surveillance van, informed Johnson that two FBI special agents were on their way and would be on the McMillan site imminently to deal with the Russian.

"There is something else," Vic said.

"What?"

"Francis Wade has shot himself in the cemetery. I've just heard from Dover. Blew his own head off with a handgun."

Johnson paused. "My God. He must have been in a very bad place."

"Awful," Vic said. "Listen, I've got Dover trying to call me. I'll speak to you in a minute." He ended the call.

Shevchenko remained flat on the ground with Jayne's Walther trained on her. As Johnson stepped back toward her, the Russian lifted her head.

"I want to make a suggestion, an offer," she said.

"An *offer*? Is that an offer to tell me where my kids are? To tell me where your damned boyfriend Severinov has put them? That's the only offer I'm interested in."

There was a pause. "We can discuss that," Shevchenko said. "There is something else I want to say first."

"I'm all ears," Johnson said. What the hell was coming now?

"I just want to tell you one thing," Shevchenko said. "If I get kicked out of the States, then Moscow will send me to the gulag or quite possibly somewhere worse than that."

"Good. It's what you deserve," Johnson said in a level tone. He was sorely tempted to kick her in the ribs.

"Maybe," Shevchenko said. "But if you keep this quiet, if you don't make this public, I'm prepared to work for you—for the CIA, for MI6—in Russia."

Johnson laughed out loud. "Work for us? You've got to be joking. You can't be serious?"

Jayne snorted. "Come off it," she said. "Do you really think we're going to buy that? Are you completely mad?"

There was silence for a few seconds, broken only by the sound of sirens getting gradually louder.

"No, I am not joking," Shevchenko said, her voice sounding strained and croaky. "I am deadly serious. If Yasenevo discovers this operation has gone wrong, I am finished."

"You mean you didn't have a countersurveillance team looking after you?" Johnson asked.

"No. I decided against that. I was working alone. And there is one important point here: I am about to be promoted to head of counterintelligence in the SVR, as deputy director. They like me. The director of the SVR likes me. I should be returning there soon to take that role. If the CIA and MI6 want me to work for them, in that position, I will do it."

"Bloody hell," Jayne said. She looked at Johnson, who shook his head.

"You're talking bullshit. You seriously expect us to believe that?" Johnson said, wagging his finger at Shevchenko. "You can put your goddamn offer . . ." But his voice trailed off.

He had been about to use more forceful language to tell Shevchenko she could put her offer somewhere quite personal. But something stopped him. Instead, he turned to Jayne. "I'm going to give Vic a quick call back. Just keep that gun on her."

Johnson stepped several yards out of Shevchenko's earshot and called Vic.

"Vic, I've just been propositioned by Shevchenko," he said quietly when the call was answered.

"What do you mean, propositioned?" Vic's voice sounded tense.

"Get this, right. She's saying she's about to be promoted to deputy director in charge of counterintelligence at Yasenevo. And she's offering to work for us, and for the Brits.

She knows she's a dead duck in Moscow if they find out she screwed this up."

"It's bullshit, Joe. Tell her to go jump in a lake. She'll be in handcuffs in a couple of minutes."

"That was my reaction. I told her exactly that."

"Tell her again."

Johnson glanced over his shoulder. Jayne still had her gun trained on Shevchenko, who remained prone on the ground.

"But what if it's not bullshit?" Johnson asked. "I want to question her about my kids before the feds get a hold of her. And if she's really considering flipping to us, I might be able to squeeze out of her what we need to know."

"Look, we can grill her about your kids, but recruiting her is a nonstarter," Vic said. "I'm heading over there now. One of the feds is giving me a lift to the McMillan entrance gate."

"You're always telling me you're desperately short of high-level sources inside the SVR."

"Yes, correct. But we do have SOYUZ now."

"On the American desk. A counterintelligence deputy director would be a different ball game altogether."

"For God's sake, Joe, what planet are you on?" Vic snapped. "No chance. I'll see you in a few minutes, okay?"

"Okay, fine."

Johnson knew better than to continue the conversation with Vic in that frame of mind. Maybe he was right, anyway. He ended the call, put his phone back in his pocket, and strode back toward Jayne.

He heard a screech of brakes from the direction of the main entrance to the water filtration site on First Street NW, about sixty yards ahead of him, and looked up to see two black cars pulling up next to the gate. Two men in dark suits got out of one of them and hurried toward the gate. That must be the feds, he figured.

As Johnson drew nearer to Jayne, his phone rang in his

pocket. He took it out to see it was Vic calling him back. Johnson jabbed at the green button.

"Joe, tell the feds to cuff Shevchenko but to hold off until I get there before doing anything else. I'll be just a couple of minutes, right? Shepard said he would call them himself, but I'm just telling you in case he doesn't get to them first."

"What do you mean?" Johnson asked.

"I've just had a quick think about Shevchenko. I want to talk to her about what she suggested to you. But whatever you do, don't tell those feds what she said."

* * *

Thursday, July 31, 2014
　　Washington, DC

When Johnson, his forehead freshly bandaged by an FBI nurse, and Jayne arrived outside the secure interview room on the fourth floor at the J. Edgar Hoover Building, he found Vic waiting in the corridor.

The room, adjacent to the meeting rooms in the counter-intelligence division offices they had used the previous day, was being guarded by two armed agents.

Vic took Johnson and Jayne a short distance down the corridor, out of earshot of the guards.

"Dover and Shepard have agreed to my suggestion," Vic said. "They get it. They're going to keep all this undocumented until we've had a chance to properly interview her. Then they'll decide how to play it."

"Good," Johnson said. "You can't trust that woman any further than her nose sticks out, but you're right to explore it."

Vic nodded. "I think so. Like she says, she's dead in the

water if we send her home in disgrace. But if she's really in line for a promotion to head up Directorate KR—which may be bullshit—and if she could funnel even a fraction of what crosses her desk to us, then I think it's worth checking out. We'll grill her on your kids first. That will give us some idea of whether she's being genuine or not; then we can go in hard with the other stuff."

"Good," Johnson said. He felt relieved that Vic was approaching the interrogation with his kids at the top of the agenda. Time was of the essence, and his friend was correct: if Shevchenko wasn't prepared to help them in tracking down his family, they could probably discount what she might offer on the intelligence front.

"There is one thing I was thinking, though," Johnson continued. "Recruiting her is going to require the mother of all cover-ups, especially in terms of Wade's death. I don't see how it is doable." He was already feeling quite uncomfortable about it.

"Yes. It's difficult. But actually it may be workable," Vic said. "We know Wade was depressed and had marriage difficulties. There were also no other witnesses at the cemetery, thankfully—no Russian countersurveillance. Leaving her CS team at home was a smart move, given what happened. Take Shevchenko out of the picture, and it could be seen as a very unfortunate case of suicide. I've just spoken to Veltman, and he also thinks it can be done. So does Dover. Veltman is broadly supportive, but we need to see what comes out of this meeting. Persuading the president might be a different matter."

The door behind him opened, and Dover emerged and walked over to them.

"Do you two want to come in?" Dover asked.

Vic nodded. "There will just be us?" he asked, keeping his voice low. "No other agents? I don't want anyone else to hear this. And turn your recording equipment off, Simon. I don't want any bugs running. We need a complete vow of silence over this until we're all agreed on where this heads."

Dover grimaced slightly. "Agreed, and the recording kit is already off, don't worry. But we need to get a move on. We haven't got long to resolve this."

"One other thing," Vic said. "We don't tell her immediately what happened to Wade. That can come later. We can use him as leverage."

Johnson shook his head. If nothing else, his old friend was certainly an opportunist as well as a strategist. That was probably why he'd succeeded in the cutthroat environment that was the CIA.

Dover nodded, then strode to the door and held it open for them.

Vic entered first, followed by Jayne. While he was following the others, Johnson surreptitiously started the voice recorder app on his phone and pushed it back into his pocket. Like Vic, he didn't want any official FBI record of the conversation that was about to occur, but he did want his own recording, just in case—particularly to ensure he had an accurate record of anything Shevchenko might say about Severinov and his kids.

In the center of the room, on a wooden chair next to a small interview table, sat Shevchenko. Her hands were handcuffed together, and dust and dirt still covered her dark-blue cotton shirt from when she had fallen at the McMillan site.

Dover sat next to Shepard on the opposite side of the table from Shevchenko and indicated wordlessly to three other chairs next to them. Johnson, Vic, and Jayne sat down.

"Right," Dover said, his eyes fixed on Shevchenko. "You have a proposal. Tell us about it."

Shevchenko leaned back in her seat. "Can you remove

these handcuffs first so I can talk without pain. They hurt like hell."

Dover took a key from his pocket, leaned over, and unlocked the cuffs, which he removed and pushed into his pocket. "Okay, talk."

Shevchenko repeated, more or less word for word, what she had said to Johnson earlier about the almost certain consequences she faced if she were sent back to Moscow in disgrace, then reiterated the offer she had made.

"If you want someone in high places in the SVR, I will do it," she said. "But you need to decide quickly. The longer I go without getting in touch with Yasenevo and informing them that today's operation was a success, the more likely they are to think I've been compromised. They will sever all contact. Then I'm done for, and you get no benefit either."

Vic gave a sardonic laugh. "I'm sure that's true. But we can't possibly trust you. You're just trying to save your own skin. You're a shameless careerist."

Johnson knew his friend was simply trying to provoke a reaction, so he followed his lead. "The useless shit you're likely to feed us and take our money for won't be worth the paper it's written on."

Shevchenko looked at him. "I will want payment, yes, of course. But if you want me to prove that I mean what I say, that I am making an offer in good faith, then I can give you several pieces of information right now that will be anything but 'useless shit,' as you call it."

"There is only one piece of information I'm interested in —at least to start with," Johnson said. "You talk about acting in good faith. If so, I would like the answer to a simple question."

It was time to put her to the test, based on the draft email shared between her and Severinov that the NSA had hacked into.

Shevchenko drummed the table with her fingers. "Try me."

"I want to know where my children and my sister are. Your man Severinov has taken them to Russia. But I don't need to tell you that, do I? I want to know exactly where."

Rightly or wrongly, Johnson took the slight nod of approval that Vic gave in his direction as a cue to go one step further.

"If you don't tell me, or if you lie to me, we'll put you all over the front page of *The Washington Post* and on CNN before we put you on a plane back to Moscow."

Shevchenko folded her arms. "All right. I'm not sure your CIA director would be in agreement about doing that, but anyway, I will tell you my thoughts. The truth is I don't know for sure."

"Bullshit. You must have some idea," Johnson said, his voice rising a couple of tones.

"My guess is that he will have taken them to his Krasnodar oil refinery in Tuapse. It belongs to Severinov's company. He might try and tell you they are somewhere else."

"Your *guess*? Why do you say that if you don't know?"

"It's the obvious place. It's his main business site on the Black Sea coast and accessible if he took your kids by boat from the Mediterranean, which I understand is what happened. I don't think he has other sites on the Black Sea, although I could be wrong about that."

Johnson scrutinized her. Was she telling the truth? His gut feeling was yes. She probably didn't know for sure, but what she was suggesting made sense, despite the long distance between Cannes and Tuapse. He didn't dare think about it for fear of welling up. That could come later.

"How can we confirm this?" Johnson asked.

Shevchenko shrugged again. "You can't, not without me

asking Severinov. And I have no need to know—none at all. So that might make him suspicious."

"Have you ever been to the refinery? Do you know anything about it?" Johnson asked.

"No, I have never been there. He only mentioned it a couple of times, so I know very little about it. He did say it was a huge site, bordering on the sea. That is all I know."

It crossed Johnson's mind that Severinov might try and seek some kind of support from Russian security services if an attempt was made to rescue his family.

"How are Severinov's relations with the Kremlin currently? And with your intelligence services?" Johnson asked.

Shevchenko shook her head. "He is under huge pressure. Things have gone wrong. A few years ago, he was the golden boy. Now that is no longer the case." She pointed a finger briefly at Johnson. "That is partly thanks to you."

Johnson shrugged. "Would he request and get help from the president, or from the FSB if he needed it? What about if we tried an exfiltration to rescue the kids?"

"I don't know. I think there is much doubt over how much support he could expect these days. I would say no. He will have his own private security force, of course."

Johnson spent another five minutes asking questions to ascertain if she had any other information that might be helpful but drew nothing of significance from her.

Is that enough? Johnson wondered.

He leaned back in his chair and glanced at Vic, who gave an imperceptible nod. He took it to mean Vic was satisfied with what he was hearing.

Perhaps they should leave it there and move on to other matters, Johnson thought. That was perhaps as much as they could get from the Russian regarding Johnson's family, at least for now.

"All that may be helpful," Johnson said to Shevchenko. "The test will come when we try to get the children back. If we find you have misled us, you will pay a price." He looked over at Vic.

"Let's talk about intelligence matters," Vic said, turning back to Shevchenko. "I'm not prepared to consider coming to any arrangement with you unless you can provide some high-value information that is useful to the United States. And I mean something really significant—not crumbs from the table."

"I was expecting this," Shevchenko said.

"I'm sure you were. So talk."

Shevchenko rocked back in her chair and stared at him. "All right, here's a taste—at no charge. And a big taster. You might want to know who provided Director Kruglov with the identities of the CIA agents you have lost in Moscow very recently.

Holy shit, Johnson thought to himself.

There was silence in the room for a few seconds. Vic leaned forward and folded his arms on the table, eyeballing Shevchenko.

"Are you serious?" Vic asked.

"Yes. I am serious." Shevchenko looked at each of them in turn. "You want the name of your traitor right now?"

"You don't mean the four agents who your friend Bernice Franklin kindly betrayed last year to Moscow Center?" Vic asked. "Do you mean the recent ones?"

"The recent ones. Three in Moscow and one in Buenos Aires."

"Go ahead," Vic said, his eyes now narrowing a little.

"Try Nizam Fisher."

Johnson vaguely knew of Fisher because Vic had spoken of him a few times in a positive way, but he had never met him. From memory, he was a senior officer of Armenian extraction who worked on the Russia desk and had in the past served at the Moscow station. He could see Vic battling to keep his composure.

"That's crap," Vic said eventually. "I don't believe you."

Shevchenko threw up her hands. "No, you don't believe me. Of course you don't. Your counterintelligence team might need a kick in the, how do you say, the *priklad*. In the ass. Go and kick them and get them to check. Fisher went to the other side a long time ago."

She folded her arms and glared at Vic. "Just don't jump on him immediately. Be subtle. Otherwise it will be obvious who gave them the name. Leave it a few months."

"All right, we've noted it. We'll have to verify it—sooner, not later, though. What else?" Vic asked. "Tell us about Francis Wade."

"What about him? Where is he, by the way?"

"We have him in hand. He's not here," Vic said. "I assume he's the source of the shit about the Malaysian jet and Ukrainian military assistance?"

Shevchenko just nodded.

Vic didn't add that a quick check of the flash drive recovered from Shevchenko had showed it contained a draft of the Ukraine bill due to go to Congress and the Defense Department's Ukraine military strategy. It also had Wade's fingerprints on the case.

"How did you recruit him?" Jayne asked. "And when?"

"The bread has been baking in the oven for a long time," Shevchenko said. "I had him the moment I saw him with her. I saw the body language, saw the look in his eye. A look that should not have been there, because he is a married man, and so is she, but not with him."

Jayne leaned forward and propped her chin in her right hand. "You saw him with whom?"

Shevchenko laughed for the first time, but it was a sarcastic, slightly harsh laugh. "With a woman who is now a key player in a plot being hatched by the Kremlin to influence your politics. Although she doesn't yet know it, I suspect."

Johnson tried to avoid rolling his eyes.

"Right. So tell us," Jayne said.

"It is Martina McAllister."

Johnson felt as though he had been electrified. He was struggling to believe what he'd just heard. Martina McAllister, the twin sister of Nick McAllister, the Republican front-runner for president of the United States. He looked at Vic, who was staring at Shevchenko and grasping the arm of his chair so hard his knuckles were showing white.

"An affair with *Martina McAllister?*" Vic asked eventually. His voice rose in tone and incredulity as he completed the sentence. "You're not serious?"

"Yes, I am serious," said Shevchenko calmly. "Now you are understanding me."

"Screw me," Vic said. "How does Martina McAllister fit into this plot you're telling us about?"

"She is the intended route to her brother—the plan in Moscow is to gradually compromise her, then her brother, by introducing them to certain Russians. First the introduction is to her. That is step one. And we make clear she can't say no. In fact, neither she nor Wade can say no and back out without being engulfed in a huge scandal over their affair."

Johnson got up and walked to the window as Shevchenko continued talking. He was itching to get on with planning the operation to rescue his kids and sister, but he knew they had to go through the process with the Russian first.

The window looked out over the FBI building's internal open-air courtyard, where, somewhat incongruously, some office staff were gathered near the famous sculpture of three people next to an American flag, which was titled *Fidelity, Bravery, Integrity*. Most of those in the gathering were clinking champagne glasses to mark some kind of celebration, perhaps someone's retirement, Johnson surmised.

It all seemed utterly inappropriate under the circumstances. Shevchenko might not be lacking in bravery, but her fidelity and integrity were off the bottom of the scale.

He turned round and faced Shevchenko just as Vic was asking her about step two.

Shevchenko folded her arms. "Step two is to ensure she then introduces the Russians to her brother. We want to slowly make the relationship increasingly conspiratorial without him realizing it is happening. By the time he does, it will be too late. He will be in up to his neck. In Russia we call it *kompromat*."

"Yes, I know very well what you call it," Vic said. "We all do."

Johnson tried to take it in. A Russian operation to compromise the likely next president of the United States, using his sister and the national security advisor as conduits. It wasn't unbelievable, but it was massively audacious. In the same moment he felt a sense of outrage that they would even contemplate it, yet also triumph in that he had uncovered it.

Shevchenko was looking at him and Vic alternately. "Is that enough?"

Vic pursed his lips. "You could be lying. I have no idea whether it's true or not. We'll have to check it out and discuss it. I would like a lot more detail. Does this operation have a name?"

Shevchenko shook her head. "Not specifically."

It obviously did have a name, but Johnson decided not to push it immediately, and neither did Vic.

Johnson glanced at Vic and raised an eyebrow. He was wondering whether Vic was going to tell Shevchenko about Wade.

Vic picked up the cue. He leaned forward across the table

toward Shevchenko. "Before we go, there's one thing you need to know about Wade that might cause a difficulty."

Her eyes narrowed and she inclined her head. "He's dead?"

"Yes. I'm afraid so."

"I thought I heard a gunshot after I left the cemetery. Was that it? You bastards shot him, then. Well done."

"He committed suicide."

Shevchenko remained silent for a few moments. "It doesn't surprise me," she said eventually. "And it removes the problem of keeping him quiet if I work for you. Dead men can't tell tales, can they? You probably know that he was a depressed man on medication. I felt a bit sorry for him in that sense—he was highly intelligent, very capable, but mental health is a fragile thing, and he was behaving in illogical ways. He was vulnerable, which opened the door for me. His death doesn't change anything regarding him and Martina, though. Moscow will revisit her. They will put someone else in place here in DC after I have gone back, and they will continue the operation after a few months. I'm sure your president will enjoy hearing about Wade and her."

Vic gave a wry smile. "That's our next hurdle. Don't think this deal with you is all wrapped up. The president might not be easy to persuade. And there's another thing. How do you explain Wade's death to your people in Moscow, given that it happened immediately after your meeting? Won't they be suspicious?"

"I already told them about his depression, and they know about the affair. They also know he was due to hand over the military papers and legislation on Ukraine, and I said he was nervous about it. It won't come as a big shock, I don't think. We will see. I think it is explainable providing there is no public comment about me."

This woman was without doubt a mistress of lies and

deception, Johnson thought, watching her as she spoke. She probably *could* pull it off in Moscow.

Johnson looked around the room. On the far wall was a small FBI logo mounted on a plaque. That would do. He quietly took out his phone from his pocket, switched it to camera mode, then lifted it and snapped a picture of the entire room, including Shevchenko, with the logo in the background.

Vic stared at him. "What was that for?"

"Team photograph."

"A team photograph?"

"Yes," Johnson said. "It will be my insurance policy, in case all this goes tits up. Proof she's been fraternizing with the main enemy. It will be her one-way ticket to the gulag, if required—and if I don't get my kids back."

"I've told you, you can trust me. And good luck with your kids," Shevchenko said. "You might need to be quick. Severinov is not a patient man."

CHAPTER THIRTY-SIX

Friday, August 1, 2014
Washington, DC

The overwhelming urge to jump on a plane to Russia and head directly to Tuapse was one that Johnson had to fight hard in the hours following the meeting with Shevchenko.

By the time Vic, Johnson, and Jayne finally left the FBI's offices at one o'clock in the morning, they had held a long series of discussions about possible ways to exfiltrate Johnson's family, including the potential use of Navy SEAL units. But they had not yet been able to come to a conclusion, mostly due to one critical missing ingredient: certainty over exactly where his kids and sister were being kept.

Johnson sent a message to Alex Goode at the NSA, first to ask if there had been any progress with efforts to trace boats sailing between Cannes and Tuapse, and second to ask him to try hacking the refinery's computer network again for anything that might be helpful. Specifically, he wanted a plan or map of the layout and the function of the various buildings and production units. That would be vital to their plan.

Meanwhile, Vic had secured agreement from Veltman to proceed with the plan for Shevchenko, providing the president was in agreement once the strategy had been explained. They were now bracing themselves for a meeting at some point in the coming hours with the president and Paul Farrar to explain the strategy.

After no more than four hours of fitful sleep, Johnson woke at just before six, telling himself he must keep his mind focused on what was now very necessary: to carefully plan a rescue operation that was going to require some thought and ingenuity.

To add to the complexity, an email from Veltman to him and Vic arrived while he was making coffee, saying that the White House wanted to be kept fully informed of what was happening with Johnson's family because of the close linkage between that and the fast-emerging Russian *kompromat* operation. The president was insisting on signing off on any rescue plan devised by the team.

Johnson groaned. How long would that take?

More red tape. More delays.

Five of the seven days Severinov had allotted for the required White House statement on Ukraine had passed so far. In two more, his kids and sister could be no more.

The email also congratulated Johnson for his quick thinking and actions in trapping Shevchenko. *Good work, Joe, with Shevchenko. You may have snatched us a victory from the jaws of defeat. Still a long way to go though*, it read.

As soon as they were ready, Johnson and Jayne drove with Vic to Langley and made their way to Vic's office on the seventh floor. Vic's red-headed executive assistant, Helen Lake, found them a room along the corridor where they could work temporarily, and there the planning really got underway.

Helen had been at the CIA since the early 1980s and had known Johnson when he worked at the Agency. Vic had rescued her from her previous role as assistant to the disgraced Near East Division chief, Robert Watson, whom she had disliked. Vic had given her a job as his executive assistant and had then taken her with him after his promotion to the seventh floor.

While the executive IT team was setting up secure internet connections for Johnson and Jayne, they waited in Vic's office as he frantically caught up with progress on the various work streams that were now underway.

Vic and Dover had decided the previous night that the FBI and CIA needed to be kept well away from any announcements about Wade's death to minimize the chances of people connecting them to it.

"Apart from anything else," Vic told Johnson, "there's no point in making things worse for Wade's family by telling the world he was spying for the Russians. He's dead, so disgracing him by announcing it now won't do any good. My guess is that details of his affair with Martina will emerge somehow at some point, and people will assume that his tangled personal life was the main factor in his suicide. Which is kind of true."

Johnson continued to avoid involvement in the machinations intended to cover up exactly what had happened. But both Vic and Dover had a couple of very good friends at the top of the Metropolitan Police Department in DC, and between them a plan was rapidly devised. They appeared to be well practiced at it.

Someone at the White House had informed Wade's wife and family of his death late the previous night. Once that had been done, at around eleven o'clock, the news had broken online following a carefully crafted briefing just before midnight by the White House press secretary to *The Wash-*

ington Post, *The New York Times*, and a couple of Washington television channels.

The next day, news organizations accordingly continued to portray Wade's death as a suspected suicide but stressed that confirmation of that would only come following the usual medical examiner's investigation. The rest of the media swiftly followed up the stories in a similar vein, producing a torrent of coverage that rapidly went international as the morning progressed.

It was the number one story on most broadcast news bulletins and online news sites for several hours, but thankfully, none of the media appeared to have any idea of the true background to Wade's demise.

Shevchenko had remained overnight in an accommodation room at the J. Edgar Hoover Building. At around breakfast time, she had dispatched a secure message to Kutsik and Kruglov at Yasenevo, telling them that she had obtained the expected documents at the meeting with TITANIUM as planned before his subsequent suicide. She reassured them that she didn't think she had been compromised since he had already passed over the flash drive to her and said his death was not a shock. She promised to dispatch more details when she had them.

Neither Martina or Nick McAllister had yet reacted to the news about Wade, but then, that was the last thing Johnson had been expecting.

Vic and Veltman were in constant touch with Deacon and others at the White House, trying to pave the way to getting President Ferguson's agreement to the Shevchenko deal and to provisional plans for the exfiltration of Johnson's family. They would need to meet Ferguson face-to-face, but not until sometime later in the day.

Helpfully for Vic, Deacon appeared to view the recruitment of Shevchenko as a gamble worth taking. Establishing a

senior source inside Yasenevo was a prize indeed, if it went
according to plan. His feedback was that one of the president's main concerns was, understandably, about the cover-up
relating to Wade's death.

With so much going on, Johnson couldn't help reflecting
that the CIA director was correct: there was still a very long
way to go. A significant number of people knew what had
happened, and there was a distinct chance of the truth
leaking out about Wade, not least during a death investigation. And if that truth did emerge publicly, it would certainly
sink the plan for Shevchenko.

However, Johnson mentally put that to one side. He
needed to concentrate on getting his children and sister back.

As soon as the internet connection was up and running,
Johnson logged on to his laptop. Immediately, he found an
email that had been sent to the address listed on his website.

*Johnson, I have your two children and your sister on my
property. I am still waiting for the White House statement
about Ukraine. Time is running out. Once I get that, if you
want your family back, you will need to fetch them. Come
alone, no US military, special services, or any other armed
support. If you disobey this instruction they die immediately.
The address is below. Reply to this email to tell me when you
are coming. Any attempt to make an unannounced visit will
also result in their deaths. We have dealt with each other long
enough now for you to know that I mean what I say.*

There was an address on Marta Street, Tuapse, which
Johnson immediately checked using a satellite map. The
neighborhood was very near the Krasnodar refinery, and the
street comprised detached properties on large plots, less than
half a mile from the Black Sea coast.

Shevchenko's words came back to him. *My guess is that he*

will have taken them to his Krasnodar oil refinery in Tuapse . . . He might try and tell you they are somewhere else.

This was bullshit, Johnson thought. Severinov had made a token reference to the statement he wanted from the White House about renouncing further military aid for Ukraine. But he must know that wasn't going to happen. And the fact he had included an address before getting the statement gave the game away: all he wanted was Johnson.

It was obvious what would happen. Severinov would wait until Johnson arrived and would then simply attempt to dispose of all of them—him, his kids, and his sister. That would be his problem solved.

But blatant and unsubtle as Severinov's bad intentions were, Johnson still couldn't ignore the email. He knew he would have to go—and Severinov knew it too.

The difficult question remained, though: How the hell was he going to do it?

* * *

Friday, August 1, 2014
Washington, DC

As was so often the case, it was Jayne who came up with the answer. Earlier, while Johnson was busy discussing Severinov's email with Vic, he overheard her making a series of phone calls.

Now, she was busy on another call, this time to her former boss at Britain's Secret Intelligence Service, Mark Nicklin-Donovan.

Nicklin-Donovan was now director of operations at the SIS, otherwise known as MI6, effectively making him deputy to Richard Durman, chief of the service who was known simply as C.

"I've just been doing some research into the refinery," Jayne said as she put the phone down. "I know quite a bit about refining following my work on the Iraq and Iran oil and gas sectors, the security implications from disruption there, remember?"

"Yes, I do. And?"

Jayne placed both hands behind her head, elbows sticking out, as she sometimes did when she had something significant to say. "In particular, I noticed production had stopped recently, so I did some digging to find out why. They've got a turnaround underway there."

"What's a turnaround?"

"It's a scheduled stoppage to allow regular maintenance to take place. Contractors fly teams in from all over the world to carry out specialist jobs. The refinery will be crawling with strangers while the turnaround is going on."

"Is that a good or bad thing?" Johnson asked. "I doubt Severinov would want to keep my kids on-site if there's a lot of people around."

"Depends," Jayne said. "I got hold of a site plan, and it's a massive complex, like all refineries. He could probably easily keep them somewhere there, and nobody would know. There will be scores of buildings scattered all over it. But the point is that there will be a huge number of people coming and going. And—"

Johnson interrupted. "So we could be refinery maintenance workers?"

"Correct. We could be, indeed. It will be the perfect cover for us to get into Russia and perfect for getting into the refinery."

"I hope you have a friendly maintenance company in your little black book, then, because I don't."

"Strangely enough, I do. I spoke to Mark just now and got clearance from him to call them. A firm called ORM, Octane Refinery Maintenance. They're British. I've just come off the phone to the managing director. We go back a long way. He got me into Iran's Abadan refinery on the Gulf a few years ago, and they are working on the Krasnodar turnaround."

Jayne explained her thinking. ORM was operating a twelve-day shift system, with a new set of workers flying from London to Sochi each time the shift was due to change. The plan was to fly from London with the next shift team into Sochi airport, a three-hour drive farther down the Black Sea coast from the refinery toward Georgia. Then they would travel by bus to Tuapse, where the team was based in a local hotel.

Johnson pursed his lips. "Isn't there a risk someone else on the team drops us in the shit? That they tell Severinov or one of the refinery managers what's going on?"

"That is highly unlikely," Jayne said. "ORM's MD is an old hand at this game, shall we say. Alf Hill. Ex-army guy. He has developed one or two good contacts at intelligence services, me and Mark included, and he is remunerated well for his services. He keeps his mouth shut, and he pays his people to do likewise."

"He's effectively on the SIS books, then? A spy?"

Jayne shrugged. "A businessman, with side interests."

Johnson remained silent for a few seconds. Again flashing up like a projector slide in his mind was that same picture of his children and sister chained up somewhere dark, terrified as hell, traumatized, and wondering whether they would get home alive.

The plan that Jayne had sketched out so briefly sounded convincing in outline. But there was a massive amount of detail to work out and very little time to do it. One mistake, and he and his children would be dead, he knew that. But what was the alternative? He couldn't think of one.

"How long would it take to get in?" Johnson asked.

"Alf has a flight leaving London first thing on Sunday morning with the people for his next shift change. They use a private aircraft. We could be on it if we can get to London tomorrow."

"Right," Johnson said. "Suppose we get into the refinery and we somehow find my kids, my sister. What then? How do we all get out?"

Jayne scratched her head and looked out the window. "The last Black Sea exfil operation I worked on, which was pulling someone out of the Crimea, we used a Turkish trawler from Istanbul. I figure we could do the same again. The rig's captain did a superb job. It was the third or fourth time we had used him for various things, but that was the most difficult operation."

"A Turkish trawler, in Russian waters?"

"Yes. At night," Jayne said.

"How does that work, then?"

"We got the guy on the beach to guide the boat with a wristwatch radio beacon. Then a small inflatable came in from the trawler, no lights on, to fetch him."

Johnson tried to think it through. "What would happen if an FSB coast guard patrol boat found the trawler in Russian waters?"

"Don't think about that, Joe. You'll drive yourself crazy. That Russian Black Sea coastline is enormous. It's more than three hundred miles long. The chances of being picked up by a Russian patrol at night is slim."

"I think what you're suggesting is good," Johnson said. "We need to put a small team together. Vic would love to join us, but he obviously can't—he's got his hands full. I'm thinking I'll get Neal involved."

He was referring to Neal Scales, who along with Vic was an old colleague and friend from Johnson's CIA days in Islamabad in the late 1980s. He was now number three in the Directorate of Operations since Vic had promoted him and was one of the shrewdest operators in the Agency. Like Vic, he liked to get his hands dirty despite his seniority, sometimes even when he might be better advised to take more of a management role. Old habits died hard.

Neal had already texted Johnson a couple of times over the previous two days to express his concern about the ordeal his kids and sister were going through. Now Johnson sent him another message asking if he could spare some time for a chat.

While they were waiting for Neal, Johnson received an email from Goode at the NSA, sent to both him and Vic. It emerged that the National Reconnaissance Office had found it almost impossible to track individual yachts starting from Cannes, as there were so many on the Mediterranean in that area. So they had instead started at the other end, Tuapse, and backtracked using the much smaller number they had found in that segment of the Black Sea.

The result was that they had identified a small yacht that had arrived in Tuapse the previous day after sailing from Cannes on the day of the kidnap.

Unfortunately they had not been able to obtain any coast guard shipping communications with the boat as of yet, and they could not give any guarantees, but they were 95 percent certain it was the boat they were seeking. No others that had sailed that route. Goode also attached a detailed plan of the refinery site.

All that was enough for Johnson. It corroborated what Shevchenko had suggested was the most likely destination for his family and what Severinov had written in his email.

Twenty minutes later, Neal walked into the room Johnson

and Jayne were using as their office for the day. A tall man whose slim build belied his wiry strength, he strode straight to Johnson.

"Hi, buddy," Neal said. He shook Johnson's hand, then gave him a hug and kissed Jayne on the cheek.

"I just want to say straight out that we'll get them back," Neal said. "Don't worry. We'll do whatever it takes."

"You might regret saying that," Johnson said, attempting to smile.

Neal ran his hand through his slightly unkempt blond hair and sat at the table where Johnson and Jayne had set up their laptops. "No, I won't. I'll just imagine it's my kids, then it's easy." His own children, aged twenty-one and seventeen, were only a little older than Johnson's.

"Well, thanks, and I appreciate it," Johnson said. He turned to Jayne and asked her to explain to Neal the exfil plan she had conceived.

Neal listened carefully. When she had finished, he asked a few questions about the refinery, and then a few more about the trawler.

"Alf thinks it would be much easier to manage if he takes only two of us to the refinery, which will be me and Joe," Jayne said to Neal. "Perhaps you can manage the trawler end of the exfil from Istanbul?"

Thankfully, Neal just nodded and didn't ask the question that remained in Johnson's mind: Would the Russians sink the trawler if they spotted it?

He didn't really want an answer to that.

* * *

Friday, August 1, 2014
White House, Washington, DC

. . .

Vic, Veltman, and Shepard had been sitting in the small meeting room for more than an hour when Charles Deacon, whose black glasses seemed even farther down his nose than normal, finally beckoned them into the neighboring Situation Room main conference room.

In Vic's experience, the position of Deacon's glasses was a good barometer of how his boss, the president, was feeling. Sure enough, that proved to be the case.

"He's not in a good mood," whispered the president's aide as the trio walked past him. "I'm not staying. Over to you. Good luck." He headed off toward the stairs.

Deacon's assessment proved to be spot-on.

"What I want to know from you three so-called intelligence gatherers is how the hell my national security advisor was leaking all manner of confidential material to a Russian spy while also having an affair with the sister of a high-profile politician—my main opponent no less—and you knew nothing about it until that very Russian spy told you?" Ferguson barked without preamble and without inviting the three men to sit.

Vic certainly didn't want to shunt the blame onto Shepard. But given that it was an FBI responsibility, he and Veltman waited for him to speak first.

"Sir, it's a good question," Shepard said. "I've already spoken to the director, and he has ordered an inquiry. We will report back to you as soon as we know more. We recognize it's critical, and it will be completed as quickly as possible."

Ferguson, who was in his usual position at the end of the table, shook his head. "Sit down," he said.

The three of them sat in a row along the side of the conference room table.

"I've only got a few minutes, so you'll have to listen," Ferguson said. "As you can imagine, I'm extremely angry about what has happened. Losing Wade in these circumstances is a disaster right now. I've read the details from you all about the proposal to use Shevchenko as a penetration agent in Yasenevo, and quite frankly, I'm damned nervous about it."

"I understand that, sir," Veltman said. "We are too, but we have a straightforward choice. Either we go for the Shevchenko offer, or alternatively we hold her up as an example of how far the Russians are trying to influence politics and the next election in this country. In the latter scenario, we kick her back to Moscow on the next plane and to a probable death in a Siberian prison. We then shout at the Russians for a week or two. I would understand if you wanted to go down the latter route, but I would prefer the former. It's a gamble, but think it could potentially give us far more long-term value."

Ferguson leaned back in his chair and folded his arms. He said nothing for several seconds, surveying the three men in front of him in turn. "All right. But if it goes wrong, and it turns out she's pulling the wool over our eyes, you know what I would do with you three, don't you?"

Vic didn't need the president to spell it out, and he was certain the others didn't either. That was the biggest issue with being promoted to the kind of level he was at now: he had to take responsibility when things didn't go according to plan, as well as the credit when they did. It was a double-edged sword that, as some of his predecessors had found, could occasionally prove professionally fatal.

"Sir, we believe it is worth the risk," Veltman said. "It could give us a highly valuable asset inside Russian intelligence at a time when we currently only have one other of any value, and he is very new to us, so it is difficult to gauge how he will perform."

"As long as she doesn't play a double game," Ferguson said. "I'm from the skeptical school. And if all this leaks out, which has to be a distinct possibility, then the game is finished. And I could be finished too."

Veltman nodded. "We have taken all actions we can to ensure that doesn't happen. We immediately compartmentalized it so only those who need to know are informed. Thankfully that has worked so far. The longer that stays airtight, the greater the likelihood of us getting away with it, particularly once we are through Francis's death investigation and funeral."

The president stroked his chin. "When is Shevchenko due to go back to Moscow?"

"Any day now, but the order hasn't come yet. On our end, we're working to keep her here until Joe Johnson has his kids and sister back," Vic said.

"Yes, that makes sense," Ferguson said. "If things go really badly wrong, we could use her as some kind of bargaining chip. But in terms of Johnson's kids, my strong preference would be to send a SEAL team in to get them back."

He looked questioningly at Veltman first, then Vic.

"I understand your point of view," Vic said. "The issue we have is that Severinov has made it clear that if SEALs or any other military are sent in, he will immediately kill the kids and sister. And we don't know exactly where on the refinery they're being held. Joe says he couldn't live with himself if he agreed to send them in and something went wrong. He doesn't want to risk it. He would rather do it himself. Then he would have only himself to blame. But he's an extremely capable guy. I'd back him to pull it off."

The president gave a slight shake of the head. "I'm sure he is extremely capable, from what I've heard. Well, I hope you're giving Johnson maximum support behind the scenes, then?"

"Yes, sir, of course. We're working out plans right now."

"Johnson has done very well, it seems to me," Ferguson

said. "Especially with pinning down who was responsible for shooting down the Malaysian plane, finding the troll factory, and tracing Shevchenko. But if those kids die, it will likely be me who will be the target of flak in the media for not insisting on sending the SEALs in. I'm not sure I Iike that."

Vic pursed his lips. *Typical politician, more worried about his own image than anything else.*

"That's not necessarily the case, sir," Vic said. "If the worst happens, which hopefully it won't, I think we could explain—"

"You know damn well how these things work," the president interrupted, his voice level, his eyes fixed on Vic. "I would without doubt be targeted. Portrayed as weak and indecisive in the face of Russian hostility. That's how the frigging papers and TV operate. There would also be another online and social media barrage. I can't afford that—not in the current political climate with another election around the corner. So know this: if it goes wrong, it's you who made this decision, and you alone."

PART FOUR

CHAPTER THIRTY-SEVEN

Sunday, August 3, 2014
Sochi, Russia

Most of the group of petroleum engineers who were scattered around the Boeing 737-300 were sleeping as the jet began its descent across the eastern Black Sea toward Sochi.

Johnson, who was woken from his fitful doze by the slight bump as the plane's trajectory changed, looked around the cabin from his window seat on the port side of the aircraft. It was no more than half full.

Although there were a few younger men, the majority of those on the refinery maintenance team were gray-haired, bespectacled, slightly paunchy veterans. Johnson felt that he fit in very well.

Jayne, asleep in the seat to Johnson's right, stood out a little more because there were only three other women in the group of fifty-two people.

The company's managing director, Alf Hill, was in the row

in front of them, reading documents on an iPad and scribbling notes in a spiral-bound notebook.

Unlike the others, Johnson had struggled to sleep. There was too much to think about. The recurring color picture of his kids tied up somewhere dark, wouldn't go away.

Johnson, Jayne, and Neal had traveled on a daytime flight from Washington's Dulles Airport to London's Heathrow Airport, at which point they had split up. Neal flew from Heathrow to Istanbul, where he was meeting one of Jayne's former MI6 colleagues and the trawler captain. Meanwhile, Johnson and Jayne took a cab to Gatwick Airport to meet up with Hill. There was no way Johnson was going to give Severinov his travel plans, so he had not replied to the oligarch's email.

The flight to Sochi, operated by a private charter company, had taken off from Gatwick at around one in the morning, and the journey of nearly two thousand miles had taken four hours and forty-five minutes.

Johnson glanced at his watch, which was not his normal Citizen timepiece but a chunkier device with a two-inch face. Apart from telling the time, which was a quarter to nine in Sochi, it also contained a GPS location beacon that would transmit its location with pinpoint accuracy to a receiver that Neal would give to the trawler captain.

Based on what Hill had told them at the preflight briefing, they should be in Tuapse by early afternoon. They would then rest for a few hours and head to the refinery around quarter to nine that evening. Maintenance was continuing around the clock in order to get the turnaround finished in the shortest time possible and get the site back into production. The group was starting on the night shift.

Operating at the refinery under cover of darkness suited Johnson. While they were waiting to move to the site, he and Jayne could prepare a plan. He had persuaded Hill to spend some time with them once they arrived at the hotel. Specifically, Johnson had asked him to show them the refinery layout on a large-scale map that Hill had acquired for the maintenance project.

Hill had introduced Johnson and Jayne to a handful of the others in the group at Gatwick, but most took little interest. Perhaps that was partly due to the late hour at which they were departing, but maybe they were used to strangers joining their work teams.

The vast majority of the spare parts and equipment that Hill's team required had been shipped directly to the refinery well in advance. However, there were some additional specialist components that they needed to take with them. Therefore, at Gatwick, several crates had been loaded into the cargo hold of the Boeing. Hidden deep inside one of the crates, among spare parts for electric motors and pumps was a locked box supplied by the CIA station in London. It contained two Beretta M9 pistols, six spare magazines, and six M84 stun grenades, as well as other equipment including infrared night-vision goggles, a handheld thermal imager, and a reel of black tape.

At the bottom of the box was a container holding five pieces of C4 explosive the size of cigarette packets, together with five even smaller remote detonators and two wireless control units that could operate multiple detonators.

Hill assured Johnson that customs in Sochi were highly unlikely to carry out more than a superficial check of the crates, based on his previous experience at the airport.

The plane continued its descent over the sea, and Johnson peered out of his window over the port wing. The morning sunshine lit up the mountains that surrounded Sochi on the eastern side.

Johnson reflexively patted his trouser pocket, where he had placed his passport. There had been no time for Vic's team to create a new cover identity for him, and he couldn't reuse the Philip Wilkinson legend deployed on his previous visit to Russia a week and a half earlier. So he had switched to his second false identity, that of Don Thiele.

As with his Wilkinson legend, the Thiele identity included a thoroughly backstopped set of papers and documents, including a US passport, credit cards, bank cards, a driver's license, and a birth certificate. There were even fake LinkedIn and Facebook accounts. It all checked out. Provided Johnson was careful to pay off the credit card bills and the bank accounts remained in credit, he never encountered a problem.

Thiele was supposedly a fifty-seven-year-old single man with no dependents who was a US oil industry consultant—the occupational details had been added to his documents only in recent days. Johnson deliberately kept it vague. The photograph in the passport showed him with his usual short-cropped semicircle of hair and with circular wire-rimmed glasses that made him look like an academic. Since the glasses he normally used with the Thiele identity were at home in Portland, he had obtained a similar prescription-free pair from the disguise department at Langley, and his hair was starting to grow back after being shaved for his last stint in Russia.

Jayne, meanwhile, was traveling under one of her favorite legends, Carolina Blanco, a British national born in 1962 in Buenos Aires of English parents; she was carrying a passport in that name that looked nearly as old as its owner, complete with a shabby, scratched cover. She was supposedly a human resources consultant who was assessing the performance of the engineering staff.

Half an hour later, the group was trudging off the plane from the private jet apron and into the VIP terminal, next to the new international terminal building.

The modern steel structure was still heavily adorned with banners, posters, and advertising featuring the Winter Olympics, held in the city only five months earlier and used relentlessly by President Putin to raise Russia's profile around the world.

Johnson had not visited this part of Russia before, but rather than absorb the atmosphere, his entire focus was on getting through passport control unscathed. After two tumultuous covert visits to the country within the past three months, he was forced to breathe deeply and slowly in an attempt to slow his heart rate, which he could feel had picked up despite his years of experience in such situations.

Logic told him that the FSB could not have details of the legend he was using here and that his passport had always functioned internationally when he had previously used it. The Russian visa that the Athens CIA station had inserted into the Thiele passport was of high quality.

But on the other hand Severinov definitely was expecting him in Russia, even if he did not know how or when or where he might arrive. And despite Shevchenko's doubts over whether Severinov could call on Russian security services for assistance, he knew very well that the oligarch had good personal connections inside both the FSB and SVR, as he had clearly demonstrated in their last encounter.

The Octane team lined up in front of two passport control booths, manned by two thin-lipped male officers whose gray faces suggested that they had been on shift duty all night. They worked quickly, taking no more than a brief glance at each of the British members of the contingent as they passed through the checkpoint.

By chance, Johnson found himself at the left-hand desk at the same time as Jayne arrived at the right-hand one.

The Border Service officer took his passport, looked at it,

then pushed it under an electronic scanner. While it was processing, he looked up.

"American?"

"Yes," Johnson said.

To his alarm, Johnson noticed a purple light glinting from the scanner. This was an ultraviolet device, designed to catch forgeries.

"What is the purpose of your visit?" the officer asked in heavily accented English.

"Business."

"Are you with this group, the British?" The officer indicated toward the other members of the team.

"Yes."

This had not been the process on arrival in Moscow on his previous entry. Johnson could see out of the corner of his eye that Jayne had already been waved through the booth next door.

The officer withdrew the passport from the scanner and glanced down at it. "Have you been to Russia before?"

Johnson, not anticipating the question, hesitated briefly while mentally reassuring himself that he had never used the Thiele passport to enter Russia previously. "No, my first visit."

"Where is your destination?"

Now Johnson was feeling more uneasy. He felt he had no choice but to be honest, given he was with the group. "I will be working on the refinery at Tuapse. The Krasnodar refinery."

The officer nodded, slowly closed the passport, and handed it back to Johnson. "Enjoy your stay here—Mr. Thiele." He indicated with his head that Johnson could continue.

Johnson walked through the control area and joined Jayne, who was standing with Hill.

"Problems?" Hill asked.

"I hope not. Just a few questions. Had I been to Russia before, where was I going to, that sort of thing. My passport went through an ultraviolet scanner. But it seems okay."

Hill shrugged and Jayne shook her head.

"It was all straightforward for me," she said.

"Singling out the Americans," Johnson said.

Once all the party had completed passport checks, they passed through the terminal, and Hill guided them to two buses that stood waiting in the landscaped pickup area.

Hill took a seat in front of Johnson and Jayne on the first bus. "We should be at the hotel in about three hours," he said.

Johnson nodded. That sounded about right for a ninety-mile journey on a winding coastal road. He stared out the bus window. Four men were loading some of the smaller wooden crates that had come on the aircraft into the cargo bay of the bus. The larger ones were being put into a truck. At least they had all come through customs intact. Of the forty or so boxes, only one had been searched, Hill had told them, and that was not the one containing the hidden weapons.

Beyond an elevated section of highway that ran alongside the northern fringe of the airport, green hills rose into a blue sky, punctuated by a white church bell tower and a giant set of five colored Olympic rings fashioned from tubular steel girders that were mounted on a pedestal.

A row of three Russian police cars, all white with blue stripes along the sides, stood behind a line of trees and bushes that divided one area of the open-air short-stay parking lot from another.

This was going to be tricky. Johnson absentmindedly fingered the beacon watch on his left wrist. It crossed his mind that a lot depended on the device.

CHAPTER THIRTY-EIGHT

Sunday, August 3, 2014
Tuapse, Russia

The River Tuapse Hotel, where the Octane team was staying, was a four-story building that looked as though it dated from the Soviet era, and it stood in a slightly run-down residential area to the south of the refinery.

As it turned out, it was also only about three-quarters of a mile from the property that Severinov had instructed Johnson to visit to find his children.

Inside, the hotel proved to be far more comfortable and well equipped than it appeared on the outside. He and Jayne dumped their bags in their shared room, and Johnson took first turn in the shower.

Afterward, he ordered coffee from room service and logged on to the shared email account that Shevchenko and Severinov had been using; Goode's team had provided him with access.

Since he had last checked the previous day, Severinov had left a short message.

The kids and sister are at the refinery here now. We are ready to deal with Johnson when he shows up. How is Operation Pandora progressing?

Unsurprisingly, there was no reply from Shevchenko.

Johnson tried to keep himself on an even keel when reading the message about his children and Amy. At least he knew they were alive and had confirmation of where they were.

But what was Operation Pandora? It was the first he had heard of it, and neither Vic's team nor the FBI had it on their radar, as far as he was aware. Was it the name the SVR had given to the operation Shevchenko had been working on with Wade, or McAllister, or something else? She had certainly neglected to mention it while being grilled at FBI headquarters.

He showed the note to Jayne after she emerged from the bathroom.

"That's helpful," she said. "What does he mean by 'we'? Does he have a bloody army there waiting for us? And what's this Pandora?"

"No idea," Johnson said. "But we'd better go and see Alf and start drawing up our battle plans."

Once Jayne was dressed, they headed to Hill's suite farther down the corridor.

He already had his detailed map of the refinery site spread out on a coffee table, along with a set of aerial photographs, and proceeded to talk them through the various operational units and the function of the other buildings.

The refinery site was enormous. Johnson hadn't quite grasped the scale of it until Hill pointed out the distances involved. Its western end was near the sea, and it ran inland in an easterly direction for about one-and-a-half miles. The site was a third of a mile across in some places.

"Where the hell do we start?" Jayne asked.

"I don't think it is quite as bad as it looks," Hill said. "Most of these units and buildings are operational—mainly tanks for crude oil or fuel storage or fuel production units." He pointed to a series of enormous cylindrical white tanks on the aerial photographs. "Your man Severinov wouldn't be able to keep the kids in these."

Hill drew a red line with his pen around most of the section of the refinery that lay west of the highway that ran south out of the town, bisecting the site. "Those are the units under maintenance for the turnaround. So that rules out those areas."

He also drew a red line around the tanks, which were almost all east of the highway, farthest away from the coast. "This is the tank farm, as they call it. They won't be there either."

Hill put a red line around another group of four buildings west of the highway. "These are where we and a bunch of other maintenance contractors are based and where our equipment is stored during the turnaround. Those will also be nonstarters for you. They are busy as hell."

Johnson stared at the map. Hill had eliminated at least three-quarters of the site. That was helpful in one sense, but only if he was correct.

"So where *do* we start looking, then?" Johnson asked.

Hill marked two groups of buildings at the western end of the site, nearest the sea. "These are not operational refinery buildings and are not being used by maintenance contractors. They are for equipment storage, vehicles, administration offices, and so on. The turnaround teams will not be in those buildings, so if Mr. Severinov is keeping your kids on-site, that's where they might be."

Johnson studied the map. What Hill was saying seemed to make logical sense.

"How do you get from the western part of the site to the eastern on the other side of the highway?" Johnson asked.

"There's a tunnel that runs beneath the highway so refinery vehicles can cross easily, here," Hill said, marking it on the map.

Hill seemed quite unfazed by the idea of helping smuggle a couple of foreign spies into a potentially hostile situation on a site owned by a company to which he was contracted.

"I'd just like to thank you now," Johnson said. "I know you're putting yourself and your business at risk with this."

Hill shook his head. "No need. When I was younger I worked in the British Army for several years in military intelligence, which is why I've been interested in helping MI6. I know the game. I've had the occasional hiccup before doing this kind of thing, but I've just blamed it all on a nonexistent head of human resources. Don't worry. I'll talk my way out of it, if necessary. Anyway, I know Jayne from way back. She says you are good, and I believe her."

He hesitated, then continued. "I've got kids of my own, so I can imagine what it's like."

Johnson nodded. "Okay. I appreciate it."

He went back to the map of the refinery and asked Hill to explain what the different units were and, in particular, what was in the numerous cylindrical steel tanks on the eastern part of the site.

Hill pointed out the larger tanks, some of them as large as 140 feet in diameter, he said, which mainly contained crude oil prior to processing, and the smaller ones, which contained refined fuels, ranging from jet fuel for airlines to diesel and gasoline for domestic use, and also specialist products, such as liquid petroleum gas and the feedstocks for petrochemical plants.

Johnson scanned the aerial photographs again. Toward the eastern end of the site were two tanks that stood by themselves, separated from the others by a long stretch of what looked like waste ground. Beyond them, after another stretch of waste ground, were four more tanks that appeared to be in the advanced stages of construction.

"What are those?" Johnson asked, pointing to the pair of tanks that stood alone.

"Those are diesel and gasoline tanks for the fleet of road tankers that transport fuel from the refinery all over the country," Hill said. "The trucks fill up at this loading gantry here." He pointed to a long row of pumps next to the tanks.

"And these other four, the ones that look like they are being built?"

"I understand they are new tanks for specialized products, maybe for the petrochemical industry."

"Thanks, interesting," Johnson said. "Success lies in preparation, as my old boss at the Office of Special Investigations always said."

"The fuels are all highly flammable. I would stay well away from all of them," Hill said. "Severinov won't be keeping your kids anywhere near them, I imagine."

"I hope not. Now tell me, where's the electricity substation?"

Hill pointed to a unit at the eastern end of the site, beyond the four tanks under construction, separate from all the other units and the tanks. "That provides power for the whole refinery."

Hill took two Octane security passes on lanyards from his pocket and handed them to Johnson and Jayne, along with white plastic protective helmets, yellow high-visibility vests, and safety glasses from a bag in the corner of the room. "Helmets, glasses, and vests are compulsory on-site. Sorry, might be annoying."

Johnson nodded. "Annoying, maybe, but they'll help give us some anonymity too if everyone looks the same."

He glanced at the security passes. They had bar codes and the photographs Jayne had sent to Hill a couple of days earlier. In Johnson's case, the photograph was the same as in his Thiele passport, which showed him with a light beard. It wasn't a heavy enough growth to hide his features, but it made him look different. Accordingly, Johnson had not shaved for two days, which meant he already had a long stubble.

"Where are the site entrances?" Johnson asked.

Hill explained that there were three entrances. The main one led off the highway that bisected the site and into the western section of the refinery. There was a secondary entrance in the western section, not far from the buildings Hill had pinpointed as the most likely location for Johnson's children to be kept. Another secondary entrance led off the highway and into the eastern part of the site, near the tank farm.

"They only allow visitors and contractors to use the main entrance. The other two are for emergencies—in case of a fire or something like that to allow firefighters in—or for special truck deliveries. They guard them, but the gates are shut usually."

Johnson nodded. "How do the passes work? What checks are made?"

"They will electronically scan the bar codes upon entry, which allows their system to record the names of people going on-site," Hill said.

As work was continuing twenty-four hours per day on the site, it would look fairly normal for Johnson and Jayne to be there in protective gear during the night, Hill said.

Johnson pulled his phone out and took several photographs of the refinery map and the aerial photos.

There was a knock at the door, and two of Hill's colleagues appeared carrying the equipment box belonging to Johnson that had been extracted from the bundle of electrical equipment. It was intact, and to Johnson's relief, the seals were unbroken.

The men placed it in the corner of the room and left.

Hill looked at Johnson and Jayne. "I don't think I can do much more for you. I can't take the risk of delegating any of my people to work with you. That wouldn't be fair to them. I can transport you onto the refinery site on the bus, though."

"There is one more thing," Johnson said. "What checks do security make when you take the buses onto the site?"

"They do check," Hill said. "A guard comes on the bus at the gate and looks at everyone's identity lanyard. They will look beneath all vehicles with mirrors and so on."

"Do they go through the cargo hold?"

"With anyone they don't know, they are very thorough. They know us very well, so they usually just open it and have a look. It's just boxes in there. If there are staff with lanyards on the bus, they are less concerned about the cargo."

"Can we hide in the hold so they wouldn't see us if they checked?"

Hill shrugged. "I guess so. You could hide inside one of the larger cardboard crates. They are long enough to get into, and we have a few empty ones. I can slide two in there for you. Easy."

Johnson had noted earlier that the cargo hold was a flat space roughly three feet high beneath the seating area, accessed via doors on both sides of the bus. It had areas that were hidden behind parts of the vehicle chassis that were not visible without actually crawling into the space.

Johnson paused, thinking. He turned to Jayne. "We'll hide

in a box. I don't want to take the risk of being checked by guards. Severinov is certain to have given them a photograph or description of me, if not of you."

"I agree," Jayne said.

"It will be a bumpy ride, but it's not far," Hill said. "We'll be meeting in the hotel lobby at about eight thirty. Come down then, and the two buses will depart from here at eight forty-five. You can go on the first one. Then after that, you are on your own."

* * *

Sunday, August 3, 2014
   Tuapse

The bus came to an abrupt halt, causing Johnson to slide slightly forward inside his cardboard crate; then came a loud hissing noise as the vehicle's air brakes activated. The sound seemed far louder in the cargo hold than it had earlier in the day en route from the airport, when Johnson had been in the soundproofed passenger cabin above where he and Jayne were now lying.

The bus vibrated a little as the engine was turned off, and then came another mechanical sound, which Johnson presumed was the passenger door opening, followed by the sound of voices speaking in Russian from outside.

In the crate next to his, Jayne remained silent. The openings of both boxes faced forward, and they had been pushed right up against the front wall of the cargo compartment, largely hidden from the view of anyone glancing in by at least twenty other boxes.

Both of them had small black backpacks containing a Beretta M9, three spare magazines, three M84 stun grenades, and a pair of infrared night-vision goggles. Johnson's bag additionally contained the handheld thermal imager, the five pieces of C4 explosive, and the wireless detonators. They each carried one of the detonator control units.

There came the thud, thud, thud as footsteps went up the short flight of steps that led into the bus's passenger cabin, and then more voices. Johnson could make out enough of the conversation to know that security guards were checking the lanyards of the Octane maintenance crew. There were regular beeping sounds, which Johnson assumed came from the electronic device the guards used to record the bar codes.

Eventually, there were more footsteps in the stairwell, followed by the loud groaning of metal on metal as the door to the cargo hold opened.

Johnson closed his eyes.

"What is all this?" a deep Russian voice asked.

"These are the usual spare parts for our work on the refinery," Hill's voice replied. His clear tones were quite distinctive. The men must be standing no more than a few feet away. "They are mainly electrical and mechanical parts to replace worn-out ones on the unit we are servicing for the next few days. Same as always."

There was silence for a few seconds. Then the sound of a wooden box being dragged across the surface of the cargo hold, followed by a loud grunt, presumably as either the guard or Hill lifted it out of the hold.

"Open it."

"Sure, no problem," came Hill's voice. He didn't hesitate. He was a cool customer, that was for sure.

Johnson heard a creaking, splintering sound as the box was opened.

"These are relay switches for pumps," Hill said.

"Okay. Close it up. Next box."

Surely they're not going through all the crates, Johnson thought.

He lowered his head, shut his eyes, and pressed his face to the floor. He heard a virtual repeat of the same inspection process with a second box. Now he could feel droplets of sweat trickling down his forehead.

There was a pause. By that stage Johnson's entire body was so tense, he felt he was going to seize up completely. He remained motionless, facedown.

Then the process was repeated for a third box.

We're screwed. There was nothing he could do but wait for the worst to happen.

But after the third box had been ripped open, there was a short silence. "You can continue. That is enough," the man with the deep voice said eventually.

To Johnson's massive relief, the cargo door was slammed shut seconds later. The passenger door was also slammed shut, and then came the throaty roar of the powerful diesel engine as it was restarted, followed by another hiss as the brakes were released.

The bus began moving forward through the security check zone and onto the refinery site.

* * *

Sunday, August 3, 2014
    Tuapse

When he'd acquired the refinery, it had not been possible to find a suitable villa to buy in Tuapse. So Severinov had long ago built his own, high up in the wooded hills east of the town. The property, a six-bedroom, single-story affair, over-looked the River Tuapse, which had icy blue waters that twisted and turned their way from the mountains to the coast, and from his verandah, Severinov had distant views of the Black Sea. The eastern end of his refinery was also just visible.

He and Pugachov had finished dinner by quarter to nine and retired to the lounge, where he asked his butler to fix both of them a glass of his favorite Madeira wine from the Koktebel winery, across the Black Sea in the Crimea.

Just after the drinks arrived, Pugachov's phone rang.

The FSB colonel had arrived in Tuapse the previous morning following the arrival of the yacht that had carried Johnson's kids and sister.

Tkachev and his men, two of whom spoke fluent French, had done an excellent job in kidnapping and delivering Johnson's kids and sister, as ordered. Now Severinov did not want to make any mistakes this time with Johnson, who he knew for certain would turn up at some point.

There had been no response to his email, as expected, but that made little difference.

The previous Wednesday, an alert had flashed up on Severinov's laptop screen warning of a possible unauthorized attempt to access it. He had instantly closed the machine down and disconnected it from the refinery network. His IT team had not been able to identify where the attack had come from or who had carried it out. But clearly, the CIA or the NSA had to be at the top of the list of suspects, and Johnson was on their team.

Pugachov glanced at the phone and answered it. He listened for several seconds, then checked his watch.

"Why the delay in informing me?" Pugachov asked, leaning forward in his chair and catching Severinov's eye.

Again, he listened. "Not good enough," Pugachov said. His voice was flat and menacing as he rattled off a series of questions and then listened to the answers.

Finally, Pugachov slapped his thigh angrily. "We will discuss this another time. You had better have your excuses ready." He ended the call.

"What's that?" Severinov asked.

"My FSB contact in Sochi thinks Johnson might have gone through the airport earlier today. There was an American, tall, vaguely fitting the description, but under a different name. He was with a group from a British company that is working on the refinery."

Severinov stiffened. "Working on the turnaround? At my refinery? When did he arrive at Sochi? What was his name and company?" The questions were coming like machine gunfire.

Pugachov looked away. "Earlier. At lunchtime. He's not a hundred percent sure, but the man's name was Thiele. Don Thiele. He told the Border Service officer at passport control he was working for a company called Octane Refinery Maintenance, ORM."

Severinov put the wine glass down on the table. "*Lunchtime?* That's hours ago. So he must be in Tuapse by now. He could be on the site. For God's sake. Why didn't they—"

"I don't know, Yuri," Pugachov interrupted. "The passport officer was probably half asleep. He only sent the notification to our office when his shift finished. But he did say he wasn't sure. Probably just covering his ass for reporting it late."

Severinov swore again. "Was he traveling alone or with backup? What about that SZR assistant director, Marchenko? The one who was with him in Rostov? He might be there too. He was using the cover name Venclova."

"He isn't sure. He thinks alone, although it is difficult to be certain because he was with a group from ORM."

"We'd better get down to the refinery now. Give Tkachev a call and warn him. I'll call head of security."

Severinov shook his head as he tapped the number on his phone. The security team had been given photographs of Johnson two days earlier and warned that he might try to enter the site. The number of staff on duty at both the main entrance and the two secondary entrances had both been increased, and they had been told to rigorously check everyone entering, particularly given the number of external contractors around.

All were under strict instructions to hold Johnson if spotted. However, if correct, the name Thiele was a new one. Severinov had given his team the Wilkinson alias that Johnson had used previously.

Tkachev and a couple of other security guards were in charge of the kids and the sister, who were being kept locked up in a disused storage building on the southern part of the site.

Severinov grabbed his Makarov from the coffee table and shoved it into his waistband, then put a spare magazine in his pocket. Then he strode out the door and across his driveway toward his black Mercedes, rattling out instructions to his head of refinery security, Kirill Yanayev, on his phone as he went. Behind him, Pugachov was doing likewise on the phone with Tkachev.

CHAPTER THIRTY-NINE

Sunday, August 3, 2014
  Tuapse

The bus came to a halt and the engine was turned off. The cargo hold doors were opened.

"Come out, quickly," said Hill, speaking in an urgent whisper. He began pulling boxes out of the way so they could crawl out.

Johnson and Jayne scrambled out of the cargo hatch and put on their hard hats and yellow reflective vests, hung safety glasses around their necks on straps, and slung their backpacks over their shoulders. Now they each looked no different from the army of other contractors who were milling around.

They were just in time: a group of four security guards walked past the bus, all dressed in distinctive green-and-yellow reflective jackets. None glanced in their direction.

The last scraps of daylight had disappeared, and the entire refinery site was brightly lit by a mixture of powerful floodlights and low-energy streetlights. The bus had stopped outside a pair of two-story buildings that Hill explained were being used as a base by the various contractors who were doing work during the turnaround. Octane had three rooms in the left-hand building, to where staff members were now carrying the boxes that had also been in the hold.

Johnson took a few moments to get his bearings, recalling the refinery layout from the map that Hill had shown them earlier, which he had committed to memory as best he could. The entrance the bus had used was off the main highway that ran through the center of the refinery site, and they were now a couple of hundred yards to the west of the gate.

"Thank you," Johnson said, turning to face Hill. "We'll try and stay out of your way now."

"Yes, and good luck," Hill said. "I hope you don't need it. Remember, the head of human resources hired you, not me, if anyone asks. Not me. Understood?" He said it with a straight face.

"Completely understood," Jayne said. "You've already done more than we could have expected."

"Yes, extremely helpful," Johnson said. He took out his phone and tapped out a short two-word encrypted message to Neal in Istanbul: *On site.*

By that stage, he expected the trawler to be nearing Russian waters.

Johnson then waited. As soon as he spotted a group of contractors heading in the direction they wanted, he and Jayne tagged on a few yards behind them, trying to appear as though they were part of the same bunch.

The route took them westward through the site. On both sides of the road were multiple pipelines of different sizes, some supported on metal stands that were head high, others on concrete supports that were lower. The pipelines branched off in some places toward huge steel production units built from an incomprehensible tangle of vessels, pipes, and valves that Johnson guessed would normally be belching steam and pumping out oil products of various types. Not now, though. None of the units were operational, but all were busy with a swarm of workers wearing the ubiquitous yellow or orange safety jackets and white hard hats.

It took more than ten minutes to walk through the forest of production units, by which stage the group they had started out following had largely dispersed.

Visualizing the map, Johnson cut off the road and followed a footpath that took them around a long workshop built from corrugated steel and from which the raucous sound of metal drills, lathes, hammers, and other high-powered electric tools was coming.

Beyond that was a small parking lot, then a tall brick building with an industrial roller shutter vehicle door on the left side, perhaps twenty feet high. Next to that were some flat-roofed brick buildings.

Johnson paused at the point where the path led through an archway between the workshop on one side and a brick wall on the other.

"Let's just see the lay of the land here," he said softly. Based on what Hill had told him, they were at the section of the refinery they were looking for.

Jayne pointed. "See beneath that covered area? Two guards. One with a holstered gun."

Johnson followed her gaze to a sheltered area at the left of the warehouse with the roller shutter door. These guards had dark uniforms rather than the green-and-yellow worn by most at the refinery. "I see them," he said.

"Two more in that truck to the right of the building," Jayne said. "The Toyota pickup."

Indeed, Jayne was correct. Behind the windshield of the

Toyota that stood to the right of the building with the shutter door, he could just about make out two more guards.

"Sharp eyes," Johnson said. "Just move out of their line of sight."

They edged to their right, behind the brick wall, so they weren't visible to the guards.

"So what are they guarding?" Jayne asked.

Johnson ran his eyes across the flat-roofed brick buildings beyond the one with the shutter door. Then he spotted another two guards in a small prefabricated hut next to the second flat-roofed brick building.

"They've got these buildings sewn up like Fort Knox," Johnson said. "Let's circle around the back and have a look."

They followed the brick wall toward the river, which brought them to another path that ran westward behind the buildings that were being guarded. The path ran within forty yards of the buildings in some places, although there were a few pine trees in the space between.

"Not sure if this is a good idea," Johnson said. The yellow high-visibility vests and white helmets they were wearing were a double-edged sword. They offered some anonymity in one sense, but on the other hand made it impossible to simply fade into the shadows.

Then two men wearing similar protective gear appeared coming along the path toward them, walking at a brisk pace.

"Come on, let's go for it," Jayne said. "It will look natural, like them. Walk confidently. Then we'll get a look at the rear of those buildings. We can just keep walking and return another way."

"Agreed," Johnson said. They stepped out and walked quickly at a sharp pace along the path, avoiding eye contact with the two men as they passed them.

Another security guard was ambling slowly along a path right next to the rear of the building with the shutter door, and yet another sat on a low wall behind the first flat-roofed building.

"My gut tells me this is it," Johnson muttered. "No other buildings on-site have this much security. And these guys have different uniforms."

They continued walking at pace in a loop that took them a couple of hundred yards away from the buildings they had pinpointed and back to their vantage point next to the arch between the corrugated iron workshop and the brick wall.

Just as they arrived there, a black Mercedes 4x4 braked sharply to a halt, throwing up a hail of gravel in the parking lot forty yards ahead of them, in front of the second flat-roofed building.

Two men got smartly out of the front doors and began walking briskly toward the guards in the prefabricated hut.

Johnson's scalp tightened, and he reflexively ducked behind the brick wall to his right, pulling Jayne with him.

"That's Severinov," he muttered. "And I think the other guy is Pugachov."

* * *

Sunday, August 3, 2014
    Tuapse

Severinov, followed closely by Pugachov, strode into the storage building where the head of refinery security, Kirill Yanayev, was standing anxiously, his hands clasped behind his back. Next to him was Georgi Tkachev.

"Any sign of Johnson?" Severinov asked bluntly, eyeballing Yanayev, who stood six inches taller but was visibly anxious in the face of Severinov's bullish entrance.

"No, sir. None at all," Yanayev said, his tone low and

matter-of-fact. "The photograph of Johnson went to all our officers yesterday, as you know, and we have been keeping strict checks on everyone visiting the site, but—"

"Yes, but what about Don Thiele?" Severinov interrupted. "That's the name he's likely using. Not Johnson. As I told you."

"I know that, sir. I was about to say that we are still double-checking the list, especially the ORM names, but nothing yet. Everyone who has come through security has been recorded into the system with the bar code scanners as normal. Thiele is indeed on the updated list of Octane employees that the company supplied to us yesterday. And he has a bar code allocated. There was a photograph of him looking a bit different to Johnson, with a short beard. But he does not appear to have entered the refinery." Yanayev spread his hands, palms upward, and shrugged.

"*Dermo.* Shit," Severinov said. "When did Octane people last come on-site?"

Yanayev checked his watch. "About forty-five minutes ago, sir. They all came in on two buses for the night shift. It is a new group, just arrived from London, though most have been here before. All the people on the buses were checked."

"*Forty-five minutes?*" Severinov pressed his lips tight together. "Could he have sneaked in without being checked? Did your guards check the baggage hold and the trunk on the buses?"

Yanayev nodded. "Yes, my team check the baggage hold, always. They generally open some of the boxes."

"Do they look in all the boxes?" Severinov demanded, his voice menacingly level. "Do they pull the boxes out? Could someone hide in the baggage hold?"

"They do pull some of the boxes out, yes. Not all of them, as that would take too long. Most of the buses have dozens, scores, of boxes loaded on them. And then there's a lot of trucks coming into the site too, carrying materials and equipment, as you will know. If we checked every single box, really, it would take forever. But it would not be easy to hide in those baggage compartments unseen, in my view."

"Not good enough. From now on, check all boxes going in and out. And I want everyone's bar codes recorded on the way out of the site as well as on the way in. If Johnson, or Thiele, has somehow gotten into this refinery, we don't let him out. And if he tries to come in, you hold him and tell me immediately."

Yanayev nodded. "Yes, sir."

Severinov turned and looked at Tkachev. "The kids and woman are still secure, I assume?"

"Of course," Tkachev said. He pointed toward a door at the rear of the room. "They are through there. Still tied up. If you want me to dispose of them, just say."

"No, I don't, not yet," Severinov said. "Make sure all entrances to this building are secured and locked."

"They already are," Tkachev said.

Severinov took Tkachev by the elbow and steered the Spetsnaz assassin across the room to where Pugachov was standing.

"I suspect Johnson may either be on the site or will try to get in soon," Severinov said. "He would not want to delay—his kids are here. He'll be desperate to try and get them out. We need to lock this refinery down and find the bastard."

Tkachev nodded. "I would approach this like a military search. The site is quite narrow; at a guess, I would say about four hundred meters wide. We could take ten men, spread them out in a line, and comb the place. If Johnson's here, we'll squeeze him into a corner like a fox into a hole."

Severinov folded his arms. "Yes, we'll begin by doing that. We can start here and work our way east up the site."

He looked at Pugachov. "Georgi and I will go with the

search team. Can you remain here and ensure the kids are secure, and deal with Johnson if he comes here?"

Pugachov nodded. "I'll kill him if he does."

Severinov turned around and beckoned Yanayev to join them, then started rattling out a series of orders.

* * *

Sunday, August 3, 2014
  Tuapse

"My gut tells me my kids are in one of those two buildings," Johnson said. "The one with the flat roof or the one with the roller door."

"Yes, so how do we get them out?" Jayne asked. "Damn tricky with all those guards, unless we—"

"Unless we create a good diversion," Johnson said. He tugged at the small nick in his right ear.

"That's what I was about to say. Exactly."

It often seemed to Johnson that Jayne had a built-in instinct, almost a sixth sense, for what he was thinking, and the majority of the time, her thoughts took her in the same direction as his.

They were walking eastward along the path, away from the buildings in question, toward the main entrance. Johnson felt they needed to regroup and think through their next steps as calmly and precisely as possible.

After walking for several minutes, they arrived back in an area where turnaround work on the refinery units was underway and there were more people dressed like them in hard hats and yellow vests were milling around. It gave them better natural cover.

They paused behind a large mobile crane that was not being used.

"Listen, I've got a plan in mind," Johnson said.

He went on to outline what his thinking was. Jayne listened, interjecting with the occasional question as he spoke quietly and quickly. Both recognized there was little time to play with.

After a few minutes, having agreed on the details, they set off at a brisk walk through the refinery, again heading east. They passed the building where the Octane team was based, continued beyond what looked like an administration office block and parking lot, and through the tunnel to the eastern half of the refinery.

There they found a somewhat different landscape. This was the tank farm, comprising rows of enormous cylindrical white-painted steel containers, some of them at least forty or even fifty feet high, while others were smaller. Long metal staircases wound their way in spiral fashion up the sides of the tanks to allow employees to carry out inspection work on top.

Most of the tanks appeared to be in use, but a few were obviously undergoing repairs, and workmen were going in and out of a couple of empty ones through a gap at their bases.

Johnson led the way past the tanks that were grouped together until he came to a wide-open area of waste ground that stretched for about two hundred yards. At the other side of it were the two tanks that he had identified from the aerial photographs, standing next to a long overhead gantry with pipes dropping down. This was where the fuel tanker trucks were loaded up with diesel and gasoline prior to starting their journeys to gas stations all over southern Russia.

Normally, Johnson could see that this unit would be busy with a stream of trucks. Today, during the turnaround, it remained silent and empty.

As they drew near to the two tanks, Johnson stopped. One of the tanks had a large sign on the side with black writing on a yellow background that read Gasoline in both Russian and English, and the other was marked Diesel.

"How do we know whether these tanks are full or empty?" Johnson asked. "Won't all the measurements be done remotely?"

He turned to Jayne. She was the refinery expert between the two of them.

"Yes, they'll have gauges feeding data to the control center. But there will be local field display gauges next to the tanks too." She pointed. "I can see one there."

They walked up to a half-moon-shaped unit mounted on a pipeline that ran down from the top of the gasoline tank, which towered thirty feet above them.

Jayne bent over the unit and pulled up a small protective flap on the front to reveal a digital display. "There, it's about ten percent full."

Johnson nodded. "Perfect."

He removed his backpack, took out one of the small slabs of C4 explosive and a remote detonator, then pushed a cable from the detonator into a socket at the back of the control unit. He punched a button and tapped in a secure code on the keypad to synchronize the two and to prevent the detonator from being triggered accidentally by another remote device.

"Give me your remote," Johnson said. "I'll code that as well, in case we need a backup. This will be detonator one on the keypad, okay?"

Jayne nodded, took her remote control from her bag, and handed it to Johnson, who keyed in the same code to synchronize it with the detonator before returning it to her.

Then he pushed two pin-like plugs on the back of the detonator into the soft C4 before shaping the soft explosive around the back of the detonator so that the two elements were firmly held together.

Johnson scrutinized the tank structure. Two pipelines led from near the base of the tank to join up with a larger pipeline that ran alongside the nearby road.

"What about where the pipeline joins the tank body?"

Jayne nodded. She was silent for a few seconds. "You do realize that will blow the fuel truck loading site pretty much away?"

"Yes. That's the idea," Johnson said with a thin grin on his face. "But that long stretch of waste ground is a good buffer— it should stop the explosion from blowing the rest of the refinery up with it. I don't really want to do that."

"I wouldn't be so sure," Jayne said. "Even at ten percent full."

"I think it will do a nice job."

Johnson walked to the massive tank, which was surrounded by a circle of gravel, and used some black tape to fasten the C4 and detonator to the underside of one of the two pipes that emerged from the main body of the tank.

"That's one done," Johnson said. "Next is the substation."

They made their way up the slope past the four tanks under construction that Johnson had seen on the aerial photographs. At the base of each of the tanks, a couple of the huge steel panels that formed the bottom of the tank wall had yet to be welded on, allowing workmen to walk or drive vehicles in and out of the bottom of the vessels, which Johnson guessed were at least 120 feet in diameter.

They all had steel stepladders that curved their way around the structure like a snake up the side of the tank to an observation platform at the top.

Farther eastward up the slope, parked on the edge of the road near the last tank under construction, stood two old

Toyota pickup trucks that appeared to have been left by workmen.

At the top of the slope, near the refinery's eastern perimeter fence, stood a large gray metal building with a black-on-yellow sign that in both Russian and English read Electricity Substation. A large overhead cable ran into the substation from pylons that were outside the refinery, but the cables within the refinery appeared to be buried underground. At least, nothing was visible.

A steel door into the substation had a red warning sign on it, and a row of three fire extinguishers hung next to the door.

Johnson looked around. There was nobody in sight.

"Behind the extinguishers?" he asked Jayne.

Again she nodded. Three minutes later, the pair of them were walking away, having taped a second slab of C4 and a detonator out of sight on the back of the red extinguisher cylinders. Johnson coded it as detonator number two on both remote control units.

"We need to kick this diversion thing off," Jayne said. "Before Severinov does something stupid."

"Yes, but let's do it from nearer where the kids and Amy are so we can check how people react."

Jayne nodded, and they set off back toward the western end of the site, down the slope, past the gasoline and diesel tanks next to the truck loading gantry, and over the waste ground. They were about to cut over onto the road when Johnson stopped dead.

Three hundred yards ahead of them was a line of men, thinly spread out at intervals almost across the entire refinery site, most of them wearing the distinctive yellow-and-green security team jackets. They were walking slowly toward them, very clearly looking for something.

CHAPTER FORTY

Sunday, August 3, 2014
  Tuapse

Johnson's gut twitched inside him. He ducked down behind a wall next to two dumpsters, followed by Jayne.

"Severinov's got the security after us," Johnson said. "Now what?"

Jayne had already begun to strip off her reflective yellow vest, revealing a dark navy shirt beneath, and she then removed her white helmet.

"Get that reflective gear off," she said. "Then we run back up the site. We need somewhere to hide until they're gone. There are places."

Johnson nodded and ripped off his reflective vest and hard hat. His dark-green shirt beneath made him far less visible. They both stuffed the garments and hard hats into one of the dumpsters and closed the lid.

"Let's go," Johnson said.

Doubling over, they ran back across the waste ground

toward the fuel loading gantry and twin tanks, where they paused and looked back. The line of about ten security men was now a third of the way across the waste ground, still moving steadily. However, there was no obvious sense of urgency; it didn't appear that they had been spotted.

"Keep going," Johnson said. They turned and continued running toward the four tanks under construction.

"I think we should trigger the detonator on the fuel tank now," Jayne said. "That would stop their search."

Johnson stopped and turned. He could see the line of men was approaching the fuel tank where the detonator was secured.

"It's going to cause the mother of all explosions if that tank goes up. It would kill all of them," Johnson said. He felt very uneasy about the potential death toll, although his options were running out rapidly. "And we'd need to take shelter first. The blast could take us out."

"We could shelter inside one of these new tanks," Jayne said. "The walls are an inch thick. That would protect us. Then trigger it from there."

Johnson looked at Jayne, then away again. She was right. They had few options. If they were captured, they'd be dead, as would Carrie, Peter, and Amy. He felt as though he was backed into a corner.

"Yes, okay," he said.

As they drew nearer to the new tanks, Johnson caught sight of the two old Toyota pickups beyond the tanks.

"Jayne, if we could get one of those Toyotas, could you hot-wire it?" One of Jayne's surprising skills was the ability to quickly hot-wire a car. She had learned it during her time at MI6.

"Maybe, but then what?"

"After the blast, we drive it down to the other end of the refinery, get the kids out, and use it to drive to the beach landing point. It would be a hell of a lot quicker than running."

"The blast could knock out the pickup, though."

"Drive it into the tank, so it's sheltered like us." Johnson could see that workmen had been doing exactly that with other trucks, since there were vehicle ramps leading through the gaps in all the tank walls.

Jayne paused. "All right," she said. "We'll give it a go."

Johnson took his Beretta from his backpack and shoved it into his belt. "Best get moving."

Jayne also put her pistol into her waist, then reached into her backpack and took out her heavy-duty multitool, which included a wire stripper. Johnson knew she would need it to strip the ignition wires in order to hot-wire the pickup.

"I'll go check the tank while you're doing that. I'll wait at the entrance." Johnson pointed to the second of the four tanks that stood about forty yards from where they were.

Jayne nodded and set off toward the pair of Toyotas.

Johnson walked over to the tank and, using the vehicle ramp, stepped inside.

It was like entering some kind of futuristic Roman amphitheater. The inside was an enormous, perfectly cylindrical space. The walls were made from large steel plates that had all turned rusty brown, and they were decorated with silver spots and lines where they had been welded together. They towered high above him, creating a bowl-like effect. It appeared that the tank was very near to completion. A number of scaffolding towers stood around the edge, up against the walls, and a row of industrial welding kits, oxyacetylene blowtorches, and gas cylinders lay on the floor.

As Jayne had said, the steel tank shell wall was at least an inch thick at the bottom. She was correct: that should shelter them from the blast if they triggered the detonator attached to the fuel tank a few hundred yards away.

Johnson glanced around, then walked back to the tank entrance. Before stepping out, he checked carefully to his left and right. In the distance to his left, he could just about make out the dark figure of Jayne, who had almost arrived at the two Toyota pickup trucks.

To his right, the line of security guards was visible in the distance, not far from the fuel loading gantry. He hoped Jayne would be quick, but his best guess was that they had a good five minutes before the guards got anywhere near. There was no sign of any other surveillance.

Johnson stepped cautiously out of the exit. But as he did so, he heard a slight noise to his right.

Johnson spun around. Less than ten yards away, flat against the outside wall of the tank and pointing a handgun straight at him, was the Spetsnaz GRU man, Tkachev, whose photograph he had obtained from Mikhail near Severny. There was no mistaking the noticeable scar on his left cheek.

Shit. Where the hell did he come from?

"Raise your hands above your head," Tkachev said, his lips pressed tightly together. "Now!" he said, raising his voice sharply.

"Don't even think about trying to pull that gun in your belt," Tkachev said. "Or else you get a bullet through the head. Now, ease it out of your belt slowly with your right hand, then kick it to me. Move very slowly, because my trigger finger is itching, and it won't take much. When you have done that, put your hand back above your head."

Johnson knew he had no choice. He slowly lowered his right hand and, using his index finger, flicked the Beretta out of his belt. It fell with a crunch onto the gravel.

Then Johnson kicked it in Tkachev's direction and slowly raised his right hand again.

Tkachev crouched and, keeping his gun trained on Johnson with his right hand, edged forward and used his left hand to pick up the Beretta, which he pushed into his belt. Then he slowly stood and took a couple of steps backward.

"Now your backpack. Get it off, drop it to the ground, kick it to me. And empty your pockets very slowly. Phone, wallet. Throw everything here," Tkachev said.

Johnson complied.

Tkachev placed Johnson's phone and wallet in the backpack, then put it on the ground behind him, took out his own phone and, using his left hand, pressed the keypad and held the phone to his ear.

"It is Georgi," Tkachev said in Russian. "I have the American, Johnson, near the new tanks, beyond the fuel loading station. I have his gun. Where are you?"

There was a pause as Tkachev listened. Then he spoke again.

"I am sure you will want to finish this yourself?"

He waited for a reply, then nodded. "I thought so. You can just walk up here with the security guards, in that case. See you in a minute." He ended the call and replaced the phone in his pocket.

Johnson assumed that he had just spoken to Severinov, who, judging by the conversation, was not far away.

Bastard.

* * *

Sunday, August 3, 2014
Tuapse

Severinov had felt as tense as a coiled spring but now allowed himself to relax a fraction. The end was in sight for Johnson, and he was determined to make it a memorable one.

He pushed his phone back into his pocket, checked the

Makarov that was stuffed into his jacket pocket, and walked briskly across the stretch of waste ground. The area was covered in gravel and crushed stone while awaiting development into yet another refinery unit.

As he walked, he overtook several of the refinery security team who had been walking in a long line while combing the site for any sign of Johnson. He might have known that it would be Tkachev who would outthink Johnson and trap him, not his bunch of half-incompetent security officers who wouldn't know the ass from the elbow of an infiltrator.

As he drew near to the four new tanks that were nearing completion, he could see Johnson standing just outside the entrance to the second one, his arms held in the air, with Tkachev a few meters away.

He stopped next to Tkachev, who had his pistol pointed straight at Johnson, and stared at the American, who remained motionless.

"Finally, Mr. Johnson, finally," Severinov said. He took another step toward Johnson and scrutinized him for a moment. "In Russia we have a saying: death is not found behind mountains but right behind our shoulders. You appear not to have checked over your shoulder tonight. And that means our long acquaintance must finally end."

Johnson shifted from one foot to the other, hands still aloft, but said nothing.

"How long has it been now?" Severinov continued. "Twenty-six years since our first encounter in Afghanistan, I believe. You are a fool who doesn't know when to stop. Now tell me—are you alone, or do you have that helper of yours, Marchenko, with you this time, or perhaps the British woman?"

"He is in Kiev, not here," Johnson muttered.

"That is lucky for him, although I am not sure I believe you." Severinov glanced around the area but could see no sign of anyone else. "Anyway, if he or someone else is on this site, we will find them."

Johnson looked at him nervously. "Shooting me won't help you. Your leaders in Moscow will still stab you in the back— or from behind your shoulder, as you put it. It will simply make you even more of an international target than your part in shooting down that Malaysian airliner already has. You are an intelligent man, Yuri, but you are not applying that intelligence well."

"It is you who has failed to apply intelligence to your situation, Johnson. I instructed you very clearly to extract from your president a statement that there would be no more supplies of weapons or missiles to Ukraine. I gave you seven days—and those seven days are now up. Instead, it appears that the United States is going to increase its commitment. You will bear the consequences for that, as I warned you."

Severinov took another step toward Johnson, who didn't blink. "You underestimated me. Remember, whatever we do is for the glory of the *Rodina*, the Motherland. It is one big Russian operation."

"Ah, a Russian operation. Your active measures. Is that Operation Pandora? Is that the one?" Johnson asked. "Was the Malaysian jet part of Pandora? The troll farm in Rostov?"

Severinov had to stop himself from doing a double take.

Who the hell has leaked that?

The only other person he knew of who was aware of Pandora was Anastasia Shevchenko, who had confidentially told him about it in the first place because she was working on it.

So how did Johnson know about it, and why mention it now?

"Operation Pandora?" Severinov asked.

"Yes, you know all about Pandora, don't you?"

"I don't know anything about that," Severinov said, recovering himself quickly. He grinned at Johnson. "And whatever you know isn't long for this earth. Wave goodbye to it. Wave goodbye to your kids, your sister." He grinned at Johnson.

"All right, you will do what you will do," Johnson said. His voice had a resigned air about it. "But can I just see my kids and my sister one more time before you do it?"

Severinov was silent for a couple of seconds, contemplating. Perhaps this was a way to double the impact, to leave a lasting legacy of what he was about to do to Johnson. Perhaps his children and his sister should witness it.

"You would like them to see me shoot you dead, would you?" he asked.

A look of scarcely disguised horror momentarily crossed Johnson's face, which he was clearly battling hard to quell.

"I just want to say goodbye," Johnson said quietly. "You can't make them see me die."

Severinov grinned. "Actually, I think that's an excellent idea."

He turned to Tkachev and pointed into the oil tank behind him. "Put this idiot in the center of the tank. Make him stand there while I fetch his kids and sister. Then they can watch him die."

Severinov glanced up at the inspection platform at the top of the flight of steps that curled up the side of the tank. "I tell you what—they can go up there and get a grandstand view of it. Did you ever see Spanish bullfighting in the arena? Or that film *Gladiator*?"

Tkachev laughed. "*Gladiator* I have seen many times."

"That's what it will be like. Except I'll use a pistol instead of a bull or a sword."

He noticed that Johnson had gone pale. For a second he thought the American's knees were going to buckle, but he must have recovered himself, because he remained standing.

As they spoke, three security guards from the search team

arrived at the tank. Severinov told one of them to accompany him to fetch Johnson's kids and instructed the other two to remain with Tkachev. "It is possible that the American has his Ukrainian friend, Marchenko, with him on the refinery, or maybe someone else. You two keep a lookout for anyone here while Georgi keeps a watch on him," he said, pointing to Johnson. "Is that understood?"

The men nodded their agreement.

Severinov turned to Tkachev. "I've got my car just down the road. I'll bring the kids and sister back in the security truck with this guy." He indicated toward the guard he had designated to accompany him. "It will be quicker if I go with the car. You keep this *bljad*, this son of a bitch, in the tank. If he tries anything, just shoot him dead."

He watched as Tkachev pointed toward the center of the tank and told Johnson to go and stand there.

Johnson, who clearly realized he had little choice, walked to the middle of the huge tank, his hands still raised, then turned and faced Tkachev, who placed Johnson's backpack up against the wall of the tank and then stood at the entrance.

"Good," Severinov said. "I'll be back in ten minutes."

He walked off at a brisk pace toward his Mercedes ML 4x4, which he had left parked near the fuel truck loading gantry and about seventy meters from the diesel and gasoline tanks that supplied it. The security guard followed a couple of paces behind him.

Severinov crossed the waste ground. He was now feeling much more upbeat. The thought of handing out a death sentence to Johnson after so long was positively uplifting.

He turned to the security guard, who was lagging behind. "Come on, we need to move quickly." The guard increased his pace to catch up.

But as Severinov resumed his stride, now within fifty meters of his car, there came an enormous, earth-trembling explosion from the gasoline tank in front of him that imme-diately shattered his eardrums.

In the same moment a fireball erupted, spreading outward and rising far into the night sky and causing a flash of light so bright that Severinov was blinded instantly.

The last thing Severinov knew was a sensation of intense heat as his body was thrown backward. The force of the explosion ripped him off his feet and lifted him ten meters into the air, blowing him back with tremendous force against a steel pylon, where his body was shattered and shredded, leaving it so mangled that days later, Russian investigators had to carry out a DNA test to identify his remains.

* * *

Sunday, August 3, 2014
    Tuapse

Jayne eventually picked herself up off the floor of the enormous oil tank where she had been thrown on her back by the blast. She picked up the remote control unit, pushed it into her backpack, and staggered a little unsteadily to the gap that formed an entrance to the structure. She poked her head cautiously around the edge of the thick steel tank shell wall and involuntarily gasped at what she saw.

Orange flames were soaring hundreds of feet into the darkness, illuminating the dense black cloud of smoke that was also rising. Despite the blaze being several hundred yards away, she could feel the heat on her face and hands.

Even as she watched, another smaller explosion boomed into the night as some other vessel or pipeline caught fire.

"Bloody hell," she muttered. From her position at the

mouth of the fourth of the tanks under construction, she peered at the entrance to the second.

That was where she had last seen Johnson. She had been about to force open the door of one of the Toyota pickups to hot-wire it when she had glanced back at him, only to see him raise his hands into the air as another dark figure appeared near to him.

Realizing what had happened, she had run from her exposed position to the nearest cover, which was the fourth tank. There she threw herself to the ground just outside it and watched.

There was little doubt who the two men holding Johnson were: one was Severinov, whom she had seen earlier in the day and whose authoritative walk and body language she recognized from videos she had seen of him. He was the one in charge, directing the other man, who she presumed was Tkachev, and the three security guards who had turned up.

She was tempted to blow the detonator immediately when Johnson had been forced into the tank at gunpoint. She realized that in there, the tank walls would protect him to some degree from the blast. But something made her wait.

Then as she watched Severinov—she was sure it was him —head back on foot toward the fuel loading gantry and twin tanks, with one of the security guards following behind him, she knew that was her opportunity.

There was absolutely no alternative, that much was clear in her mind. Her guess was that if Severinov hadn't shot Johnson on the spot, he was certain to do so soon, probably inside the tank.

It was a literal choice between Severinov's life and Johnson's—and probably hers and Johnson's family's lives too.

And so she had taken the remote control from her backpack, switched it on and, after taking cover behind the steel wall inside the tank, pressed the button.

The twin explosions as the gasoline and diesel tanks went up, separated by no more than a second, had been deafening and forceful.

Even in Jayne's relatively sheltered position, the blasts had reverberated around the cylindrical tank, half deafening her and knocking her off her feet. The fall bruised her spine and shoulder, and she immediately cursed herself for her foolishness in not lying down before triggering the detonator. But she was alive, and she was certain that Severinov was not.

What she didn't know was whether Johnson was alive.

Jayne felt her hand shaking and realized she was in a state of shock. But despite the chaos and her confused state, she forced herself to concentrate and to process what she was seeing.

On the ground next to the second tank opening, she could see two motionless figures in reflective jackets. They were the two security guards she had seen. Were they dead? Unconscious? And where was the other man, Tkachev or Pugachov? She couldn't see him, but she knew she had to get to the tank and check what had happened to Johnson.

Jayne took the Beretta from her waistband, flicked off the safety, dropped to her knees to lower her profile, and began to crawl toward the second tank. The ground was rough and covered in the detritus from the building works: bits of metal, old rivets, screws, lumps of cement. They all dug into her knees and hands as she crawled.

Her senses were now on red alert, completely overloaded.

Was Tkachev or Pugachov there in hiding, ready to take her out as she drew closer?

Had he shot Johnson?

Or—the truly unthinkable outcome—had Johnson died in the blast she had triggered?

She had to keep going.

Jayne crawled level with the third tank, which was empty.

Gradually she drew closer to the second tank.

Still there was no movement, no sign of anyone alive.

* * *

Sunday, August 3, 2014

Tuapse

Carrie, exhausted, had her eyes closed as she tried to doze, when there came the deafening boom of a huge explosion somewhere nearby. In the same instant, all the windows of the room in which they were imprisoned were blown inward, throwing fragments of glass everywhere and causing the door of the room to slam shut.

Something hit her on the side of her face, and she screamed instinctively and loudly, as did Amy, who was lying next to her on the piece of rough carpet. Peter, who was asleep, made a guttural noise and jerked awake.

Carrie tried to pull herself upright but was hampered by the bindings that held her hands firmly behind her back and her ankles together.

Then all the lights went out, and they were thrown into complete darkness.

Carrie screamed again.

This was a never-ending nightmare, like one of the horrible psychological thrillers she had often watched on television at home with her friends and then wished she hadn't.

She could feel the trickle of something warm down the side of her cheek. Was it blood on her face? Had she been cut? She couldn't get her hand to her face to check, and she couldn't see anything anyway.

"Oh my God," she said, her voice faltering, and she began to cry. Her tears turned from a trickle into a flood, and her crying from a sob into a full-throated roar of despair.

Where is my dad?

There came the sound of a frantic, panicked conversation in Russian from the room next door, where she knew from her last trip to the toilet that several security guards had been sitting and watching television. But now the power had gone off, and the TV was silent.

She tried to stop her sobbing to listen, but she couldn't understand a word of the conversation. The door opened, and someone shone a bright flashlight at them for a couple of seconds, then slammed the door shut again.

The voices grew louder, and footsteps clattered on the concrete floor as the men piled out of the neighboring room into the corridor. Another door slammed shut.

The loudest sound then was from the wind, which was blowing through the broken glass, causing one of the wooden window blinds to flap and clatter against the window frame.

But above it, Carrie gradually began to hear a distant roar, with crackling and occasional smaller explosions. She could smell smoke and burning. It smelled bad and sickly, like the scent of burning rubber, which she had once come across when a neighbor at home set fire to some trash and a couple of old bike tires from his garage.

"My God," she muttered to herself.

Carrie tried to make sense of what had happened. There had been a big explosion, and presumably all the guards had gone to either help or run to safety, leaving them trapped alone in the dark.

Another sob choked her.

What would Dad say? Come on, pull yourself together. That's what Dad would say.

Carrie stared into the darkness. She couldn't move, and

neither could the others, because of the bindings on their wrists and ankles.

What would Dad do?

Think of a solution. That's what he would do.

Maybe she could find something to cut the bindings.

Then she remembered that as one of the guards had walked her down the corridor to the toilet, she had seen men in the neighboring TV room eating with knives and forks. Perhaps there were still knives in that room.

Carrie turned herself around, somehow got onto her knees, and started to inch herself toward the door. She would have to open it with her teeth.

"Carrie, where are you going?" Amy asked.

"I'm going to look for a knife. I'm going to cut us free," she said. "And then we're going to get out of here."

CHAPTER FORTY-ONE

Sunday, August 3, 2014
  Tuapse

The first thing Johnson saw when he opened his eyes was Tkachev crawling slowly across the concrete base of the oil tank, hauling and heaving himself along by his hands and elbows.

Behind Tkachev trailed his bloody and mangled right leg, which appeared to have been badly injured below the knee. His left leg was also twisted and sticking sideways at a strange angle.

Johnson realized he must have only been unconscious for a very short time, but the back of his head throbbed, and his shoulder felt as though it had been hit by a truck.

He winced at the sudden flood of pain and had a sharp recollection of what had happened: the enormous explosion, the flash of sun-bright light, the sensation of being hit in the midriff by a full-force gale, and the uncontrollable tumble several yards backward onto the tank floor.

The inside of the tank was illuminated in a ghostly way by a flickering orange light, which Johnson realized must be coming from the intense blaze burning a few hundred yards away, where the fuel tanks had exploded.

Johnson's gaze returned to Tkachev and the gory, bizarre red line he was painting behind him on the new white cement. The trail led some distance from near the entrance of the tank, presumably where he had been deposited by the force of the blast. He was bleeding at a considerable rate.

What the hell is he doing?

Then, through the haze, he saw where the Russian was headed. He spotted, ten yards ahead of Tkachev and roughly halfway between the two men, a pistol lying on the concrete floor. It was his, Johnson's, Beretta that Tkachev had taken from him only a short while earlier. Presumably the Russian's own pistol must have been lost in the explosion.

The sight sent a shot of adrenaline through Johnson that immediately masked some of the pain he was feeling. He jerked himself to his feet, his mind telling him to run forward toward the gun. He had to get there first.

But his body had other ideas. Perhaps it was due to the shock of what had happened, the pain he felt, or perhaps just low blood pressure, but he was immediately overcome by dizziness and spun sideways to the floor.

Johnson then forced himself to scramble to his knees, battling to overcome a sense of disorientation. He knew he had to reach that gun, because Tkachev was still somehow hauling himself toward it. Johnson began to crawl as fast as he could.

Despite the Russian's injuries, he was somehow using his arms to propel himself at a steady rate and was almost to within touching distance of the gun. He lifted his arm and, now at full stretch, appeared to push himself forward.

Johnson, converging on Tkachev from the other direction, launched himself and brought his right hand down toward the gun at exactly the same time as the Russian, who grabbed Johnson's wrist in his right hand, using a grip that felt like some kind of industrial clamp.

He momentarily eyeballed Tkachev, whose cheek scar was standing out white against his face in the gloom.

Johnson twisted his wrist in a bid to escape and, at the same time, tried to grab the gun with his other hand. But Tkachev had the same idea, and his left hand also descended toward the Beretta.

This time, it was Johnson who seized Tkachev's wrist in an attempt to stop him, leaving the two of them bizarrely locked together, their hands crossed over, holding tight onto each other's wrists like a pair of wrestlers.

The Russian had by far the stronger upper body, arms, and wrists. But it became instantly clear to Johnson that Tkachev's terrible lower body injuries had left him quite unable to do much more than heave himself around like a walrus. Surely he couldn't last much longer, given the amount of blood he was losing.

While still clinging to Tkachev, Johnson swung his body and legs around and, with all the force he could muster, launched a kick at Tkachev's lower limbs with his right boot, which had reinforced rubber toe caps. The kick made solid contact with the messy remains of Tkachev's right leg.

The Russian let out a tremendous roar of pain and weakened the grip he had on Johnson's right wrist.

It was enough for Johnson to wriggle his hand free.

In the same movement, he grabbed the butt of the Beretta and rolled sideways, letting go of Tkachev's left wrist.

Johnson rolled for a second time as fast as he could, putting himself out of the Russian's reach, and then crawled farther, ensuring he was a safe distance away.

He then pressed off the safety on the Beretta and, from a sitting position, leveled it at Tkachev.

Without speaking, Johnson got to his feet, his dizziness dissipating.

"I should kill you, you murderous bastard, for what you did in shooting down that airliner," Johnson said. "But you're going to bleed to death anyway with those injuries, and I'm not going to waste a valuable bullet."

He steered a wide berth around Tkachev, who having lost his battle to reach the pistol, had sunk belly-down to the floor. He was groaning softly, his body apparently surrendering to the inevitable.

Johnson unsteadily made his way toward the entrance of the giant tank. Outside, he could see the motionless bodies of the two security guards who had been with Tkachev.

Bloodstains were visible near the bottom of the inch-wide edge of the rusty steel plate that formed the tank wall, and the trail of blood from Tkachev's leg began on the floor below. Johnson's best guess was that the explosion must have propelled the Russian into the steel plate, which had acted almost like a knife as his legs slammed into it.

Got to get my kids. Got to get my kids.

As he walked, a shadow appeared at the left side of the entrance, and Johnson raised the pistol, his senses again on full red alert.

But the figure that emerged slowly and cautiously from behind the outside steel wall of the tank was Jayne, also carrying her gun, her backpack over her shoulder. He immediately lowered the gun and flicked on the safety.

"Thank God," she said. She moved toward him and flung her arms around his neck, giving him a tight hug that lasted several seconds.

She broke it off and stood back. "We need to get out of here," she said.

"My kids," Johnson said, pushing his pistol into his belt. "We need to get to them. My sister." He still felt dazed and struggled to enunciate what he was feeling. "What about Severinov?"

"Severinov is dead. One hundred percent dead," Jayne said. "He was very near the tank when I detonated it. No chance."

"Thank God for that."

"We will need to walk to find your kids. Those Toyotas are wrecked. It's complete chaos. The power's gone off across the whole refinery."

Johnson hadn't realized the power had gone down because the flames from the blazing fuel tanks were throwing off so much light. "That might help us. The security people will be panicking, and we'll be less obvious."

"Let's go," Jayne said. "Are you okay to walk?"

"I'll walk in any state if it means getting my kids and sister safely out."

Immediately outside the fuel tank entrance, Johnson spotted a GSh-18 pistol lying in the gravel. It must have been Tkachev's weapon, which he had dropped when hit by the blast. He picked it up.

Then Johnson noticed his own backpack, which was still lying on the floor against the tank wall. He removed his phone and wallet from it, then put the GSh-18 inside the backpack before slinging it over his shoulder.

Johnson glanced back at Tkachev one more time, just to make sure. The Russian was now lying silently on the concrete surface of the tank floor.

Johnson and Jayne set off on the road that led westward through the refinery. To their right lay an utterly apocalyptic scene. Burning fuel from the tanks had spread across a wide area, and the flames had engulfed the entire fuel truck loading gantry.

The wreckage of what looked like a Mercedes 4x4 was blazing furiously near the gantry. Johnson assumed it was probably Severinov's vehicle.

In the distance, Johnson could hear the sound of several sirens. He guessed that before long, a mass of fire, police, and ambulance crews would have descended on the site. It was even more important, then, that they got out quickly.

This was a blaze that would likely take a day or two to put out. As they walked, Johnson checked his watch, which thankfully Tkachev had not thought to take from him. It was half past eleven.

As he glanced up, he saw two men walking rapidly up the road toward them about a hundred yards away. He was certain one of them was Pugachov.

Johnson grabbed Jayne by the arm and pushed her into the narrow gap between two buildings to their left. One of them appeared to have lost part of its roof in the explosion. Johnson clicked off the safety on his Beretta and crouched behind a concrete post, braced for the Russians to come after them.

But they didn't. Johnson watched as the men passed by, walking almost at trotting speed. One was definitely Pugachov. The other was in a green uniform and was carrying a black case with a red cross on it, so he was presumably some kind of paramedic. The pair were seemingly oblivious to their presence. Johnson guessed they were going in search of Severinov and Tkachev.

They waited a few moments to be certain the men had gone, then continued. They saw several security officers on the way, but all were running around frantically, shouting at each other, dragging hoses, and trying to organize fire crews, stretchers, and first aid equipment.

Ten minutes later, they arrived at the two buildings they had pinpointed earlier as being the most likely to be holding

Johnson's children. Someone had placed a few emergency lanterns in certain places, but otherwise the site was largely in darkness.

Johnson stopped outside the first building with the giant shutter door. The guards who had been outside earlier were gone, and a row of windows high up on the wall had been blown in. "Let's see if we can get in here first."

The shutter door remained closed, so Johnson walked to the left side of the building, where a pedestrian door was hanging open. The building, like the others, was now in darkness, so he turned on the flashlight on his phone.

He stepped carefully through the entrance into a corridor. Another door was to the right, which Johnson also opened. He found himself in a vehicle garage on the other side of the shutter door and pointed his phone flashlight.

"Shit," Johnson said involuntarily. In front of him stood a white Volvo truck with a red lowboy semitrailer attached to the back of it. Johnson took a few steps and directed the flashlight upward. On the lowboy was what looked like a military tank, except this one had three enormous, slim white-tipped missiles mounted on the top.

"What is *that*?" Jayne said behind him.

"It's the goddamn missile launcher. The Buk. This must be the one they used to shoot down the Malaysian jet," Johnson said. "The NRO traced it back to the port here, then lost sight of it. It's got a missile missing."

They both stood staring at the vehicle. On the floor, fragments of broken glass were scattered everywhere from the windows that had been blown inward by the explosion.

"Jayne, take some photos of this. I'm going to search the back of the building."

He strode quickly past the missile launcher, opening the doors of three rooms that led off the garage. They were all empty.

While Jayne used her phone to take photographs of the Buk, Johnson returned to the corridor and searched the remaining rooms in the building. There was only a storage area and a toolroom that contained vehicle maintenance equipment.

"Come, we'll try the other building," Johnson said. He turned off his flashlight and led the way out and across a concrete walkway. The guards that had been at the hut outside the flat-roofed building earlier in the evening were gone.

Johnson carefully opened the door of the flat-roofed building and stepped inside, turning on his flashlight again. He found himself in a large, empty room that ran across the full width of the building. A door at the rear of the room was open, and once again, fragments of broken window glass lay on the floor.

Johnson paused. He could hear a faint noise coming from somewhere. A scraping sound.

He strode to the door at the rear of the room, which led into a corridor.

Johnson cautiously moved along the corridor, with Jayne close behind. There were a few doors that led off it at intervals, and Johnson opened all of them as he went, but all the rooms were empty.

He paused again. The scraping noise was louder now, and he could tell it was coming from the rear of the building.

Trying to tread silently on the concrete floor, Johnson edged his way toward the door where the noise was coming from, which was ajar.

There was a trail of fresh blood on the concrete corridor floor that led from the room next door, which Johnson checked with his flashlight. There only a television, several chairs, and a table with dirty plates and cutlery on it.

He moved to the door where the noise was coming from,

slowly put his eye to the two-inch-wide opening, and lifted his phone flashlight.

Johnson gave an involuntary yelp, a sound that Jayne was later to describe as a primeval howl, at what he saw.

There in the room was his daughter, Carrie, her hands tied behind her back and ankles lashed together, with a black-handled steak knife between her teeth, using it to try and cut through bindings that were tying Peter's wrists.

His son was on his knees, head down, holding his wrists up behind his back as best he could so his sister could saw at the plastic ties.

"Carrie!" Johnson called. "Peter!"

Amy, who was lying on the floor behind them, was the first to react.

"Joe, thank God."

Carrie dropped the knife from her mouth onto the floor, which Johnson could see was covered with glass fragments.

"Dad!" Carrie called. She burst instantly into tears. Peter turned himself around, falling off balance in the process, and also began to cry, as did Amy.

Johnson rushed into the room and placed his hands on his daughter's and son's heads, torn between the urge to embrace them and the driving need to get them out and to safety.

"It's going to be okay. I love you. But be quiet. We have to get out of here quickly," Johnson said.

He picked up the steak knife from the floor and quickly sliced through the plastic ties that bound his daughter, son, and sister.

The room stank of vomit and stale sweat.

Blood was trickling down the side of Carrie's face from a cut at the top of her cheek, not far under her eye. He took a handkerchief from his pocket and instructed her to hold it to the cut. His flashlight showed trails of what looked like dried vomit down the front of her shirt.

"Don't talk, just follow me and Jayne," Johnson said. At the top of his mind was the fact that while Severinov and Tkachev were no longer a threat, Pugachov certainly was.

CHAPTER FORTY-TWO

Sunday, August 3, 2014
   Tuapse

Johnson stopped on his way out of the flat-roofed storage building and grabbed five green-and-yellow security jackets that were hanging on hooks in the corridor. He instructed the others to put them on and also took white hard hats and safety glasses from a box on the floor and handed them out.

"Just walk confidently, as if you belong here. Don't speak to anyone or make eye contact. Follow me," Johnson instructed.

For a second, the deep irony of the moment flickered across his mind. His children were now part of an operation of the very type he had previously only given them very sketchy details of for fear of worrying and frightening them. But he buried the thought and concentrated on the task in hand.

Such was the chaos at the stricken refinery that their journey out was far easier than Johnson had envisaged.

The flames were illuminating the massive clouds of smoke being thrown upward with an eerie orange light from beneath, like a scene from a science fiction movie.

A couple of panicked guards yelled instructions at them, but when Johnson continued walking, there was no follow-up. The men ran off to do something else.

It became obvious that the refinery security team was rudderless and without leadership. The large number of maintenance contractors on the site were heading toward the exits, shouting at each other and with phones clamped to their ears.

Where the hell is Pugachov?

The FSB chief was nowhere to be seen.

Johnson led the others past the storage and administration buildings and headed toward the secondary entrance on the southern side of the refinery. He knew it emerged onto a street that went down westward toward the beach where they needed to be for the arranged exfil.

As they drew nearer to the secondary entrance, Johnson could see that the white steel security gates had been opened and two fire engines were coming in, their blue emergency roof lights flashing, followed by three ambulances.

A single security guard stood next to a red-and-white traffic boom, which had been raised to allow the vehicles through. At the right-hand side of the gate was a small prefabricated security hut.

For possibly the first time in the whole operation, something was going right. As the fire engines came in, Johnson led the way out along a path that ran alongside the road, past the hut, and into the street. The others followed. The guard ignored all of them, too focused on the task of getting the emergency vehicles through.

Several other people in protective clothing and helmets

were also out in the street, gathering in groups, holding anxious discussions, and pointing at the fire.

Johnson turned right and led the way down the street toward the beach, past the refinery wall to his right, with its high concrete wall and vicious-looking razor wire on top.

When they reached the beach, he twisted and pulled out the knob on his watch that activated the GPS location beacon, which would then alert the trawler captain, who Johnson hoped was somewhere offshore within easy reach of the designated meeting point.

Fleeing the refinery felt like an escape from a prisoner of war camp. But the job was only half done. Until they were safely out of Russian waters, there could be no celebration.

* * *

Monday, August 4, 2014
Tuapse

The five of them were waiting huddled between two clumps of bushes at the rear of the beach, half a mile south of Tuapse and just below the express railway line that ran along the coast south toward Sochi.

Johnson's biggest fear was that police or, worse, Pugachov and his FSB crew would catch up with them before they could escape out to sea.

A vision kept rolling through his mind of a unit of FSB officers emerging from over the railway line, searchlights glaring, and grim-looking men in dark suits wielding AK-47s surrounding them.

If not that, then once they got out to sea, that a high-speed FSB coast guard ship would hunt them down.

The orders to halt blaring over the loudspeaker, the rifle shots across the bows, the armed officers clambering aboard.

Johnson tried to put such negative images out of his head.

It was half past midnight by the time he finally noticed the black inflatable dinghy coasting toward the beach, its outboard motor making little more sound than a low murmur.

The boat was a hundred yards away from them, and so stealthily did it glide to shore that Johnson only realized it was there because of the sound of waves slapping against its rubber bottom and stern.

Johnson took Peter by the elbow and pointed at the boat. "Come on, let's go. Stay close to the bushes until we reach the boat."

There was only a quarter moon, and for the most part that was hidden behind intermittent clouds. In the darkness, Johnson could not see the trawler that they were to be taken to. He just had to trust that this arrangement was going to work.

They made their way along the top of the beach until they drew level with the black inflatable, which was now floating ten yards from the edge of the water. Then they ran directly to it.

In their hurry to get aboard, none of them bothered to remove their shoes and socks as they splashed through the shallows. A man in a dark hoodie helped them clamber aboard.

"Name?" the man asked in English, with a heavy Turkish accent.

"Joe Johnson."

"Good." He nodded briefly, then turned his attention back to the motor at the stern of the boat. He reversed the craft slowly, the engine at little more than idling speed, turned it around, and set off directly out to sea.

Johnson scanned the shore as they edged away from it. There was no sign of pursuit vehicles or police. There were no whistles blowing or rifle shots. Just the flames and smoke from the blazing refinery rising dramatically high into the sky behind the darkened beach, plus the wailing of a siren somewhere near the town.

The man, a heavily muscled type who looked to be in his forties and who spoke good English, introduced himself as Deniz and explained that he was first mate on the trawler. "You are lucky tonight, very lucky. The coast guard, the police, the authorities, they are only interested in the oil refinery on fire."

"How do you know?" Johnson asked.

"I listen to the FSB coast guard patrol on the radio," Deniz said. "They are not concentrating on the sea tonight. I think there was a big accident at the refinery." He spread his hands wide in imitation of an explosion.

"That is good," Johnson said. "Yes, I think there was an accident."

Johnson put his hand on Jayne's thigh, next to him. He found that she was shivering in the chilly night air, or maybe it was a delayed reaction to what they had just experienced.

After about ten minutes, Deniz throttled the engine back, and out of the darkness, the black hull of the trawler loomed up.

"This is our boat," Deniz said as he maneuvered the inflatable alongside the stern of the trawler and grabbed a metal ladder.

Not a single light was showing aboard the trawler, which Johnson realized was not the old fishing boat he had been expecting. This was a sleek, modern vessel that looked more like a high-speed yacht.

Once they had scrambled aboard and the inflatable had

been quickly hauled up onto davits at the stern and secured, the trawler's diesel engines growled into life. Almost immediately, the boat accelerated away, gathering pace very quickly.

Deniz took them all into the main cabin, which was far more luxurious than Johnson had envisaged, with long, broad padded seats, a fully equipped galley, a dining table, and a television. On the table were two plates of sandwiches, together with cookies and drinks on the table, but the children and Amy ignored them and headed straight for the seats where they collapsed, exhausted.

Deniz brought the trawler's captain, a gray-haired, dark-skinned man named Emirhan, and a second mate, Yusuf, who introduced themselves briefly to Johnson and Jayne, then disappeared again. It turned out that they were the only three crew members.

"We have a long journey," Deniz said, his forehead creased with deep frown lines. "Nearly five hundred nautical miles to Istanbul. Perhaps twenty-two or twenty-three hours. You need to sit and relax. I have informed Istanbul and your friend Neal, that we are on our way."

"Yes," Johnson said. He glanced over his shoulder to make sure that his children and Amy, still sitting on the padded seats at the far end of the cabin, were properly out of earshot. "But how far to safety?"

Deniz shrugged. "Russian waters reach twelve nautical miles offshore. So not too long. But to be honest, that means nothing. They could chase us a long way. They don't care about territorial waters and that kind of shit. This boat is fast, maybe twenty-three knots. But their FSB boats are faster, of course."

"How fast?"

Another shrug. "The Svetlyak or Rubin patrol boats? Maybe twenty-eight or thirty knots."

Johnson grimaced. "What could happen if they catch us?"

Deniz hesitated before answering. "They could sink us if we are in their waters and they do not like the story I tell them. They might sink us outside Russian waters. But we have a good start, and sinking us would cause a big row, and I hope . . ."

His voice trailed off, and he pointed to the seats. "Your children need sleep. Your sister needs sleep. You and your wife need sleep. You can rest now."

Johnson nodded. "Thank you. Jayne's not my wife, but she probably does need to sleep, and my children and sister definitely do. I will wait until we are out of the territorial waters."

He knew there was little likelihood of him sleeping for the entire journey—not until his children and his sister were safely on Turkish soil.

But Johnson felt he did need to lie down. The impact of what had happened to him and his family in the past few hours and days had started to hit him, and he too was now feeling utterly exhausted.

He and Jayne made their way to the rear of the cabin and sat on the padded bench facing Carrie and Peter, who were leaning against each other's shoulders, their eyes still wide with fear.

* * *

Monday, August 4, 2014
   Black Sea

Bright sunshine and the deep-throated honk of a ship's horn awoke Johnson, who was lying on his back on one of the trawler's seats. He checked his watch. It was past eight o'clock, and he had slept for more than five hours.

Jayne was still asleep, as were the children and Amy.

There had been no Russian coast guard boat, no pursuit. They must be safe now. *Thank God.*

He watched Jayne's chest rising and falling steadily as she slept, her dark hair falling over her face. On so many levels, Johnson felt he owed her a huge debt yet again.

The speed of thought, decisiveness, and timing she had shown in triggering the detonator at the refinery had been spot-on. It was a big step to have taken, knowing the consequences of such a large explosion. But she had in a stroke saved the lives of Johnson and his family.

Furthermore, Severinov's death had removed a huge thorn not just from Johnson's flesh but from that of the United States generally. It seemed that, coupled with Tkachev's almost certain demise, some justice had been handed down to those who had been chiefly responsible for blowing three hundred people out of the sky, even if Johnson would rather have put them in court.

Johnson was also well aware that Severinov's death had removed one of the largest concerns about potentially deploying Shevchenko as a United States agent in Moscow. The relationship between Severinov and Shevchenko could easily have been a security threat to that arrangement.

He felt he had much to relay to Neal in Istanbul and Vic in Washington, but although they were now a long distance from Russian waters, Johnson knew it would still be risky to open up communications. With Pugachov still functioning, the FSB would undoubtedly be monitoring all channels, and his only option from this boat was satellite phone, which was not secure.

Those conversations would have to wait.

Johnson slowly raised himself and made his way forward through the cabin to the cockpit, where he found Deniz at the wheel.

The first mate's deeply weather-beaten face creased into a smile for the first time, and it made Johnson realize that he too had not smiled for a long time. He grinned in response.

CHAPTER FORTY-THREE

Wednesday, August 6, 2014
 Washington, DC

After a series of phone calls between Veltman and President Ferguson's aide, Charles Deacon, the summons had come.

Somewhat to Johnson's dismay, given his state of exhaustion and jet lag after a Turkish Airlines flight back to Washington from Istanbul the previous afternoon, the president had asked to see Veltman, Vic, Johnson, and Jayne in the Situation Room at six thirty that evening.

Johnson explained the situation to his family, who were sitting in the living room of Vic's house, where they were now all staying until they could return to Portland. His children and Amy, still visibly in shock from their ordeal, said little as Vic's wife, Eleanor, supplied them with mugs of coffee.

It was not surprising, Johnson told them, that the president wanted him to join a briefing on their investigation and the rescue mission. Ferguson had after all been heavily involved in discussions about the operations involving

Shevchenko and the refinery rescue. But he did think he might be given a little more time to recover first.

The prospect of a meeting with the president meant Vic and Veltman first needed to speak to Shevchenko again. They needed to be clear on how the arrangement she had proposed would work once she flew to Moscow, which was scheduled to happen the following day. The president was certain to grill them about it, and they needed answers.

Veltman invited Johnson along to the Shevchenko meeting too, not least so that he could tell her about what had happened to Severinov and the events at the refinery. They were keen to gauge her reaction.

"I guess we might find out what she really thought of the bastard," Johnson said to Vic.

"I doubt it," Vic said. "She's an opportunist. She probably only bedded him for either financial gain or career advancement. Same reason why she's getting into bed with us."

Johnson smiled at his friend's cynicism. But he knew he was correct.

There was another reason Johnson wanted to see Shevchenko, though, and he was ready with his questions for when she arrived.

They were gathered in a CIA safe house on Prospect Street NW in Georgetown, a gray-painted town house with a short flight of wrought-iron steps up to the front door and shutters at the windows, near to Georgetown University. It was a fifteen-minute drive from Langley, although the surveillance detection route they had taken turned that into nearly an hour. They didn't want to run the risk of any Russian embassy surveillance tailing them if Shevchenko was involved.

Also at the meeting was the CIA's deputy director of counterintelligence, Ricardo Miller, a notoriously dour character in the long tradition of spy hunters at the Agency. Vic had explained that Veltman was insisting on his presence, not least to cover his own ass given the risk that Shevchenko could be playing a double game of some kind with them.

They were all sitting on sofas in the living room, and Johnson had just begun his second strong coffee of the afternoon when there came a cautious single knock at the door followed by a sharp double knock.

"That will be her," Vic said, jumping to his feet.

Dover and Shepard had allowed Shevchenko to go back to the apartment she had been renting in the Woodward Building. The view was that she was highly unlikely to simply flee, given the likely consequences, and that the best way to ensure her plan remained undetected by counterintelligence at the Russian embassy was for her to continue with life in as normal a way as possible until the time came for her to fly home.

Vic returned to the room, ushered Shevchenko in, and poured her coffee.

Johnson still found it incredible that here was a woman whose professional fortunes hung so precariously in the balance that now she was prepared to become a traitor to the country for which she had previously been a star in the making. He reminded himself yet again that although they were in a position to make or break her, they needed to proceed with caution.

Is it really wise to bring the fox into the henhouse?

He didn't like the idea of recruitment by coercion, and neither did Vic, but she seemed happy to go along with it.

Shevchenko took a seat and accepted the coffee and cookies that were offered, while Vic introduced Miller, who was the only one there she didn't know. She stared at him, her forehead creased. In contrast to the previously arrogant, somewhat proud demeanor she had previously carried, she now seemed contrite, almost humble.

After apologizing for being slightly late following a ninety-minute surveillance detection route, she explained that on the face of it, Yasenevo appeared to have accepted her account of the reasons and circumstances behind the suicide of her mole, Francis Wade.

She had told her boss, Kutsik, that it was entirely due to the affair Wade had been conducting with Martina McAllister and the pressures that that had wrought inside his marriage. Her story had been given legs by the fact that some details of the affair were starting to leak into the media, which had already run a couple of speculative stories about the couple. There would inevitably be a lot more over the coming days as journalists got their teeth into it.

And confirmation that Shevchenko seemed to have escaped trouble at home over Wade's demise had come in the form of a secure phone call she had received that morning from Maksim Kruglov to formally offer her the post of deputy director in charge of Directorate KR, as she had forecast.

"I accepted immediately," Shevchenko said with a slight smile.

"Congratulations," Vic said. "It is some achievement."

Veltman, Johnson, and Jayne also added their congratulations. Miller remained silent, his arms folded, peering at Shevchenko through thick black-rimmed glasses.

Vic seemed to be struggling to get his words out, seemingly scarcely able to believe that Shevchenko had actually had the appointment confirmed. It must be like winning the lottery for him, Johnson couldn't help thinking.

However, Shevchenko's behavior also told Johnson that she did not know about the fate of Severinov. Hardly surprising, given that media coverage of the Krasnodar refinery blaze had been almost nonexistent in the US; even in Russia, where most media outlets had covered it, no journalists had so far latched onto the fact that Severinov had died. That wouldn't be the case for long, Johnson was certain.

He was considering how to bring up the subject when she saved him the trouble.

Shevchenko caught Johnson's eye. "I hope you managed to get your children back safely?" she asked as she sipped her coffee.

Is she sincere? Johnson wondered.

"Yes, I did, thank you."

"How are they doing?"

Johnson hesitated. Both Carrie and Peter had been impacted by their ordeal in different ways, as had Amy, for that matter. They were all confused as to how a family holiday had led to such a traumatic outcome, and angry too, not least with their father. There was no doubt he would need to spend a lot of time talking with them as soon as he could extricate himself from the current round of discussions. They would probably need counseling too. But he wasn't going to go into all that with Shevchenko.

"They are okay, considering the circumstances," Johnson said. "I was just pleased to get them back, although the rescue operation was not without some drama."

"I heard there was a fire at the refinery. An explosion."

So she knew that much, then.

"There was. And there were casualties, unfortunately."

There must have been something in his tone. Shevchenko put her coffee cup down slowly. "Are you trying to tell me something?" she asked. "Is he dead? I sent him a message this morning, but there was no reply."

Johnson paused before answering. "I am sorry to tell you, but yes, Severinov is dead. He died in the explosion late on Sunday night."

Shevchenko stared at the floor for several seconds. She showed no emotion.

Eventually she looked back up at Johnson. "Well, that solves one problem." Her eyes flicked to Vic and Veltman. "He would have been a security risk for me if I was to work for you."

That opened the door for Johnson to bring up another issue that he wanted to get out in the open.

"You mean because you tended to confide in him when you shouldn't have?" Johnson asked.

Shevchenko gave a short sigh. "Yes, I confess I did. We worked together for a long time. I think he would have been trustworthy had I continued the relationship with him."

"But if you didn't? Had you been thinking of not continuing it?" Johnson asked.

She nodded. "I had been thinking of ending it. It had run its course. It had no future. And then . . ." She didn't finish the sentence, but she didn't need to.

Vic leaned forward. "And one of the things you confided in him about was Operation Pandora, is that right?"

A flicker crossed Shevchenko's face, and she sank back into her chair, folding her arms. "*Bozhe*. God. Did he tell you about that? Or have you been hacking my emails?" She looked first at Vic, then at Johnson.

Miller ran a hand through his curly ginger hair, which was receding on both sides of his scalp. A look of concern flitted across his face.

Vic ignored him and stroked his chin. "This is where trust hits the road. I asked you last week whether the *kompromat* operation regarding McAllister had a name, and you said no. So, please, tell us about Operation Pandora, Anastasia."

Shevchenko hesitated. Whether it was for dramatic effect —and she was quite an actress—or because she was debating whether to give away another secret, Johnson wasn't clear.

"What I have told you about Wade and McAllister and McAllister's sister, and about those agents the CIA has lost in recent times—all that is the tip of a very large iceberg that is floating in the direction of America right now," she said. "Operation Pandora is the name of a much wider set of active measures to influence and compromise and infiltrate political America and corporate America, at many levels, going right up to the top. It is designed to run for many years in a strategic and systematic way. Trying to disrupt the next election is only one part of that. It is not partisan, aimed at any one party, but opportunist. Believe me, if we could have gotten to President Ferguson the way we have been trying to get to McAllister, we would have done so."

Johnson leaned back and folded his arms. "Well, screw me," he murmured.

He had expected there might be a few snippets of high-quality information from Shevchenko as she sought to establish trust in these early days. But she was throwing the entire kitchen sink at them.

Shevchenko sipped her coffee. "I'm not yet seeing the detail of how Pandora will be delivered in the future. But in my new role, I will see much more of it. Yaseveno and the Kremlin will be on red alert for any signs of infiltration that could impact Pandora, and counterintelligence will be central to that, of course. It will run for years."

Veltman had been listening to the conversation carefully. Now he stood and walked to a large ornate fireplace, turned, and folded his arms.

"Who is running Pandora?" Veltman asked.

Shevchenko pointed upward with her index finger. "It goes right to the top. The president. And his shitty assistant, Igor Ivanov."

"Is there anything written down, any papers, plans?" Veltman asked.

Shevchenko shrugged. "Not that I have seen. There may be. But they are probably locked in Ivanov's safe."

"That's another task for you in your new role, then," Veltman said. "But I have another question. As an intelligence professional, and a very good one, what is your view on recruitment by coercion?"

Shevchenko gave a thin smile. "Like you are recruiting me, you mean?"

Veltman nodded.

"It is not the ideal method. You never quite know what might happen. But we are all opportunists, aren't we? You, me, all of us."

"What is your end game, your route out, if we go through with this arrangement?" Veltman asked. It was a fair question.

"You are asking me if I want to retire in Russia or California?"

Again, Veltman nodded.

"That depends on whether I get caught or not. I might quite like the idea of Monterey instead of Moscow."

"We had better have a good exfil arrangement in place, then," Veltman said.

"Speaking of which, what are you doing about Nizam Fisher?" Shevchenko asked.

Miller leaned forward. "My counterintelligence team is all over Fisher," he said. "From a suitable distance, of course. We're going softly but thoroughly with him. As we agreed, we don't want to do anything that will put a red flag next to your name in Moscow."

Shevchenko nodded. "I'm pleased to hear it. I do not want to end up in the Moskva River."

Veltman checked his watch. "We need to get to the White House soon, so let's talk practical arrangements."

They spent the next half hour drafting an outline plan for covert communications with Shevchenko once she was back into harness at Yasenevo, which would be run by Ed Grewall's team at Moscow station. They also discussed two possible exfiltration options should she be discovered and agreed that Langley would put something concrete together. Veltman also agreed that a monthly stipend would be paid into a numbered account in Zürich for Shevchenko, the amount to be decided soon. Johnson had little doubt it would be far more than he was earning.

Eventually, Veltman stood and shook hands with Shevchenko. "I look forward to working with you. I trust it will be a productive arrangement."

"Yes," Shevchenko said. "Just one final request. Day-to-day handling and covcoms will of course be run by your Moscow station. But I would like to maintain some operational contact here with these two." She pointed at Johnson and Jayne. "They are not CIA staff, and I like that. But they are operators. Good operators."

Johnson caught a glimpse out of the corner of his eye of Miller rolling his eyes. The counterintelligence chief let out a sigh.

Veltman shrugged. "That would depend on the operation. It's an unorthodox approach."

"Unorthodox is one word for it," Miller said. "I could think of others."

"Let's discuss it later, Ricardo," Veltman said. He looked toward Vic, who nodded, and then to Johnson and Jayne, raising his eyebrows as he did so. They both also nodded their agreement.

"We could work with her, if and when appropriate," Johnson said cautiously.

"Right, then," Veltman said. He turned back to Shevchenko. "It will obviously depend on the circumstances, but it is a possibility, yes. Let's see what leads you come up with first."

* * *

Wednesday, August 6, 2014
  Washington, DC

President Ferguson had a long list of questions that he was
working his way through, prompted on occasion by Deacon,
who sat to his right in the Situation Room with Paul Farrar
while Veltman, Vic, Johnson, and Jayne occupied the left side
of the conference room table.

After expressing his relief that Johnson's "gamble," as he
put it, of not using a SEAL team had paid off and that he
had managed to get his kids back safely, he started with
queries about Shevchenko, then listened as Veltman gave an
update.

"First, we have just had another meeting with her,"
Veltman said. "The Russian active measures op against us is
code-named Operation Pandora, and it's far more extensive in
scope than we thought. She says, and these are her words not
mine, that the Wade and McAllister *kompromat* is the tip of a
large iceberg floating in our direction."

"Pandora? Tell me more."

Veltman outlined what they had learned from Shevchenko
so far. "She has limited knowledge of it as of yet, or so she
claims. We hope to get more once she starts her new role."

The president whistled through his front teeth. "It is
astonishing that they think they can get away with this," he
said. "The Malaysian airliner, the troll factory bombardment,
the blackmail of Wade, the compromising of the
McAllisters."

He turned to Johnson and Jayne. "I'm not someone who
goes overboard in praising people, but I want to say, for the
record, that you have both done an outstanding job to get to
the bottom of what has been going on. I've read the briefing.
Well done. Right down to getting photos of that missile

launcher at the refinery. I am very grateful to you, and Paul is doubly so." The president glanced at Farrar.

The photographs that Jayne had taken of the Buk launcher at the refinery had been included in a CIA briefing that had gone to the White House and to Farrar's office that morning. Discussions were ongoing as to whether they should be made public, but Veltman's view was to keep them confidential for now.

Farrar leaned forward, his hands clasped together. "I am, indeed, in both of your debts. Getting the truth won't bring my wife and kids back, but at least it will help bring some closure."

"Thank you," Johnson said. "I've just been trying to do my job. We both have. I wouldn't be here if Jayne hadn't acted so quickly the way she did."

"I would agree with that," Veltman said. "They have done a very good job. And in terms of the *kompromat*, sir, it is also worth bearing in mind that in most cases, people slip into these situations without realizing that it is happening, and then it is too late." He paused for a second, then added, "Presidents are not exempt."

Johnson was more than slightly taken aback that Veltman had voiced what everyone else was probably thinking. He knew for sure he would have felt too intimidated to have done so himself, but that's what the director of the CIA was paid for.

Ferguson pursed his lips. "Thank you for that shot across the bow," he said, a slight note of sarcasm in his voice. "Right, so you've recruited her, this Shevchenko—we're in bed with a blackmailer." He rolled his eyes slightly. "And she's going to keep us properly informed on the composition of this iceberg, of Operation Pandora, is she? You think we can trust her to do that?"

Veltman shrugged. "Impossible to know until she is back

in her new role. My instinct is that this could work well. The only issue is that what she is proposing to do is very high risk. If she gets caught by her own counterintelligence operation, then . . ."

"Yes, I am sure that she will go straight to Butyrka jail and reap the usual Russian reward for espionage," the president said. "It is up to you to do your best to make sure that does not happen. But fine, I am giving your proposals for Shevchenko my unwritten approval."

"Thank you, sir. She also made a slightly unusual request. She insisted that Joe here, together with Jayne, are two of her prime points of contact on this end when possible."

The president frowned. "That's unorthodox. I don't like the sound of that. I appreciate that Joe and Jayne are skilled at what they do, but my worries are around security."

Johnson was thankful that Veltman, anticipating a potentially negative response from the president, had chosen not to bring Ricardo Miller along to the meeting. There was no doubt that Miller, already skeptical about deploying Johnson and Jayne to help handle Shevchenko, would have jumped in with a series of negative points at this juncture. Instead, Veltman was able to subtly smooth over the president's concerns.

"Yes, but in practice," Veltman said, "they both work hand in glove with Vic, and they follow our processes, so I don't foresee any issues. Of course, we will see how things unfold from her end first."

Ferguson became aware that Deacon was gathering his papers together. He obviously had another meeting to get to.

The president scrutinized first Johnson, then Jayne. "All right. I need to go now, but I trust that you won't screw this up, then."

"We'll try and make sure that doesn't happen, sir," Johnson said.

"You've got a good track record. I like the work you've done. I might make more use of you both myself," Ferguson said. "There may be certain tasks in the future that might suit your particular skill sets. But if you're going to walk the high wire, then it is a long way down. Remember that."

Ferguson stood and began to walk toward the door.

Johnson nodded. "Yes, sir. Understood. And if you think we might be useful to you, I would be honored to assist."

EPILOGUE

Friday, August 8, 2014
Portland, Maine

The August sunshine, with temperatures rising into the mid-eighties, had given a languid feeling to Portland. For the first time in more than three weeks, Johnson felt able to relax.

He sat on a comfortable outdoor sofa on the porch that ran across the rear of his house and sipped a glass of his favorite Belgian-style white beer from Allagash, a local craft brewery just off the turnpike northwest of the city.

The grass needed cutting, and there was a pile of other jobs that needed doing indoors and out, but they would have to wait.

Jayne was lying with her head resting on his thigh, eyes closed and almost asleep, and Carrie was in a chair tapping away on her phone, which beeped at regular intervals as new messages arrived from her friends, presumably anxious to know how she was. She still had bandages around her wrists and ankles where the plastic ties had cut into her.

Peter, who also still wore bandages, sat in another chair with his headphones on, listening to music and stroking Cocoa, who had scarcely left their sides, still seemingly unable to believe that his beloved family had finally returned home.

Had it really been only four days since they had been striding through a blazing refinery in Tuapse, in scenes akin to a TV disaster movie, looking for his children? It hardly seemed possible.

It was a similar feeling to those he often experienced after returning from a tough operation. The contrast between the two scenarios—home and operational—was so marked that it left him with a kind of disconnect.

He sometimes asked himself which one was real life. Of course, they both were, but it was not easy to reconcile them. There had been little time for such rumination this time. His entire concern had been for his children and the impact that their kidnap, incarceration, and traumatic escape had made on them.

Johnson glanced at Peter, then Carrie. He was intensely proud of how they and Amy had responded. The sight of Carrie with a knife between her teeth trying to free her brother in a situation where at any point a security guard could have returned and found her was something that he would never forget.

Both of his children had lost about nine pounds during their ordeal. Amy had lost even more weight. Johnson was grateful that his sister had been with them. She'd kept it together more than he could have imagined. But he was worried about all of them.

Jayne opened one eye and looked up at him. "What's on your mind, Joe?" she murmured.

Johnson didn't reply but just pointed to his right and left, toward his kids. Jayne nodded. She understood. That was what he liked about her—she was always on the right wavelength.

"Would you like a coffee?" Jayne asked. "I'll make one for you."

"Thanks," Johnson said. "That would be great."

Jayne got up and wandered off to the kitchen.

As soon as she had gone, Carrie put down her phone and turned toward her father. "Ali just can't believe what happened to us. She thinks I'm making it up."

Alison was one of Carrie's best friends. Johnson had told his kids in no uncertain terms not to tell their buddies anything about their ordeal, and Vic had taken him aside and underlined the point to him. But it was almost impossible for him to enforce in practice, and he guessed Carrie had probably let on more than she should have.

He decided to let it slide. Actually, it might be a good opportunity to chat.

"I'm sure she can't," Johnson said. He drained his beer and put the glass down. "How are you feeling about it all now, Carrie?"

She frowned. "I'm okay, I think. Although I did wake up in the night thinking I was on that floor in the refinery instead of in my bed. I felt confused for a moment and thought, Why are my hands free and not tied behind my back? Maybe I'd been dreaming about it."

"It wasn't a nightmare, then?"

"No, not that."

"That's good." Johnson paused and scratched his ear. "Look, I know I've said this a hundred times already, but I'm so sorry for what happened. It was my fault. I should have seen it coming. I should have predicted what might happen. And I feel like I failed you all."

"It's not your fault, Dad. How could you know he would do that?"

Johnson shrugged. "Well, it's my job to foresee these things, kind of."

He saw out of the corner of his eye that Peter had removed his earphones and was listening.

"I agree with Carrie, Dad. Don't blame yourself," Peter said. "I did think we were going to die at one stage, but I knew you'd get us out of there. I was confident in you."

"Hmm, well, I'm glad to hear that, but I was thinking it might be a good idea if we all see someone who's a specialist in talking through these things. It was very traumatic and—"

"Dad, no, I'm not seeing a shrink," Peter said. "I'm fine."

Johnson tried not to smile. His kids were far too much like him, pretending everything was all right when it likely wasn't. But they were resilient, that was for sure. Still, he didn't want to let anything hidden to fester.

He decided to leave it for now and perhaps return to the issue in a couple of days.

"Fine," Johnson said. "We'll keep it in mind, though. Sometimes you can get delayed shock from these sorts of things without realizing it. Just make sure you let me know if you're not feeling great, okay?"

"Okay, Dad," Carrie said. She returned to her phone just as Jayne came back carrying the coffees, which she deposited on the table next to the sofa before sitting down next to him.

While his kids were definitely tough, he had noticed occasional flashes of anger at nothing, an unwillingness to communicate, which wasn't like them, and a tendency to eat their meals quickly and then disappear. Now Carrie was having dreams and disrupted sleep too. The brief conversation he had just had with them was the first time they had opened up at all about what had occurred, even though he'd tried to gently broach it at least once a day since their return. Previously they had shut him down.

In contrast, he had already had a good chat with Amy,

who was predictably blaming herself for what had happened and for not being more alert that night in Cannes outside Natalia's house. He'd told her that she should not even think of blaming herself, that rather it was his fault. At least Amy accepted that she needed professional counseling and had already found someone through a friend. She would be okay, and was trying to chill out with Don, who had been massively relieved to have her home safely.

Johnson eyed his kids again. He would leave it another day or so and then take them out individually for a coffee or an ice cream or a walk and try to talk to them a little more. What had happened undoubtedly must have affected them. He just wasn't sure how it would emerge in the months and years to come.

Johnson picked up the coffee mug.

By now, Shevchenko would be back in Moscow following her overnight flight. She was an intriguing character. A thorough professional in most ways, a tough cookie, yet liable to the occasional mistake, to human error, which had changed the course of her life. It would be interesting to see how that situation evolved.

His gut feeling was that she might not be a straightforward person to deal with. Time would tell.

Johnson took a sip of his coffee. And as for the president, well, it had been an experience to meet him for the first time, that was for sure.

What might come out of that relationship, if you could call it that? It was difficult to say.

But Johnson didn't need reminding that the further he stuck his head above the parapet, the more rarified the atmosphere and the more likely he was to get shot at. What was it the president had said?

If you're going to walk the high wire, then it is a long way down. Remember that.

No pressure, then.

* * *

THE NEXT BOOK:
Book 1 in the NEW *Jayne Robinson* series
The Kremlin's Vote

If you enjoyed **The Black Sea**, and indeed the whole Johnson series, you'll probably like the next book. It is **The Kremlin's Vote**, book 1 in a new series running in parallel with this one, but with Johnson's colleague **Jayne Robinson** as the main character.

The **Jayne Robinson** series consists of contemporary spy thrillers, while the Joe Johnson series will continue to focus on backward-looking war crimes investigations, albeit with a strong element of espionage as always. And don't worry—Jayne will also continue to appear in the Johnson books!

You can buy my paperbacks from **my website shop** at a significant discount to Amazon, particularly if you buy the bundles on offer. I can only currently ship to the US and UK though. Go and visit:

https://www.andrewturpin.com/shop/

To give you a flavor of **The Kremlin's Vote**, here's the blurb:

Defending the West . . . **Why has a top United States official been gunned down outside a quiet British pub? A trail of deception misleads the CIA . . . And intelligence operative Jayne Robinson is viciously targeted**

during a high risk foray into Russia to get the truth.

In this first book in a dramatic new spy series, Robinson is covertly deployed by the CIA in a deniable operation to handle one of its biggest assets in the Kremlin—recruited by her.

But instead, she finds herself grappling to get to the bottom of an apparent threat that seems likely to engulf the White House.

The mission becomes unexpectedly, and deeply, personal for Robinson . . .

Can she outwit one of the Russian foreign intelligence service's most deadly operatives?

Nothing is what it seems in this vortex of deception and deceit.

As she gets closer to the reasons for the killings, the stakes rise . . .

Will Robinson overcome the threats from all that modern Russian spycraft can throw at her?

The Kremlin's Vote, book number one in the new **Jayne Robinson series**, is a gripping espionage thriller with unexpected twists that will be difficult to put down.

* * *

ANDREW'S READERS GROUP AND OTHER BOOKS IN THE SERIES

If you enjoyed this book, I would like to keep in touch. This is not always easy, as I usually only publish a couple of books a year and there are many authors and books out there. So the best way is for you to be on my Readers Group email list. I can then send you updates on the next book, plus occasional special offers. There's no spam and you can unsubscribe at any time.

If you would like to join my Readers Group and receive the email updates, I will send you, **FREE** of charge, the ebook version of another Joe Johnson thriller, *The Afghan*, which is a prequel to the series and also to the Jayne Robinson series, and normally sells at $4.99/£3.99 (paperback $11.99/£9.99).

The Afghan is a thriller set in 1988 when Johnson was still in the CIA. Most of the action takes place in Afghanistan, then occupied by the Soviet Union, and in Washington, DC. Some of the characters and story lines that emerge in the other books have their roots in this period. I think you will enjoy it!

The Afghan can be downloaded **FREE** from the following link:

https://bookhip.com/RJGFPAW

If you only like reading paperbacks you can still sign up for the email list at that link to get news of my books and forthcoming releases. Just ignore the email that arrives with the ebook attached. A paperback version of *The Afghan* and all my books is for sale at my website, where you will find large discounts on bundles of my books. I can currently ship to the US and UK:

https://www.andrewturpin.com/shop/

Have you read the other thrillers in the Joe Johnson series?

Prologue: *The Afghan*
1. *The Last Nazi*

2. *The Old Bridge*
3. *Bandit Country*
4. *Stalin's Final Sting*
5. *The Nazi's Son*
6. *The Black Sea*

And the **Jayne Robinson** thriller series so far comprises:

1. *The Kremlin's Vote*
2. *The Dark Shah*
3. *The Confessor*
4. *The Queen's Pawn*

To find the books, just type "Andrew Turpin thrillers" in the search box at the top of the Amazon website sales page — you can't miss them!

IF YOU ENJOYED THIS BOOK PLEASE WRITE A REVIEW

As an independently published author, through my own imprint The Write Direction Publishing, I find that honest reviews of my books are the most powerful way for me to bring them to the attention of other potential readers.

As you'll appreciate, unlike the big international publishers, I can't take out full-page advertisements in the newspapers or place posters on the subway.

So I am committed to producing books of the best quality I can in order to attract a loyal group of readers who are happy to recommend my work to others.

Therefore, if you enjoyed reading this novel, then I would very much appreciate it if you would spend five minutes and leave a review—which can be as short as you like—preferably on the page or website where you bought it.

You can find the book on the Amazon website by going to the Amazon website and typing "Andrew Turpin The Black Sea" in the search box at the top.

Once you have clicked on the book's sales page, scroll down to "Customer Reviews," then click on "Leave a Review."

Reviews are also a great encouragement to me to write more!

Many thanks.

THANKS AND ACKNOWLEDGEMENTS

Thank you to everyone who reads my books. You are the reason I began to write in the first place, and I hope I can provide you with entertainment and interest for a long time into the future.

Every time I get an encouraging email from a reader, or a positive comment on my Facebook page, or a nice review on Amazon, it spurs me on to press ahead with my research and writing for the next book. So keep them coming!

Specifically with regard to *The Black Sea*, there are several people who have helped me during the long process of research, writing, and editing.

I have two editors who consistently provide helpful advice, food for thought, great ideas, and constructive criticism, and between them have enabled me to considerably improve the initial draft. Katrina Diaz Arnold, owner of Refine Editing, again gave me a lot of valuable feedback at the structural and line levels, and Jon Ford, as ever, helped me to maintain the authenticity of the story in many areas through his great eye for detail. I would like to thank both of them—the responsibility for any remaining mistakes lies solely with me.

As always, my brother, Adrian Turpin, was a very helpful reader of my early drafts and highlighted areas where I needed to improve. Others have done likewise. The small but dedicated team in my Advance Readers Group went through the final version prior to proofreading and also highlighted a number of issues that required changes and improvements—a big thank-you to them all.

I would also like to thank the team at Damonza for what I think is a great cover design.

AUTHOR'S NOTE

As always, I should begin by stressing that this book is a work of fiction and designed purely for the reader's entertainment. Although I have used a backdrop that includes some real-world events, the characters and the plot are all either from my imagination or used in a fictional sense. It would be entirely wrong to read anything more into them.

As a former journalist, however, I do take a keen interest in current affairs and news at both national and international level and I often take ideas and inspiration from real-life events and the people who take part in them.

I remember in July 2014 being shocked, although not entirely surprised, to hear that Malaysia Airlines Flight MH17, traveling from Amsterdam to Kuala Lumpur, had been shot down over Eastern Ukraine with the loss of all 283 passengers and fifteen crew. And it was this disaster that gave me the idea for part of the plot that comprises **The Black Sea**.

The incident, which occurred near the border between Ukraine and Russia, was just the latest in a conflict that had been ongoing in that region between the Ukraine government and pro-Russian separatist rebels.

Several Ukrainian military aircraft had already been destroyed in previous weeks, and it was clear that powerful anti-aircraft missile systems were being deployed by the rebels.

Of course, my account of the disaster in this book is a heavily fictionalized one, albeit drawing on some of the publicly available information that has emerged since 2014.

A notable feature of the aftermath of the MH17 incident was the wave of social media posts, emanating mainly from

Russian sources, that sought to blame various supposed culprits, particularly the Ukraine government and the CIA.

However, subsequent investigations, both official and unofficial, have made clear that the Malaysian airliner, a Boeing 777, was shot down by a Buk surface-to-air missile fired from pro-Russian rebel territory.

The main inquiry, by the Dutch Safety Board and the Dutch-led joint investigation team, concluded that the Buk unit had been transported from Russia on the day of the incident and returned afterward.

On March 9, 2020, the Dutch Public Prosecution Service formally charged four suspects—three Russians and one Ukrainian— with causing the crash of the Malaysia Airlines Boeing and with the murder of all 298 people on board. The trial got underway at the Schiphol Judicial Complex in The Hague, with none of the four accused present in court. You can follow the trial and obtain updates at: https://www.prose cutionservice.nl/topics/mh17-plane-crash

Other in-depth investigations have unearthed more valuable detail. In particular, the UK-based investigative journalism site Bellingcat, founded by Eliot Higgins, has produced a wealth of evidence showing exactly how the Russians transported the Buk launcher into Ukraine and the identities of the military officers involved in that operation.

The trial may or may not reveal whether MH17 was shot down in error, as many believe, having been mistaken at some point by someone for a Ukrainian military plane. But whatever the reason, there is no doubt that the weaponry used came from Russia.

The exact machinations that went on behind the scenes in Russia and Ukraine prior to this incident have so far remained shrouded in mystery and secrecy. In my fictional story, I have used my imagination to conjure up a version of what might have happened and I am certain that it bears only a tangential semblance to the truth.

However, the fundamental factors behind Russia's real-life involvement in Ukraine are clear. In the face of growing economic weakness at home in the years following the global economic crisis of 2008, President Putin set his country on a course of resurgence beyond its borders. He needed a positive story overseas to spin to his people to regain the esteem lost at home.

Hence the snatching of Crimea from Ukraine in early 2014, a move that Moscow justified by arguing it was simply a case of Russia taking back land that was rightfully its own. In fact, it amounted to the grabbing of another country's sovereign territory.

This was followed by the stirring up of latent pro-Russian nationalism in Eastern Ukraine, of which the Malaysian jet disaster was one outcome. The end result of these events was that Mr. Putin's ratings soared once again inside Russia.

On the other side, there has been strong support from the United States for Ukraine and other countries in the former Soviet Union's old sphere of influence in central and eastern Europe. Indeed, it is well-known that the US provided $1 billion of loan guarantees to Ukraine, as well as supplying a large range of "non-lethal" military equipment to the Kiev government. The US argues, rightly, that this was a strategically sensible move given the increased flexing of Russia's muscles outside its borders.

The extension of NATO membership to those countries formerly under the Soviet Union's influence has been another bugbear in Moscow.

The outcome is that Ukraine has become a theater of the "new Cold War," and as such it seemed fertile ground for a fictional thriller plot, constructed against a factual backdrop of Russian and American political and military strategic moves.

I have therefore had the shooting down of MH17 on a short-list of potential war crimes for Joe Johnson to investigate for some time.

The real-life and well-documented theme of Russian interference in US and European politics, using social media as a key tool, has added another layer of intrigue on which I have also drawn heavily. I have used my imagination to devise the method of interference described in this book.

It would be a mistake to try and draw parallels between my fictional characters and real-life politicians, military leaders, and intelligence agency operatives. For example, although for the sake of realism my fictional politicians do belong to one political party or another, I try to make my plots and characters as non-partisan as I can. It would certainly be wrong to infer that the story line is designed to either denigrate or support any real-life political party in any country.

Although I have deployed Vladimir Putin as the Russian president, there is no suggestion the conversations or meetings or actions involving him that are described in the book actually took place. All of these came from my imagination. Similarly, in real life Putin does not, as far as I know, have an adviser named Igor Ivanov.

There is an oil refinery at Tuapse, on Russia's Black Sea coast. However, it is not named the Krasnodar oil refinery, and it is not owned by a company called Besoi Energy, as that does not exist. To the best of my knowledge none of the tanks containing gasoline or diesel have ever exploded at that refinery, and as far as I'm aware, neither has it been used as a base for kidnappers to hold their captives.

Equally, there is no point doing an internet search for the refinery maintenance company depicted in this book, Octane Refinery Maintenance, because that is also fictional.

And readers should not try to book a room at the River Tuapse Hotel in Tuapse, because it is entirely imaginary.

In Washington, DC, the apartments in the Woodward Building on Fifteenth Street NW are, to the best of my knowledge, not used by Russian SVR spies. Equally, the exclusive Chevy Chase Club is not a meeting place where Russian spies collect leaked documents from their agents inside the US government, as far as I know.

In Rostov-on-Don, Russia, there are many office buildings along Bol'shaya Sadovaya Ulitsa, and some of them are adjacent to the status of Matvei Platov that stands in a small plaza. However, as far as I could ascertain, none of these buildings are called the Platov Business Center, because that is fictional. They also certainly do not house an internet troll company called the Web Marketing Group, because that also stemmed from my imagination and has nothing to do with the real-life Internet Research Agency based in St. Petersburg.

Glenwood Cemetery is a historic cemetery in Washington, DC, and has a row of interesting mausoleums within its grounds that are worth visiting. However, the cemetery is not, to be the best of my knowledge, a site used by Russian intelligence operatives to meet their agents.

Nor has the nearby McMillan Sand Filtration Site—a decommissioned water treatment plant dating back to the early 1900s—been the location for the kind of fictional shoot-out depicted in this book when Johnson trapped Shevchenko.

I could have worked my way through many more of the locations and buildings listed in this book, describing which are fictional and which are real, and this is not by any means an exhaustive list. However, it will give you a flavor of some of the principal ones and those which are probably of greatest interest. I hope it is helpful.

Finally, on a lighter note, I should mention that the one thing that keeps me going through all the long months of research, writing, and editing before I can publish each book is coffee. I do enjoy a good latte—it is essential brain fuel!

So when I was invited to join **Buy Me A Coffee**—a website you might have heard of that allows supporters to give the providers of their favorite goods and services a cup or two—I thought it sounded like a good idea.

Therefore, if you enjoy my books and would like to buy me a latte, I would be extremely grateful. You will definitely be playing an essential part in the production of the next book!

You will find my online coffee shop at:

https://www.buymeacoffee.com/andrewturpin

Many thanks.
Andrew

RESEARCH AND BIBLIOGRAPHY

As with my previous books, what follows is a necessarily selective list of some of the countless sources I used and read while doing my research for **The Black Sea**. It might form a starting point for those of you who like to explore some of the issues referenced in greater depth.

The two key themes running through The Black Sea are the ways in which Russia sought to obscure the truth and mislead over its role in the shooting down of Malaysia Airlines Flight 17 in Ukraine and the ongoing Russian efforts to interfere with and influence the democratic political process in the United States, including presidential elections.

I have a great admiration for investigative journalists who are prepared to put their heads above the parapet and take personal risks in an attempt to uncover the truth. This should be the job of all journalists, but the reality is that in today's media environment, the financial pressures on news organizations are such that in practice, very few are given the time and resources to carry out such work.

Those who continue to deliver outstanding work in very challenging circumstances are therefore worthy of particular praise, especially independent journalists who do not have the financial backing of larger organizations.

Bellingcat, the British online investigative journalism website run by Eliot Higgins, is one such outlet. I spent a lot of time reading through material produced by Eliot and his colleagues about MH17, and drew a great deal of inspiration and knowledge from it.

For those of you who haven't checked out Bellingcat, I recommend you do so. Their valuable work includes not just investigations into MH17, but also the Syrian civil war, the poisoning of former Russian intelligence officer Sergei Skripal in the UK, and the Yemeni civil war. They are widely quoted by mainstream media who have come to trust their methodology and accuracy.

Bellingcat can be found at: https://www.bellingcat.com/

The official Dutch Safety Board report into the downing of MH17 is available online at the following link: https://www.onderzoeksraad.nl/en/page/3546/crash-mh17-17-july-2014

If anyone is interesting in what a Buk missile system looks like and how it works, I would recommend a YouTube video from BBC News, which can be found at the following link: https://www.youtube.com/watch?v=PlcmziopqZA

Many investigators and journalists chronicled the way in which Internet trolls based in Russia pushed out huge numbers of posts on Twitter, Facebook, and other social media outlets trying to heap the blame on Ukraine for the MH17 disaster.

Apart from Bellingcat, one particularly thorough account came from Kharkiv Human Rights Protection Group, a long-standing organization specializing in helping individuals whose human rights have been infringed. Based in Kharkhiv, Ukraine's second largest city, it reported that the Russian troll campaign pumped out at least 65 million tweets trying to blame Ukraine for the disaster. See its account at: http://khpg.org/en/index.php?id=1557928691

A good account of how a Russian troll factory operates can be found in *The Washington Post*, which conducted an interview with an employee of the Internet Research Agency, based in St. Petersburg: https://www.washingtonpost.com/news/worldviews/wp/2018/02/17/a-former-russian-troll-speaks-it-was-like-being-in-orwells-world/

There are several good articles describing how the United States, chiefly through the CIA, sought to support Ukraine in its conflict with pro-Russian separatist forces in the east of the country.

One such account can be found in Forbes magazine, at: https://www.forbes.com/sites/melikkaylan/2014/04/16/why-cia-director-brennan-visited-kiev-in-ukraine-the-covert-war-has-begun/

The wider implications of the MH17 disaster for Russia and its people, for the West, and for international relations generally were discussed in great depth in a number of outlets. Two commentaries that appeared in *The Economist* at the time of the incident neatly summed up the views of many. You can find the first at: https://www.economist.com/leaders/2014/10/01/a-web-of-lies?spc=scode&spv=xm&ah=9d7f7ab945510a56fa6d37c30b6f1709

The second is at: https://www.economist.com/briefing/2014/07/24/collateral-damage

For a discussion about the range of weapons, missiles, and other military equipment that the United States provided to Ukraine during the conflict with Russian separatists, try the following article in the Ukraine-based Unian Information Agency website: https://www.unian.info/politics/10584102-u-s-could-supply-to-ukraine-surface-to-air-missiles-rfe-rl.html

If you would like to read more about the evolution of Russia following the break-up of the Soviet Union in 1991, there is a wide choice of books available. However, I would recommend an excellent account by one of the *Financial Times*' journalists, Arkady Ostrovsky, entitled The Invention of Russia.

Ostrovsky describes how Russia, which appeared to revel in its new-found freedom in the first years after the break-up, ended up in a kind of autocracy once again at the hands of Vladimir Putin and his *siloviki*. The book includes some detail on how Putin sought to influence the 2016 US Presidential election. It can be found at: My Book

For a further account of how Russia sought to try and influence the 2016 US election, I would recommend an article by a former CIA officer, John Sipher, in *The Atlantic*. It can be found here: https://www.theatlantic.com/ideas/archive/2018/08/convergence-is-worse-than-collusion/567368/

I have located a couple of the scenes in this book inside the Situation Room in the White House. For those who are interested in what the Situation Room is like, I would recommend the following video on YouTube, produced in 2009 when Obama was still president, but nonetheless interesting: https://www.youtube.com/watch?v=T7ch13ZuMu8

The highly secretive operations of the National Security Agency are a source of some fascination for many. In this book, the NSA's Tailored Access Operations unit features in a couple of scenes. For those wishing to read more about this unit, there is a detailed account in the German newspaper *Der Spiegel*, which can be found here: https://www.spiegel.de/international/world/the-nsa-uses-powerful-toolbox-in-effort-to-spy-on-global-networks-a-940969.html

For those who are interested, for whatever reason, in cemeteries, there is an interesting article on the Bellamorte website about the Glenwood Cemetery that features in The Black Sea. It can be found here: https://www.bellamorte.net/washington-dc-glenwood-cemetery-review.html

And if anyone would like to find out more about the McMillan Sand Filtration site, where Johnson captured Shevchenko in this book, an update on redevelopment plans and a photograph can be found at: https://dc.curbed.com/2019/10/31/20938082/mcmillan-development-demolition-construction-sand-filtration-reservoir

Another interesting article for connoisseurs of historic utility infrastructure about the McMillan site can be found here: http://www.bshs.org.uk/travel-guide/mcmillan-sand-filtration-site-washington-d-c

ABOUT THE AUTHOR AND CONTACT DETAILS

I have always had a love of writing and a passion for reading good thrillers. But despite having a long-standing dream of writing my own novels, it took me more than five decades to finally get around to completing the first.

The Black Sea is the sixth in the **Joe Johnson** series of thrillers, which pulls together some of my other interests, particularly history, world news, and travel.

I studied history at Loughborough University and worked for many years as a business and financial journalist before becoming a corporate and financial communications adviser with several large energy companies, specializing in media relations.

Originally I came from Grantham, Lincolnshire, and I now live with my family in St. Albans, Hertfordshire, UK.

You can connect with me via these routes:

E-mail: andrew@andrewturpin.com

Website: www.andrewturpin.com.

Facebook: @AndrewTurpinAuthor

Twitter: @AndrewTurpin

Instagram: @andrewturpin.author

Please also follow me on Bookbub and Amazon!

https://www.bookbub.com/authors/andrew-turpin

https://www.amazon.com/Andrew-Turpin/e/B074V87WWL/

Do get in touch with your comments and views on the books, or anything else for that matter. I enjoy hearing from readers and promise to reply.